THE ACCORD

A NOVEL

SUSAN S. THROCKMORTON

(MULTIPLICITY PRESS, LLC)

Cover Design by Mark Kotanchik. All other artwork by the author.

This is a work of fiction. Other than Pope Francis, Donald Trump, Hillary Clinton, and the historical figures, Emperor Constantine and Helena, mother of Constantine, Bishop Aubert of Avranche, King Philip V of France, the Knights Templar, the Knights Hospitalier, Godfrey of Bouillon, Jacques de Molay, Last Grand Master of the Knights Templar, Archbishop Sens, Pope Clement, Pope Urban II, Geoffrey of Charney, King Louis XVI of France, Marie-Antoinette of France, and Maximilien de Robespierre, referenced herein, the events and characters portrayed in this book are fictitious. Any similarity to real persons, living or dead, is coincidental and not intended by the author.

ISBN13 **978-0997065817**
(MULTIPLICITY PRESS, LLC)

LIBRARY OF CONGRESS CONTROL NUMBER:
Application pending

* * * *

*As always, to my wonderful husband,
for his encouragement and support,
and to my dear friend, Queue,
who helped me explore the mysteries
and beauty of Belgium and France.*

* * * *

OTHER WORKS BY
THE AUTHOR

THE MAYAN MANIFESTO
Available at Amazon.com, and as an eBook on
Kindle, Apple Books and
Barnes and Noble Nook

CHAPTER ONE

*By night will come through the forest of Reines
Two couples by roundabout route,
Queen of the white stone,
The monk King in gray in Varennes,
Will the choice of Capet be the cause of
Storm, fire, blood, axe...*

Nostradamus, Quatrain IX-20, published 1555

EARLY MORNING, JUNE 21, 1791, NORTHERN FRANCE

Draped in a dark wet cloak, the small man led his horse further into the copse of beech trees, hoping that the steady patter of the falling rain would muffle the sound of his steed's heavy breathing. The horse flared his nostrils and Leonard began to stroke his head, willing him to keep quiet and motionless. Leonard instinctively held his own breath as the group of 50 or more riders passed only 30 yards from his hiding place. After a few minutes, when the hoof beats began to recede into the distance, he took in a deep breath and whispered to his horse, "Balthazar, that was close." He continued patting the animal's neck, using the motion to slow the heartbeat of the horse and his own as well.

Leonard waited a few more minutes, in the relentless drizzle, before remounting his horse. *Now that the threat has passed,* he thought, *I can take my time getting to the abbaye. That group of traitors will come and go before I reach it; then I can hide the silver and the Queen's treasure and await the arrival of the King's guard.*

Riding slowly up the path through the dark forest, he mulled over the queen's instructions, wondering what could be of such importance within the small metal box that she had entrusted to him. The Queen had told him only that the contents would 'secure the assistance of the Pope,' should the efforts of the royal family to escape be thwarted. As he continued his journey northward, he could have no way of knowing that the royal family had already been captured in St. Menehould, as they attempted to reach the eastern frontier of the Empire.

The ring of his cell phone jarred him awake into total darkness. Fumbling for the phone on his bedside table, he looked at the time before quickly typing in his passcode.

"Bonjour," Jeff said, trying to sound awake and coherent at such an ungodly hour.

"Bonjour, Jeff, bonjour," came the voice of Professeur Bertrand over the phone. "Comment t'allez vous? So sorry to disturb you so early but I have exciting news."

"Oh, Professeur," Jeff replied, sitting up in bed and simultaneously turning on his bedside lamp. "Bonjour. No problem; what's the news?"

"The Ministere Culturelle in Belgium has finally responded to our requests to explore the abbaye ruins at D'Orval."

"Fantastic, Professeur," Jeff said excitedly as he jumped out of bed, already contemplating how long it would take him to dress and make it to his office at the Sorbonne.

"Are they going to allow us to dig in…?"

"Well, we mustn't get ahead of ourselves," Professeur Bertrand explained. "To start, he will only allow us to photograph and visually search the ruins. Then we shall see."

"Well, it is a start, Professeur. Perhaps your family connection had something to do with it?" suggested Jeff.

"Peut-être, perhaps," said Simône Bertrand, thinking out loud as she tapped her finger against her lower lip, wondering exactly what the Abbott of D'Orval actually knew about her family history.

"So when do we get started?" asked Jeff, talking to his phone's speaker, as he pulled on jeans and stepped into loafers, smoothing his hair as he glanced toward the small mirror on the chest of drawers.

"First things first, I would like you to continue your search at the Bibliotheque Nationale for another day for any further mention of Marie-Antoinette's papers. And I understand you have friends coming to visit this weekend?"

"Ah oui, two friends, sisters-Alex and Liz from the U.S. I'm acting as their tour guide for a few days before they start a two-month holiday across Europe."

"C'est bon. I will head up to Belgium before you and get a head start, as you say. You can join me next Monday, if that works for you."

"Perfect, Professeur. I'm planning to rent a car anyway, so I'll just keep it and drive up on Monday. Where are we staying?" Jeff asked.

"There is a small hostel in town that looks nice and has a view of the valley. I will make us reservations. Au revoir, see you on Monday."

"Au revoir, Professeur," Jeff said as he ended the call. He looked at his bed, contemplating climbing back in before reconsidering, realizing how much he had to accomplish in the next few days before Alex and Liz arrived.

Liz, funny. Jeff realized he still thought of her as Dita, the name given to her as a child by the woman who had raised her. He probably always would, but he knew that name and past were dead, if not buried. *She is Elizabeth King, not Dita Puhlya*, the story about whom only a few other close friends knew. *But what a story*, Jeff thought, as he finished getting ready and ate a quick breakfast: *twin sisters separated at birth and almost sacrificed on their 21st birthday by crazy neo-Nazis intent on saving the world at the end of the Mayan calendar on December 21, 2012.* Momentarily, Jeff was lost in memories of Chichen Itza and that fateful night. *Someone should write a book*, Jeff mused as he walked down the two flights from his apartment and headed up toward the Metro.

Eleven hours later, an IPhone alarm rang in San Francisco, interrupting the sunlit dream. Alex and Liz were walking along the Seine River. It had just rained and the sun shone on the sparkling tree leaves. An elegant older woman stooped to give her dog a treat before they continued along the quay. As the scene faded, Alex opened one eye to look at the time before hitting the snooze on her phone alarm. *Just a few more minutes*, she thought pulling a pillow over her head.

In the kitchen Liz was already sipping a second cup of espresso as she reviewed the written list before her. *I guess I'll have to go shopping today*, she thought, as she considered the missing items. Despite the fact that she had more than enough money to spend, and Alex's frequent urgings, Liz still found it difficult to spend money on herself. Deep down, she guessed, she was still the dirt-poor girl living in the barrio.

Lost in thought, Liz jumped when Alex tiptoed behind her and gave her a quick hug. "You're up early," Alex said, as she yawned and stretched her arms above her head.

"Yes, couldn't sleep," said Liz, as she turned to smile at her twin. "You came in late, " she added.

"Oh, yeah," Alex said sheepishly, "out and about with Sam-still the bad influence," she added with a laugh.

Liz nodded in acknowledgment before returning to her list.

"What are you so serious about?" Alex asked as she pulled up a chair.

"Oh, just my packing list," Liz said with a sigh, and roll of her eyes. "I mean, we leave for Paris tomorrow, and I don't have half the things on the list you made for me."

"Well, then, I guess we'll just have to cancel our trip," Alex said, sounding very serious.

"Wha...?" Liz asked before catching the joke. "Okay, fine. We can go shopping today, although you know I hate it."

"Finally," Alex exclaimed with delight. "I'll be ready in 20 minutes," Alex added over her shoulder as she ran toward her bedroom.

The next afternoon, Alex closed her backpack before sitting on the edge of her bed, phone in hand.

> "Hey, Jeff, can't wait to see you. Just finished our packing-Plane leaves at 10 PM. Grabbing an early dinner with Aunt Meg, then she'll drop us at airport. See you tomorrow.
>
> Alex"

Alex finished the text and sent it before heading into the bathroom to shower.

CHAPTER TWO

SImône exited the elevator and walked through the dimly lit garage toward her reserved parking space, one of the perks of being a tenured Professeur of Anthropology and Archaeology at the Sorbonne. As she reached her car, Simône rummaged in her purse for her phone, finding it just as it stopped buzzing. "Merde," she muttered under her breath, as she checked her recent calls. *Philippe really needs to stop calling me*, she thought with chagrin, glad now that she had missed the call from her ex-husband.

She set down her brief case in order to search again in her rather voluminous purse for her car keys. She grabbed the door handle as her other hand found her key ring. To her surprise, the door opened under her grasp before she could hit the unlock button on the fob.

"Merde!" she exclaimed again, this time loudly as she turned to look over both shoulders. *I must have forgotten to lock it*, she thought, frowning as she climbed into the driver's seat, started the ignition and pulled her red Peugeot RC2 out of her parking space. She immediately changed focus and began thinking about the task ahead-her exploration of the Abbaye D'Orval in southern Belgium.

By the time she had reached street level and turned into traffic, her thoughts had strayed almost 1000 years into the past. Her great (actually too many greats to say, she realized)-anyway-her great many times uncle was Godfroi (Godfrey) de Bouillon, a nobleman in what is now southern Belgium who had led the first Crusade to the Holy Lands in 1095 AD and was crowned the first king of Jerusalem in 1099, only to die a year later. Simône had sat beside her grandmother many times as a very small child listening to details of Godfrey and his knights and the crusade, which had been ordered by Pope Urban II and 300 of his bishops at the meeting in Auvergne in 1095 AD. Four years later, Godfrey and his army had captured Jerusalem from the Muslims rulers on July 15, 1099 AD.

Simône knew by heart the stories of the many crusades and how Jerusalem and the Holy Lands had all fallen back into the hands of the Muslims under the leadership of the great Islamic warrior, Saladin, in 1187. She also recalled that the last Crusade waged by King Louis in the name of Pope Clement from 1263 AD to 1270 AD had not been particularly successful, and that in 1291 AD, the Turks had taken Acre, on the Mediterranean coast, the last stronghold of the Knights' Templar, thereby ending their story in Palestine. But what she, like many Templar historians, longed to discover, was the truth about the elusive Templar treasure. Most believed that it had been lost when the Templars were forced to flee the city of Acre, Palestine by sea in 1291 AD-which knowledge Jacques De Molay, the last Grand Master of the Templars, presumably took with him to the grave when he was burned at the stake by King Philip of France in Paris in 1313.

Her focus returning back to the 21st century as she turned off the Rue de Grenelle toward her apartment, Simône thought about what had started her on this journey: the partially burned diary of a long dead grandson of the hairdresser of Marie-Antoinette. It seemed to contain cryptic references to a treasure belonging to the Templars, a treasure that his uncle had transported for the Queen at the time of the French revolution. Whether it was the treasure of historical myth was not clear.

Discovered in her grandmother's house two years ago, the diary had certainly piqued her interest because of its apparent age, and the fact that she quickly determined that it was written in centuries-old French. However, it was not until, after some cajoling and flirting, she had obtained the services of elderly Professor Lange in the language department at the Sorbonne that she had begun to realize the significance of the find. Now it seemed that it might actually lead to the discovery of the true nature of the Templar treasure. Even though it had been written in old French, this much was clear: the Abbaye D'Orval had specifically been mentioned, as had references to the Knights' Templar.

Simône smiled when she recalled how excited Jeff had been when she first told him about the contents of the diary. *Jeff, too bad he's so young*, Simône thought a little guiltily, knowing that as a research assistant, he was forbidden fruit.

Tant pis, Simône mused with a shrug as she pulled into the garage of her apartment building. Once inside her apartment, she kicked off her heels before rummaging through her mail and pouring herself a glass of wine. *Time to pack,* she thought as she headed into her bedroom, before realizing that the balcony doors were partially open, with her ice blue silk sheers billowing with the evening breeze. *Mon Dieu*, Simône thought, frowning slightly. *I didn't lock my car or apartment today? What is my problem?*

She glanced very quickly to her briefcase and then she sighed, unsure why but relieved that she had taken the diary to work that day. After closing and locking the doors, she grabbed a suitcase from her closet and began to pack.

"It wasn't there." And then in halting French: "Oui, yes I searched everywhere." He listened to his phone before replying: "She must have it. Don't worry-I will follow her tomorrow."

"Merde, I said I would get it."

"Ma'asalaama," he said, momentarily slipping into Arabic before catching himself. "Au revoir, demain."

The man silenced his cell phone and settled down into his car seat, his gaze never leaving the window, which was illuminated on the 4th floor of the apartment building across the street from where he was parked. "Merde," he said again to himself. "It is going to be a very long night."

Halfway down the block, the light from the street-lamp filtered through the shadowing Linden trees, leaving a mosaic of spider webs on another windshield; the man beneath sat silent, only the glow of his cigarette's tip visible inside his car. He would report this to his handler in Tel Aviv, *after finishing my cigarette*, he thought rebelliously.

Actually, this assignment is turning out easier than I thought. I'll let the Syrians do all the work and I'll take all the credit. He grinned smugly to himself before taking the last drag of the cigarette and throwing it out his open car window.

After passing through customs, Alex and Liz rode the escalator down to baggage claim. "I hope our suitcases made it, we were kind of late to check in."

"Don't worry," said Alex, unconcerned. "If they don't show up, it's just a great excuse to go shopping at all the designer stores on the Champs-Élysées."

"Oh great, more shopping," said Liz, before acknowledging her twin's joke with a nod of her head. "I'm going to use the restroom here, if that's okay," said Liz, nodding toward the ladies' room.

"Sure," said Alex. "I'll text Jeff and let him know we're waiting for our luggage. Hopefully he's not stuck in traffic."

After sending the text, Alex lugged two large back-packs from the luggage carousel onto a trolley. When Liz came out of the bathroom, Alex waived her over. "Hey, Jeff is on his way. He'll meet us outside."

A few minutes later, Jeff stopped his rental car at the curb, jumped out and ran around to greet them each with a hug and a kiss to both cheeks. "Bonjour, bonjour," Jeff exclaimed, causing Alex and Liz to grin at each other.

"So you've gone Frenchy on us?" asked Alex teasingly.

"But, of course, mais oui," said Jeff as he deposited their backpacks in the trunk. "Mon Dieu, what did you bring, Kings, the family fortune?"

The girls just smiled as Jeff continued, "Welcome to the land of great wine and food. I can't guarantee that all of the natives are friendly, but you'll meet a few here and there."

"That's okay-we're only here for the food and wine," Alex said sarcastically.

"And of course to spend time with you," Liz added quickly.

"Of course," said Jeff, a slight smirk on his face. *The King Twins, just as beautiful as ever: Alex with her blue eyes and blond hair, and the very Irish-looking Liz, with her dark hair and pale skin,* thought Jeff as he pulled away from the curb.

"So what's the plan?" asked Alex, as she began to fiddle with the radio.

"Well," said Jeff, "I was thinking we could go do the touristy things: the Musée D'Orsay, the Louvre, the Eiffel Tower. And then I want to take you out for a nice dinner at a place in Montmartre; it has a beautiful view of the city-kind of pricey but I think I can swing it."

"No, you're not paying," said Alex and Liz in unison, before laughing. "You're the poor struggling grad student," added Alex. "We're the rich heiresses-we'll pay for dinner; consider it recompense for your guide services."

"But I..." started Jeff.

"No, Alex is right. Keep your wallet in your pocket. We have to spend our money on something," said Liz, her green eyes sparkling.

"Well, if you insist, twist my arm," Jeff said, conceding the argument. *They are right, of course*, Jeff realized, trying not to let his male ego enter into the discussion. The King girls had inherited millions a few years ago when they finally discovered their family history, and he was still living the life of a paupered student. Truth be told, renting the car was already cutting into next month's budget.

"So what's first?" Jeff asked, as he turned off the airport frontage road and into traffic.

"I wouldn't mind going to our hotel for a quick shower," said Liz, leaning between them from the backseat. "We're right off the Champs-Élysées. Do you mind?"

"No problem. I really don't want to be a tour guide for two ripe Americans, no matter how beautiful they are." Alex playfully punched Jeff in the arm, though she was secretly happy that he still felt that way. It had been nine months since he had come to Paris. Alex had been happy to let their relationship evolve into just a close friendship while he was gone, although given some of their recent conversations skyping, she hadn't been sure how happy Jeff was with the arrangement. But today he seemed laid back and friendly, so Alex decided she would go with the flow too.

On the drive into the city, Jeff described what he had been doing for the last nine months in his position with Professeur Bertrand.

"Wow, that's incredible," exclaimed Alex. "You think this might actually be Templar treasure?"

"Let's not get carried away-all I know is that Professor Bertrand's too many to count great, great, like, you know, many greats uncle was the original leader of the First Crusade. A hundreds of years-old diary belonging to one of the descendants of a servant of Marie Antoinette, which the Professeur discovered a couple of years ago, describes treasure belonging to the Templars. Whether it is 'the treasure'-unknown." Jeff shrugged and removed both hands from the wheel in a questioning gesture, for emphasis. "But the diary talks about Abbaye D'Orval which is very close to the castle of Godfrey De Bouillon, so we're going to start there."

"Sounds exciting," interjected Liz. "I don't suppose there are any Nazis involved in this tale."

Jeff and Alex looked at each other before bursting out laughing. Jeff said, "Don't worry D,"-he started to say before catching himself-"Liz, I promise we will not be hanging out with any more Nazis."

"Well that's good to hear," said Liz, ignoring the slip, before sitting back in her seat.

An hour later, having showered and changed into sleeveless summer dresses and flats, Alex and Liz locked their hotel room door and continued their conversation about everything they hoped to see in Paris as they walked to the elevator. As usual, as they stepped off the elevator, the striking pair elicited several looks from other hotel patrons sitting in the lobby. To their surprise, however-er, the attention of one person's gaze with absent.

"Where's Jeff?" asked Liz, looking around while Alex stopped to drop off their room key at the front desk.

"You're not going to believe this," Alex said with some irritation in her voice. "Jeff is gone! Apparently he got a phone call right after we went upstairs. He told the clerk that an emergency had come up, and he had to leave. Said he'd call us in a few hours."

"Really? He just left without talking to us? That doesn't sound like Jeff. I hope nothing bad happened," said Liz, trying to hide the disappointment in her voice.

"Who knows, maybe his professor cracked the whip on him," Alex said with a shrug. "Probably not an actual 'emergency' emergency," she added, making air quotes with her fingers. "But no matter, we are big girls and we have a guidebook. Let's go explore the City of Lights."

Four hours later, just as they were leaving the Louvre, Alex's phone rang; after checking the ID, she put it on speaker.

"Hey, it's me. I'm so sorry I ditched you."

"You better have a good excuse, Stahl, or we're firing you as our guide," Alex said, not yet ready to forgive him for disappearing.

"I know, I know, but wait until you hear... Simône," Alex looked at Liz and raised her eyebrows at the use of the first name, but remained silent.

"She's gotten permission for us to explore the Abbaye ruins. I guess she charmed the monk in charge. She's like that... Anyway," he continued breathlessly, "we only have this weekend, because I guess there is some kind of photo shoot starting Monday for some Belgian government publication. And so..."

"And so," Alex said, completing his sentence, "you need to go out there instead of hanging out with us, right?"

"That sucks," said Liz to no one in particular.

"Look, ladies, I'm really sorry and I feel like a jerk for bailing at the last minute but this is literally a once-in-a-lifetime opportunity. I'm actually at the Sorbonne right now gathering up all of our research and equipment."

"But I have an idea, four researchers are better than two. What would you think about going out there with me tomorrow? I told Professeur Bertrand about you, and your academic backgrounds in archaeology and anthropology, and she was excited to have you join us. She even agreed to pay all of your expenses for the weekend-hotel, meals, etc. She said, 'the more the merrier.'"

When neither Alex nor Liz spoke, Jeff continued. "It is beautiful country. You could see northern France and southern Belgium and then I could put you on the train back to Paris from Reims on Sunday night."

Alex and Liz looked at each other for several seconds before shrugging in unison.

14

"I think it sounds like fun," Liz said. "I want to see Belgium and we hadn't included it on our list of places to visit. What do you think, Alex?"

"I guess it's okay," said Alex grudgingly. "As long as we have time to see everything we planned when we come back."

"And as long as there are no Nazis!" added Liz with a laugh.

"I swear," responded Jeff quickly. "No crazy ancient Mayans either."

"Okay, we're in," Liz and Alex said together, causing Jeff to laugh, relieved.

"So I'll come by your hotel at 7:30 to pick you up for the dinner I promised you. I'm paying since I changed our plans. Try to look decent," teased Jeff.

"Well, you know we don't have too much to work with, but we'll give it our best effort," said Alex. "See ya," and she ended the call.

"Seems like everywhere we go with Jeff, we find adventure," Liz commented as they headed down the steps into the Metro.

"Let's hope it's a 'I just had a fun vacation; want to see my home movies' type of vacation, and not an 'I almost got sacrificed to a Mayan God' type of adventure,'" said Alex.

CHAPTER THREE

After reaching the Belgian border, Simône decided to head straight for the abbaye. *I'll spend an hour exploring so I know the lay of the land when I photograph the grounds tomorrow*, she thought. Unlike in most parts of France, it appeared that this area was still surrounded by virgin forest-lush, green and overgrown. She wondered if some of the trees that seemed to reach toward her car as she passed had stood there since the time of the ill-fated queen. The light rain and dark, low-lying clouds gave a somewhat ominous feeling to the journey. Attempting to shake off the feeling of-what-dread, she supposed, which seemed to grow stronger as she reached the country road leading to the abbaye, she muttered, "ridicule."

The abbaye is just the home to kindly old monks-nothing to worry about, she reassured herself as she left the highway, following a local road until she reached a long drive heading onto the abbaye grounds. Once inside, she waited in a reception room in the main entrance building before being escorted by a young, silent, robe-clad monk into the office of the head of the abbaye.

Looking around quickly as the Abbott approached her, Simône saw that the room was appropriately austere, with unclad floors, and an ancient desk, although somewhat anachronistically holding a large computer monitor, and a phone charger, along with a time worn leather covered Bible.

"Abbott, again I must thank you," Simône said, hesitating before extending her hand, which the man grabbed warmly. He fit the image Simône had imagined, clad in a light brown robe, and leather sandals, his grayish-blue eyes alert, yet seemingly kind. "I certainly could have waited until after the photo shoot…"

"Nonsense, my dear, once we learned of your family connection to the esteemed Godfrey, I certainly could not refuse you. But I must warn you. These ruins have been picked over for hundreds of years after being almost completely destroyed during the revolution. Truthfully, I am surprised anything is still standing."

"I understand, Abbott; this is just the beginning of my search, as I said when we spoke earlier this week. I don't really expect to find anything here but I have to faire l'effort (make the effort), non? Before moving on to other possibilities."

"Oui, I understand. But such a big job; it is only you?"

"Oh no, Dieu merci! I have three assistants coming tomorrow to help me. I just thought I would explore a little tonight and take some pictures in preparation."

"Ah, oui. Well, bon chance! If you need anything, I will be here in my office until 7 PM. After that, the gates will be locked and inaccessible. We have no phones within the abbaye proper," he said apologetically.

"Oui, of course. I understand. But I should be finished long before 7."

"D'accord, then, Professor Bertrand."

"Au revoir, Abbott, and again, merci beaucoup."

Simône returned to her car for her iPad before paying for entry into the grounds. *Hauntingly beautiful*, she thought, as she entered the original abbaye ruins and then stopped to admire the still standing main stone frame and arched doorways of what was once, she was sure, a magnificent church, first consecrated in the 1100's by Cistercian monks, destroyed and then rebuilt in the 1300's, Simône recalled from her research. In 1793 AD, the abbaye had been burned to the ground by French troops, in retaliation for aid the abbaye's residents had provided to Austrian troops.

17

But perhaps, the real reason for the destruction had been something different. *Peut-être*, considered Simône, *the troops had been searching for something-something they believed Marie Antoinette had sent there before the revolution. And in their furor after not finding it, razed the abbaye. Far-fetched*, Simône admitted, *but not impossible*. After standing for another minute studying the still magnificent ruins, she began section by section to methodically take notes and pictures on her iPad.

Montmartre of Moulin Rouge fame, a large hill located in the 18th Arrondisement in the northern section of Paris, was historically the area where most well-known artists, such as Van Gogh, Monet, Picasso, and Modigliani, lived and worked at the beginning of 20th century Paris. Although no longer the home to the type of artists who illuminated the area during the Belle Epoque, it was still a regular draw for tourists who came to see the Basilica de Sacre Coeur and to check out the easels of the second rate artists who daily set up shop in the shadow of the white dome of the cathedral. And tucked in amongst the many overpriced, tourist dives that littered the hill were a few authentic French restaurants with magnificent views of the City of Lights.

When the three musketeers arrived at the restaurant, a few minutes before 9 o'clock, Madame Vasseur, the proprietress, greeted them warmly. Like most French bistros, the tables inside were small and quite closely spaced, and the restaurant seemed to bubble over with the conversation of the patrons filling every table. Alex and Liz looked at each other, wondering how long they would have to wait to be seated. But they were pleasantly surprised when Jeff and Madame Vasseur continued threading their way through the dozen or so tables to a door at the back of the restaurant beside the bar. Following on Jeff's heels, they found themselves on a small but elegant terrace lined with flowering plants, and a sole table, which overlooked the rooftops of the entire city.

"Oh my God, this is beautiful!" exclaimed Alex, before rewarding Jeff with a brilliant smile.

Jeff winked at her before saying, "merci beaucoup!" to their hostess as she seated them. "Andre told me to let you choose our menu; I'm sure he knows what he is talking about. I will leave everything in your very capable hands, Madame."

"Ah, bon," said Madame Vasseur, with a smile and a clap of her hands. "Bon appétit!" she added, before retreating to the interior of the restaurant.

"How did you score this?" asked Liz, clearly impressed, once their hostess had left the terrace.

"This restaurant is owned by the family of one of the other grad assistants in my department at the Sorbonne. He owed me a favor for some help I gave him on one of his projects. They usually only use the terrace for family gatherings but when I told him about you two coming, he put in a good word with his aunt, and 'voila!'"

"Well, it is incroyable!" said Liz.

Soon their waiter had appeared with a very tasty bottle of red wine, and a freshly baked loaf of bread. While they drank and talked, darkness settled over the horizon and the lights of the city began to sparkle, like stars laid out below them on a carpet of dusky purples, blues and grays.

As the meal progressed, the three dined on a delicate salmon paté garnished with a perfectly poached quail's egg, a rich coq au vin in which they sopped their bread to savor every drop of the delicious gravy, and pot de crème chocolat for dessert.

The man, cap pulled low, wearing what appeared to be a construction worker's clothes, pulled a satellite phone from his oversized coat pocket and dialed.

"He is still there with two girls. Americans, maybe?"

After listening to the caller, he said, "How the hell should I know?"

And then, "These fancy places take hours just to serve some food. Pah!"

He again listened to the reply on the other end before responding.

"No, he doesn't have it-why would he? I tell you, this is a waste of my time."

The voice on the other end yelled, "So where is it?"

"It's with the woman, the professeur, I'm sure!"

He grimaced and kicked the ground with his toe as the person on the other end of the phone gave a long-winded reply.

"Alors, I will wait until he leaves, but finish searching his apartment, vitement! And leave no trace of the search. Even the Monseigneur can't help you if you get caught. A l'heure."

As he ended the call, he instinctively reached for the pendant hanging from a chain around his neck-a dragon being stabbed with a sword in the shape of a cross-and then he crossed himself for good measure.

"I don't think I can eat another bite," said Alex.

"This food is amazing, but I'm stuffed," agreed Liz, before pushing her half-eaten dessert away.

Jeff, who had just finished his last spoonful of pudding, grinned as he patted his stomach.

"Pretty amazing, right? And Andre said we get the locals' discount, which makes it even more incroyable."

"I know what I will be dreaming about tonight, French food," said Liz.

After Jeff paid the modest bill and they thanked Madame Vasseur profusely, the three began walking down the hill to the closest metro station, Les Abbesses.

At the entrance, Jeff said, "This is where I leave you. My apartment is just a few more blocks down the hill. I'm going to walk off my dinner. But you can catch the Metro here and it will get you within a block of your hotel."

"Yes, we rode it today; we know the stop," said Alex.

"Okay, so I will pick you up bright and early tomorrow morning."

"We'll be jet lagging, but we will be ready," said Liz.

"Yes, having consumed at least three espressos," added Alex.

"Okay, well, bon noir, mes belles amis," said Jeff, with a wave as Alex and Liz walked down the steps into the Metro.

CHAPTER FOUR

"You won't believe what happened to us last night!" Alex said excitedly as she and Liz climbed into Jeff's car.

"Don't tell me-kidnapped by neo-Nazis."

"You're so funny," said Alex, rolling her eyes. "No smart aleck, but we did get locked in the Metro."

"I guess speaking Spanish isn't that helpful when the PA system is in garbled French," added Liz. She and Alex recounted their adventure, starting with missing the last train at their stop because they had not understood the announcement, finding locked doors at two exits, and running for what seemed like miles in the warren of tunnels before encountering a mysterious stranger who had arrived seemingly out of nowhere to rescue them and show them the way to the one unlocked exit.

"Kind of weird, really," said Alex in conclusion. "I mean, he claimed he had missed the last announcement also, but he definitely spoke French. I heard him on his phone; we shared a cab with him back to the Champs-Élysées."

"Oui," agreed Liz. "Definitely French, although with a weird accent, but I have no idea what he said. Although..." She paused, reconsidering.

"What?" Alex turned to the backseat to look at her sister.

"Well, he was talking really quietly but..."

"But?" asked Alex, feeling sometimes as if she was pulling teeth from her reticent sister.

"Well, I thought I heard him say something like, 'tout a l'heures,' and then, 'Belgium.'"

"It means 'see you soon.' But Belgium?" Jeff continued. "That is a coincidence, I suppose, but not that strange. France shares its northern border with Belgium-so there are probably lots of Belgians in Paris."

"Who knows? Maybe you misunderstood him. The cabbie was rather belligerently demanding payment right about then, as I recall," added Alex.

"Yeah, you're probably right," replied Liz, not sounding totally convinced. She sat back in her seat and pulled out a book to read.

After reaching the outskirts of Paris, Jeff turned on to the A4 and headed north. He provided running commentary as they drove through the French countryside, passing field after field of yellow-flowered plants.

"What is that plant?" Alex asked.

"I think it is called Rape. They use it to make Canola oil. You see it all over northern France," Jeff explained.

Four hours later, having stopped at Reims for lunch and a quick walk through the beautiful Gothic cathedral gleaming with sunlight like a multi-faceted jewel, where Kings of France were once crowned, they reached the Belgian border.

"The forest is really dense," commented Alex, looking at the stand of dark trees and bushes, which encroached on the two-lane road onto which they had just turned.

"Yes, we'll have to be careful," said Jeff playfully, glancing over his shoulder at Liz. "Lions and tigers and bears, oh no!"

"No, no lions, or even a Tin-Man," laughed Liz, "but I suppose there could still be a wild boar here and there. Most of the wild animals were killed or died off when Europe's forests were almost completely deforested before the Industrial Revolution."

"Aren't you a smarty-pants?" teased Alex.

"No," said Liz, blushing. "I just learned about it when I took a history class on pre-industrial Europe."

"Okay, well then, semi-smarty-pants," Jeff said, before tossing a quick grin toward Liz in his rearview mirror.

By the time they reached Bouillon, the home of Godfrey and his iconic castle, a steady rain had begun to drench the cobbled streets and brightly colored awnings of the small town.

"I hope I get better reception here. I've been trying to reach Simône all day, but the cell reception is horrible," said Jeff as he pulled the car in front of the hostel where they would be staying.

"Too bad it's raining," Alex said with a frown as she exited the car. Dense fog blanketed the area, blocking all visibility to the town below. "I bet the view is amazing when it is clear."

"Don't worry," Jeff replied. "I think it rains every day here," gesturing to the very green trees, bushes and tall grass surrounding the parking lot, "but it will clear up."

"Hope so," said Alex, looking out at the dark line of rain clouds, which were drifting down the surrounding hillsides.

Once inside, they were greeted by the clerk at the front desk, a young man listening to music with headphones. When they walked in, he removed the headphones and looked at them for a moment as though appraising them. He initially began speaking German but immediately switched to passible English when he realized they were Americans.

"Welcome to our humble abode, ladies and gentleman. My name is Godfrey, and I am at your disposal," he said sardonically, gesturing with his hands.

"Merci beaucoup, Monsieur," said Liz. "I am Liz King and this is my sister, Alex. And our friend, Jeff Stahl. Hopefully you have two room reservations for us."

"Yes, I've been expecting you, but not expecting such a good-looking group. Who will be with whom?"

"Oh, I will be with my sister," Alex said quickly, avoiding the questioning look from Jeff.

"But of course," said the clerk, who had noticed the unspoken exchange and attempted to hide a smirk as he turned to get two old iron keys from hooks on a large board on the wall behind the desk.

"And Professeur Bertrand, she is staying here again tonight, oui?"

"So she isn't here?" Jeff asked, sounding somewhat concerned.

"No, Monsieur, although I am expecting her any time."

"I think she should be here shortly. Do you serve dinner here at the hostel?" asked Jeff.

The clerk looked over both shoulders as if to check that the coast was clear before saying, "Yes, but to be honest, you would do better eating at one of the cafés in town. The cook here-not so bon. Vous comprenez?"

"Yes, I think we understand," Jeff said, with a chuckle. "Thanks for the tip. Well ladies, why don't you check out your room and get settled in?" Jeff added, turning to Liz and Alex.

"Okay, sure," agreed Alex and Liz. They headed up the stairs at the back of the lobby. Their room located at the end of the second floor hallway, was simple, but comfortable, with twin beds, facing a window overlooking the town below. Liz began to unpack a few things from her backpack while Alex checked out the bathroom down the hall.

Jeff, who had stayed in the lobby, which offered free Wi-Fi and better cell service, checked his texts before dialing a number.

"Hello, Professeur. Finally. I was beginning to worry," said Jeff. "I've been trying to reach you all day."

"Oh sorry, Jeff. I just lost track of time. And the reception at the abbaye is horrible. But the abbaye itself is fascinating. I spent most of the day photographing the grounds."

"That's terrific! I'm looking forward to seeing everything tomorrow. I wanted to let you know that we arrived. There is dinner available at the hostel but…"

"Don't worry. We can do better than that, je pense. There is a café in town with wonderful mussels, and good local wine. I am driving into town now. I want to shower and print out a few of my pictures to show you."

"Let's meet in the lobby in say, an hour and a half," suggested Jeff, turning to give thumbs up to the clerk, as he headed up the stairs to his room.

"D'accord, see you then," agreed Simône, as she turned into the parking lot of the hostel.

Two hours later, the group sat drinking local red table wine as they waited for their orders of mussels and bread to arrive.

"First, I want to thank you both for joining us," said Professeur Bertrand. "And please, call me Simône, for we are new amis, friends." She raised her glass in toast to Liz and Alex. "When Jeff told me about you two, I realized you would make wonderful additions to our quest. Has Jeff told you much about what we are doing?"

"Only that you are searching for something that might lead you to Templar treasure," Liz said, a note of excitement in her voice.

"C'est vrai, you are correct," said Simône, with a smile.

"But perhaps I should explain. I don't really think we are looking for treasure, in the traditional sense-gold or silver. No, I think we are searching for something much more precious."

"Like what?" asked Alex, her interest piqued.

"It is still a mystery," Simône said, shrugging her shoulders. "But from what I've read in the diary I found… You told them about it? Ah oui," she asked, looking just momentarily at Jeff, who nodded, before continuing. "I suppose some people might think that it concerns no less than the future of mankind."

Jeff, Alex and Liz looked at each other in surprise as the Professeur continued.

"According to the diarist, his uncle, the queen's hairdresser, was entrusted by the queen with a document right before the French revolution and told to hide it at the abbaye. Why she chose that location we may never know, but if the document does concern the Templars, then perhaps it makes sense. This area contributed many knights to the Crusades-even a relative of mine, Godfrey of Bouillon."

"Yes, Jeff told us; that is amazing," said Liz, shaking her head.

"Or who knows? Perhaps it was destined," added Simône.

"What do you mean destined?" asked Alex.

"Well, I suppose you have heard of the quatrains of prophesy by Nostradamus?"

"Yes, of course," answered Alex, nodding her head in agreement.

"Well, one of the many prophesies attributed to him suggests that a couple, a 'Queen of the white stone' (supposedly a reference to Marie-Antoinette and a scandal involving a diamond necklace) and a King in gray, will travel through the forest, causing some type of war and violence. Many believe this references the royal family's attempts to escape France on the eastern border before the revolutionaries who were quickly gaining control could take them captive."

"The quatrain also mentions a second couple traveling through the forests of Reines (which many believe referred to Reims). Some historians suggest that this is a reference to the Queen sending someone-perhaps the hairdresser Leonard-on some type of secret trip on her behalf. Such a theory of course, has always just been based on speculation and conjecture," Simône admitted.

Simône looked at Jeff, who nodded silently, as if he was agreeing that she should continue.

"But now perhaps we have actual evidence that such a secret trip occurred. Most historians believe that if such a trip was made, it was to bring actual treasure to the North for future use by the Royals and the Royalist troops. But I think that given the diarist's focus on a document, perhaps the riches were not the true treasure."

"So what does the diary say about this document that makes you think it was or is so valuable?" asked Alex.

"That is what is so intriguing," Simône said, leaning forward and lowering her voice, causing the other three to huddle in as well.

She looked around, before saying, "The diary does not reveal the contents of the document itself. But it claims the document was contained in some type of tube, and that there was writing on the outside of the rolled document contained in the tube."

"What did it say?" gasped Liz.

Simône paused a moment, seemingly for dramatic effect, before continuing. "A rough translation is:

Knights of good will, spread the message far and wide.
The peace will be obtained
Heaven's treasures and cross, combined,
By promise of the three, with arms laid down.
And all men of good heart
Have pledged and hold that
God provides one sovereign end
'Ere grace or fire for each and every soul."

"Wow, that's profound sounding," Alex said, eyes wide. "What do you think it means?"

"I suspect, given the times and places where the Templars were active, 'the three' refers to the three religions: Christianity, Judaism and Islam, and some agreement between the three. I think that is supported by the phrase 'heaven's treasures and cross combined.'"

"'Heaven's treasures' could definitely refer to stars and the moon, prevalent symbolism in the Jewish and Islam faiths. And of course, the cross reference is obvious. Now how such an agreement became secret treasure of the Templars, je ne sais pas!" Simône said in conclusion, shrugging her shoulders and turning her palms upward in question.

Alex and Liz sat silent for several seconds considering the possibilities.

"I would bet the reference to the three religions would've been of great interest to the church, and by extension, the Knights Templar," Jeff said, thinking out loud.

They each stared into their glasses as if they held the answer, before Liz asked, "Do you really think there might have been some type of peace agreement between the three religions at the time of the Templars?"

"Not likely, but I suppose it is possible," Jeff replied. "Either at the time they were in Palestine or sometime before their arrival. There are documented periods of time when the three religions lived in relative peace."

Simône nodded as Alex and Liz listened with rapt attention.

"Before the crusades, there was a period of tolerance that existed in Jerusalem and Holy Lands as a whole. Perhaps some détente was reached which formed the basis of such an agreement," Jeff said.

"Certainly the discovery of such an agreement might have a profound effect in the present day on the state of world relations, particularly in the Middle East," interjected Simône.

"So if such an agreement was reached, why have we never heard of it?" asked Alex, her eyes shining with question.

Professeur Bertrand shrugged her shoulders again in her very French way before answering. "There are many possibilities, I suppose. Remember, at the time of the Templars' control of the Holy Lands and through the time of their ultimate demise, the church-the Catholic

Church-actively sought the destruction of the Muslim religion."

"Well, and vice versa, I assume, correct?" asked Liz, with a slightly furrowed brow.

"Yes, that is true. Muslims continued attacks in the West long after Isobel and Ferdinand regained control of Spain in the late 1400's."

"And what do you mean by demise?" asked Alex.

"Now that's where the story gets interesting, and the reason we are here in this charming village of Bouillon," said Jeff, sitting forward in his seat. "May I?" he said with a look at Simône, clearly deferring to the Professeur.

"Mais oui, but of course," she said, gesturing for him to continue.

"First, I guess I should tell you about the history that led to the Crusades and the formation of the Knights Templar. Until the 300's AD, Christians were openly persecuted and killed for their beliefs. They had to worship in secret, if at all. But in 302 AD, the Emperor Constantine is said to have converted to Christianity after seeing the sign of a cross in the sky during a major battle. Once he passed the edict of Milan in 313 AD, guaranteeing religious freedom to Christians, the Christian religion began to spread throughout the empire."

"But I thought the Templars were active around 1000 AD," said Liz, looking confused.

"Well, Constantine's involvement is just the beginning of the story. In addition, Helena, the mother of Constantine, already a devout Christian, who revered the holy city of Jerusalem, was determined to spread the Christian faith. She traveled to Palestine in 326 AD in search of holy Christian relics, and in particular, the one true cross. While she was there, she was responsible for converting a number of structures from pagan temples to Christian churches, as well as building the Church of the Nativity in Bethlehem and the church on the Mount of Olives in Jerusalem."

Jeff took another sip of wine before continuing.

"But, most importantly, she was responsible for the construction of the Church of the Holy Sepulcher, supposedly built over what many believe was the location of the tomb of Jesus. She returned to the West in 328 AD, bringing with her many allegedly Christian relics. The relics she brought back stoked the fires of Christian fervor to visit the historic lands and sites she had encountered in her travels," Jeff concluded.

"It's interesting that a woman had such power and influence, in the 4th century, no less." Alex looked at Liz and Simône, who both smiled in appreciation.

"Yes, that's true," agreed Jeff, not taking the bait. "Once the pilgrimages started in earnest, the numbers of Christians visiting Palestine steadily grew over the next three centuries. But then, along came Mohammed and Islam in the 7th century."

"However, although Muslims now controlled the Holy Lands, something resembling a truce existed, I guess you would say," Jeff said, before stopping to take a drink of his wine and eat some of the mussels which had just arrived.

CHAPTER FIVE

"Don't stop the story now," said Liz, encouragingly. "You still haven't gotten to the Templars."

"Ah, the Templars," said Jeff, wiping some juice from his chin. "Patience, we are almost there."

Outside, the rain had stopped and the last bit of sunlight glimmered on the horizon down valley. Inside the café, table candles had been lit, imparting a warm glow that held at bay the encroaching darkness.

Jeff took one more sip of wine and pushed away his now empty plate before continuing.

"From the latter part of the 7th century and for the next 300 plus years, the pilgrimages continued sporadically. But by the early 11th century, traveling to the Holy Lands had become quite dangerous. Pilgrims were stopped, robbed, sometimes murdered by various marauding groups. In particular, the Seljuk Turks, a fierce band of warriors who had sworn allegiance to Islam, posed an increasing danger to those penitents hoping to reach Jerusalem. The problem got so bad that in 1095 AD, Pope Urban II called a meeting of High-Church officials and archbishops in Auvergne, France and pled for a crusade to retake the Holy Lands."

"Under Godfrey of Bouillon, some 50,000 knights who had answered the Pope's call marched toward Palestine. Upon reaching Jerusalem, they took the city in a bloody siege that lasted 40 days, from June 7th to July 15, 1099 AD. From that time forward, Jerusalem was ruled by a Christian king until the Muslim tribes, under the leadership of Saladin, retook Jerusalem from the crusaders in 1187 AD."

"So if the Templars found some treasure in Jerusalem, it would have been during that 88 year period when Christians ruled the city?" Alex asked.

"Yes, I suppose that could be true," Simône replied. "There have been stories told throughout the last millennium of treasure found by the Templars under the Temple Mount. Some historians believe that they dug into and beneath the Temple Mount during the Christian reign in Jerusalem. They definitely had access to that area while they were in control. In fact, we know that they even kept their livestock and other supplies in certain areas beneath the mount. So it is certainly possible that they engaged in excavation or archeological exploration during that time period."

"Except, the story isn't quite complete," Jeff said. "The Templars still had control of parts of Palestine for another 100 years after the Muslims retook the city. There are other sacred and historical areas such as the Monastery at Mount Carmel, which we know the Templars controlled at various times during the crusades. They had a post, Pilgrims' Castle, which guarded that route for pilgrims coming from the seaport of Haifa to Jerusalem. In fact, it wasn't until 1291 AD that the last Templars were forced to flee Palestine by sea with the fall of Acre on the Mediterranean coast."

"And remember," Jeff added, "traditional wisdom holds that the Templar treasure was just that, actual treasure-gold, silver, jewels-they had accrued over the hundreds of years since their founding. As bankers and major landholders throughout Western civilization and the Middle East, it is believed that they had untold wealth, wealth which seemed to have vanished without a trace when their Paris Temple was raided on Friday the 13th, 1307 by soldiers acting on behalf of Philip IV, King of France. At the Temple and throughout France, over 2000 Templars, servants and staff were arrested."

"Why? What had they done?" asked Liz.

"That's just it," answered Jeff. "Probably nothing, but King Philip owed large sums of money to the Templars. And Philip had a nasty habit of clearing his debts by arresting those to whom he was indebted, such as Italian bankers or Jews, seizing all of their assets and then throwing them out of France. Conventional wisdom holds that his arrest of the Templars was his way of canceling large war debts accrued during the reign of his father."

"But of course, he could not do that to the Templars-throw them out of the country." Simône interjected. "They were French, not foreigners, and although they had lost some favor with the Church after losing the Holy Lands, they still had some supporters and power."

"So how did King Philip get away with it?" asked Alex.

"Because, ma cher, he accused them of heresy, the one charge the church could not ignore," Simône responded. "He arrested them in the name of the Inquisition, fully sanctioned by the church. All but the few who escaped-less than 30-were subjected to horrible forms of torture, such as being drawn on the rack or having their feet burned until the bones fell out, in order to get them to confess to various acts of apostasy: everything from spitting on the holy cross to acts of homosexuality and idol worship. Subject to these horrible tortures, even the bravest of the Templars, including the head of the order, the grand master, Jacques De Molay, confessed."

"So was there any truth to the charges?" Alex asked, her voice revealing her disbelief.

"Unlikely," said Jeff, shaking his head as he took another sip of wine. As the waitress walked by, he motioned for the check.

"And at first it looked like the Pope might intervene. After all, the Templars were basically an arm of the church, and the arrest of the Templars under the secular power of Philip probably was not well received by Pope Clement."

"What did he do?" Liz and Alex asked in unison.

"Pope Clement issued a Papal Bull, a ruling," replied Simône, taking on the role of storyteller as Jeff paid the bill and divvied up the last of the wine among their four glasses.

"He declared that Philip had acted illegally and that he must surrender control of the Templars and their assets to the church. When Philip refused, the Pope was forced, I guess you would say, to issue a second Bull to all of the Kings throughout Europe, commanding them to arrest all Templars and their properties in the name of the church. By doing that, he was letting it be known that he was taking charge of the Templar issue."

"But in the meantime, Philip continued to deny the Pope access to his prisoners who he held in Chinon, France. Finally in July 1308, Pope Clement interviewed 75 Templars who Philip had sent to him in Poitier."

"And?" Alex and Liz asked, again in unison, wide-eyed.

"The Pope apparently found that the Templars were not heretics, that their initiation practices were perhaps strange but not truly a denial of their Christian beliefs, and absolved them."

"So they were freed?" asked Liz, hopefully.

"Well, that is where the story really gets strange. There was a document only recently found in the Vatican libraries in 2007, the Chinon Parchment, which apparently contains those findings of absolution. But for whatever reason, those findings were never made public back in the 1300's. In May 1310 AD, Philip had 54 Templars, who had recanted their confessions, burned at the stake on the grounds that they were relapsed heretics."

"And the Pope did nothing?" Alex asked, sounding indignant.

"Apparently he continued 'to consider' the matter," Simône said, shaking her head. "And ultimately, Pope Clement issued another Papal Bull in March of 1312 AD, which ruled that although the Templars were not heretics, their reputation had become so stained that they could no longer act as an effective arm of the church. And he subsequently granted all of the Templars' assets (which had been seized by Philip and the other European monarchs) to the Knights Hospitalier."

"So Philip didn't get the treasure after all?" asked Liz, sounding satisfied.

"Unfortunately, he did. In fact," said Jeff, jumping in, "he extracted a large sum from the Knights Hospitalier, claiming he was owed it for his efforts in bringing the Templars to justice."

"Oh brother," said Alex with disgust.

"Then, having made a determination that satisfied Philip without unduly disgracing the Church, the Pope apparently washed his hands of the remaining Templars who were still in Philip's dungeons. Philip, with the help and sanction of the particularly bloodthirsty Archbishop of Sens, the one who had signed the death warrant on the unfortunate 54, determined that he could let the four most senior Templars, including Geoffrey of Charney and the Grand Master himself, Jacques De Molay, starve to death in prison."

"But instead, Molay and Charney recanted their confessions once again. As relapsed heretics, according to church law, Philip could now burn them to death, as he had the 54 Templars who had earlier recanted. And so, on March 18, 1314, the two were burnt at the stake on an island in the Seine River, in sight of Notre Dame Cathedral," said Jeff, solemnly.

"And the Pope never intervened?" Liz asked in disbelief.

"No. In fact, with his dying breath, Jacques De Molay, supposedly cursed Philip and Pope Clement, both of whom died within the year."

"Serves them right," said Liz indignantly, sitting back in her chair with her arms across her chest.

"And more importantly, neither Philip nor the Church ever found the bulk of the Templars' treasure."

"It just disappeared?" asked Alex incredulously.

"Well, ma cher, that is a story for another day, peut-être," said Simône, looking at her watch. "Jeff, it is after 9. I think it is time to call it a night," she added, looking around at the empty café and the proprietor who had been glancing at their table repeatedly for the last half-hour.

"Oh, right," said Jeff. "So Professeur, what is our schedule for tomorrow morning?"

"Shall we meet out at the abbaye tomorrow morning at 9 AM? The sun will be up by then, and we should have plenty of light to begin our search."

After Simône gathered her things and headed out the door, Jeff turned to Alex and Liz. "Ladies, after you," said Jeff as he held the door for them. Five minutes later, they were back at their lodgings.

"Well, good night, and thanks for the Templar history lesson. It is all fascinating," Liz said, giving Jeff a peck on the cheek before walking away through the lobby toward the dormitory stairs.

"Yes, thanks, Professeur," said Alex, following Liz's example with a quick kiss on the cheek, leaving Jeff with a disappointed look on his face.

When Alex reached their room, Liz began to pepper her with questions, as they got ready for bed. "So what gives; why are you giving the poor boy the cold shoulder?"

"I'm not; I think it's just... I don't want things to be complicated on this trip. This is about you and me, right sis? Not some guy."

"Fair enough," said Liz. "But you know, I don't think ones like Jeff come along that often. I wouldn't leave him hanging for too long. If you're not careful, the Professeur might just snap him up."

"Very funny, although I admit they did seem pretty cozy when they were finishing each other's thoughts during the tale of the Templars," Alex said, somewhat pensively.

"Ah, jealousy!" said Liz with a laugh. "Remember, I'm the one with the green eyes. Bon noir, ma soeur," said

Liz, before turning off the bedside lamp, leaving Alex alone in the dark with her thoughts.

The next morning, as Jeff drove down the long, forest-lined road to the Abbaye, Alex and Liz talked excitedly about their upcoming treasure hunt.

"So what are we actually hoping to find out here? I mean, we are talking about something that might've been hidden here over 200 years ago. And from what I've read about the Abbaye, it was almost destroyed shortly after," said Alex.

"And I still don't really understand exactly what all this has to do with Templar treasure," said Liz from the backseat.

"Well, you heard what Simône said. "The riches of the Templars were probably dispersed throughout Europe at the time they were captured on that very unlucky Friday the 13th," Jeff said.

"I've always hated Friday the 13th," said Alex with a frown.

"Me too. But putting that aside," continued Jeff, "there has always been a myth about some other treasure discovered by the Templars, something priceless that had great meaning from a religious standpoint. Perhaps even something that marauding soldiers would have considered insignificant or even worthless."

"But certainly something like the document described in the diary that Simône found would have been destroyed-burned or something-when the Abbaye D'Orval was burned to the ground," Alex said.

"Probably," admitted Jeff, "but you never know-we have to at least look. Admittedly, it's just the beginning of our search. Who knows where this may lead," said Jeff, as he pulled the car into the abbaye's parking lot.

CHAPTER SIX

EARLY MORNING, JULY 23, 1793, L' ABBAYE D'ORVAL

Brother Bernard, looking decidedly older and much wearier than his twenty–one years in his mud-stained robes, opened his eyes to the cold, bleak light of dawn. Pungent smoke pervaded the air, filling his nostrils. He stifled a cough as his lungs tried to expel the thick, acrid air that enveloped him. As his eyes adjusted to the light, he blinked to stop the stinging sensation.

The night before, during the maelstrom, he had left his hiding place in the church to sneak past soldiers who were intent on destroying every last abbaye structure, many already alight with hell's fire; he had crawled through the dark to his present hiding place, a copse of prickly bushes, which stood at the edge of the clearing that delineated the perimeter of the once resplendent abbaye grounds. He choked back a sob as he thought about the violence, the death, the slaughter of several of his beloved brothers: gentle Timothy; the funny, yet brilliant Pierre, scion of a great family, who had forsaken all to humbly serve God; and Francoise, who only had taken his vows a month before. All dead, viciously slaughtered by the marauding mob because the three monks had refused to divulge where the abbaye's gold was hidden. Bernard wiped away tears as he wondered what had happened to the rest of his brothers.

The killers claimed that they sought liberté, égalité, fraternité, *or even justice,* the words they had shouted during the rampage, but Bernard saw clearly that they acted

39

for the most craven of all reasons-for gold, for treasure. *Yet*, he thought hopefully, taking a deep breath, *perhaps they did not discover the real treasure,* the treasure that the Abbott had entrusted to his care two years before when a stranger had appeared at the abbaye seeking sanctuary.

Bernard knew that the man had come on a secret mission for Marie-Antoinette, la Reine de France, bearing not only silver Ecus (coins), but also something else, something that the traveler described as "much more precious." Presumably, the traveler, a man named Leonard-supposedly a servant of the Queen herself-had shared the nature of the contents of the small metal box with the Abbott. Bernard could not say. He only knew that after speaking with Leonard, who had arrived shortly after a troop of soldiers had come and gone after unsuccessfully looking for the man on the abbaye grounds, the Abbott had instructed Bernard to hide the box safely on the grounds, but had made him vow to reveal the hiding place to no one but the Abbott, and to guard it with his life. But Bernard had never gotten the chance to tell him the location he had chosen.

A few hours later, having been fed and reprovisioned, the mysterious Leonard had safely galloped away from the Abbaye, minutes before the same troop of soldiers had returned and taken the Abbott into custody, declaring him an enemy of the revolution. Over the protests and pleading of the monks, Abbott Godard had been beaten, chained and blindfolded before being thrown like a sack of grain over the back of a pack mule, one of three tethered behind the horse of one of the soldiers.

"Fear not my brothers. God will protect you," he had shouted out, despite his distress. And then, even as blood watered the soil beneath his beaten body, he cried out, "Bernard, do not forget your vow."

At this, one of the soldiers had struck him, rendering the old man unconscious. That was the last time that Bernard had seen the Abbott, an unconscious sack of humanity. A few weeks later, word reached their golden valley that their dear leader had been taken to the dungeons of what had once been the Abbaye du Mont St-Michel. Now desecrated with the blood and suffering of many Christian martyrs who had died at the hands of the revolutionaries, Bernard knew that until recently, it had been regarded as one of the most holy spots in western Christendom.

Bernard, who wondered wretchedly if God still resided there, or anywhere in France, for that matter, slowly pulled his aching body out from under his prickly sanctuary and cautiously looked around, surveying the devastation. He listened for several minutes for any noise suggesting life, but was only rewarded with the sound of the breeze rustling through the trees surrounding the clearing, and the popping of still glowing embers and the settling of burned timbers.

With great sorrow, he walked toward the smoldering ruins of the abbaye, noting that some portions of the abbaye's exterior walls still remained standing. As he reached the interior of what had been the churchyard, he saw with hope that the wall, which had encased the hiding place of 'the treasure,' as he thought of it, appeared to be intact, albeit covered in black soot. Walking past, he arrived at the area where the beautiful church had stood. Just yesterday, he had sung mid-day prayers here with his brothers. Now only the tortured skeleton of that holy place remained. Choking back another sob, he used the back of his hand to wipe away tears before crossing himself, and then continued with his inspection. The beautiful illustrated Bible, which had held a place of honor on the altar, was now just a pile of black and gray ashes. Shaking his head in anger, the young monk turned in a full circle, noting grimly that nothing made of wood remained.

So, no ladder, he thought. He had hoped, futilely, that the one kept in the corner near the altar to light candles in the second story windows might have survived the flame, affording him a means of retrieving 'the treasure.'

After a moment spent staring around forlornly, he gasped, startled by a sound behind him. Jerking around, he saw that the noise came from one of the abbaye's curs that now came up to him whimpering, no doubt, for both food and comfort.

"I know, boy, it is terrible!" agreed Bernard, squatting to pet the small black and white dog. "I'm not long for this God-forsaken place. I just have to figure out how to get 'the treasure' and then I'm leaving." The dog, his oversized black eyes fixed on the man, seemed to be asking to be included in the man's plan. Bernard hesitated a moment before saying, "D'accord, you can come with me. You are the only family I have left, I guess."

He gave the dog one more pat on the head, before standing up to look around once more, considering his options. He thought for a moment before exclaiming, "Peut-être, there is still a ladder in the orchard."

Excited into action, he ran back through the grounds to the clearing where he could circumnavigate the perimeter of the ruins more easily. The small dog, now sure of his welcome, trotted dutifully along behind him. Within minutes, the monk had reached the far side of the grounds where acres of fruit trees stood, untouched by the fires.

"Dieu merci," he said, again crossing himself, as he spied an eight-foot, wooden ladder, leaning against an apple tree laden with almost ripe fruit. Bernard quickly mounted the first three steps, and picked several pieces of fruit, with which he filled his pockets.

He hesitated, before picking one more and climbing down. "Waste not, want not," he said to the dog waiting expectantly below. He ate most of the red globe in a few ravenous bites before offering some to his companion. The dog sniffed the proffered piece of fruit before whimpering pitifully, indicating his disappointment.

"Sorry, boy, but I don't have anything else," he said, putting his empty palms under the dog's muzzle. "But perhaps the Lord will provide. We will look for other food before we leave. Perhaps a few scraps yet survive."

Having finished his meal, the monk laboriously hoisted the heavy ladder under his right arm, and slowly carried it back around to the churchyard.

I hope I can remember the exact location, and that it is still here-it's been two years, he thought. Once he had positioned the ladder in what he considered the likeliest spot, he tucked his robe up around his legs and into his leather belt, creating pantaloons of a sort. *"Wouldn't want to break my neck climbing this thing after escaping murder by those cutthroats,"* he thought. After carefully climbing to the top rung of the ladder, he looked around to ensure that no one had appeared to thwart his mission, before he began to push on stones in the area where he recalled the hiding place had been positioned. He searched unsuccessfully for several minutes before realizing that the heavy smoke damage had confused him as to the location.

Climbing down, he looked at the wall for a few moments before repositioning the ladder to his left. This time his efforts met with success. Approximately fourteen feet up, he found a partially mortared seam between two stones, which he himself had set two years before. Using a large nail that he had found during his search of the church grounds, he dug into the mortar until he was able to pry loose one of the stones. After several minutes of exertion and some bloodying of his knuckles, he had removed the remaining stones concealing the opening.

"Watch out, dog," he said, as he dropped the last one at the base of the ladder. Inside the niche sat a small metal box, the exterior blackened by smoke, but otherwise miraculously intact. A smile lit his soot-covered face, as he once again uttered thanks. "Thank you, Lord, and you, blessed Virgin, for preserving this treasure-surely a sign that it is as sacred as the Abbott said."

Crossing himself, he then grabbed the box, which only weighed a few pounds, with his right hand, and used his left to climb back down. Upon reaching the ground, he decided to take his prize back out past the clearing, still wary of being discovered.

He sat down behind his original hiding spot, the copse of bushes, and looked at his companion, who sat wagging his tail. After the monk was satisfied that he could not be seen from the clearing if someone wandered by, he carefully pried the blackened box lid open on its hinges, wiped his hands on his robe, and then, holding his breath, lifted a six-inch, intricately carved wooden cylinder from the box.

Red wax, from what he assumed had been a royal seal, had melted-no doubt from the heated stones of the niche in which the box had been concealed-partially covering writing on the outside of the tube. Finally exhaling, he took his time unscrewing the metal cap before emptying the contents of the tube onto his lap. Holding the roll so that a stream of sunlight illuminated the writing, Bernard began to decipher the message, which seemed to be written in a form of Latin that he had only seen in a few very old manuscripts in the abbaye's library. His eyes grew wide as he read the script. When he had finished, he cried out, "Mon Dieu!" startling the dog, which had fallen asleep at his feet.

The young monk thought for a minute before he carefully replaced the missive in its tube, which he then, as carefully, returned to the metal box. He then rose to his knees and began to pray. After almost an hour of supplication, punctuated only by the snoring of the pup, Bernard arose.

Having received an answer to his prayers, he again climbed the ladder. He would take the box and its contents but leave a message should Leonard or the Abbott or someone acting on their behalf come to reclaim it. Standing precariously on the top rung so that he could see inside of the stone hiding place, he used his nail to carve a message-the message, which had come to him in his prayers-on the ledge closest to the opening. Bernard sweated and strained as he put his full weight into the grinding of the lettering into the solid stone. When at last he finished his task, he wiped the sweat from his brow, and looked toward the sun, estimating that at least two hours had passed. Satisfied, he climbed quickly down the ladder, and lowered it so that he could carry it back into the woods.

"Come," he said, hesitating, before adding, "Chanceux (Lucky). I shall call you Lucky, for you and I have survived when we should not have. Perhaps the Lord has put us together for a purpose."

After he had hidden the ladder in thick bushes twenty feet inside the forest tree cover, he turned to the dog, who had been trailing at his heels and said, "Why don't we go scrounge for some food in the larder below the kitchen? Perhaps God will continue to provide."

When he reached the subterranean larder, he found the door at the bottom of the stairs ajar. He lit a partially burned torch that he had picked up in the smoldering ruins. Stepping inside, he discovered that barrels of food stores had been knocked over, their contents—grain, dried fruit and vegetables—strewn and trampled across the earthen cellar floor. But in the darkest corner, missed by the rampaging soldiers who had been more interested in gold than sustenance, the monk rejoiced to find a cache of dried meats hanging from a timbered beam.

After failing to reach the string of meats by standing on his tiptoes, he rolled one of the wooden barrels over, up righted it, and after several tries was able to balance his feet on top of opposite edges of the open barrel top.

Using a knife also missed by the marauders, he cut the cord holding his find, which promptly fell between his feet into the barrel. Throughout Bernard's endeavors, Lucky stood below barking excitedly.

After awkwardly dismounting, and throwing a piece of meat to his new friend, the monk found an empty grain sack, fashioned it into a rough backpack, and then stuffed it with the meat, the apples he had picked earlier, some dried fruit and the treasure box. As he worked, he spied the last item on his mental list, an animal skin bag hanging near the door. Grabbing it, he took one last look around before climbing the stairs up to ground level and the still smoking ruins.

"C'mon Lucky, one last stop before we can depart." Swinging his makeshift backpack over his shoulder, Bernard circled back around the perimeter until he came to Mathilde's fountain. Kneeling, he said a quick prayer of thanks before dipping his clasped hands into the cool, sweet water and bringing them to his mouth repeatedly. Meanwhile, Lucky had helped himself to a drink as well. When the thirsts of both man and beast had been quenched, Bernard filled his skin canteen, and then arose, as he said a silent prayer for his lost or scattered brothers, before heading down the road leading away from the abbaye.

"Perhaps, if you and I are lucky, Lucky," he said, smiling slightly for the first time that day, "we will find shelter by nightfall." When he reached the edge of the abbaye grounds, he resisted the urge to look back; instead, he continued walking, his small, faithful black and white companion trotting at his heels.

CHAPTER SEVEN

Natalia sprinted the last fifty yards before stopping to check her split time. She doubled over for a moment, hands on her knees, taking long slow breaths. When she finally stood up, she smiled briefly as she watched the sun just peaking over the horizon, its rays casting streams of pink and orange through the layers of clouds which floated just at the top of her line of sight. A Tel Aviv morning at sunrise. When Natalia found herself in some far corner of the globe, a frequent occurrence these days, she often thought of this scene, the constant motion of the Mediterranean lapping the shore as the morning mist rolled off the water.

How many times as a teenager had she done this same run, faster and faster, until she had run herself into a full track scholarship at UCLA? And now seven years later, here she was, home again, if only briefly, before heading out again on her next adventure, her next mission.

Although she was just one of many young Israelis who went abroad for their educations, Natalia, unlike most of those students, had been groomed from her early teens, like the last two generations of her family, as a Mossad agent. Fluent in five languages, she had traveled extensively throughout her high school and college years, and understood the geopolitics of the Middle East better than most world politicians.

Natalia, acting on what was now second nature, looked around surreptitiously at the various passersby, fellow early morning runners and walkers, as she stretched, before jogging back to the lot where she had parked her car.

7:15. Good, plenty of time, she thought, *to go home, shower, change and eat before meeting with Ari,* her division chief, at 9:30. He had mentioned something about babysitting some archeologists in France-*not sure what that is about, but guess I'll find out soon enough.*

Jeff, Alex and Liz found Simône in the abbaye's bookstore, speaking in rapid French to one of the clerks. Catching her eye, Jeff waved her over and said, "Bonjour. How did you sleep?"

"To be honest, not very well. I spent a couple of hours rereading the diary and then I was too wound up to go to sleep. Maybe a few hours," Simône said with a shoulder shrug.

"Moi aussi," Jeff responded. "So what are our marching orders?"

"Well, I thought we could start with a short walk around the ruins. I can give Liz and Alex the five-franc tour and then we can divide the grounds into quarters and begin our search."

As they walked through the ruins, Simône pointed out various rooms and their probable uses when the abbaye was still functioning in the 1700's. When they reached the northwest corner of the ruins, they stopped to look into a small fountain fronted with a greenish-tinged, worn bronze plaque.

"This is the Mathilde fountain. The story of her involvement in the Abbaye is quite fascinating," said Simône. "According to legend, Countess Mathilde of Tuscany, the aunt of Godfrey of Bouillon, was a widow who one day accidentally dropped her wedding ring into a spring located on this spot. After she had gone into a nearby chapel to pray for her treasure's return, a trout rose to the surface of the waters with the ring in its mouth. In her excitement, she cried out, 'Truly this is a val d'or (a golden valley).' To show her gratitude to God for the ring's return, she decided to provide the funds for a monastery to be built on this site. The legend also explains the coat of arms of the abbaye, which includes a trout and a ring."

"Is it possible the treasure is in the fountain?" asked Liz, leaning over the edge to look down into the water.

"It isn't very deep, really no place to hide anything," answered Jeff, shaking his head. "It seems unlikely, and besides, probably too obvious a location for Leonard to use as a hiding place."

"So what are some other possibilities?" Alex asked, furrowing her brow in thought.

"Perhaps somewhere around what was then the church. Remember, the abbaye was still functioning when Leonard would have come here. He wouldn't have had access to the private rooms of the monks," Simône replied.

"Then maybe we should all start there-search all of the ruins around the church," Alex suggested

"That was our thinking," agreed Jeff."

After gathering their belongings, they headed as a group through the church's arched doorway into the area surrounded by partially standing stonewalls ranging from approximately 10 to 20 feet in height.

"As you can see, most of the walls are of new construction, built to hold the remaining pieces of the original walls destroyed by the French troops. So I wouldn't spend much time there; focus on the original masonry only," Simône said, while pointing out the different areas of stonework.

"Okay, will do," Jeff replied. "If you're going to start here, Professeur, I'll take the north side. Alex, why don't you take the west, and Liz, the south? Okay?"

"Sure," Alex replied, and Liz nodded in agreement.

After nearly two hours of searching, kicking and pushing on individual stones and pillars of the remaining structures, the hot, dusty and empty-handed Alex and Liz returned to the nave of the chapel's ruins, where Jeff and Simône stood in discussion.

"Cheer up, mes chers," said Simône. "We must not give up so easily. We are at the beginning of our search. And even if we find nothing today, it doesn't mean the treasure doesn't exist, just that it is not here now. Let's take a break and get something to eat in the café here on the grounds."

"They have found nothing I as I suspected. This is a waste of time. You can tell Achmed to tell the sheikh I said so."

"Probably not a good idea to upset the sheikh. Just keep watching and report back if anything happens," said the man on the other end of the phone call.

"Unlikely," grumbled the young, dark-haired man, clad in typical tourist attire-shorts, T-shirt, running shoes, with backpack and cell phone. As he ended the call, he continued to walk slowly around the ruins, pretending to show interest in the various informational signs.

CHAPTER EIGHT

As they walked toward the café, Alex asked, "Professeur, last night you said the mystery of the missing Templar treasure was a story for another day. What did you mean by that?"

"Oh, just that perhaps all of the Templar treasure didn't go missing after all. If Marie-Antoinette did have a document discovered by the Templars, it could only have come from one source."

"From who?" asked Liz, who had slowed her pace to listen to the Professeur's answer.

"King Philip, bien sûr. His troops raided the Templars' compound on that fateful Friday the 13th. They certainly would have found anything hidden in the Paris headquarters."

"And you think it somehow was passed down through the French monarchy?" Liz asked.

"Makes sense. Perhaps it was a trump card they held onto, knowing it might come in handy with the church one day. It would also explain why Pope Clement allowed Philip to burn Molay at the stake, even after Clement had determined that the Templars were innocent of heresy. Philip would have had something to hang over Clement's head, to insure his silence," Jeff interjected.

"Just makes me despise Philip even more," Alex said, with disgust.

The others nodded in agreement as they reached the entrance to the café. An hour later, the searchers reentered the ruins, having satisfied their appetites with delicious abbaye-made bread, cheese and beer.

"I'm ready for a second round," said Alex, cheerfully.

"Me too," added Liz with a grin.

Simône smiled at Jeff. "Excellent decision to add them to our team, Jeff. Their enthusiasm alone shall bring us success, I think."

"Simône, maybe we should look at the diary again. Maybe there is something that we missed?" said Jeff.

"I've read it a hundred times, but all right," agreed Simône, despite sounding doubtful.

"We'd really like to see it," said Alex, eagerly. At this entreaty, Simône withdrew an object from her leather satchel and placed it on the worn stone altar around which they had gathered.

It looks like a shroud protecting the secrets of a centuries-old mystery, thought Liz, as Simône donned soft cotton gloves, and after looking over both shoulders to ensure that no one other than their group was within the general area, unwrapped the material protecting the diary. Once revealed, Liz and Alex could see that the object in question was a very ancient looking leather bound journal of sorts, its top right hand corner partially burned away. In addition, the rest of the book was scorched and blackened along the edges and back cover.

"As you can see, I'm afraid it is not in very good shape," said Simône.

"Do you know how it was damaged?" asked Liz, as she stood beside Alex who was leaning forward to get a closer look.

"No, unfortunately; nor do I know how it came into my grandmother's possession. But given our connection to the area, and Godfrey, perhaps she found it during the course of her research. She was a renowned Templar historian. In fact, she wrote several books about the Crusades. Surprisingly though, despite the many years I spent listening to her Templar stories, she never told me about this discovery. "

"Really, that's kind of weird!" said Alex.

"Well, she suffered from dementia in the last few years of her life, so perhaps, she just forgot," Simône said, a note of sadness in her voice. Alex grimaced, realizing too late the insensitivity of her comment.

"But nevertheless, we have it now," said Simône, as her gloved hands slowly opened the book to a page which had been marked with a thin piece of velum.

"You both have referred to it as a diary, but it seems sort of strange that the nephew's diary would contain such specific information about his uncle," said Alex, a question in her voice.

"You're right, of course," answered Jeff, after glancing in Simône's direction. "I suppose it would be more accurate to call it a biography. The pages at the beginning of the journal contain information about the life and background of the author, a Parisian gentleman writing in the mid-19th century. It appears he saw himself as something of a historian who gathered information about this great uncle through various family members-perhaps even through something written by Leonard himself. Although, of course, we have no original source material from Leonard. Who knows, perhaps he pictured himself as a writer, and he hoped to publish the story one day. But whatever the case, his account seems to be singular. In all of our research, we have found no other mention of this journal, diary, whatever you want to call it."

"Which is why it is so extraordinary," said Simône. "Of course, it could just be total fiction," she added, "but given his details of his uncle's journey, and his description of the Abbaye D'Orval that seems consistent with the manner in which other historians described the abbaye at the time of the revolution, I... we believe it is at least an authentic recounting of his uncle's story, as the author understood it."

"Is this the page which contains the 'Knights' Call' that you told us about?" asked Liz, leaning closer.

"Yes," said Simône with excitement, pointing to the middle of the page, which contained French words that looked to Liz to be written in couplet form. "Liz, that's a great name for it, by the way."

"So does it say anything else about the 'treasure' or where to find it?" asked Alex, again leaning forward as though physical proximity to the book might cause it to surrender its secrets.

"Well, the writer says that when Leonard reached the Abbaye D'Orval, he hid silver and a small box containing treasure entrusted to him by the Queen, a 'treasure,' which she believed would ensure the Pope's assistance in freeing the royal family should their attempts to escape the revolutionaries be thwarted."

"How?" asked Alex. "By blackmailing the church, like you suggested, earlier."

"Unfortunately, nothing in this book specifically answers that, but apparently Leonard also believed that the secret in the box had been in the possession of the Royal family since the time of Philip IV," said Simône.

"How do we know?" interjected Liz.

"Well, despite being a loyal servant, Leonard apparently also had a healthy interest in self-preservation. We can only surmise, but perhaps he thought it made sense to learn this very important secret himself, in case he found himself in need of divine, or at least papal, rescue from the revolutionaries at some point in time."

"According to the nephew's account," said Jeff, jumping in, "Leonard opened the box before hiding it, and found the royal seal of Philip IV on a very ancient looking carved wood cylinder."

"And?" asked Liz, with anticipation.

"The seal on the tube he found had been broken- we can only assume by someone in the French Royal family who succeeded Philip, but truthfully, we probably will never know. But according to our diarist, it was on the outside of the tube that the 'Knights' Call,' as you referred to it, was found, and inside was an ancient piece of rolled parchment."

"So do you think Leonard looked at the parchment and found some type of peace treaty?'" asked Alex.

"I agree with Simône. We may never know," answered Jeff, with a shrug. "But what else could it be: the agreement, accord, peace treaty, whatever the 'Knights' Call' references? I mean what else could it have been?" asked Jeff again, rhetorically. "Why else would Marie-Antoinette have believed it would hold such power over the Pope and the Church?"

"So after all that, surely the diarist tells us where the treasure was hidden!" said Alex with certainty.

"Perhaps he did," said Simône, "but unfortunately the pages after this section are either illegible or missing." As she said this, she turned through the book to reveal a section of missing pages, and then a few that were scorched and unreadable.

"Oh, you've got to be kidding!" said Alex, with disgust.

"Ah, but never fear, my dear Ms. King," Jeff said with a smirk. "We are not entirely thwarted."

"C'est vrai, very true" said Simône, also smiling. "One of the reasons we are here today is because of my assistant's great skill and hard work."

Jeff nodded at the compliment before Simône continued.

"Fortunately, some of the correspondence and papers of Marie-Antoinette, written after the royal family was taken into custody, are preserved in the national archives."

"Really, I'm surprised they weren't all destroyed by the revolutionaries," said Liz.

"Yes, it is somewhat surprising but perhaps there was an educated person among the captors who appreciated the historical significance of her correspondence. Anyway, thankfully, some do still exist."

"It took months of searching," added Jeff, "but only last month I happened upon a letter from Leonard that we believe was written only two months after the Royals were captured."

"And it told her about the location of the treasure?" asked Liz.

"No, it was much more obscure. Leonard, of course, could not write anything that might call attention to himself, the journey he had undertaken or the treasure, which had been entrusted to him. So instead he wrote to inquire about the health of his Majesty, the Queen, and their children."

"How does that help?" asked Alex, sounding annoyed.

"Well…" Jeff said mysteriously, a glint in his eyes, "at the end of the letter, we think he may have included a coded message."

"Which was?" asked Alex, somewhat impatiently.

"'Like the royal kings of old, look to the heavens and let your faith be your salvation.'"

"Huh?" said Alex, confused. "That doesn't give any information on the treasure or its location."

"Yes, taken literally, it explains nothing, I agree. But in light of the mission he had undertaken for the Queen only two months before, it may be quite significant. It seems likely that Leonard would have made some effort to let the Queen know where he had hidden what might be her only chance of freedom. If, and I admit, it is a big 'if,' that was his intention, we just need to figure out its meaning to find the original hiding place of the treasure."

"Okay," said Liz and Alex, in unison, looking at each other as though accepting the challenge. "I guess 'kings of old' could refer to Philip IV. And 'look to the heavens and let your faith be your salvation'-I don't know," continued Liz. "I suppose, taken literally the phrase could refer to prayer," said Liz, thinking out loud.

"And probably would have been interpreted that way by her jailers," added Alex.

"I doubt either Leonard or the Queen believed that prayer alone would save the Royals' necks but…" Liz paused before continuing, "but if it was meant to be a clue, perhaps it did refer to an actual location."

56

"A location here at the Abbaye," said Alex in a hushed tone. And I think I might know where..."

"Yes?" Simône asked in anticipation.

"Well, assuming Leonard did hide it here on the grounds, and like you said before, he wouldn't have gone into the private quarters of the monks, his only other option would have been in or around the church, right?"

"Right," answered Jeff, a question on his face.

"So which walls of the church and church yard are original?" continued Alex. "Which ones are we sure weren't destroyed by the French revolutionary troops?"

"If the bricks show fire damage, as we discussed before, they are most likely original," answered Simône.

"And look to the heavens..." said Alex, raising her gaze to the top of the wall closest to them.

"So you think he was just referring to something 'raised,' like at the top of the church?" asked Jeff.

"Did you see something on your search that meets that description, Alex?" Simône asked expectantly.

"There is an area in the far corner of the church-yard, where I was searching... I'm not positive but it looked to me like there was once an opening there. There are the older smoked stained stones with some lighter gold-colored ones filling the middle section."

"Where? Show me!" Simône said, with a gasp.

It's over there," said Alex, pointing toward the area where she had searched that morning. Alex, Liz and Jeff began moving in that direction before Simône stopped them. "Just a moment, let me secure the diary."

It took her a few minutes to cautiously rewrap the fragile parcel and place it in her satchel. By then, Alex had already located the corner section of wall, which she had described to them. The stone wall stood approximately 20 feet high; the first 15 feet was comprised of darkened ancient looking irregular shaped stones with lighter more symmetrical stones and modern masonry resting on top.

"See, that area about fourteen feet up?" Alex said, pointing. "Doesn't it look like there might have been an opening there, where the stone is lighter?"

"Yes, it is certainly possible," agreed Simône. "Perhaps it was even the location of the abbaye's 'precious reserve,' a place for preserving relics and official church documents. I read there was one here at D'Orval located somewhere on the premises. Most churches of the time had some place for hiding precious possessions. Of course, if that was it, at the time, it would have had a wooden door or other covering."

"So how do we get up there?" asked Liz, craning her neck to look up at the space.

"Unfortunately, not in the same manner that Leonard would have. He probably could have accessed it with some type of ladder kept on the church premises. Who knows, if it truly was his hiding place, perhaps the monks assisted him if he told them the object was a holy or religious one. They certainly would have had no great love for aiding the irreligious revolutionaries," Simône explained.

As they continued to consider the possibility, Jeff rummaged through his backpack, before extracting a pair of gloves. After putting them on, he studied the wall for a moment before placing his right foot in a crack where a piece of stone had been chipped away. As the three women watched, he carefully worked his way up the wall, searching for foot and handholds as he climbed.

"Wow, new skills?" asked Alex, impressed.

"Yeah," answered Jeff from above them. "After that experience of getting trapped in the Mayan cenote, I decided to do some climbing training. I started climbing on the wall at my gym a couple of times a week. I haven't done it since I got to France, but I still have the hang of it, no pun intended."

"Ha ha, well, you go, Spiderman," said Alex.

Having pulled himself up to the level in question, he held on to a jutting block with his left hand while he used his right to examine the light colored stones. At first they held fast, but after some effort, he felt a slight movement. "I think I can probably move some of them with some effort," Jeff said, sounding excited. "I don't think they are mortared in, just crammed into place. Stand back ladies," Jeff said as he grinned down at them.

"What are you going to do?" asked Simône, sounding slightly alarmed.

"I'm just going to try to remove a stone or two so that I can see inside the opening, if there is one. I think if I can move this one," he said with a grunt, "the one below will come loose as well. It's...coming," he said breathlessly, just as the one-foot square stone came crashing down to the ground with a resounding "thunk" that reverberated off the closest ruin walls.

"Merde!" Simône shrieked, muttering the swear word before turning slightly red. "You will have every monk in the place after us with pitchforks."

Alex and Liz looked at each other before bursting into laughter.

"Sorry, Professeur," said Jeff sheepishly. "I'll try to keep the noise down. Alex, I have a flashlight in my backpack-hand it up."

Alex retrieved it quickly and then followed his same route up the wall until she could hand it up to his outstretched arm. She jumped back down, landing in a crouch, before quickly backing away, just in case any more stones came tumbling down. In the meantime, Jeff had managed to loosen another stone, which he also dropped down once Alex was safely out of the way. With flashlight in hand, he leaned precariously to the right in order to look into the chasm he had created.

"Careful up there," said Liz, wondering if they could possibly catch him should he lose his balance.

"Can you see anything? What is up there?" asked Alex, who was standing on her tiptoes to try without success to see up into the dark space.

After a few moments of silence punctuated only by Jeff's rather labored breathing, he answered, disappointment apparent in his voice. "If there was anything up here, it's not here now. The hole goes back about two feet. I think you were right, Professeur. It definitely looks like it was used for storing something. There are holes on the side that look like they might once have held hinges; there are some rusty looking stains. But the inside is dark like the stones around the outside; I think it probably was exposed to fire. I imagine anything in here would have been burned to ash."

As Alex, Liz and Simône waited, Jeff continued to slowly inch his light around the confines of the small box-like space. He was about to begin his descent when a few lighter colored lines about 6 inches from the edge of the base of the box caught his eye.

"Hmm," said Jeff, out loud.

"What? What is it? What do you see?" asked the three women all at once.

"Well," he said, laying his flashlight down in order to use his free hand to move the remaining two stones over to the area that he had already cleared.

"What, you're killing us down here," exclaimed Alex.

"Someone has carved something here, on the edge of the opening. It is still partially covered."

"What does it say, Jeff? Don't keep us in suspense," admonished Simône.

"I'm not sure, Professeur-looks French. Uh-get me a piece of paper. I will try to do a rubbing of it."

Jeff, who was starting to tire after balancing himself on the wall for several minutes, struggled to push the last stone in until he had uncovered what appeared to be the complete message. Having found some pieces of blank paper in his backpack, Alex again scaled the lower reaches of the wall and handed Jeff the paper and a lead pencil. Jeff laid the paper over the carved message and secured it with the weight of the flashlight before awkwardly making the rubbing with his free hand. Once he was satisfied that the entire carving was legible, he again requested help.

"Alex, climb back up. I don't want to mess it up by dropping it in the dirt."

Alex sighed and rolled her eyes at Liz before climbing up once more. Jeff carefully handed the paper to Alex, who just as carefully passed it into the waiting hand of Liz. Alex quickly hopped down and then stepped aside as Jeff clambered down the wall. Alex began laughing as he turned around, seeing that his hands, clothes and even parts of his face were covered with a grayish-black soot.

"You look like you have been cleaning chimneys," Alex said, chuckling.

"Yeah, I'm definitely going to need a shower. Hey, help me move these stones against the wall so they are a little less conspicuous. Maybe they'll just look like they fell out."

"Yes sir, boss," Alex said, with a salute of her hand.

Liz and Simône had already taken the precious piece of paper over to the altar and were studying it intently.

"Can you read it, Simône?" Liz asked hopefully.

Suivez la fleche de Michel

"If it is literal, it is simply 'follow the arrow of Michel, Michael,'" said Simône, as Alex and Jeff joined the discussion.

"So what does it mean?" Liz asked again, turning to Simône.

"Je ne sais pas-I don't know," said Simône. "It raises so many new unanswered questions. First, does it even have anything to do with what we are seeking, and if so, who left the message and for whom? Obviously, not for us. Was it left by someone who found the treasure hidden by Leonard?"

"It seems unlikely that French revolutionaries would have left a message about where to find the treasure-they would have just taken it or destroyed it," reasoned Jeff. " And besides, it seems a little esoteric for the commoners who made up the revolutionary guard."

Alex and Liz nodded in agreement. "Who is Michael?" asked Alex.

"Who knows, it could just be a meaningless religious message left by a monk, unrelated to any Templar treasure," Jeff said with a shrug.

"I am assuming the reference is to the Archangel Michael. Saint Michael, to us Catholics," said Simône.

"Yes, but why would someone go to the trouble of carving that in what was just a rudimentary safe? I mean, if Simône is right, what does the Archangel Michael have to do with some old bones and church papers?" Liz asked.

"I agree," said Alex. "It seems like quite an effort if it wasn't intended as some type of message to someone."

"Maybe someone found the treasure after Leonard left it here and recognized that it was something significant, something that needed to be protected, and so he or she took it but left a coded message for whomever might come seeking it," Liz speculated.

"Well, it couldn't have been any Knights Templar," said Jeff. "They were gone long before the 1700's."

"Or so we think," said Simône. "As you know, there are many people, even some respected academicians, who believe that later societies, fraternities like the Free Masons, were actually secret continuations of the Templars, which adopted their core beliefs and traditions."

"Yes, I know, Professeur, but in reality, didn't those organizations just adopt some of the underlying pageantry of the Templars, like the crosses, etc."

"You are probably correct, Jeff, but never forget, many myths have some basis in fact, in ancient history. Even some part of the tale of King Arthur, the warrior king, who was portrayed as bringing the Anglo-Saxon tribes of England together as a nation, probably derives from actual history," Simône said.

"But, back to the matter at hand, I think perhaps we should adjourn to the hostel, shower and meet at 6 in the lobby. In the meantime, think about what the message might mean. I assume that within all of our brilliant minds lies the answer. I am going to confess our little masonry project to the Abbott before I leave. It seems only appropriate."

"Oh, okay, Professeur, sounds good. Do you want to take the rubbing?" asked Jeff, extending the paper toward her. Simône considered for a moment before saying, "no, it is your discovery. Why don't you safeguard it for now, along with the diary," Simône said, handing him the bundle.

"Okay, sure, Professeur," said Jeff, surprised. "Well, ladies," Jeff said, turning to Alex and Liz, "let's head back."

"Okay, we're ready," agreed Liz and Alex as they grabbed their daypacks and walked with Jeff toward the visitor center parking lot.

CHAPTER NINE

Simône headed in the opposite direction, walking toward the office where she had first met the Abbott.

She rattled the door handle to the Abbott's office before realizing it was locked. *Oh well, I'll call him tomorrow,* she thought, secretly relieved to be able to postpone the discussion of their recent vandalism of the Abbaye grounds. *I guess I'll have to make a contribution to the abbaye's charitable fund or something,* she thought, before turning her attention to what was really on her mind, the day's discovery.

"Follow the arrow of Michael." Simône definitely was not a religious scholar but she did have a working knowledge of the heavenly cast of characters revered by the various major religions; icons and religious motifs frequently played a significant role in archeological explorations.

Let's see, she thought, as she headed through the parking lot to her car, *there are many famous Michaels in history but only one of great religious importance. If the message refers to the Archangel Michael, he is considered a significant figure in all three major religions, Judaism, Christianity and Islam.*

Specifically referenced in the book of Daniel as "a great prince who stands up for the children of your people," the Jews believed that Michael had rescued Daniel from the furnace and had saved Isaac from being sacrificed by Abraham. Over the centuries, Michael became known as the patron or protector of the Jews, despite the fact that sainthood was clearly a Christian, and specifically a Catholic, notion.

In the Christian religion, Simône knew that Michael would battle and prevail over Satan and his forces in the end times as foretold in the New Testament Book of Revelations. *And Michael*, she recalled, *is even mentioned in the Qur'an in the Sura Al-Baquara, as being an angel and messenger of Allah.*

Interesting, thought Simône, as she started her car, and failing to notice the dark sedan, which had backed out of the space two down from her, pulled out of the parking lot. *The 'Knights' Call' seems to reference all three religions and Michael is revered by all three religions. Surely that is not just a coincidence. Perhaps we did find Leonard's hiding place*, Simône mused, excited to share her new ideas with Jeff and his friends. As she pulled out from the abbaye's lane onto the main road, she checked her phone for messages. *Damn, no service. Weird, I saw other people using their phones at the ruins. Oh well*, she thought, dropping it into her purse.

"So what should I do? I'm right behind her."

"Does she have the diary?" asked the voice on the other end of the phone.

"No-she gave it to the guy; he kept the rubbing too, but she must know what is in it."

"Then grab her, she'll tell us," said the disembodied voice.

"What about the guy and the two girls?"

"She's the one in charge. We'll deal with them later."

"D'accord," said the driver, before ending the call.

Simône was lost in thought as her vehicle traversed the stretch of road that traveled through the densest part of the forest a few miles outside of Bouillon. She suddenly was snapped back to the present when a black sedan came speeding up behind her.

Hey, slow down, idiot, thought Simône, as the car came within a few feet of rear-ending hers, and then quickly jerked into the other lane. Two seconds later the driver of the other car pulled in front of hers, accelerated about a 100 yards down the road and then slammed on his brakes, bringing the sedan sliding to a stop in the middle of the road, blocking both lanes of travel. Simône, who had been traveling slightly above the posted speed of 80 Km, put all of her weight on her brake pedal, barely managing to come to a skidding stop only a few feet from the other car.

"What the hell?" Simône said out loud in a mixture of irritation and fear.

She had just unbuckled her seatbelt and had begun to exit her car when the driver of the other car emerged. Simône noticed nothing about him except the large gun he held in his hand.

"Jesus!" Simône screamed. She slid back into her seat and without bothering to shut her car door, threw the gearshift into reverse and began backing quickly down the road from which she had just come. She had backed only 40 to 50 feet away when her assailant began shooting, taking out her windshield and one of her front tires.

In reaction, Simône reflexively jerked the wheel, causing her small sports car to go careening backwards into the roadside ditch. Given the steep angle of the embankment, Simône's efforts to open her door were thwarted by the deep scrub oak into which the car had settled. By the time Simône had managed to crawl across her console and open the passenger door, the shooter had reached her and was motioning with his gun for her to get out.

As Simône exited the car, she realized she had little chance of escape; the trees and brush presented an impenetrable barrier and she knew from the past two days that very few cars traveled this stretch of road. Adrenaline pumping, she exited the car yelling, "Who are you? What do you want? I don't know you..."

"Ah, but I know you, Professeur Bertrand. Simône Bertrand, correct?" asked the gunman, a sickening grin on his face.

Simône recoiled, a feeling of panic beginning to engulf her as she realized this was not some case of mistaken identity or a random carjacking.

"I can see by the look on your face that I am correct. And now, you must come with me."

"What? Hell no, I'm not going with you," Simône said, a quaver in her voice.

"Well then, I will have to shoot you," said the young man matter-of-factly, in what Simône was beginning to realize was some sort of Middle Eastern accent. As she looked at him, she sensed that he would do so without hesitation; in fact, he would probably enjoy shooting her, if she tried to run.

"What do you want? This is a mistake..." she kept repeating, yet she knew what he wanted, knew this had to something to do with their discovery. She started to ask about Jeff and the girls but stopped herself, realizing that mentioning them might put them in danger if they weren't already there.

My car is undrivable, Simône realized. *Hopefully, he will take me into town and I can figure out a way to escape*, she thought, still holding out some hope that this mercenary, if that's what he was, just sought information about their discovery at the Abbaye, information that she would happily reveal if only he would let her go unharmed. But Simône's hopes began to fade as he secured her hands behind her with metal handcuffs, taped her mouth shut and forced her into the trunk of his car, before driving away.

CHAPTER TEN

The woman, 5'6", with shoulder length, brunette hair and an athletic build, wearing dark, nondescript clothes, moved quickly and silently from the Bouillon side street into the idling car.

"So what's happening, Davide?" she asked, apparently startling the man at the wheel who had been reading something on his cell phone.

"Crap-how do you do that? What are you, a stealth ninja?" asked Davide, sounding slightly annoyed.

"Well, for someone who does as much surveillance as you, I'd think you would learn to keep your doors locked," said Natalia, laughing. "Anyway, enough chit-chat," she continued. "Bring me up to speed. I've been driving from Paris for the last three hours; I haven't received an update since then."

"I've watched them all day. They found something out at the abbaye-some kind of carving or writing."

"Where in the abbaye?"

"In the walls surrounding the yard, near the church ruins-about fifteen feet up-some kind of storage area or box. The three inside have the rubbing they made of it."

"Do you know what it says?"

"No, I was waiting for you to arrive-we'll go back tonight after dark.

"How do we get to it?"

"Same way as the guy did-you'll climb up while I stand and watch."

"Of course," said Natalia, "we can't expect you to get your hands dirty."

"You are younger, and I admit, in much better shape than me. And I am your superior. So, yes, you can climb and I promise to try to catch you if you fall."

"Wonderful," said Natalia, with a roll of her eyes, as she sat back in the passenger seat. "I'm going to take a little nap. Let me know if anything exciting happens."

"Yes, of course," Davide said, with a chuckle.

CHAPTER ELEVEN

When the car finally came to a stop, Simône tried to listen for any identifiable sounds, which might give her a clue as to where she had been taken. She heard one of the car's doors opened and shut, and then footsteps moving away. After several minutes passed without any further discernible noise from her captor, she began to kick the lid of the trunk, hoping that the noise would attract attention from someone in the area. She kept it up for several minutes until her feet began throbbing in her now ruined shoes, and she felt slightly breathless, having sucked up much of the oxygen in her cramped prison.

After resting for a moment and taking slow, deep breaths through her noise, since her mouth was still covered, she decided to try kicking out one of the taillights, something she had once seen in a movie. Given that her hands were still handcuffed behind her, she realized she would have to squirm around until her back was facing toward the rear of the car. She had finally gotten into position and was reaching toward her feet to attempt to locate the light, when she heard footsteps approaching on what sounded like stone.

Barely breathing, she remained perfectly still as the trunk lid opened.

"Ah Professeur, have you been napping?" asked the same surly voice she recognized from earlier. "Sorry to disturb you, but the time has come for our little talk. An associate and I have a few questions for you about your recent activities."

As he said this, he grabbed her under the arms and pulled her roughly from the trunk, scraping her left arm on the trunk latch, before dropping her in a heap on the ground. "Oh dear, so sorry, I was told not to damage the merchandise," he said, with a sarcastic grin.

Simône glared up at the man, maybe 25 years old, approximately 5'8' in height, dark brown hair and olive complexion, dressed in typical tourist attire-shorts, black polo shirt, tennis shoes-and mirrored sunglasses, which hid his eyes. But he looked familiar. *Perhaps I have seen him around the Sorbonne*, she considered.

Looking around, she saw that they were in a small cobblestoned courtyard surrounded on three sides by tall gray stone walls. A ten-foot high electronic sliding steel gate blocked the fourth side of the enclosure. Almost immediately, Simône knew where he had brought her-Godfrey's castle. She was heartened by the fact that it was still light; *perhaps I can get the attention of some tourists on the grounds*, she thought, wondering where the main entrance was located. She glanced quickly up at the sun, trying to estimate the time.

"I can see the wheels turning, Professeur-I'm sure you know where we are. Unfortunately for you, we are on the opposite end of the castle from where the mindless tourists roam. Given the very thick walls, and the river below us, you could scream at the top of your lungs and no one would hear you, n'est pas."

Having said this, he reached down and ripped the tape from her mouth. "Anyway, I have a job for you," he said, roughly grabbing her injured arm and jerking her to her feet. He then unlocked the handcuffs that had been restraining her wrists.

Simône saw that he was once again pointing his gun at her and she was certain he was willing to fire it.

"Get your phone from your backpack," he said, handing her the leather satchel that he had confiscated earlier. Seeing no alternative, she complied.

"Now you are going to call the hostel in town and leave this message for your friends," he said, handing her a piece of paper with a handwritten script. "We don't want them worrying about you, do we?"

Simône frowned, realizing that he must have been watching them for a while, knew about Jeff, and probably Liz and Alex too.

When Simône did not reply, he added. "And say it exactly as written. I'm listening to every word," he said, emphasizing this by waggling the gun in her direction.

Simône quickly read the script and then proceeded to place the call; a female clerk at the hostel answered it.

"Yes, this is Simône Bertrand. Oui, bon soir."

"Oui, I need to leave a message for Jeff Stahl."

She listened a moment before continuing.

"Yes, can you take it down word for word so that you can give it to him when he returns?"

"Oui, merci."

Simône read the message she had been given, but after hesitating briefly, added a reference to 'visiting the sights her uncle had told them about.' Her captor responded by putting the gun to her temple and signaling her to stop speaking.

"Alors, merci, au revoir," said Simône, as the man grabbed her phone and ended the call, before dropping it into her satchel, which he threw angrily into the trunk.

"What was that bullshit about your uncle? That wasn't in the script!"

"I just thought if I suggested some sightseeing before they returned to Paris, they would have no reason to think there was anything to be concerned about," Simône said, trying to keep her voice from trembling.

The man, who had removed his sunglasses to wipe his brow, looked at her suspiciously, trying without success to figure out if she had played some sort of trick on him. As he stood there seeming to strain what she supposed were his few active brain cells, Simône noticed a tattoo of two tear drops below the outer corner of his left eye, indicative, she assumed, of time he had spent in prison somewhere.

"Nice tattoo," Simône said, unable to restrain herself, but then immediately regretted the comment when he exploded.

"Shut up, you heathen bitch," he said, punctuating the retort with a hard slap to her face that caused her to stumble back against the car.

"Follow my directions from now on, if you want to keep breathing."

"Sorry," Simône said, rubbing her throbbing left cheek.

"Come on, enough screwing around. We're going inside."

Her captor motioned for her to walk in the direction of a large wooden door located in the lower left corner of the wall that faced the fence. When they reached it, he pushed with some force and the door creaked inward on ancient hinges, revealing a dimly lit set of stairs leading downward into the bowels of the castle. When Simône hesitated at the threshold, he gave her a shove, causing her to almost miss a step as she descended into the near darkness.

Simône counted her progress down the steps until she reached the number twelve, at which point she stepped onto what felt like moss-covered dirt underfoot. In front of her, lit only by her captor's flashlight was a stone-lined passageway ending in a six-foot wooden door.

She stopped short of it, waiting for some direction. Instead, he reached past her and turned a large metal doorknob with a very modern looking lock. The man's action revealed a small low-ceilinged room, *not much larger than a pantry*, Simône thought, which held three chairs and a trunk in the corner. It was illuminated only by a battery-powered lantern, which cast long shadows into the four corners of the space. But she also saw that there was a second, smaller door on the opposite wall. *It might just be some sort of storage closet*, Simône thought, trying not to show too much interest.

After restraining her again with her hands behind her back, he said, "Sit down," and pushed her toward one of the metal chairs. Simône almost fell again as she sat down awkwardly.

"Now you are going to be a good little prisoner while we wait for my partner."

After approximately ten minutes of total silence, the man, who had been looking at something on his phone, said, "I have to leave for a little while. Don't bother trying to escape. I've got the only key." With that, he abruptly stood up and left the room through the same door by which they had entered.

Jeff, Alex and Liz reached the hostel at about 4:30; they headed upstairs to shower and change, having agreed to meet downstairs for a beer at 5:30.

"So what do you think the carving means?" asked Liz, as they dressed in jeans and casual sweaters.

"Not sure. More importantly, do you think I should wear these cute high-heeled Michael Kors sandals that I brought?" asked Alex, modeling them for Liz, who was finishing drying her hair.

"I wouldn't. Have you seen those cobblestones-total ankle breakers," said Liz, always practical.

"Okay, fine, you are probably right," said Alex with a pout, as she replaced the heels with a pair of Vans.

"You'll thank me later," said Liz with a slight smirk.

When they reached the lobby a few minutes later, Jeff was nowhere to be found. Instead, they were waved over by the same clerk who had checked them in the day before.

"Allo, I have a message for your friend, Jeff." He reached into one of several numbered cubbyholes behind him and pulled out a handwritten phone message. "Here, the last clerk said she forgot to give this to him when you came in-guess it is from the other guest with you, Madame Bertrand."

Alex took the piece of paper and began to read out loud to Liz.

"I'm so sorry - a family emergency has arisen back in Paris. I am driving down immediately. I will call you as soon as I can. Enjoy the sights that my uncle told you about.

Simône"

Alex finished reading and then looked back appraisingly at the clerk. "Who did you say took this message?"

"Elsa, she just went off duty."

"Can we speak with her?'

"Unfortunately, she has the next few days off-said she was going on holiday."

Alex frowned. "Did she say she had actually spoken to Simône-Professeur Bertrand?"

"Oui, I believe so-said Madame Bertrand called and had her write down the message for Monsieur Stahl."

"Okay, thank you," said Alex, before grabbing Liz's arm and pulling her to the opposite corner of the lobby. "This is strange!" said Alex, her voice barely above a whisper.

"What do you mean?" asked Liz.

"This message doesn't make sense," she said, as she began to text Jeff.

"Get down here NOW!"

As she looked up from her phone, she saw that Jeff had just come bounding down the stairs, a big grin on his face.

"What's up? Can't go even an hour without me?" he asked, teasing, as he held up his phone to show her the text, which he had just read.

"No-it's not that," said Alex, shaking her head.

Jeff came over to them quickly, sensing something was wrong. "Is everything okay?"

"I'm not sure," replied Alex, still speaking in almost a whisper, causing Jeff and Liz to form a small huddle around her. "But I think something weird is going on."

She paused as she handed the paper bearing the message to Jeff. "This message from Simône doesn't make any sense."

Jeff read it twice before looking up at Alex and Liz. "I see what you mean. Obviously I have never spoken to any of her uncles. I've never even met any of her family."

"Why would she say that, then?" asked Liz.

"I don't think Simône left this message," Jeff said, sounding worried. "Or if she did," a frown creasing his brow, "I think it may have been under duress. Maybe she's trying to let us know."

"Do you actually think something's happened to her? I tried to talk to the woman who took the message but she's gone, left on vacation. The clerk said she'd forgotten to give you the message before she left."

"Dammit, I should have stopped at the desk when we came in! I didn't even think..." said Jeff, his voice trailing off.

"It's not your fault," said Alex. "There's no way you could have known."

"So what do we do?" Liz asked.

"Let me try to call her-maybe we are overreacting," said Jeff, trying to remain calm, yet clearly concerned.

The girls sat together, anxiously waiting as Jeff tried the multiple numbers he had for Simône.

Finally he said, "I've tried every number, work, home and cell; they are all going to voicemail."

"Is there anyone else you can call in Paris? Someone who lives close to her or knows her well?" Alex asked.

"Not that I'm aware of. I suppose I could call the university but there probably won't be anyone there on the weekend."

"And she's not married?" asked Liz.

"No, divorced just six months ago-kind of an ugly one, I guess, so probably no help there."

"Let's check her room," suggested Alex. "If her things are gone, then she probably did come back here, pack up, and head back to Paris."

"I agree. If so, no harm, no foul; if not..." Jeff let the alternative hang in the air.

After a few minutes of explanation, the front desk clerk, Godfrey, agreed to let them into her room. "I'm not really supposed to do this," he said, hesitating at her door, before using his master key.

"We won't tell a soul," said Alex, encouraging him with a smile.

Once inside, they saw that the room was neat, as though the housekeeping staff had just cleaned. Simône's monogrammed bag sat undisturbed in the corner, and an inspection of the closet revealed her organized clothes and shoes.

After filing out of the room and thanking the clerk for his help, they followed him back to the lobby. Once he was out of earshot, Alex, who looked as if she was about to burst, said, "Oh my God! She really is missing. I thought we were just being paranoid. So should we go to the police? I don't want to be overly dramatic but..."

"Maybe we'll have to...let me think for a minute. I know Simône; if she left this message, she was trying to tell us something-like...like her location," Jeff said.

"She talked about her uncle. She knows you don't know any of her uncles, but..." Suddenly Liz's face lit up. "Could she have meant the one uncle we do know about?"

77

"Of course, you're brilliant!" said Jeff, sounding excited. "She knows we know about Godfrey-maybe that is the clue."

A few seconds passed as they considered this possibility.

"His castle!" Alex and Liz suddenly said together, before looking around to see if anyone in the lobby was listening. They saw that the clerk had left the front desk momentarily, and the one couple sitting in the other corner of the lobby seemed engrossed with something on their laptop.

"It's 5:45," Jeff said, checking his phone. "Simône and I went to see it a couple of months ago when we first came to look at the Abbaye. I think I remember that it is open to tourists until 7 this time of year."

"Let's go then," said Alex, who was already headed for the door. Over her shoulder, she added, "Even if she isn't there, at least we can check it out and maybe we will see something to help us figure out what's going on."

Jeff and Liz needed no further prompting. But as they left, Jeff decided to leave a message for Simône, on the off chance she came back. "Listen," he said to Godfrey, who had just resumed his position behind the front desk, "if Simône, Professeur Bertrand, should call or come back while we're gone, will you tell her we took her uncle's advice?"

"Uh, sure," said Godfrey, distractedly, without taking his eyes off his phone on which he was typing a text, as Jeff headed for the lobby door.

"It looks like they are headed to dinner," said Natalia, stretching her arms out in front of her and rolling her shoulders back to relieve the muscle tension from sitting for hours. "Seems unlikely that they could get into any trouble in this sleepy little village."

"Yeah, once they're gone, we'll head out to the Abbaye and check out their find," said Davide. "We'll have to wait until dark, though, at least nine, before we can sneak onto the Abbaye grounds. We should get something to eat now. I saw a café around the corner that looked okay. We can go there.

"Alright, but let's make it a quick recon at the abbaye. My instructions from Ari are to keep an eye on the Americans, not to go sightseeing at some old ruins."

"True, but if it weren't for those ruins and what they are looking for, they wouldn't be here in the first place, and we'd be sitting eating real food in a café in Tel Aviv."

CHAPTER TWELVE

A few minutes later, Jeff parked his rental car in the main lot at the bottom of the hill; at the top, the large medieval castle loomed. As they walked quickly up the cobble-stoned-drive, Jeff gave them a brief history of the fortress.

"Historians believe that some form of the structure was built here several centuries before it was first mentioned in a historical text in 988 AD. It was owned at that time by a Duke of the House of Ardennes (Godfrey, the uncle, was the 5th and last in line.) He had to sell the castle in 1096 AD to Prince Otbert, Bishop of Liege, in order to raise money to help finance the First Crusade that we told you about. After that, it passed through numerous hands, including several French kings, but because of its hilltop location overlooking the entire valley and the River Semois, which runs through it, the castle continually served as a fortress to repel invaders passing through the area."

"It's in incredible shape; I never would have guessed it was so old," said Liz, with a gasp, slightly out of breath, as they reached the level where the drawbridge granted access to the main courtyard of the castle. If they had stopped to look, they would have enjoyed a beautiful view, a canopy of treetops, the shimmering sunlit river far below and the gray-tiled roofs of the houses that lined it. But on a mission, they headed straight for the kiosk to purchase admission tickets.

From a distance, the castle had looked like it was covered in plaster or stucco, but as they reached the entrance, they could see that the walls had been constructed over the centuries with countless levels of gray stones, held in place by the weight of those that rested above. As they walked through the small, dark passageway, which linked the outer drawbridge with the foot-thick wall lining the inner courtyard, their senses were immediately assaulted by the accumulated sights and smells of more than a millennium: moss-coated walls, stones stained by water, blood and fire, and the ghostly scent of the untold legions of man and beast that had sought protection within its keep.

Once inside the courtyard, they spotted a small group of tourists had gathered around a man dressed in medieval-looking clothes, his left arm sheathed in the leather gauntlet of a falconer. On his arm perched a magnificent bird, its dark wing-feathers glistening, hooded yet alert, waiting for the moment when his master would release him to the air, to freedom.

"I wish we could stay and watch," said Liz pensively, "but I know…"

"Next time, kiddo," said Jeff. Liz nodded gravely in acceptance.

After reviewing an informational placard with a diagram, the three decided to spread out in order to quickly explore the different areas of the castle, planning to meet back in the courtyard in 15 minutes.

"If you see anything out of the ordinary, come back immediately-don't do anything heroic. I mean it!" said Jeff, looking pointedly at Alex and then Liz, who both nodded solemnly in agreement.

Fifteen minutes later, they reconvened in the center of the now vacant courtyard, as the last of the tour bus operators corralled their charges for the trip back to Reims and the champagne that awaited.

"Anything?" asked Jeff.

Both Alex and Liz nodded in the negative. "Well, at least we tried," said Liz.

"Any other ideas?" asked Alex.

"While I was waiting for you, I tried calling all of her numbers again. I really am worried," admitted Jeff. "She's usually a stickler about returning messages. It just isn't like her not to call within an hour or two."

"So now do we go to the police?" asked Liz, a catch in her voice.

"I guess so," said Jeff, sounding dejected. "Although, I'm not sure what the local cops are going to do, particularly since she left a message saying she had returned to Paris. I doubt they will believe our idea about a coded message. Let's go back to town, just in case she's shown up," he added, not sounding very hopeful.

After having eaten a quick dinner, the Israelis headed out toward the abbaye, just missing the three Americans, who were returning to their hostel.

At the edge of town, Alex, who was looking at her IPhône, said, "You know, I've been thinking. Simône seems pretty tech savvy. She has all of the gadgets, including a laptop, iPad and iPhone, right?"

"Yeah, she is and does, why?" Jeff asked.

"Well," Alex continued, "I have 'Find my phone' enabled on my phone and laptop. I've never used it, but if she has it, maybe we can find her location if her phone still has some juice."

"Yeah, but don't we need her laptop for that?" asked Liz.

"Yes," Jeff said, thinking out loud, "but I think I know how we might get it. Let's get back into her room. She had her iPad with her out at the abbaye but I bet her laptop is in the bag we saw in her room."

"Now all we have to do is to convince Godfrey to let us back in," said Liz, sounding unsure.

"It's probably better if we don't all go traipsing back in there. I'll go alone. Do you have any idea what the password for her laptop could be?" Alex asked Jeff.

"I'm thinking," he said, massaging his temple with his free hand as he drove.

"Well?" asked Alex and Liz together after several seconds had passed.

"One of the classes that Simône teaches is a seminar on preeminent archeologists. It is her favorite class-she uses the biographies of the various archeologists to teach the history of the science in an interesting way. Maybe she used one of their names."

He paused for a moment before continuing. "I don't think she would use a birthday or anything obvious like that; she's too smart. So yeah, I think maybe she would use one of her favorites. Try Boucher de Perthes. He was the French archeologist who first discovered primitive tools here, proving that early man had populated Europe."

"And if that isn't it?" asked Alex, doubt in her voice.

"Call me when you get to the room. I'll do some quick research online while you're using your charms to persuade Godfrey to let you break and enter."

"Don't worry; I've got this," said Alex. She took off her sweater to reveal the tank top she was wearing underneath, applied some lipstick and mussed her hair slightly as Jeff pulled the car into the parking lot, trying to conceal the look of amusement on his face.

"He doesn't stand a chance," Jeff said under his breath, as he pulled out his laptop from the backpack beside him and began to type.

Leaving her purse in the car, Alex took only her room key, and her cellphone, which she hid in her jeans underneath the back of her top. She went running into the lobby, arriving slightly breathless as she approached the front desk.

Godfrey, who was in his usual pose-headphones in place, phone in hand-looked up and then smiled when he saw Alex approaching alone.

"Oh good, you're still here," Alex said, sounding almost desperate.

"Oui, Mademoiselle," he said encouragingly.

"I'm such a ditz sometimes," said Alex, leaning over the desk toward him. If my head wasn't screwed on... " she continued, before Godfrey interrupted.

"What can I help you find?"

"Well, I think I know where I left it-my phone, I mean. I think I must have laid it down on the bed when we went to search Simône's, Professeur Bertrand's room. I know you're busy; I really hate to bother you but...If you could, maybe, just give me a key, I could run up there quickly and check?" Alex said, ending her entreaty in a question, and an apologetic smile.

"Pas de problème, Mademoiselle Alex," Godfrey said, with a grin. He immediately reached behind him and pulled the key in question from a cubby, and then handed it toward Alex. As she tried to take the key, he pulled it back, slightly out of her reach.

"But, of course, you will owe me," he said with a smirk.

"Of course," agreed Alex, ignoring his obvious intentions. "A drink with everyone before we leave town?" she asked, as she reached over the counter to grab the key from his hand, and then headed for the stairway to the second floor rooms.

"I was thinking something more private," she heard over her shoulder, before she turned the corner at the top of the stairs.

"Yeah, right," she muttered, as she reached Simône's room.

Once inside, she easily found the laptop in the bag, just as Jeff had suggested. After turning it on, she typed in the password, "Boucher de Perthes," and waited a few seconds before getting the "try again" message.

Damn, time to call Jeff, she thought, pulling his number up on her phone's favorites.

"Hey," said Jeff after one ring. "So I take it Boucher de Perthes didn't work."

"Nope."

"Well then, try Margaret Conkey. She's an American who has done a lot of work in southern France on Paleolithic cave drawings. She espouses a strongly feminist view of archeology. She rejects the idea that cave drawings were only made by male hunter-gatherers. Thinks there may have been some female historian-artists in the clan."

"I like her already," said Alex, as she tried the second name, without success. "No joy, and I'm worried, because depending on how Simône has her password protection set up, we may only get three tries before it locks up for a while. Godfrey's sweet, but I'm afraid he'll get suspicious if I stay in here too long."

"I don't know," said Jeff, sounding frustrated. "There's another guy; some archeologists don't consider his work very professional under today's standards but I suppose..."

"Who?" demanded Alex.

"Louis Felicien De Saucy. Also French. He traveled extensively in the Middle East in the 1850's and '60's. He was the first person known to have conducted an archeological dig of the Holy Land in 1863 AD. He drew the first known map of Masada and he excavated the Tombs of the Kings in Jerusalem."

"So do we try it?" asked Alex, fingers poised above the keyboard.

"I...guess so," Jeff said, finally. "Given what we are working on..."

"Okay," said Alex, trying to sound patient. "Spell it for me. Do we use the whole name or...?"

"Try DeSaucy1863, no spaces, capitalize the D and S," responded Jeff. "I think that's our best bet."

A few seconds later, the computer was unlocked. "Bingo," she said excitedly.

"Did it work?" asked Liz over the phone's speaker.

"Yeah, we're in-now where do I look?"

"Go to ICloud.com and hit 'Find my phone.' The GPS location should come up."

Alex went through the steps before letting out a gasp.

"You won't believe this," she said. "It's at the castle! It's still on and it's there!"

"Alex, we need that computer."

"I know, but Godfrey will never let me just walk out with it. So…?"

"You took your room key, right?" asked Liz, jumping in.

"Yeah, I brought it just in case."

"So, if he asks, tell him you went to our room to get my laptop. Turn it off so he can't look at it if he asks; tell him you don't know the password. And it will explain why you took so long."

"Okay, wish me luck," said Alex, before ending the call.

She quickly checked the room to make sure everything was as she'd found it, before heading back downstairs with the computer under one arm and her phone prominently displayed in her other hand.

When she reached the bottom of the stairs, she was relieved to see that Godfrey was engaged in conversation with the couple she had seen in the lobby earlier. She switched the computer to her right side away from him, quickly dropped Simône's room key on the counter, and gave the clerk a quick wave with her left hand, which now held her cellphone.

"Found it," she said brightly as she walked quickly out the front lobby door. Sliding into the passenger seat, she said, "Let's go, before he has time to think about what he just saw."

"Alright, Mata Hari," Jeff said as he pulled out of the parking lot and turned right onto the main road that would take them up to the castle's parking lot.

"Hey, I learned my flirting skills from the best, Samantha Dilis."

"I'm sure Ms. Dilis would be very proud to hear that you paid such close attention during all of those evenings the two of you spent partying and toying with unsuspecting frat boys during college," Liz said, laughing.

"No doubt," agreed Alex.

"Okay, not to interrupt those wonderful memories, but let's focus on our present problems. It's almost 7 o'clock," said Jeff, looking at his watch. "I'm not sure how we are going to get in if it is closed."

"We'll figure something out," Alex said. "Just get us there as fast as you can."

CHAPTER THIRTEEN

As they pulled into the visitors' parking lot, they saw that all of the tour buses had departed and only a few cars remained.

"I think I'll park over by that retaining wall under the tree, maybe a little less conspicuous," Jeff said. "Check the phone location again."

Liz, who sat with the computer in her lap, soon confirmed that they had arrived at the general location of the phone. Once Jeff had parked with the nose of the car up against the wall, Alex started to open her door.

"Wait a minute," said Jeff, catching her by the arm. "We need a plan. If Simône really is here against her will, the person or persons who are holding her are not going to be friendly. They're kidnappers, for God's sake. They are probably really dangerous."

"I'm sure you're right, which is why we need to find Simône before something happens to her," Alex snapped back.

Jeff and Alex continued to debate their course of action, while Liz turned to survey the parking lot behind them.

"I just..." Jeff said, before being interrupted by Liz.

"Alex, Alex, isn't that the guy...the guy we met in the metro?" Liz asked, pushing on her twin's shoulder to get her attention. "You know, the guy we shared the cab with?" Liz said, pointing out a man who had just parked and exited his car halfway across the parking lot.

"What? Who are you talking...?" Alex said, turning around to see.

"That can't be a coincidence," Liz said. "I sensed something weird about that guy that night. He must have been following us!"

"Yeah, all the way to Belgium, but if so, he obviously doesn't know you are here now. And let's keep it that way. Get down," Jeff yelled, gesturing with his hands, as the man stopped to look back over his shoulder.

A few seconds later, Alex raised her head enough so that she could see the man in the side view mirror. As she watched, he removed a bag from the trunk, before heading up the hill toward the castle.

"He's dressed totally different; he had a suit on that night," Alex said. "But I think you're right-something about the way he carries himself. And the hair color and height are right. I agree. It can't be a coincidence."

After a few more seconds, she said, "C'mon, before we lose him," then opened her door and slipped out before Jeff and Liz could say anything. By the time they reacted, Alex was halfway across the parking lot, crouching behind the man's car and motioning for them to join her. Jeff and Liz looked at each other, and then in silent agreement, got out of the car and ran to where Alex was waiting.

"He's stopped near the turn in the walkway, talking on his phone," Alex said, craning her neck to look around the car bumper, before ducking back down beside them. "Once he heads up toward the plaza we can follow him. He won't be able to see us because of the curve in the walkway."

They waited another minute before leaving their hiding place at a dead run, stopping only when they reached the top of the walkway to catch their breath. Liz took the opportunity to peer around the end of the fence that surrounded the plaza leading into the castle.

"He's going through a gate on the far side of the ticket booth," said Liz, between gulps of air. "It must lead around to the back side of the castle."

Alex, who looked like she was about to follow, stopped when Jeff grabbed her arm. "Let's wait a minute.

The door must be unlocked. I didn't see him using a key to open it," said Jeff, who had peered around the corner before crouching back beside Alex and Liz.

"Okay, he's inside," said Alex impatiently, who had continued to watch the progress of their quarry. "Let's go-oh, damn, the teller just came back to the ticket booth. Guess you'll just have to do the distraction routine this time, Jeff-it's a female teller," Alex said, with a sly smile.

"Fine, once I get her attention, you two can sneak through the gate. I'll follow as soon as I can," Jeff said.

"Shouldn't we stick together?" asked Liz.

"It'll be okay," Alex said quickly.

"How will he find us? It seemed like a maze when we were in there before," Liz said, sounding concerned.

"Oh, I've got some wrapped candies in my purse. I'll leave a trail," answered Alex.

"Let's hope the rats don't get them," Jeff said.

"Ew, let's hope there isn't any."

"Good luck with that, in a 1000-year-old castle," Liz said.

"Okay, here goes," said Jeff. "Give me a minute to distract her before you follow."

"Hello. I just finished touring the castle, which was awesome, by the way. I was wondering if you could give me some advice as to some other sights in the area?" Jeff asked as he approached the booth.

Soon he was engaged in a lively conversation with the teller, who had pulled out a map and was drawing directions to all of her favorite sightseeing locations in the region. As the dowdy middle-aged woman laughed and flirted with Jeff, who had managed to direct her attention to a stone plaque mounted to the right of the main drawbridge entrance to the castle, Alex and Liz sprinted to the gate and slipped through without being noticed.

"So what time do you get off work?" Jeff asked, with an engaging smile. "I figured you would be closed by now."

90

"Oh actually, now," said the woman, looking at the digital clock mounted behind her. "Unfortunately, I have to meet my husband in town. Otherwise, I suppose we could, perhaps ..." she said mischievously, shrugging her shoulders.

"Ah, tant pis (too bad)," Jeff said, doing his best to sound disappointed. "Thanks so much, though, for all of the information." As he walked away, he glanced over his shoulder and saw that the woman was engrossed in the process of locking both the drawbridge gate and the door to the booth she had just exited.

Jeff quickly crossed the plaza and then broke into a sprint down the hill, stopping about ten yards below, before jumping into the thick bushes that lined the hillside down to the parking lot. A few minutes later, the woman came strolling down the hill, talking on her cellphone.

"I tell you-he was flirting with me. Very cute! If only I were a few years younger. I would have taken him up on it."

She listened for a moment before laughing.

"Robert-ouffe! What he doesn't know won't hurt him."

She continued the conversation as she passed him and continued down the hill. Jeff waited until the woman's voice had faded into a whisper, before climbing out of his scratchy hiding place. *I hope that gate is still unlocked*, he thought, as he ran back up the hill, stopping just long enough to check for any tourists on the plaza before continuing to the gate.

When he reached it, he saw that someone had stuck several pieces of chewing gum into the lock, preventing the bolt from fully engaging. *Those King girls-smart*, thought Jeff, as he looked over his shoulder once more before slipping through the gate into the interior of the castle.

Once inside, he switched on the flashlight on his cellphone and immediately saw a small wrapped object ten feet in front of him. Reaching down, he picked up the object, which proved to be the piece of candy promised by Alex. After his eyes had adjusted to the dim light, Jeff continued quickly down the corridor, which curved slightly right and downward into what Jeff guessed was a subterranean level of the castle below the main courtyard where they had noticed the falconer earlier.

Fifty yards ahead in the low light, he spotted another piece of candy. Satisfied that his friends had come this way, he picked it up before continuing down the corridor, glad that he had worn rubber-soled shoes, which allowed him to proceed almost silently. Another fifteen yards ahead, he saw that the corridor forked, but he was relieved to see another small white object, leading him to the left. Jeff didn't bother to pick it up, missing the fact that what he was seeing was only an empty wrapper. Off in the corner out of sight sat three large rats enjoying an unexpected treat.

As he continued walking, the surface under his feet changed from smooth, closely laid cobblestones to rough, moss-covered stones, uneven in height and shape. Because of the uneven terrain, Jeff slowed his pace, even though it had been almost fifteen minutes since he had last seen Alex and Liz. *I must be getting close to the other end of the castle*, thought Jeff. A few seconds later his light spotlighted a large wooden door blocking the passageway.

Oh crap, thought Jeff, considering the possibilities. *Liz and Alex are safely on the other side, waiting for me...or they are now being held hostage along with Simône. Guess you've got no choice, Stahl*, he concluded. Holding his breath, he turned off his light as he pushed on the door, which creaked slightly on its hinges. Immediately he was engulfed in endless darkness. Relieved that he hadn't stepped into the kidnapper's lair, he pushed the door open further, intending to turn his light back on as he walked, and stepped into empty space. Jeff felt himself falling down a moss-covered slope before coming to a stop in a contorted heap in a foot of water. He sat up, dazed and disoriented by what had just happened, before realizing that his cellphone-his only source of light-was no longer in his left hand.

Once inside the gate, Alex and Liz had stopped to let their eyes adjust and to determine that their Paris stalker was not in sight.

"I can't hear footsteps," Liz said, after listening for a few seconds. "Should we wait for Jeff, do you think?"

"I'm afraid if we do, we might lose him," Alex said, pointing toward the darkness. "Who knows how many passageways and side hallways there are down here. I think we should go-but we won't move quickly. We don't want to run into the creep."

Turning on their phone lights, they began moving silently down the passageway, stopping every so often to listen for any sound from their prey. At one point, Alex whispered, "good call on the shoes!" Liz smiled and nodded in silent acknowledgement.

As they walked, Alex began to leave pieces of candy on the ground as guideposts for Jeff. When they reached a fork in their path, they stopped, waiting silently to hear any sound that might guide their way. Liz felt her heart beating in her chest, sure that Alex must be able to hear it. After waiting for what seemed like an eternity of heartbeats, Liz, wide-eyed, turned to Alex as the sound of what was certainly the creaking of an old door hinge echoed from the passage to the right.

"Gotcha!" Alex whispered gleefully. She reached into her purse and grabbed another piece of candy, dropping it behind her as they headed even further into the foundations of the crusader's fortress. Some 100 feet further along, they reached a wooden door in the left wall of the passageway. Hearing voices, they stopped, both instinctively holding their breath until they heard the conversation continue, confirming that their arrival had not been detected.

"Let's turn off our lights," whispered Liz, "in case you can see under the door."

Moving to opposite sides of the door, their backs against the wall, the sisters stood silently, straining to hear the conversation on the other side. The voices faded in and out as, it seemed, two men moved closer and further from the door.

"Al-Bazheeri won't tolerate failure...the meeting with the Iranians ... too important ... must be found and destroyed ...no evi ... reconcilia ... the three...no attention to Bouillon or the ... baye."

Suddenly the voices became clear, as though the two men had stopped close to the door. "I'm going to leave now so that I can set things up before his arrival," said the voice of the man who seemed to be in charge. The other man answered in the affirmative with what Alex thought was a thick Arabic accent, much like that of one of her college track teammates from Saudi Arabia.

Continuing, the leader said, "Wait for an hour-I don't want her screams to be heard. Once it is dark, all of the maintenance staff will be gone from the grounds. Get the information, dump the body and get back to Paris. We're meeting with Al-Bazheeri as soon as his plane arrives. Probably 2 AM-don't be late! Ma'assalama.

"Ma'assalama," said the other man.

Immediately, they heard the turning of the doorknob.

"Go," whispered Alex, as she grabbed Liz and sprinted frantically in the opposite direction from which they had come. They managed to slip just beyond the curve of the passageway before the door opened, casting a triangular shaped pattern of light into their darkness. Making no attempt to be quiet, their Paris stalker appeared in the doorway, stopping to light a cigarette, before pointing the beam of his flashlight back down the corridor leading to the exit. Although they hadn't been able to see him strike the match, the pungent smell of sulfur hung in the air, even after his footsteps had faded away.

"What about Jeff?" asked Liz, her voice barely audible.

"That scumbag isn't bothering to be quiet. Jeff will-hopefully-hear him and have a chance to hide."

"Where is he? It's been at least 15 minutes since we left him," Liz said anxiously, checking the time on her phone.

"I don't know. Maybe he had a hard time ditching his new girlfriend," Alex replied, trying to sound unconcerned.

The sisters stood silently in the dark for a moment, as the reality of their situation engulfed them.

Finally Liz turned on her flashlight and whispered, breaking the silence that that begun to weigh upon them, "What do you think we should do? You heard those guys; if we don't find Simône soon, he'll kill her."

"I know, I know," said Alex. "It's 7:45. Last night it didn't get dark until at least 9, so that gives us a little time. I think we should wait for Jeff; hopefully he will show up soon."

"Okay; let's wait another 15 minutes, but then I think we have to try to find Simône. You heard them-'dump the body in the river.' Remember, somebody rescued us. I guess it is our turn to rescue Simône."

"Yeah, I guess so," agreed Alex reluctantly, giving her sister a quick hug. "I think it's safe to go back by the door-that creep's gone. He's gone to meet the 'great' Al-Bazheeri," she said with deep sarcasm. "Otherwise, Jeff might not realize we're down here if he heads in this direction."

After peering around the corner to make sure the coast was clear, Alex and Liz resumed their positions on either side of the door. They stood uncomfortably for a few minutes before finally sitting down on the cold stone floor to wait.

Okay, Stahl, that was incredibly stupid, Jeff thought angrily. After a few seconds of soaking in the darkness, he began searching the area around where he had landed. Hopefully, there are no rats or snakes in this tub, Jeff thought, grimacing. As he searched, his fingers encountered inches of thick mud, small stones and other ancient detritus. Finally he found his phone, wedged firmly under his right buttock. "So, not a stone," Jeff said out loud, feeling even more stupid as he carefully wiped his precious discovery on his collar, the only part of his clothing that was only slightly damp, and not mud-covered and drenched.

"Thanks, Mom!" Jeff said to the darkness, now extremely grateful for the waterproof phone case-the early birthday present-he had received last week in a care package from his mother. He almost hadn't opened it, thinking he would be really adult and wait until his actual birthday; but now he was really happy that the little kid in him had prevailed. *Smart kid*, thought Jeff, as he switched on the phone's light to assess his situation.

"Awesome," Jeff said sarcastically, seeing that he was in a cistern of sorts. The mossy slope behind him was much too slippery to climb, and in front of him loomed an eight-foot stone wall. I'm really getting my money's worth out of that wall-climbing class I took. *Luckily this is a very old wall, missing a number of stones. And there is obviously no one around to prevent me from climbing it since there is no way they wouldn't have heard me when I fell,* thought Jeff, who couldn't help chuckling, despite his situation.

Jeff surveyed his options for a moment before cramming his phone deep in the front pocket of his jeans, and beginning his climb. Once he reached the top, he pulled himself as noiselessly as possible over the edge

96

onto the rough stone floor. Resting for a moment, Jeff heard only his own heavy breathing, punctuated by the steady drip of water from somewhere overhead, and a slight rustling of what he guessed were resident rodents.

Time to get out of here. Jeff shone his light down the corridor; he was surprised to see that it came to an end a mere 20 feet in front of him.

"What the ...?" he said aloud, before cringing as the sound echoed for several seconds around him. Moving closer, he saw that a solid stone wall blocked the passage. Clearly, he had come the wrong way.

Nice job, Alex! he thought, angrily. But immediately he realized that the mistake must be his. *She wouldn't have sent me in the wrong direction.*

Deciding he shouldn't waste any more time, he surveyed the wall behind him that bordered the left side of the cistern. Doing his best imitation of the Spiderman that Alex had mentioned earlier, Jeff slowly found hand and footholds across the twelve-foot opening. When he finally reached the other side, his knuckles were bleeding and he was sweating profusely. He stopped only long enough to wipe the slime from the soles of his shoes before passing back through the door and running back down the passageway. Once he reached the fork, he listened before peering around the corner. The absence of light reassured him as he began walking toward what he hoped was Alex, Liz and Simône.

Jeff had taken only a couple of steps when he was stopped short by the smell of cigarette smoke wafting up the corridor toward him.

"Dammit," he said silently, knowing that it could not be coming from any of his friends, none of whom smoked. Switching off his light, he reversed direction and walked as quietly as he could back toward the fork. After turning the corner, guided only by his hand skimming the wall beside him, he continued another 10 yards, before flattening himself against the wall. As he waited, barely daring to breath, he saw the beam of a flashlight glancing off the ceiling of the corridor to his left.

Seconds later, the man, who Alex and Liz had followed through the gate, walked by, smoking a cigarette and making no effort to be quiet. When it was evident that the man was not stopping, and the beam of his flashlight was no longer visible, Jeff exhaled slowly, suppressing a cough brought on by the smoke from the strong unfiltered cigarette. He waited until he could no longer hear the shuffling gait of the man before edging back toward the fork. Once he was sure that he could not see any flashes of light, he turned on his phone light, and began walking in the opposite direction.

CHAPTER FOURTEEN

Jeff walked slowly, just in case there should be any other surprises awaiting him. However, soon he encountered a very welcome sight: Alex and Liz, some 30 yards in front of him, sitting on the floor on each side of another wooden door.

"There you are!" Jeff exclaimed, running to them.

"Shh!" they hissed at the same time. "There is a guy on the other side of this door," Liz whispered, pointing over her shoulder with her thumb.

"Okay," Jeff said, dropping his voice to a whisper as he squatted down beside them.

"What happened to you?" asked Alex, stifling a snicker as Jeff's light revealed the condition of his clothing.

"Long story. Let's just say I took one step too far-down the wrong fork," he added for clarification.

"Oh, sorry," said Liz, smiling at him with sympathy.

"So what's happening here?" Jeff asked, refocusing the conversation.

"Like we said, there's a guy ..." Alex stopped, looking at him questioningly. "Wait, how did you get by Paris stalker guy? He just left not two minutes ago. He must have passed right by you."

"Luckily, I smelled his cigarette smoke-was able to hide. I have a sensitive nose, you know."

"Yeah, I remember," Alex said. "I had to stop wearing that perfume-very nice perfume, I might add-that Liz gave me for my, our birthday last year. Anyway, that creep," she continued, pointing down the corridor, "he's apparently the 'head' creep,'" making air quotes with her fingers.

Liz added, "There's another guy in there; he has Simône, we think, and he said he is planning to kill her, after he questions her once it gets dark. Which gives us, by my estimation, about an hour to figure out a rescue plan."

"Okay, not good," said Jeff. "But at least she's alive and we know where she is." He paused for a moment before asking, "So you haven't gone beyond the door; don't know what's on the other side?"

"No, but after 'that' guy came out, I could hear the other guy pacing back and forth." Liz said in response. "He walks really loudly, like he's agitated, or something. Anyway, finally he walked away. Not sure but it sounded like he walked to the right of the door, and climbed some stairs before opening another door."

"How could you tell-about the stairs I mean?" Jeff asked, sounding doubtful.

"Well, you know, when you come to stairs, you hesitate, and then you speed up, quicken your pace, and the sound of your footsteps is louder. I guess because you are putting all of your weight on the one foot."

"Interesting observation. Are you an expert in stepology?" Jeff asked, teasing.

"No, it's just that I used to listen for my moth … for Roberta when she came home drunk. I didn't want to get caught off guard. Over time, I guess I just learned to recognize the sound of steps on stairs."

Alex and Jeff looked sympathetically at Liz, not knowing what to say, sorry to have made Liz remember that sad period of her life. After several seconds when the silence grew uncomfortable, Liz said, "Anyway, that's how I know."

"Well," Alex said cheerily, willfully changing the tone of the conversation, "that information is going to come in very handy. By my calculations, I'm guessing that 'right' of the door is toward the southwest end of the castle, opposite of where we entered at the gate. So maybe he went outside. I say we open this door and find Simône.

"Look, let's not be too hasty," Jeff replied, sounding a cautionary note to Alex, who, if nothing else, was always a woman of action.

"Fine. Then I have another idea," Alex said, conceding the point. "There are three of us-all very physically fit and should I say, very attractive." She waited for the laugh that didn't come. "Irrelevant, I know, just saying, trying to add a little humor to the situation. Anyway, let's make a loud noise. If he comes out, we jump him. Three against one."

When neither Liz nor Jeff responded, she continued. "It has to be a noise-not music or voices. We don't want him to be sure that it's people. If he doesn't respond, we'll at least know he isn't waiting on the other side."

After considering, Jeff asked, "Okay, what noise?"

"I have a gong noise on my phone," Liz suggested. "From the warm up for my Tai Chi class. "Would that work? It's pretty loud."

Alex gave her a "really" look.

"It might work," agreed Jeff. "It's better than anything I have."

"So where should we stand?" Liz asked.

"Let's turn our lights off. Liz you stand next to the door and stick your foot out to trip him. Alex and I will jump on top of him and restrain him once he, hopefully, trips."

"Alright," Liz said, without much confidence.

"Oh, and Jeff, take off your belt," Alex said.

"What? Why?"

"Don't argue; take it off. We'll need something to tie him up."

"Uh, okay," Jeff said, not sure he liked the idea. "Let's get in position. Turn off your lights before you play the sound, Liz."

Liz laughed. "Why do I feel like the Three Stooges?"

"Hopefully not," said Jeff.

Once they were in place, Alex said, "Sound the gong, three times."

As Liz had promised, it was quite loud, echoing off the stone walls around them.

The three stood in darkness waiting. Finally Alex whispered, "Do it again but open the door just a crack. Maybe he can't hear it through the wood."

"If you say so," said Liz. She slowly opened the door, holding her breath, until she could feel an almost imperceptible crack between the door and stone surround, before sounding the gong again.

Another minute of total silence passed before Jeff said, "I think we're safe. Let's go." He stopped to rethread his belt through the loops of his pants, before hitting the button on his phone to illuminate his screen. "This will give us a little light without being too bright. He went right so we're going left."

"What if there are others?" Liz asked, hesitating.

"We only heard the two, right?" Alex asked, reassuring her. "And all of the conversations were between Paris Stalker guy and the other guy. The one with the strong accent."

"I hope you're right-guess we'll find out," said Jeff, as he stepped through the doorway. "Stay right behind me," Jeff whispered over his shoulder.

They had taken only a few steps before encountering a locked door.

"So what now?" Alex asked.

"Well, I think we have to risk it...Simône, Simône," Jeff said, not quite yelling.

The tension between them was palpable as a few seconds passed. Finally, they heard a faint reply. "Dieu merci!" and then, "Jeff, is that you? I'm in here! Help me! I'm handcuffed!"

"The door's locked," Jeff yelled. "Is there a deadbolt you can reach from your side?"

"No, and he took the key."

"Okay-we'll try to figure out a way to open it," he said, turning to Alex and Liz. "Any suggestions?"

While he had been leaning into the door talking to Simône, Alex had been examining the lock. "I'm pretty sure I can pick it."

"What?" Jeff exclaimed, total surprise in his voice. "You've done this before?"

"I admit that I did sneak out a few times in high school. Our butler, one of Senora's henchmen, was always locking me out. So finally I had one of my friends on the track team with-shall we say-a past, teach me the basics. Nothing you can't learn on the internet," she said, when Jeff gave her a look.

"Anyway, I've got my trusty 10-tool Swiss army knife that Samantha gave me right after our little adventure in Mexico," she said, pulling it from her purse. "I no longer go anywhere without a weapon."

"Now all I need is a second thin piece of metal, like a..."

"Will a bobby pin work?" asked Liz, pulling one from her hair.

"Perfect," said Alex. Jeff and Liz watched in awe as Alex inserted first a thin nail file type tool from her knife into the lock, before pushing the head of the bobby pin in beside it. "This could take a couple of minutes. I'm kind of rusty."

"Hurry!" said Liz, who had turned to keep an eye on the stairs at the southern end of the corridor.

While Alex worked, Liz ran to the top of the stairs and found another deadbolt that could be locked by hand. Securing it, she retraced her steps to join the others.

"I locked the door at the top of the stairs, in case he comes back."

"Good thinking," said Jeff, giving her a smile.

About a minute and several swear words later from Alex, they heard a clicking noise from the bolt.

"Voila!" Alex said, proudly, before turning the handle and pushing the door open. Inside, they found a wide-eyed Simône, sitting handcuffed to a chair.

"I've never been so happy to see anyone in my life. I heard them saying they were going to kill ..." Simône stopped, her words almost a sob.

"No worries, Professeur. But let's get you out of here before those thugs come back."

"A slight problem," Simône said, gesturing with her head to the metal handcuffs.

"Quel problème?" Jeff asked, smiling. When Simône frowned in question, Jeff continued, "Alex, it turns out, along with her many other talents, can pick locks."

Alex had already kneeled down behind Simône, to begin picking the cuffs. Just as she inserted the bobby pin into the lock, they heard a loud sound from the outside corridor, as though someone had kicked the door at the top of the stairs. Next came a series of gunshots, presumably to try to breach the lock.

"Hurry!" Simône said, in desperation.

"Why don't you and Liz go before he get's into the corridor?" Alex asked, without looking away from her task.

"No way!" Jeff and Liz said in unison. "We're not leaving you," added Liz.

Alex fumbled, dropping the pin. *Get it together, King*, she thought to herself, taking a deep breath and willing herself to ignore the gunshots echoing behind her, as she picked up the pin. While she continued to work, Jeff and Liz barricaded the door with the two remaining chairs and the trunk from the corner. Just as she felt the latch of the cuffs releasing, she heard another shot, a crash, and then steps moving quickly in their direction.

"We're trapped," Liz said, trying to keep the panic out of her voice.

"Do you know where that door goes?" Jeff asked, looking at Simône, who had taken off the cuffs and was rubbing her wrists.

"It might only be a closet, but I wondered…"

As she spoke, Jeff went over to examine it. "I don't think so. It opens in, seems unlikely for a closet. And there is some loose mortar around the door, as though someone tried to seal it at some point."

"Alex, Liz, come here. Let's try to push it open. On three."

"One, two…" Just as Jeff said "three," they pushed their shoulders against the door, which gave way, as the barricaded door opposite shuddered but held as someone tried to push in from the other side.

"Time to go, ladies," Jeff said, switching on his flashlight. Having learned his lesson, he quickly swept the beam on the floor in front of him before stepping through the doorway. The floor was solid, but to his surprise, when he pointed the light out in front of him, he found himself in the same corridor he had left only twenty minutes earlier. He ushered the three women through and pushed the door back into place, realizing now that what he had seen earlier was an optical illusion. Rather than bricks, the backside of the door was merely painted wood, expertly disguised to resemble the surrounding stone. He also noticed that there were large metal rings set into the stone that corresponded to a ring-shaped handle on the door.

Jeff had absorbed all of this in the split second before he said, "Liz, Alex, turn on your lights. There is an eight foot drop down there on this side of the door-don't ask."

As he spoke, explaining what they needed to do to reach the other side, he continued to hear the pounding on the other door, knowing that the barricade would soon give way.

"There are some obvious handholds on the rocks and a slight ledge on the sides-it's about twelve feet across. But for God's sake, hurry, this guy is about to get through!"

Alex, who had run ahead, and had already crossed over the chasm, was holding a light for the other two women and urging them to hurry.

Jeff again removed his belt and looped it, fastening it as tightly as possible between the two metal rings. *That won't hold for long*, he thought pessimistically. As he retreated, he saw that Liz was just finishing her crablike passage across. Jeff, who had the advantage of having traversed the space less than an hour before, moved quickly across, finding familiar handholds. He was just about to swing himself from the wall into the waiting doorway when the door leading back to Simône's abandoned cell flew open, and shots began ricocheting in his direction.

The man, visible in the doorway to the lit room, shot wildly, unrestrained, as though he had lost the ability to control his direction of fire. As the barrage continued, Jeff landed in a crouch in the doorway, before feeling a breath stopping, searing jolt in his left shoulder, which propelled him face forward onto the cold stone floor.

"Jeff!" screamed Alex, rushing toward him.

"He shot me," he gasped in disbelief. After a second's hesitation, Liz and Alex grabbed him under his arms and dragged him forward so that Simône could shut the door, providing him cover.

"Can you move?" asked Alex, kneeling beside Jeff as tears streamed down her face.

"Yes, I think so," Jeff said, his breath ragged. "We have to get out of here."

"But the blood…" said Liz, staring at her hands.

"I know," Jeff said, breathing shallowly, "but we have to go!"

They could hear their pursuer now, yelling, presumably cursing, in Arabic, on the other side of the cistern. He fired off more shots, only a few of which seemed to strike the ancient wooden door.

Jeff got to his knees and then stood up slowly, with the help of Liz and Alex, who was visibly shaken by Jeff's condition. Feeling with his right hand, they watched as he searched the left side of his chest for a bullet hole. "Good, I think it went through-I've heard that's good. I'm glad it didn't hit any of you."

"Let's go," he said weakly, gesturing down the corridor with his bloody right hand. At his urging, the women, with Jeff trailing behind, began to run down the corridor, intent on beating their pursuer into the light that awaited them at the other end of the castle. When they reached the gate, panting heavily, Alex opened it and carefully looked out before motioning them forward.

"He's not out here but if he came around by the other fork he could come at any time. Can you keep going?" she asked Jeff, who was looking ashen.

"Yes, go," he said softly, the pain evident in his voice.

"I'm afraid we better keep running all of the way to the car," Alex said apologetically, still breathing heavily from their pace.

What they didn't know, couldn't know, was that their assailant had fallen victim to his own carelessness. As they ran down the hill to the safety of Jeff's car, Simône's kidnapper had hobbled back through the corridor, up the stairs and into the courtyard, intent on finding them and finishing his task. *I'll kill all of them, filthy infidels*, he thought. Minutes later he sat in his idling car, breathing raggedly, his life flowing out of the wound in his thigh, the wound to his femoral artery caused by one of his own ricocheting bullets, his own senseless rage. As darkness fell, he spoke his last words, "Allahu Akbar," before lapsing into unconsciousness, while his cellphone buzzed unanswered on the car seat beside him.

CHAPTER FIFTEEN

When they finally reached the car, Alex, who was now operating on a combination of adrenaline and anger, took charge and began issuing orders.

"Let's get Jeff into the back seat with his feet up to keep him from going into shock. Liz, sit back there with him. Keep him awake and put pressure on both sides of the wound."

Simône, who seemed dazed by everything she had just endured, responded only when Alex yelled, "Simône!" sharply. "You're shotgun-let's move!" Simône looked at her with confusion, before finally getting into the front passenger seat.

As their car sped out of the parking lot, racing into the village, Liz alternated between looking over her shoulder for any pursuers, and talking to Jeff, urging him to remain conscious.

"Simône, is there a hospital, clinic, anything here?" Alex asked desperately.

"I ... I don't know. I'll call ... who should I call?" Simône asked, starting to cry.

"Do you still have your phone?" Alex asked, speaking quickly. "The number from the hostel should be in your 'recents,' since you left the message there this afternoon."

"No, I'm sorry, he kept my bag. My phone was in there ..."

"Oh right, no worries. It's on mine. Here," she said, handing her phone to Simône. "Call them. Don't tell them that Jeff was shot-just say he is injured and needs emergency care. I don't want to get the local cops involved;

who knows who might be working with these murderers," Alex said, angrily.

Simône took a few deep breaths to steady herself, before finding the number on the phone and placing the call on the speakerphone. When Godfrey answered and she identified herself, Godfrey interrupted chattily, "Oh, bon soir; I didn't know if we would be hearing from you again."

Before he could continue, Simône cut him off. "Listen, please! My friend Jeff has been injured. We need a doctor-immediately! Is there one in the village?"

"Oh no, what happened?" asked Godfrey.

"No time," Simône said. "The doctor?"

"Ah oui, just a veterinarian I am afraid, but there is a clinique near Virton. Anyway, Dr. Chernot-second street over when you first come into town. Five houses down, red door. I hope ..." Godfrey started to say before Simône ended the call.

"You heard him, only a veterinarian, but he should have sutures, and pain meds," Simône said, looking back with concern at Jeff. By the time they reached the house in question, Liz's jeans were soaked with blood and Jeff was moaning lowly. Alex screeched the car to a halt, causing the right front tire to jump the curb, upsetting a trash bin, which clattered noisily into the street, spilling its contents.

In less than a minute, the red door opened and a young, 30ish-looking man stepped out. "What is happening out here?" he asked in French, surveying the scene.

After looking at Alex, who subtly shook her head "no," Simône told the man that they had been out hiking and some unknown person, presumably a hunter, had shot at them through the woods. "We don't know who it was," she concluded, shrugging her shoulders and turning up her hands in question. "Please, can you help us?"

The doctor came around to the side of the car and looked in. "Mon dieu, I'm not a surgeon. But..." he said, looking at their desperate faces, "bring him in." He hurried to open the door wide as Simône, Alex and Liz dragged Jeff, who was still dripping blood, out of the car to his feet and maneuvered him up the stairs into the house.

Within seconds, Jeff was on an examining table being attended to by Dr. Chernot.

"I thought we would never get out of there," Davide said with disgust. "Since when are there armed monks at night at church ruins?"

"I don't think those were monks," Natalia answered, shaking her head. "Most monks that I have met don't carry semi-automatics. Ari warned me that detractors of Pope Francis would not want what they are hunting to come to light. Apparently it is just the type of thing that he would probably champion. Perhaps they are part of Archbishop DeVito's splinter group-the intelligence I have read suggests that he isn't very happy with the Papa."

"Well, that was close. And you certainly took long enough."

"Okay, next time you climb the wall in the dark with a pencil and paper in your mouth, and make the rubbing while hanging fifteen feet above the ground," Natalia snapped back, giving him a dirty look that he ignored.

"Never mind, let's find our little group, shall we? Make sure they are tucked in safe and sound."

As they pulled into the parking lot of the hostel, they both noticed that the car that Jeff had been driving was not visible.

"Oh, hell! They aren't here. I hope they haven't ditched us; Ari will be very pissed," said Davide, before adding some choice swear words in Hebrew.

"Let me go in and ask if they are still checked in. I'll tell them I am another friend from Paris. You, they'd never believe," she added, looking at him, before hopping out of the car and running up the steps into the lobby.

Inside, Natalia put on a sweet smile as she approached the male clerk at the desk. "Allo, bon soir, Monsieur! Comment-t'allez vous?"

"Well, thank you, Mademoiselle, et vous?"

"Bien, merci."

"How can I help you? Do you need a room?"

"No, actually, I am here to visit some friends who are staying here. Professeur Bertrand's group."

This statement brought a frown to the clerk's face.

"Monsieur?" Natalia asked, noting his reaction.

"I am afraid I have bad news-I just got a call from the Professeur. Her friend, Jeff, has been injured somehow. I sent them to Dr. Chernot, our veterinarian. We have no medical doctor in town," he concluded apologetically.

"Tell me where, quickly!" Natalia said, brusquely.

"The second street over, red door, halfway down." By the time he had finished the sentence, Natalia was already out of the front door. She jumped into the car, startling Davide who had been relaxing, smoking a cigarette. "Trouble-let's go. The guy-some kind of injury-sounds serious. Two streets over, red door," Nicole said.

Davide, who was used to her shorthand, had already started driving at the word 'trouble.' Within two minutes, he pulled up behind Jeff's badly parked car, and they jumped out, guns in hand.

CHAPTER SIXTEEN

Dr. Chernot finished washing his hands before gesturing to the three women huddled in the corner of the room.

"Your friend is very lucky. The bullet went cleanly through, and I don't think it hit bone or any major artery or he would have lost a lot more blood. I have cleaned the wound, cauterized the bleeders I could find, and stitched up the layers I could reach without surgery. But you must get him to a hospital as soon as possible. I can call an ambulance but it would take a while to get here."

"No, thank you." Alex said, quickly. "We will drive him ourselves. To Reims-quicker," she added, in explanation.

"Doctor, we are so grateful for your help," Simône said, diverting his attention. "What do we owe you?"

He looked at them for a moment, as though trying to read their thoughts, before responding. "Perhaps we should just chalk this up to an interesting experience. By law, I am not supposed to work on people, so I don't think I can charge you. It is strange though; I don't think that the gun he was shot with was a hunting rifle, more like a handgun given the size of the wound. And it isn't even hunting season around here for another month."

"Exactly," said Liz, quickly, "which is why we were so shocked to have this happen just hiking in the woods."

"Where did you say you were?" the doctor asked, a note of suspicion in his voice.

Alex and Liz turned to Simône, who hesitated before answering. "Oh, on the Sentier de Semois. The trail by the river. A few miles down. It is beautiful, non?"

"Yes, very," the doctor answered, his eyes narrowing, before he continued. "Well, I have sedated him. He can walk but he will be groggy for a while. He will be in significant pain when it wears off. Again, you must promise me to get him to a hospital as soon as possible tonight. Here is my card. Have his doctor call me, if he has questions and I will explain the specific care I provided. And hopefully, I will not lose my license," he said, frowning.

"Absolutely; yes, we will; as soon as possible," the three responded in chorus.

Before the doctor could change his mind or ask any more questions, they helped Jeff off the examining table and slowly walked him to the door.

"Au revoir and thanks again," said Simône, as Liz opened the front door.

Hearing the approaching voices, Natalia and Davide positioned themselves on each side of the front steps. "If it is just them, let me do the talking. We don't want to scare the hell out of them!" Natalia said, in a whisper.

The door opened and the group slowly stepped out, shutting the door behind them. Alex, who was in front, was walking backwards while attempting to guide Jeff down the stairs as Liz and Simône supported him under each arm. When she reached the street level, Alex happened to glance to the right, before exclaiming, "Oh my God, Natalia?"

The rest of the group froze, before looking left at the woman who stood pointing a gun at them. Simône, who was on Jeff's right, gasped as she sensed, before seeing, a man to her right, also armed.

"Hello, Alex," said Natalia, lowering her weapon. Seeing this, Davide did the same. "I assume he was shot? No bad guys with you, I take it?"

"What … uh, yes, he was shot, and no, no bad guys now," Alex said, looking extremely confused. " But what are you doing here?" she asked, her eyes wide.

Natalia surveyed the street, before saying, "I will explain everything but we must get you out of here. Clearly you have encountered some major trouble, so I guess we didn't do a very good job."

"What job?" Liz asked, totally befuddled by the conversation.

"Our job to guard and protect you," said Natalia, sounding distraught. "But really, we have to get out of here."

"By here, do you mean Bouillon?" asked Simône, joining the conversation.

"Yes."

"Sounds like a great idea. Simône, Jeff, Liz. This is Natalia Shain. I ran track against her in college-you know-in California, but she is from Israel," Alex said, looking at her questioningly.

"It is a long story. But all that matters now is that you know me. You can trust me. I will explain everything. But not here! You need to get in your car and follow us. Can he travel?" Natalia asked, looking at Jeff.

"I think so," replied Alex.

Natalia turned to Jeff who had been listening, eyes barely open. "Jeff, correct? If we go to Reims, we will raise all sorts of suspicion and interest, which you don't want right now, I imagine. Do you think you can make it to Paris? It looks like the vet did a pretty good job of patching you up. I have a friend-doctor-in Paris who can take care of you."

"Wait a minute, Natalia. I don't know what the hell is going on and I'm not risking Jeff's life just because we knew each other in college," Alex said angrily.

Jeff looked over at Natalia for a moment, appraising her. "No, Al, I'm okay. The bleeding has stopped and he gave me some IV fluids. I can make it to Paris. It's just a little over two hours and a half, especially at this time of night, no traffic."

"Are you sure?" Alex asked, concerned.

"Yeah, I'm okay," Jeff reassured her.

114

"I assume we shouldn't go back to the hostel for our suitcases?" Alex asked, looking at Natalia.

"I wouldn't, unless what you have there is worth your life," Natalia said, matter-of-factly. "And, I think we should switch cars. That way, if we run into your 'bad guys' again, they will focus on us, not you. Can you drive a gear shift, Alex?"

Alex nodded in the affirmative as they switched keys and she and Liz gathered their purses and backpacks from their car.

"Let's try to stay together on the road. What is your cell number?" Natalia asked Alex.

Natalia quickly entered it into her phone and texted Alex to check it. "Okay, if you have any problems, call or text me. Otherwise, meet us at the address I am texting you now. It is a clinic in the 4th Arrondisement on the right bank in the Jewish quarter. But before we go, give me a thirty second description of your bad guys."

Alex turned to Simône, who said," Middle Eastern- he, my kidnapper, spoke Arabic. Dark hair and eyes, maybe 5'8", mid-20s. He had a tattoo with two teardrops beneath his left eye." As she said this, she unconsciously rubbed her cheek.

"They talked about meeting some Iranians and someone named Al-Bazheeri. That's all I heard."

"The other guy was about 5'10', dark hair, brown eyes, olive complexion, older, maybe 50. It also sounded like a Middle Eastern accent to me, and he spoke French, English and probably Arabic, as well," Liz added.

Natalia and Davide looked at each other before he spoke, "Very good. By the way, I'm Davide. Her partner. We are Mossad, Israeli intelligence, in case you haven't figured that out. It sounds like the bad guys you encountered are some Syrians we've been looking for. You are lucky to be alive. Let's try to keep it that way."

All four nodded grimly to the Israelis before climbing into the borrowed car. Forty-five minutes later they had crossed into France and were headed south to Paris.

CHAPTER SEVENTEEN

They reached the outskirts of Paris at 1:30 AM, exhausted and starving. On the edge of town, Simône had taken over the driving, after convincing Alex that she was no longer in shock, and that she could navigate through the city more quickly than Alex. They lost Natalia during the delay, but twenty minutes later, Simône pulled the car to a stop in front of the address that Natalia had given them. One lone streetlight dimly lit the cobbled street and Jeff's car, which sat parked in the shadow of the building.

"I hope this is it," Alex said, hopping out of the front passenger seat to open the back-seat door behind her. As she helped Liz with Jeff, Simône went to talk to Natalia, who had appeared in the doorway of the closest building.

"Is there someone who can help us bring him in? He is pretty much dead weight at this point and we are all exhausted."

"Yes, of course." Natalia turned around in the doorway and said something in Hebrew into the room. Seconds later, two six foot men came down the stairs, gently took Jeff under each arm and carried him inside as Simône, Liz and Alex followed, slowly climbing the stairs.

Inside, they found a brightly lit doctor's waiting room, decorated with photos of beautiful celebrities. "Plastic surgeon, I'm guessing," Alex whispered to Liz, as they followed Natalia into the next room.

"You're right," Natalia said, over her shoulder. "Yuri is a very successful plastic surgeon-does all of the rich and famous here in Paris."

Liz looked around, surprised, before Natalia added, "Not here of course. He has a fancy clinic off of the

Champs-Élysées. But some of his clients, who are more rich than famous, prefer a more discrete setting, so they come here. Yuri, by the way, is also a very skilled trauma surgeon. He was a field surgeon for the IDF, the Israeli Defense Force, before opening his private practice here. Don't worry. Jeff is in excellent hands."

"Even as we speak," she added, pointing toward another door, which seemed to lead into the surgical suite. "He will be patched up quickly-no questions asked."

Natalia gestured to a corner table, which held a coffee maker and mugs.

"What else can I get you?"

"A bathroom would be nice," Alex said quickly. "And we haven't had anything to eat since lunchtime."

"Yes, of course, I'm sorry. I should have realized ..." Natalia said, pointing to the restroom before heading into the outer waiting room, where she spoke in Hebrew to Davide, before returning to the three women who were now drinking coffee.

"Davide has gone to wake up a friend down the street who owes him some favors. We will have some sandwiches in a few minutes."

"Oh, thank you," said Liz.

"But while we wait," Natalia said, "perhaps you could give me some details on what happened. The last time Davide and I saw you," looking toward Simône, "you were at the Abbaye, and you two and Jeff," she said, pointing toward Liz and Alex, "were leaving your hostel for what we thought was an innocent dinner."

"So what went wrong?" Natalia asked, turning first to Simône, who began to recount what had happened after she left the Abbaye. And then Liz and Alex joined in when she reached the point where she was forced to leave the message for them at the hostel.

"That was very smart of you, by the way," said Liz, smiling at Simône."

They then finished the harrowing story, concluding with Jeff getting shot, and their encounter at Dr. Chernot's office.

"So it sounds like you never actually revealed the information from the diary or what you found at the Abbaye?" Natalia asked.

"No, they were actually quite disorganized and inept," Simône said, with a slight smile.

"Yes, it certainly sounds like it," Natalia agreed, with a laugh.

"So where do we go from here?" Alex asked Natalia. "We have been talking about this for the last three hours on our drive and we want to continue our search, but not if we would be risking our lives."

"Well, if the 'treasure' is what you believe it to be-it would be an extraordinary find. Because you know so much already and given what you've been through, I will tell you what I know ..." Natalia paused as one of the two men came into the room carrying several bags of food. All interest in the conversation died as Simône, Alex and Liz dove into the piles of sandwiches laid out before them.

After they had each devoured a large sandwich and chips, Natalia laughed before saying, "I always was in awe of your ability to eat, Alex. I remember from some of our track meets."

Turning to Liz, she said, "She would beat me in the 800 and the mile and then down a huge amount of food. And stay skinny. In truth, I kind of hated her, and admired her, all at the same time. But I never knew that she had a sister; she never talked about you. Were you a college runner too?"

Alex and Liz looked at each other before Alex said, "Well actually, Natalia, it is a very long and complicated story. We never even knew the other one existed until five years ago. And we're not just sisters, we're twins. We were separated at birth by some truly evil people who killed our parents, tried to steal our inheritance and almost killed us."

"Oh my God, that's horrible!" Natalia said, looking back and forth between them.

"Hey, but we're together now," Liz said, trying to change the uncomfortable subject.

Natalia was about to ask for further details but their conversation was interrupted by a gowned doctor who had entered the room through the door Natalia had earlier indicated.

"Oh good," Natalia said, getting up to make introductions.

"Alex, Liz, Simône, this is Dr. Yuri Landau." The three women immediately noted that the mid-30's man with dark, curly hair and deep blue eyes, who smiled back, bore a striking resemblance to Natalia. "And I should say, my cousin," Natalia added, with a grin.

Yuri smiled again, before saying, "Good news, ladies. Your friend, Jeff, will be fine. Luckily he is quite strong and in very good shape. The bullet did not do any irreparable damage to the bones, ligaments or tendons in his shoulder. It passed cleanly through. And thankfully did not fragment along the way."

"Thank you, doctor," Alex said, eyes glistening.

"Can we see him?" Liz asked, giving Alex a hug.

"Actually he is getting dressed with the help of my nurse. He is sedated so he must rest-I would say at least 48 hours. And his left arm will be in a sling for a while. Here are some pain meds and antibiotics," he added, reaching into his pocket for two large bottles, which after a brief hesitation, he handed to Alex.

"You will be his nurse, I take it?"

"Uh, yes," Alex said, turning slightly red.

Simône added, "We all will. He will be well taken care of, I assure you, Doctor."

"Thank you, Yuri; you can send me the bill," said Natalia, before giving him a hug and a peck on the cheek.

119

"Oh, מזה שכח מזה (forget it)," he said in Hebrew. "Let's just say that we're even."

"Okay," Natalia agreed as the door opened and Jeff, his left arm in a sling, wearing someone else's button-down shirt instead of the blood-soaked one he had arrived in, walked out slowly, accompanied by a cute, 20-something nurse.

"He is ready to go. Quite a handful, this one." She smiled at the waiting women, who rushed forward.

"Careful," Jeff said with a slight grin. "I'm still a little out of it-don't knock me over."

"No, sorry; oh, right; mais oui," said the three.

Simône and Natalia switched keys as they said their good-byes.

"Alex, a minute of your time," Natalia said, as they headed for the door.

"I am sure you realize it by now, but these guys are bad dudes, killers. We think they are an offshoot of a Syrian jihadist group-basically in competition with Al Qaeda-trying to establish a reputation here in Europe. You need to proceed very cautiously, if at all," Natalia said, a worried look on her face.

"I understand," Alex said solemnly. "After what happened, and Jeff getting shot..." She stopped with a catch in her voice. "I don't know what we'll do-I guess we'll regroup. I think we'll change hotels and have Jeff stay with us for a few days while he convalesces. Not sure about Simône. Do you think we should call the police?"

"Probably not unless you want to spend a week being questioned by the Belgium police. I will have one of my associates follow up in Belgium. Did you leave things at your hostel? Yes? Then I will have them picked up for you. I wouldn't go back up there, even though I suspect your terrorists are long gone and have scurried back into the hole from which they came." Natalia looked pensively at Alex for a moment before continuing.

"Well, we've got each other's numbers. Text me and let me know where you are staying so I can have your things dropped off. In the meantime, if you get the sense that you are being followed or watched, call me immediately. I've got access to a lot of resources here in the city," she added, vaguely.

"Okay, thank you! I can't tell you how grateful I am. It's so weird though, such a small world …"

"No kidding, Alex King. It is a very, very small world these days," Natalia said, giving Alex a quick hug before turning to talk to Yuri who was deep in conversation in Hebrew with Davide.

Alex shook her head and wiped a tear from her eye as she opened the door leading to the street. Liz and Simône had already carefully situated Jeff in the back seat by the time Alex joined them.

"So?" asked Liz, looking expectantly toward her sister, who sat by Simône as she drove toward their hotel.

Alex shrugged before saying, "She says they are quote 'bad dudes.' Nothing we didn't already know. Probably Syrian jihadists. Clearly they don't like what we are doing."

"They obviously don't want the 'Knight's Call' to be found. The idea of the three main religions coming to some sort of accord is definitely not consistent with their worldview. They want to see all of the other world religions subjugated or eradicated," Simône said, agreeing.

"So do we just give up our search?" Liz asked, a furrow creasing her brow as her green eyes flashed with anger.

Jeff, who had remained silent up to that point, shook his head vigorously and said, "No!" vehemently, despite his drugged state. "Screw them. It just makes me want to find it more. No way am I going to let those bastards win! They made it very personal when they shot me."

Alex looked at him for several seconds before bursting out laughing. Soon Simône and Liz joined in.

"Well, okay then," replied Alex, still grinning, as though something had been decided. "Let's go to our hotel and pick up our bags and clothes."

She stopped, looking at Liz's clothes, which were caked with Jeff's dried blood.

"Given the fact that you are still covered in blood, maybe Simône and I should go in, pick up our luggage and stuff and check out, while you wait out here in the car with Jeff. And Liz, maybe you can book us some rooms online. Any suggestions, Simône?"

"Ah, oui, there is a very nice, quiet hotel near the Tuileries Garden. I don't think our would-be assassins will have heard of it."

"Great then, it's a plan," muttered Jeff, who was still following the conversation, eyes shut.

After checking out of their hotel, stopping by Simône's, and picking up some clothes and toiletries at Jeff's apartment, they finally reached their new lodgings at 8 AM. Bleary-eyed, the four slowly stepped out of their car. Simône surrendered the keys to the valet before they walked into the hotel, secured their room keys and headed upstairs to bed.

CHAPTER EIGHTEEN

Five hours later, Alex rolled over to find the source of the beeping that had interrupted her dream of biking through the Loire Valley with Jeff and Liz. They had just stopped in front of the chateau where they were scheduled to attend a wine tasting when the beeping began. She tried to hold onto the image of the beautiful 17th century castle, but to no avail. The scene faded as she awoke to a darkened room. Shaking off sleep, she could hear Liz sleeping soundly on the next bed.

Alex rubbed her eyes, before focusing on the bedside clock: *1:10 PM. Wait, what?* she thought, before the emotions, memories and smells of the last day came flooding into her mind.

Jeff! her mind screamed, now fully awake and concerned. "Liz! D! Wake up!" Alex said, almost yelling as she fumbled for the bedside light.

"What? Huh!" Liz asked, disoriented as she sat up, before wrinkling her nose in disgust at the smell wafting up from her still blood soaked clothes.

"Oh my God! I smell disgusting," said Liz, smelling her shirt as she hopped off of the bed and began stripping down to her underwear.

Before Alex could respond, Liz had run into the bathroom and started to shower. Ten minutes later she emerged, wrapped in a towel, her hair dripping wet, but clean. "Okay, I feel human again. Don't freak out; my bloody clothes are soaking in the tub. Thankfully we have a separate shower."

While Liz had showered, Alex had called Jeff and Simône to confirm that all was well. An hour later, they sat

eating lunch in the lobby restaurant, tired, but clean, freshly clothed and ready to take on the rest of the day.

"I think we should go to my office." Simône said.
"Perhaps we are being watched, but Jeff and I have a
wealth of information there on the Templars that may help
us decide how to proceed."

She stopped for a few seconds, considering, before
continuing. "True, we did not find the 'Accord,' but the
Templars were very smart, very meticulous. I cannot believe that there was only one copy produced of such a
precious document. I'm assuming that there were three
originals of the document to begin with, one for each of
the signees. But even if the Templars only found one ..."
Simône mused.

"From what we know of the Templars, who were
quite secretive in their dealings, they likely would have
made several copies and hidden them in different locations for safekeeping."

"So where do you think we could find one?" Liz
asked, dropping her voice and leaning forward.

Jeff grimaced slightly as he adjusted his sling, before answering. "I was thinking about that very question
this morning as I was showering. I've been so drugged,"
he said apologetically, "but I think the water hitting me in
the face finally woke me up. St Michael's line has to be the
answer!"

"What do you mean?" asked Alex, not following his
thought process.

"Ley lines."

Alex shrugged, a look of confusion on her face, still
not understanding.

"In Britain, ley lines traditionally referred to straight
track ways or geographically fairly straight lines that could
be drawn conceptually to connect interrelated historical, or
mystical sites. From a religious perspective, these lines
can refer to places where allegedly there were sightings of
historical, mystical, spiritual or even biblical figures."

124

"Remember the inscription we found at the abbaye, 'follow the arrow of Michael.'"

"And?" Alex asked.

"And since we think the Michael referred to was St. Michael, the 'arrow' could refer to his ley line which intersects with some of the places where people believe they have seen visions of him. So after I woke up in the shower, I did some online research on him."

"Didn't you sleep at all?" asked Liz, concerned.

"A little, my shoulder was hurting, anyway..." answered Jeff, ignoring the look that passed between the three women.

"So tell us about St. Michael," Simône said, before taking a sip of her espresso.

"Well, as I am sure you know, he is venerated as an archangel in all three major religions: Christianity, Judaism and Islam. In the Jewish religion, St. Michael is seen as an advocate who intercedes between God and his chosen people. He is considered to be 'the prince of Israel, who helped Daniel in his dispute with the angel of Persia,'" Jeff quoted, looking down at some handwritten notes he had brought to the table.

Continuing, Jeff said, "According to the Christian tradition that the Apostle John wrote about in the Biblical book of Revelations, Michael leads God's forces against Satan. Revelations 12:7-9 says that in John's vision, war broke out in heaven; Michael and his lesser angels fought against the dragon and his angels, finally casting out the dragon, 'that ancient serpent known as the devil or Satan, who leads the whole world astray.'"

"What about in Islam?" Alex asked, listening intently.

Jeff looked down at his notes again before answering. "In the Islamic faith, believing in angels is actually one of the six tenets or articles of faith. In Sura 2 Al-Baqarah, ayat 97-98, Archangels Gabriel and Michael are both mentioned:

'... whoever is an enemy to Allah and his angels and messengers, to Gabriel and Michael-then, Allah is an enemy to those who reject faith.'"

"Sounds like using St. Michael as the guide or sign post for finding an accord entered into by the three religions actually makes sense," Liz said, excitedly.

"Yes, I think it does. And the reason I think the arrow reference is to the ley line is because St. Michael didn't use a bow and arrow. He is almost always depicted with a sword or spear used to kill a dragon. So if it isn't an arrow, it must be a metaphor; a ley line makes sense."

"So if this is correct, we have to determine where St. Michael's line runs. Where has he been sighted over the centuries? That is where we will start our search," Simône said.

"What do you mean by sightings?" Alex asked, skepticism in her voice.

Simône gave a slight smile before nodding at Jeff, encouraging him to continue.

"That's the thing," said Jeff, leaning forward, before frowning as pain shot through his shoulder. "There have been multiple sightings of St. Michael over the centuries. Weirdly, based on those sightings and other locations devoted to worship of the archangel, you can draw a line, a ley line-I guess you would call it-from the Mount St. Carmel monastery in Israel, all of the way northwest to a small island off of the coast of Ireland, 'Skellig Michael' where devout monks lived for centuries before the time of the crusades."

"Mount Carmel, which looks down over the city of Haifa on the Mediterranean coast, is recorded in the Old Testament as the place where the prophet Elijah battled and defeated 450 priests of the pagan god, Baal. Later, several holy hermits are said to have lived there in a cave, praying for the arrival of the Virgin who would give birth to the Jewish Messiah. Ultimately, two millennia later, by the time the Templars reached the Holy Land at the time of the crusades, a Carmelite order dedicated to the Virgin Mary and Elijah had established a thriving monastery on the site."

"Interesting, but what is the connection to St. Michael, if any?" asked Alex, doubtfully.

"Well, there isn't a direct connection, I guess. Some of the holy sites, along St. Michael's line that runs from Ireland to Israel, do not claim to be places where he actually appeared, but the religious societies or peoples who lived there were deeply devoted to him. Also, perhaps there is a connection because Michael is the patron saint of warriors and Elijah is revered by all three religions as a fierce warrior for God in his defeat of Baal's priests. And if the Templars did find an 'Accord,' it had to have been somewhere in the Holy Land, maybe even at Mount Carmel."

"Michael was the patron saint of the Crusaders, then?" asked Liz.

"Well, certainly one of them."

"How many different locations are there on this line?" asked Alex. "We can't possibly go to all of them."

"Yes, that's true. It's a long list:" Jeff said, looking at his notes,

"-Skellig Michael off the coast of Ireland;

-St. Michael's Chapel in Corn Brea in Cornwall, England;

-Mont St. Michel in Brittany, off the French coast;

-Bourges, France;

-Sagra di San Michele in Piedmont;

-San Michele at Castiglione di Carfagna;

-Monte Sant' Angelo, Monte Gargano, all in Italy;

-Kerkyra; Delphi; Delos; and Lindos, all in Greece;

-and, lastly, Mount Carmel."

"It could take months to visit all of these places," Jeff conceded, as he finished reading.

"And besides, we know it couldn't have been a Templar who may have found the treasure at the Abbaye

D'Orval, since they were all dead by the 18th century," said Alex.

"Obviously, but whoever found it may have recognized the potential link to the Templars, and acted accordingly. Granted, it is a long shot, but it is the only one we have," said Jeff.

"What we need to do is figure out what the person who left the message was trying to tell us," Simône said. "I don't think he, or she, wanted us to actually follow the entire line but peut-être just to consider all of those locations, without making it too obvious. Or when they took the document, perhaps they didn't know where they would be able to hide it? Which one is the most likely location given what we know?"

"I think we would just be guessing without more information," Jeff answered.

After a few moments of silence, Simône asked, "Then, why don't we split up the list of locations, and do some research this afternoon? I will look for any with a Templar connection and perhaps Alex and Liz can determine the one's where St. Michael allegedly appeared. I suspect the nexus of those is where we should start our search. I can get you day passes to the Sorbonne's main library," she added, looking at Alex and Liz. "Meanwhile, I'll review our research at my office and you, Jeff, can stay here and rest."

Jeff started to protest but decided it was a lost cause when he saw the looks on the three women's faces.

"Stop being such a tough guy and take your pain meds so you can get some sleep," Alex said. "I can't believe I'm admitting this, but I-we-actually need your mind in working order."

"Yeah, okay," Jeff agreed, with a sheepish grin.

"Simône, you should be careful. They may still be watching us. We don't want you to be kidnapped again," Liz said."

"I appreciate your concern but you must not worry. When we stopped at my apartment, I got my pistol."

"What? I didn't think they were allowed in France!" Jeff said, surprised.

"They are very restricted but my ex-husband was-is-a police officer, and he got me a license for sport shooting. We used to go to the range regularly. I am actually quite good, a French Annie Oakley."

They all laughed before Alex said, "Well, let's hope you aren't also a Calamity Jane."

CHAPTER NINETEEN

After Jeff left, the three women finished their coffee and paid the bill. "I think we should return the car to the rental place since the 'bad guys' may know what it looks like," Alex said, as they walked out of the restaurant. 'But first, we need to try to clean off the blood on the back seat."

"Then we need some hydrogen peroxide," Liz said matter-a-factly.

Alex and Simône looked at her in surprise. "No big deal," she said. "I cut myself one time and I had to get the blood out of the carpet before Roberta came home."

Alex nodded her head in understanding, while Simône looked baffled but decided not to ask.

"Okay, so where do we get hydrogen peroxide?" asked Alex.

"I think there is a pharmacy around the corner. I saw it when we were driving in. I'll go get some," Liz said.

"Not by yourself, you won't!" said Alex, adamantly. "We don't know if those crazies are still watching us."

"Okay, fine. You can be my bodyguard."

"In the meantime, I'll grab another espresso and then have the valet bring the car around," Simône said.

An hour later, after much scrubbing and conversation, they finished the task, having deftly avoided the inquiries of several passersby.

"At least you can't see the blood anymore," Alex said, satisfied.

"Let's hope they don't have any CSI's in training on their cleaning staff at the car rental place or we'll be hearing from the local police," Liz said, smirking.

Once they had returned the car, the three women took the metro to the Cluny-Sorbonne stop. After exiting the station, Simône gave them a brief walking tour of the area down the Rue des Ecoles before turning onto the Rue de la Sorbonne.

Alex and Liz saw that the entire block to their left was occupied by a huge stone building. About halfway down the block, they entered through a massive green door flanked by columns into a high ceilinged hall.

"This is the reading room," Simône said in a whisper. Ornate light green paint covered the walls of the 200-foot long hall topped with a 20-foot ceiling decorated with gold leaf and inset paintings.

"It's beautiful," gasped Liz. "It looks more like the interior of a palace than a library."

"Yes, major renovations were made a few years ago, restoring it to its former glory," Simône said proudly. "Let me introduce you to Giselle, one of the librarians, and a student of mine. She can help you with your research. She will give you unfettered access to the collection."

"Thanks, Simône. What are you going to do?" asked Alex.

"I'm going to review the research in my office, and I also have a few phone calls to return. Text me when you are ready to quit for the day. I imagine I am only good for a few hours after last night."

"Me too," said Liz, stifling a yawn.

After the introductions had been made with Giselle, Simône bid them 'adieu.'"

"So what do you think? Should we split up the locations?" asked Alex.

"I was thinking I could do research online," Liz said, pulling her laptop from her backpack and you could see what books they have referencing the historical claims of the apparitions of Michael."

"Sounds okay to me," agreed Alex. "Good thing you left your backpack in the car when we came back from the abbaye the other day, or your computer would still be MIA like mine is. I hope we get our stuff back from Natalia soon."

"Yeah, but at least we got new toothbrushes at the drugstore. My teeth were beginning to feel kind of fuzzy," said Liz. Alex headed for the circulation desk, as Liz began to type, periodically adding notes to a separate document she had created.

After a few minutes of searching the digital card catalogue, Alex requested help from Giselle in locating the appropriate stacks. Ten minutes later, she plopped an armful of books next to Liz, and sat down. "Guess I have my work cutout."

Two hours later, Alex finished reviewing the last of her cache of books. "I think I have found everything I can in these books. Most of them are repetitive," said Alex, as she stretched her arms above her head.

"I could probably find online articles for days," Liz said, "but most of them are repetitive too, and besides, I'm exhausted. Should we text Simône?"

"Sure, I will," said Alex, pulling out her phone and typing a message.

"Simône, we are beat. Ready to leave the library. Where should we meet?"

A minute later Alex's phone buzzed and she picked it up to read the response.

"Unfortunately, I am still tied up. Why don't you and Liz head back to the hotel and have dinner with Jeff. I will call in an hour or two."

"Everything okay?"
Alex texted back, wary after the previous day's events.

132

"Yes, fine. I am with my ex-husband.
Will explain later. Take care, S

"So where are we meeting her?" Liz asked.

"We're not. Said she's tied up; will meet us later."

"I hope she doesn't mean literally-we've already been there, done that," Liz said, wryly.

"Yeah," agreed Alex, with a laugh. "No, I think she is alright. Sounds like she is meeting with her ex-husband. So, she's with the 'police,' perfectly safe, I imagine. We'll go back to the hotel and have dinner with Jeff. He's probably been sleeping all afternoon. We better feed him or he'll starve."

"If you're sure she's okay."

"I think so-no hidden messages in the text," Alex said, holding her phone out so Liz could read it.

They stopped by the circulation desk to thank Giselle, before heading out into the warm Parisian evening.

"Wow, it's still really bright out here," Liz exclaimed.

"Yes. We're so far north, the sun doesn't set until almost 10 PM this time of year."

"That's good. We can keep an eye out for any bad guys."

"Exactly!" said Alex, as she linked arms with her sister and began to stroll up the street to the metro stop.

"I want you to tell me what is going on," Philippe Bertrand demanded, as he surveyed the wrecked interior of his ex-wife's office.

"Calm down and sit down, Philippe. Would you like an espresso?" Simône asked as she began making coffee in the small machine, amazingly intact, which occupied a space on a small corner table.

"You're not answering my question, but yes."

After she had prepared their cafés, Simône up righted a chair lying on its side in the center of the room, sat down and took a deep breath, as she thought about the events of the past 24 hours. Fifteen minutes later, Simône finished her harrowing tale. Philippe, who had let her speak uninterrupted, looked at her appraisingly.

"Premier, I am glad you were not hurt. You could have been killed. I know there were times I said I wanted to kill you when we were married, but ..." His voice trailed off as he looked at her, his eyes softening.

"But you would have hated it if someone else had beaten you to it," Simône said with a chuckle, breaking the awkward silence.

"Yes, precisely," Philippe said, grinning. "But you have survived and are finished with this nonsense, I presume. Laisse tomber."

"No, Philippe," Simône retorted angrily, her smile replaced with a scowl, "we are not finished with this 'nonsense,' as you put it, and I won't let it go! What we are hunting is of potentially great historical, if not religious, significance. I'll be damned before I let some fanatical thugs scare me off."

"You have always been so bull-headed," Philippe said, shaking his head. "Perhaps next time you will not be so lucky. And what about Jeff and the two young women-you seem unconcerned about their safety."

"Au contraire, I am very concerned," Simône snapped back. "But that is why we need to finish our search and make our findings public. That is the only thing that will ensure our safety."

Philippe looked around her office before saying, "I'm not sure anything will protect you at this point, but apparently it is not my concern." He paused for a moment before asking, "So, was anything taken? Do you wish to make a report?"

"No. I think they were searching for the diary and the rubbing I mentioned-Jeff has both. The rest of this," she said, pointing to the files and papers strewn across the floor, " is just our research-nothing particularly revealing. They either don't know what we know or they think we have actually found some type of treasure."

"And 'they' are?"

"I assume accomplices of the Syrians that the Israeli agents told us about."

"Well, if you won't stop the search, at least take some advice. Carry your handgun at all times."

"Yes, I have it here," Simône said, rising and pulling it from her oversized purse.

"Do you have enough ammunition? You know it is very difficult to come by under present regulations."

"Actually, I squirreled some away the last time we went target shooting."

"Pourquoi, were you planning to shoot someone?" Philippe asked, his eyes narrowing.

"No," Simône said, laughing. "Of course not. I just thought it would be good to have some should the need arise, which regrettably, apparently it has," she added.

"Well, d'accord," Philippe said, towering several inches above Simône, as he stood up to leave. "Then I will leave you, ma cher. But Simmy," he paused at the door and looked back at her over his shoulder, "be careful. I meant what I said: I can't protect you from these guys. No one can."

Simône nodded silently as the door closed behind him, his words lingering hauntingly even as the sound of his footsteps faded down the hallway.

She continued to brood on the conversation for a few moments before shaking her head to exorcise the memory. *Merde, I guess I better get this cleaned up*, Simône thought. By the time she had restored her office to some semblance of order, reorganized and gathered the research she still needed to review, and exited the building, making a mental note to call security about the damaged door lock, the city lights of Paris were on full display.

I wish I had my car, Simône thought ruefully. Unfortunately, the owner of the Bouillon repair shop, who she had telephoned and hired to locate and tow her abandoned car from the ditch, thought it would be at least two weeks before it was repaired and drivable.

That fils de pute (son of a bitch), Simône thought, cursing the man who had kidnapped her, unaware that his remains had been found earlier in the day and delivered anonymously by some of Natalia's cohorts to the morgue in Bruge, Belgium. Nor could she know that even as she walked to the metro, Interpol was in the process of determining his identity, which eventually would lead to a search for his fellow jihadists, or the fact that he had died accidentally by his own hand, robbing him of a martyr's death-an unsolved mystery.

Simône lacked any of this information, which might have relieved some of her anxiety. As she walked, she continually surveyed her surroundings and looked repeatedly over her shoulder. *Thankfully*, Simône thought, *there are plenty of students wandering around.* She sighed with relief as she boarded the train that would take her back to the Tuileries station. The only other inhabitants of her Metro car were an elderly couple deep in conversation about a movie they had just seen. She shut her eyes and leaned back in her seat as the train began to accelerate.

"She just left her office-headed for the metro. Should I follow her?" asked the man into his cellphone, as his gaze followed Simône down the street.

"Yes, but keep your distance, Brother. We don't want to tip her off that she is being surveilled. She is more likely to reveal the location of the diary if she thinks she isn't being watched. It was ill-advised to leave her office in such a mess. We don't want the police involved."

"Yes, I'm sorry, but when you texted and told me she had arrived at the library with the two girls, I knew I didn't have much time to search-I had to be quick!"

"I trust you were at least wearing gloves?"

"Of course. Do you think I'm stupid?"

The man on the other end of the phone call was momentarily silent, before saying, "Brother, we are each blessed with singular gifts. That is all I will say. Report back tomorrow morning. Sancte Michael Archangele, defende nos en proelio *(May St. Michael defend us in battle)*."

"Yes, Monseigneur, au revoir."

As the man ended his call, he touched the pendant at his neck and crossed himself, before lighting a cigarette as he crossed the street to hurry after his quarry.

CHAPTER TWENTY

Simône reached the lobby restaurant of their hotel just as Alex, Jeff and Liz were finishing dinner.

"Bon soir, mes amis," said Simône, purposefully putting a cheery note in her voice. "How was your dinner?"

"Comme ci, comme ça," answered Jeff, who had just cleaned his plate with a piece of bread, before pushing it away.

"Well, it may have just been 'so, so,' but you scarfed down every bite," teased Alex.

"Yeah, well you try getting shot. Healing takes a lot of energy."

"Oh, right," said Alex, grinning. "Maybe you should order another plateful."

"You ..." Jeff started to say, before Liz, who was used to their banter, interjected. "How are you, Simône?"

"Comme ci, comme ça," Simône repeated. "When I got to my office, I discovered that in my absence, someone had broken in and searched it, trashed it, actually."

"Oh no, that's horrible!" exclaimed Liz, sympathetically. "Was anything missing?"

"Nothing was taken, so I'm assuming it was the same group we encountered in Belgium. They must have been searching for the diary, which thankfully we had with us."

She stopped for a moment, before asking anxiously, "We do still have it? With everything that has happened in the last two days, I realize that I haven't even asked about it."

"No worries; I'm not taking any chances," Alex said, pulling a large manila envelope from the purse at her feet.

138

"Jeff gave it to me at the hostel before we went to dinner ... God, just last night! That seems incredible. Sorry, I'm rambling. Anyway, I put it under the seat in the car, didn't want to leave it at the hostel when we went looking for you. So, bottom line, it's safe."

"Merci," said Simône, visibly relaxing. "And thank you for saving my life. I realized as I was sitting on the metro that I truly do owe each of you my life. If you hadn't shown up when you did ..." She stopped, overcome with emotion.

"We're the four musketeers," Liz said lightly, grabbing Simône's hand and giving it a squeeze. "All for one and one for all, right?"

"Right!" said Alex and Jeff together. "I feel like we should have swords or something," Alex said, joking.

"No need, mes amis. We have this," Simône said, patting the purse at her side.

The other three nodded knowingly, before Jeff asked, "So, what was Philippe doing at your office? Is he stalking you?"

"Oh, no," Simône said, with a chuckle. "Actually I called him. I thought I should get his advice-find out if he thought I should file a report."

"And did you?"

"I thought about it but decided not to-given what has happened here in Paris the last couple of years, the terrorist attacks, I was afraid we might become embroiled in a much larger investigation. They might have even confiscated the diary and our research if it seemed to be connected to terrorists. I decided it wasn't worth it."

"So does he think we are still in danger?" Liz, who had leaned forward, asked in a low voice.

Simône shrugged her shoulders. "Peut-être. But he says there is nothing the police can do to protect us, so what's the point of getting them involved."

"You might be right. Remember what Natalia said: if we have even a suspicion that we are being followed or watched, we should call her. I didn't spend that much time around her when I was running against her in college, certainly never knew that she was in Mossad." Alex stopped and looked into space for a moment as though she was reviewing her history, before continuing. "But she always seemed-what's the word-solid. You know, reliable. I trust her."

"Then so do I," said Liz, smiling at her twin.

"And if she thought we were in serious danger, she would tell us?" asked Jeff.

"Definitely," answered Alex, without hesitation. "I think ..."

She stopped in mid-sentence as their waitress approached to clear the table and give them the check.

After she left, Liz asked, "What were you going to say, Alex?"

"Oh, never mind," Alex said, shaking her head.

They sat silently for a moment before Simône said, "I am anxious to find out what you found in your research but my exhaustion is winning out. So I hope you will forgive me if, as you say, I call it a night."

"No problem, Professeur," Jeff said quickly. "Why don't we meet tomorrow for breakfast at-let's say-9 AM, and formulate a plan of attack."

"Wonderful," said Simône, her voice sounding tired. "Demain (tomorrow)," she said before walking slowly across the lobby to the elevator bank. A few minutes later, having paid their bill, Alex, Liz and Jeff followed. Jeff got off at the 2nd floor; Liz and Alex exited on the 5th floor where their suite was located.

In their room, they found Belgian chocolates on their pillows. I think I have had enough of Belgium," Liz said, as she dropped the candy in the nearest waste bin.

"I'm with you, sister," said Alex, who followed suit. "Besides, if I ate that, I would be awake for hours, and my pillow is calling me."

Within 10 minutes, the sisters were sleeping soundly in their beds.

CHAPTER TWENTY-ONE

"Bon jour." Simône, who seemed much more lively after a good night's sleep, waved as Liz and Alex approached her lobby table. "Where's Jeff?"

"Oh, Mr. Sleepyhead? He should be down pretty soon. I called him about 15 minutes ago. Woke him up-sounded pretty out of it. Must be the pain meds."

"No kidding, Al. You heard what the doctor said. He's not even supposed to be doing anything today," Liz said.

"But you know Jeff; that's not happening."

"What's not happening?" asked Jeff, who had silently walked up behind Alex.

"Oh, you staying in bed all day resting."

"That's right," said Jeff, plopping down in the one empty chair at the coffee table at which they were sitting. "And by the way, I feel great. As you know, I am of hardy German stock. A little thing like a hole in my shoulder isn't stopping me." He grinned and ran his hand through his dripping wet hair.

"A couple of days ago you were Spiderman. Now you're Superman?" Alex said. "Next thing we know, you'll be leaping tall buildings.

"It's a shame you weren't faster than that speeding bullet, though," said Liz solemnly, before cracking a smile.

"Ouch! Uh yeah, guess that would have been good," Jeff agreed, as he readjusted the sling holding his left arm in place.

Simône smiled slightly before saying, "Would you like to stay here to eat breakfast or should we venture out? There is a very nice café around the corner where the croissants are magnifique," she exclaimed, putting the fingers of her right hand to her lips, in the gesture of a kiss.

"Sounds great," said Liz.

After a short walk past the gardens down the Rue de Rivoli, they arrived at a small restaurant with three outdoor tables, and as many inside. The owner, a petite, fashionably dressed, 50ish woman came bustling forward to kiss Simône on both cheeks, before saying, "Bon jour, bienvenue. Comment-allez vous? (Hello, welcome, how are you)."

"Bien, et vous?" asked Simône, reciprocating the kisses.

"Ah, bien." She looked quickly around before steering them toward a table in the corner.

The occupant of the table, a young man clad in a suit and tie, briefly looked surprised before quickly gulping down the remaining espresso in his small cup, and throwing a few euros on the table.

"Merci, Jean-Pierre. I must use the tables for larger groups, tu comprends?"

"Pas de problème, Madame," he said, before heading out onto the street. A teenage boy who had been watching the exchange from behind the pastry counter, quickly hurried over to clean and straighten the table and chairs.

"Ah, merci, Madame Desmarais, but I feel badly; we ran the poor man off.'

"Do not worry, Simône; he's my nephew," she said, with a wink. "I give him his coffee for free most of the time. He can't expect to loiter here all day."

"C'est ça," Simône agreed, before ordering espressos and pastries for the entire group. Once their order arrived, they pulled their chairs close to the table in order to keep their conversation private.

"So tell us what you learned yesterday," she said, directing her gaze at Alex and Liz.

"Well," said Alex, looking down at her pad filled with handwritten notes, "to start, I learned that there have been numerous sightings of St. Michael over the centuries. Even some as recently as the 20th century. The first recorded sighting of St. Michael was in 490 A.D. at Mount Gargano, one of the points on the ley line in southeastern Italy. Supposedly Michael appeared to the Bishop of Seponto and told him the area was under the angel's protection. There is a shrine there to Michael, and the locals celebrate the Feast of the Apparition yearly. In fact, Michael must have really liked the place, because allegedly, he appeared there at least four more times, most recently in 1656."

"But the Templars don't have a connection to Mount Gargano, do they?" asked Jeff.

"No, not as far as I could tell," replied Liz.

"And it seems unlikely that someone would hide treasure so close to Rome if they were trying to keep it hidden from the Catholic Church. Mount Gargano is on the outskirts of Rome-less than 10 miles away," said Liz.

"Perhaps," agreed Simône. "Although, since we don't know who took the document-if that's what it was-from the Abbaye, there is no telling what their true motivations were."

"I guess though if we are focusing or thinking that whatever was at the Abbaye D'Orval did have an important or meaningful connection to the Templars, it seems like there may be better candidates on the line that we should consider," Jeff said.

"There is St. Michael's Mount," said Alex, "in Mount Bay, off the coast of Cornwall. The archangel allegedly appeared there in a vision to a local fisherman in 495 A.D. But the story of the apparition seems a little suspect to me, because one author I read yesterday had done some research about the geography of the area. That historian claims that St. Michael's Mount only became an island in 1099 A.D.

"According to his citation from The Domesday (doomsday) Book, which was a land survey of England and Wales compiled in 1086 AD under the orders of William the Conqueror, the mount was surrounded at that time by a dense forest several miles from the sea. In fact, the Cornish name for the mount was 'gray rock in the wood.' But then something happened at the end of that century, maybe an earthquake, which caused the area to be covered by the sea. So it seems unlikely that 600 years before, some fisherman was hanging out in the woods and happened to see an apparition of Michael."

"I guess it's possible the story could have changed over time-maybe it was originally about a woodsman, and once the mount became an island, the story morphed to include a fisherman," said Liz.

"Either way, there doesn't seem to be any evidence of a connection between the church there and the Templars, although I guess anything is possible," said Alex doubtfully.

"And of course, there is Mont St. Michel, an island about a half mile off the coast of France, near the border of Normandy and Brittany, near Avranche. According to legend, St. Michael appeared there in 708 A.D. in a dream to the Bishop Aubert d'Avranche, who, for some weird reason, was napping at the top of the 300-foot rock mount. St. Michael told the bishop to build a small church there circling the summit, which he did," Liz said.

"About 250 years later, a monastery was started there by a group of Benedictine monks in 966. The initial foundations of the present-day church were built sometime before 1000 A.D. Over the next 200 years, the Romanesque church was gradually constructed over existing crypts and the first existing monastery structures were built against the North wall. By the beginning of the Middle Ages, a village, which had grown at the foot of the abbaye-which exists to this day-was inhabited by farmers, fishermen, and shopkeepers, many of whom sold the trinkets and souvenirs sought by visiting religious pilgrims," Liz said.

"Because it is a tidal island, there has always been some access by foot during low tides, although supposedly, crossing the sands can be dangerous because very sudden shifts of the tide can cause water to rush over that tenuous land access. And there is quick sand as well," Liz added.

"Based on the research Liz and I both did, it seems most likely that the locations on the line with a direct connection to the Templars are Mount Carmel and Mont St. Michel. When you were originally telling us about the Templars, you mentioned that they had outpost near Mount Carmel that protected pilgrims coming from the seaports to Jerusalem," said Alex.

"Yes, that's true," Jeff said.

"And based on the research I did yesterday," Liz added, "the Templars had an impressive fleet of ships during their heyday. Several historians I read mentioned that the Templars had regular contact with Mont St. Michel as it was a frequent destination for religious pilgrims, as well as a rest stop for Britons traveling through France eastward to Rome or the Holy Lands."

"If you were someone who had found some sort of treasure hidden at the direction of Marie-Antoinette at the time of the French Revolution, and wanted to safely hide it during a time of great turmoil, what seems more likely, that you would take it all the way to Palestine or to Mont St. Michel, a few days ride from the Abbaye D'Orval?" asked Simône rhetorically.

"Well, that seems obvious, Mont St. Michel," Alex said.

"But unfortunately, what seems like the obvious answer may not be the correct one," interjected Jeff.

"What you two probably don't know is what happened to Mont St. Michel during and after the French Revolution. The revolutionaries were not only violently opposed to the monarchy; they were also intent on destroying all vestiges of organized religion, in other words, the Catholic Church," Jeff added.

"Yes, but what is it about the history of Mont St. Michel that makes you think it wouldn't have been a good hiding place?" Liz asked. "It sounds to me just like the sort of religious, historically significant place that someone interested in such an important document might think would serve as a good resting place."

"But that's just it. At the time of and following the French Revolution, Mont St. Michel was used as a prison. The monks were ejected from the beautiful Abbaye, renamed Mont Libre, which was used to imprison political prisoners of the revolution. It wasn't until 1863 that the prison was closed and the Bishop of Avranche leased it back from the French government for religious purposes. About 10 years later the French government declared it a national monument and began the ongoing task of restoration and upkeep," Jeff said.

"So you can see, it's difficult to believe that someone trying to protect a document from the revolutionaries would hide it in a place under the control of the revolution," Jeff concluded.

"Yes, that is true," agreed Simône, "unless it was someone who had divided loyalties or had some connection to both the revolutionaries and the church. Or for some other reason had access to Mont St. Michel, although I don't know who that would be," Simône said, thinking aloud.

"I figure it wouldn't have been a Catholic priest or monk. Once the revolution started, they all had a price on their heads. Thousands were killed and some 30,000 were forced to leave France or be executed," said Jeff.

"That's true, but not all were put to death; some would have been imprisoned, even perhaps at Mont St. Michel. If they were willing to take an oath of allegiance to the Republic, they often escaped the guillotine. If not, they were killed, imprisoned or sent to a penal colony in French Guiana," Simône added.

146

"So is it possible that the person who took the treasure from the Abbaye D'Orval was a monk?" Alex asked.

"I imagine some clergy would've destroyed a document like an accord, if they found it. They would have thought it was inconsistent with Catholic beliefs-the idea of unity among religions," Jeff ventured.

"Exactly! In much the same way that the Islamists we encountered wanted to find it to destroy it I'm guessing," Simône agreed. "Fundamental Islamists, in particular, consider any other religion as blasphemy: non-Muslims are subject only to conversion or death."

"Yeah, I think we just saw that up close and personal," Alex said. "Any way, it sounds like a monk or priest would have been under such close scrutiny that there was the little chance of one of them smuggling a document such as an accord through revolutionary France."

"So where does that leave us?" asked Liz. "From what you have all said, it doesn't sound like there's anywhere to look for the treasure," she added, sounding discouraged.

"We haven't talked about Skellig Michael," Jeff said.

"That's true. It's at the far west end of St. Michael's line, and I suppose the Templars could have had some connection with it because they could have reached it by ship. But it is just a few hermits' beehive shaped stone huts, a small church and a graveyard perched at the top of a long, dangerous stone staircase which ascends over 600 feet up the side of the barren lonely rock, sitting eight miles off the coast of Ireland," Alex said. Looking at her notes, she added, "George Bernard Shaw described it as the 'most fantastic and impossible rock in the world.'"

"So why even include it on the line?" asked Liz.

"Well, because it was considered a mystical or holy site even before the advent of Christianity. Ancient Celts handed down legends about kings who lived or were buried there. No one really knows the actual date when the first Celtic monks came to inhabit the island or even how they got there, considering its remote location. Some historians tie them to St. Fionán, a South Kerry saint who founded Innisfallen Abbey, and others believe they were Coptic Christians who fled Byzantine Roman rule before the 7th century," explained Alex.

"There isn't a lot of recorded history of the island, but in one account," continued Alex, "the monastery was attacked in 823 A.D. and the Abbott was kidnapped, which suggests a ongoing religious community at that time. The Vikings also regularly visited the monastery, probably to plunder it. But supposedly in 993 A.D., the Viking king, Olag Tygvasson, accepted religion and was baptized there. He was later credited with introducing Christianity to Norway after he became its first King, Olaf I."

"We do know that sometime before 1044 A.D., it had been dedicated to St. Michael because there is a record of the death that year of a Aedh of Scelic-Mchici. There is also a historical record of a new church built sometime in the mid-tenth century, which was consecrated as 'St. Michael's Church.' And there is also a legend that St. Patrick, with the aid of St. Michael, had his final battle and defeated the venomous snakes of Ireland there. Then sometime in the late 12th or early 13th century, Skellig Michael was abandoned, probably because the climate grew too cold to sustain life, and its inhabitants moved to an abbaye on the mainland. And for some totally useless trivia," concluded Alex, "it was just used recently as the location for the last scene in a Star Wars movie, so now it is probably being overrun with tourists looking for Luke Skywalker."

"Well, may the force be with them. But it doesn't sound like what we are looking for. It was abandoned long before the French revolution," said Liz.

"Yes, I still think Mont St. Michel is the more likely location and I think I know someone who can help us," said Simône, before rising to pay for their breakfast and thanking the owner for her hospitality, as they headed out onto the busy street.

CHAPTER
TWENTY-TWO

Twenty minutes later, having taken the metro, the group stood on the right bank across the Seine from Notre-Dame Cathedrale, in front of the Saint-Gervais-et-Saint Protais, a 18th century church with a white stone French Baroque style facade.

"So why are we here, Simône?" asked Jeff, as they entered the empty church. Their conversation ceased as they stopped to admire the Gothic interior, with its dramatically high arched ceiling, beautiful hand carved choir stalls, stained glass, both old and modern, and sculpture from the 1600's.

"It's beautiful, isn't it?" Simône asked reverently. "They started building it in the Gothic style in the late 1400's but by the time they finished it 200 years later, the French Baroque influence prevailed on the façade."

"I was wondering," said Jeff. "The inside and outside are a little eclectic. But you're right, it is beautiful, all the same."

"To answer your question, we are here to see a friend of mine, Sister Angelique, a member of the Monastic Communities of Jerusalem. This is their home church in Paris. You might also be interested to know that members of this order also reside at Mont St. Michel," said Simône in a reverent whisper. "And she is considered a preeminent expert on the history of the clergy during the French revolution."

"Got it," said Jeff, nodding his head.

Another minute passed before a door to their right was opened by a tall, slender woman, wearing white robes, who came walking toward them. "Simône, bonjour. I was so surprised to get your text. I haven't seen you since that anthropology conference last year, c'est vrai?"

"Yes, it has been too long," responded Simône, as she exchanged kisses with the other woman. "Thank you for seeing us on such short notice. This is my research assistant, Jeff Stahl, and his two visiting American amis, Alex and Liz King. I should say, they are also friends of mine, bien sûr (of course)."

"But of course," the nun said, smiling brightly at the sisters. "And very nice to meet each of you. I have about an hour free before our noon prayers and song time. So let's sit down," she said, pointing to short brown stools lining each side of the nave.

After they had arranged themselves on the stools grouped in a semi-circle, Simône glanced at Jeff before saying, "Without going into too much detail, we are trying to determine where someone affiliated with the clergy, more specifically the Abbaye D'Orval in southern Belgium, might have hidden a document of great religious and historical significance during the heat of the French Revolution. We have some information that what we are looking for may have been taken to a location associated with St. Michael, possibly at one of the locations along the Apollo/ St. Michael's line. You know the line I am referring to, yes?"

"Yes, I do. Belief in the significance of ley lines is as old as civilization itself. So I assume you have considered the various locations along the line and narrowed down your search?" answered Sister Angelique.

"Yes, because we believe this happened during the revolution, we think whoever took the document could not have gone too far with it. For example, it seems unlikely that they could have traveled the great distances to Mount Carmel in the holy land, or even for that matter to any of the locations in the Greek islands," said Simône.

"Without telling me more than you think you should, would this document have been something that someone involved in the revolutionary movement would have wanted either to preserve, or alternatively, destroy?" asked the nun.

"That is the crux of the matter. I know as a general rule that revolutionary forces were virulently opposed to religion as a whole, and the Catholic clergy in particular," Simône replied.

"Yes, that is absolutely true. But there were exceptions. For example, Maximilien de Robespierre, one of the leaders of the National Assembly during the revolution was originally opposed to the de-Christianization of France as a tenet of the revolution, which led to the murder of many clergy. As a Deist, he believed in a Supreme Being but nonetheless, he saw the Catholic Church as a counter-revolutionary force that had to be subdued. After the initial period of de-Christianization in which all religious ceremonies were suppressed or forbidden, society began to yearn quickly for something to fill the void," Sister Angelique explained.

"In response, Robespierre and some of his colleagues announced the creation of a new religion, 'The Cult of the Supreme Being,' intended to supplant both the Church and the atheistic Cult of Reason that had grown up alongside the anti-religious fervor accompanying the revolution. Many saw this as an attempt to designate himself as Godhead. I disagree. Rather, I think he, like most people, ultimately could not live without the acknowledgement of something greater than himself," the nun added, before continuing.

"But regardless of his motivations, he was arrested and executed for this act of overreaching, among other things. Ultimately, Robespierre himself became a victim of the culture of terror and death instigated by the very groups he had led."

"So is it possible that someone who thought similarly to Robespierre might have wanted to preserve an agreement or accord that sought to create unity, or at least harmony among the three religions?" asked Simône. "Perhaps a Deist, someone who did not support any particular religion but still believed in a Supreme Being?"

Sister Angelique looked intently at her before asking, "So, is that what we are talking about? Mon Dieu! Does such an agreement actually exist?"

Simône hesitated a moment before responding. "Sister Angelique, what we are discussing must remain confidential. Someone has already tried to kill us because of the document we are seeking. I haven't said more because I didn't want to get you involved. I hope I can rely on your discretion."

"Yes, of course," the nun responded, as she looked into the very serious faces of the group surrounding her. "You have my word that I will guard your secret. But given what you have said, I must warn you. There is as much evil in the 21st century as there was in 18th century France. Even in the church, there are people driven by less than pure-often misguided-motivations. You must be very careful with whom you choose to discuss this matter. I promise you can trust my discretion, but there are others, many others, who would be very unhappy at even the suggestion that such a document existed. And it sounds as though you have already encountered at least one of them."

"You will be happy to hear that he was not a Catholic. Far from it!" exclaimed Simône. "But I understand what you are saying. I do have another question though-the original reason I came to you. Do you think it is possible that someone of the sort we were discussing could have hidden such a document at Mont St. Michel during the revolution, and if so, would it still exist?"

Instead of immediately responding, the nun looked up at a stained glass window depicting the wisdom of Solomon before answering.

"You, of course, know that the abbaye at Mont St. Michel was used as a prison during and after the revolution, or you wouldn't be bothering to ask me this question. Common sense dictates that anything taken there during the revolution would have been found and most likely destroyed."

"But, the Mont holds many secrets," she said, continuing. "A perfect example is the church of Notre Dame-sous-Terre, probably constructed in the late 900's by Benedictine monks, covered and surrounded by later construction and not rediscovered until centuries later. The fact that it remained hidden for all of those years suggests that the Mont holds its secrets well. So, who knows? I have never heard of such a document. But my order has only been at Mont St. Michel since the 1970s. A mere ripple in the waters of time that have flowed through that great abbaye. Anything is possible, c'est vrai?"

Sister Angelique shrugged her shoulders and then stood, politely ending the conversation. "And now, I must get ready for noon prayers. I wish you luck in your search, and if you should find such a document, as a historian, I would very much like to know. Very nice to meet you, Jeff, Alex and Liz," she said, shaking their hands. "Be safe, Simône, and go with God. Au revoir," she said, before silently passing back through the door from which she had earlier entered the nave.

CHAPTER TWENTY-THREE

They stood for a few moments contemplating what she had said, before filing silently out of the church into the bright mid-day Parisian sunlight.

"Well, that was interesting," Alex said, just as a car, its horn blaring, drove by, puncturing the silence. "What is her story?"

"Rather sad, really. I knew her in school. But then her parents were killed in a plane crash when she was twelve, and her uncle, a Catholic bishop, became her guardian. I think he is the one who convinced her to become a nun," Simône said.

"I wondered," said Jeff. "She didn't strike me as your typical nun, not that I know many. "

"Or any?" Alex asked, smirking.

"Too bad about her parents, though," Jeff added.

"So what exactly is a Deist?" Liz asked, wanting to change the subject from dead parents.

Jeff looked to Simône, who said, "A Deist is someone who believes that God created the universe and established moral and ethical laws controlling all human behavior, but that He does not intervene in human affairs supernaturally or through miraculous acts. Alternatively, Mono-theists believe in a single universal God. Christianity, Islam, and Judaism all hold this belief. The original divide between these religions exists because neither Islam nor Judaism believe that Jesus Christ was the Messiah."

Continuing, Simône said, "In Islam, he is a revered prophet, but they believe he was totally human, and that there is no Trinity, just one God-not three in one, as we Christians believe."

"Judaism on the other hand believes he was not the promised Messiah, but rather a false prophet, not worthy of regard. Because all three religions are 'Abrahamic' faiths, in other words, Abraham is regarded as the human religious father of all three, they each trace their origins back to the experiences of Abraham, regarded by all as the patriarch with whom God first established his ongoing relationship with mankind."

"After Adam and Eve, of course," said Liz.

"Yes. Let us not forget about Eve," said Alex. "But seriously, do you think Sister Angelique could be right, that someone who was aligned with the revolutionaries could also have been concerned with the document such as the 'Accord?'"

"Well, you heard her, 'anything is possible.' And I for one think we shouldn't rule out the possibility that someone saved the 'Accord' and hid it somewhere along St. Michael's line, probably Mont St. Michel. Now whether it is still there is another matter. Not sure how we go about looking for it," said Jeff.

"One of my good friends, Professeur Ormonde, you know him, Jeff, I'm thinking he might have some ideas. He has done extensive study of the architecture of the abbaye there, and may be able to give us an idea of where to begin our search. He also can probably tell us where we shouldn't bother looking," Simône said.

"I think we should make plans to go to Mont St. Michel. Maybe we will wait another day for you to recuperate, Jeff, and then we will rent a car and drive out. Sadly, mine is still in the garage up in Belgium," Simône said, frowning.

"And of course," she added, turning to Alex and Liz, "you are welcome to join us. But given everything that's happened, I would understand if you want to wash your hands of this craziness, and enjoy your holiday."

Liz and Alex looked at each other without speaking, before Alex said, "Oh, we definitely want to continue on the quest. But I think we should check in with Natalia-just to get her take on the situation."

Alex pulled out her phone and dialed a number in her contacts, before putting it on 'speaker.' After two rings, Natalia answered.

"Hi Natalia, it's Alex King. Actually, I was sort of surprised that we haven't heard from you. I thought I should give you a call and find out if you have any more information on the creeps we encountered in Belgium. We are thinking of going to Mont St. Michel. But we don't want to do anything stupid."

There was a pause on the other end of the line before Natalia said, "Hello, Alex, I was planning to call you today. I've been rather busy. First, I should tell you, I have all the belongings you had to abandon at the hostel. I will have them delivered to your hotel."

"Oh, thank you!" Alex said. "I had almost forgotten..."

"No problem. Second, if you look across the street toward the park, you will see a handsome young man drinking coffee, and pretending to read a book. He has been providing security for you for the past day and a half. Courtesy of the Israeli government, of course."

As they looked toward the park, the man in question looked at them and waved, a sheepish grin on his face.

"Oh!" was the only thing Alex could say in response, before waving back, as the other three stared at their outed protector.

"So how was your meeting with Sister Angelique?" Natalia asked, a knowing tone in her voice.

"How did you know ... Oh never mind. I get it. You must have a Ouija board or something. And, of course, cute guy across the street."

"Yes, he is kind of cute, isn't he?" interjected Natalia.

"Definitely. But to answer your question," continued Alex, "she seemed to think that there was at least a slight possibility that the 'Accord' we told you about ended up at the abbaye at Mont St. Michel. So we thought maybe we would take a little field trip out there, if you think it is safe."

Natalia paused again, considering the question before answering. "Well, Alex, as you obviously have discovered, life is full of uncertainty. Take the example of what happened to you and your sister. Your saga is the stuff of mystery novels. So no, I cannot guarantee your safety. But to be fair, I can tell you what I know. The 'gentlemen' and I use the word loosely, who you so unpleasantly encountered in Bouillon were Syrian jihadists who somehow had heard of Professeur Bertrand's discovery of the diary, and were apparently intent on destroying it and any chance of discovery of the 'Accord' you have been searching for so diligently."

"Each of you will be relieved to know, I imagine, that we discovered the dead body of Simône's kidnapper in his car in the courtyard of Bouillon's castle. Someone had shot him-perhaps himself accidentally-in the upper leg, and he had bled to death."

"Oh my God!" gasped Liz, before adding, "but I guess it serves him right. He tried to kill Jeff, after all."

"And almost succeeded," said Simône, frowning.

"But what about the other guy that was there?" Alex asked.

"Tant pis *(too bad),* we haven't found him. Like rats, these types are very good at disappearing back into the sewers from which they sprang. He's probably back in the Middle East by now. But given the information you provided us of their connection with Al-Bazheeri, we know he must be very high up in the organization. And we will continue to look for him."

"That's good," said Liz, sounding relieved. "So we shouldn't worry then?" she asked hopefully.

"Well, don't get me wrong. I'm not giving you the 'all's clear.' Those guys are probably not the only ones who would like to see your search fail. What I didn't tell you is that we encountered some armed 'monks'-I guess you would call them that-at the Abbaye D'Orval when we went to check out the carved words you had discovered. It's possible they were just security for the abbaye, but I haven't been able to confirm that they have regular security."

"I guess all I can say in conclusion is be careful. My guy has been watching since you got back to Paris, and fortunately, he has not seen any nefarious types lurking about. If they are there, they are better than Mossad at not being detected. And I admit I'm prejudiced, but I think our guys are the best. If someone's following you, I think we would have spotted them."

"Unfortunately, your new friend across the street has been called to another assignment. So you will be on your own if you go to Mont St. Michel. My best advice is, 'don't talk to strangers and look twice before you cross the street.'"

"Okay, thanks, Mom," said Alex, with a chuckle. "We will."

"Take care. And call me if any problems arise. I do have assets in Normandy and Brittany," said Natalia, "should the need arise."

Once the call ended, Alex said, "I'm not sure if we should be relieved, or pissed off that 'cute guy' has been following us around. But everything about this situation is weird, and I do trust Natalia. So I suppose she just had our best interests at heart when she ordered it. Or else, she is getting me back for all the times I beat her in the 800 meters."

"Yeah, I bet that's it," Jeff said, grinning. "She knew one day you'd be in France on the trail of a thousand year old document and she would get her revenge by having you tailed."

"Yep," Alex replied, nodding. "Smart girl." Liz laughed and nodded as well.

"So it is settled, you will join us?" asked Simône, after a moment.

"Yes!" said Alex and Liz together. "All for one and one for all, the four musketeers in search of the queen's lost treasure."

CHAPTER TWENTY-FOUR

"Oui, bonjour, Archbishop."

"Yes. It's Sister Angelique. Comment-allez vous?"

"Ah, bien. You said to call if anyone came asking about issues related to the church during the revolution."

"Oui, just today."

"Who? Oh, actually an acquaintance of mine, Simône Bertrand. She is a professor of anthropology and archaeology at the Sorbonne. I attended grammar school with her."

She listened for a moment before answering, "No, quite well-respected, actually. She was here with three others. Students, I guess."

"Oh, some type of agreement, an 'accord,' her word, regarding the three main religions. The document apparently disappeared during the revolution, if it existed at all."

The disembodied voice on the other end of the call asked another question, to which she responded, "Well, yes, she wanted to know about Mont St. Michel. I, of course, reminded her that it he had been a prison, and an unlikely hiding place during the revolution for a document connected with religion."

"Yes, well, it was good to speak with you as well. A bientôt," Sister Angelique said, ending a call. *Oh, I forgot to tell him about our discussion about the Deists. Probably not important*, she realized, before redirecting her thoughts to the letter she was writing.

Having agreed to give Jeff another day to recuperate, Simône spent the next day at work, catching up on
correspondence and finding replacement teachers for the
classes she would be missing in the next few days.

Alex and Liz decided to spend the day doing typical
touristy things, beginning with another visit to the Louvre
Museum, France's treasure house of art and culture. Four
hours later, after their eyes had begun to glaze over from
looking at old Masters, they ate lunch at Le Café Grand
Louvre restaurant under the pyramid in heart of the museum, before walking across the Seine River bridge to the
circular Monet Museum to view his giant murals depicting
the water lily gardens of Giverny.

Once they had toured the museum and stepped
back out into the fresh air, Liz said, "Guess the guy really
liked water lilies."

"Or maybe it was just the flower he painted best,"
Alex said, jokingly. "Should we take the Metro or walk?"

"Oh, let's walk. It's such a beautiful day! I love all
the sights and sounds of the city you can't experience underground."

"Great, but let's go wander around on the Champs-
Élysées; I want to go window shopping. We've got our
pass; we'll hop the Metro to the other end of the Champs
and work our way back."

Fifteen minutes later, they emerged from the
crowded Metro stop closest to the Arc de Triomphe. They
took in the sights of the avenue as they dodged the many
people, locals and tourists alike, who moved in human
waves down the broad sidewalk. Frequently they passed
street vendors, many illegally hawking everything from
knockoff designer purses to fake versions of expensive
men's watches. At one point, Liz stopped to look at some
counterfeit Louis Vuitton purses. As the vendor launched
into his sales pitch, Alex grabbed Liz's arm and pulled her
away.

"No way, Liz," Alex said laughing, as Liz protested
mildly.

"Look, if you want a Louis, the store with the real stuff is right there," Alex said, pointing about a block down the street. "And you can afford it, by the way, so stop being so frugal and spend some of your money. You deserve it."

When they reached the front door of the store, Liz hesitated before Alex opened the door and pulled her twin inside. Immediately a well-dressed saleswoman walked over to size them up, before greeting them after deciding they could probably afford to shop there.

"Bonjour. What may I help you with today?"

"My sister here needs a new purse," Alex said, nodding at the small nondescript leather purse hanging on Liz's shoulder.

"No, I don't need another purse," Liz said, blushing slightly. "I just think your purses are beautiful and we thought we would look around, if that is okay."

"But of course," the saleswoman said with a knowing smile toward Alex. "Take your time. Please let me know if you need any assistance."

"Why did you say that?" Liz asked in a whisper, as the woman stepped away. "I don't need another purse. This one is fine, isn't it?" Liz asked, uncertainly.

"Yes, it is," Alex said, with a reassuring grin, "but it isn't a crime to have more than one purse, you know. And besides, the prices are good here. I assure you they are cheaper than the prices at their store on Union Square in San Francisco."

"Okay, fine!" Liz said, not quite concealing her smile. Thirty minutes later, they left the store with two bags: one for Liz and one for Alex.

"I thought this was about me," Liz said with a smirk.

"Oh, it was, but there was no way I was passing up that cute wallet. I mean, it was on sale."

"Yeah, half off $1000. That's a steal!" Liz said, sarcastically. Alex grinned sheepishly before linking arms with her twin and heading up the avenue.

162

Halfway back to their hotel, the two stopped at one of the many sidewalk cafés, filled with groups of tourists drinking overpriced beer and wine, lining the Champs-Élysées.

"So, about tomorrow," Liz said, once they were seated and had flagged down a waiter to order glasses of wine. "Have we figured out how we are going to get out to Mont St. Michel?"

"I think Simône is right; we should rent a car. I don't want Jeff or Simône paying for it, though. She's already having to get her car repaired and we know Jeff can't afford it," Alex said as she and Liz each took a sip from their glasses, which had just arrived.

"This isn't bad!" Liz exclaimed.

"Funny, I remember when we first met back in college and you had never had anything to drink. Now you have become a full-fledged wino."

"Ha ha," Liz said, taking another sip before raising her glass in an air toast to her sister. "But about the car, I agree. We can afford it, and Jeff can't. And I definitely remember how that feels."

"I guess one of these days Jeff is going to have to get a job that actually pays something," Alex said.

"Or he could just be your kept man," said Liz, teasing.

"Whoa, chill. We are not really that serious. As you well know. And besides, he's damaged goods now. With that whole hole-in-the-shoulder thing."

"You're just mean," Liz said, making a face. "As I keep saying, one of these days, you better snatch him up before he takes himself off the market."

"What about you?" Alex asked, changing the subject. You've given the boot to the last three guys you dated."

"Well, you don't meet a lot of eligible guys teaching inner-city kids in Oakland," Liz said.

"So I guess we should talk to Sam when we get home. She definitely has more contacts in her cell phone than Donald Trump and Hillary Clinton combined. Ms. Dilis is quite the matchmaker. And, she introduced me to Jeff. Sort of."

"And apparently the jury is still out on that one, non?" Liz asked.

"Like I said, Jeff needs to get out of his student phase. Who knows where he'll end up and I'm never leaving you and San Francisco," Alex said.

"Okay, then we both need to find San Fran men. Or at least some Silicon Valley nerds," Liz concluded. "So what time are we meeting tomorrow?"

"Simône said she would meet us at the hotel at 8 AM. She's spending tonight back at her apartment. Guess given what Natalia said, she thinks we're out of danger."

"I hope she's right," said Liz, staring intently into her empty wine glass as though it might provide information about their future. "All I want is a nice dull vacation. If we happen to stumble across the 'Accord' and bring world peace, and you know, get the Nobel Peace Prize, so be it. But mainly, I just want to be a boring American tourist."

"Amen!" said Alex, who paid the bill before they continued their stroll up the avenue.

CHAPTER TWENTY-FIVE

Within a half hour, they reached their hotel. Once inside, they decided to treat themselves to another glass of wine at the lobby bar. Jaclyn, the bartender, greeted them with a smile as they climbed onto barstools and ordered. Having been woken by a text from Alex, Jeff joined them a few minutes later, wearing the look of someone who was slightly drugged.

"Hi ladies," he said. "What have you two been up to? Ah, shopping, I see," he said as he sat down on a barstool beside them.

"Oh, just a little," Alex said, pinching her thumb and forefinger together. "You know, just some French necessities. Trying to do our part to support the local economy."

"Right," Jeff said knowingly, winking at Liz. "I'm sure Louis appreciates that."

Jaclyn returned to offer him a glass of wine, which he declined. "Still kind of groggy," he said, talking to girls. "I took my last pain pill this morning but I think I need at least 12 hours before it is fully out of my system. Decided to lay off the booze for a while."

"Probably a good idea; you are kind of a lightweight. Figuratively, I mean," Alex said. "Actually, you are probably too heavy to carry up your room if you were to pass out after a glass of wine."

"So, we will just have to drink your share. We can't let this fine French wine go to waste," Liz said, swirling the deep red liquid in her class."

"Now you're just being mean; that's a comment I would expect from Alex," Jeff said. "But don't feel sorry for me; I have drunk my share of French wine while I have been here in Paris. One of the best things about France, you can just order a carafe of house wine at most bistros and it is usually very tasty. And relatively cheap."

"Don't worry," Alex said. "Once you are no longer a druggy, Liz and I are going to buy you any bottle you want, forget the carafe." Jeff just smiled, before taking a sip from his water glass.

"So," Alex said, "we talked and decided that we are going to rent a car to go out to Mont St-Michel. That way we don't have to worry about train schedules, etc."

"And we're paying," Liz said quickly. "No arguments!"

Jeff began to speak, but then stopped, looking at each of them. "So you two have been plotting while I was sleeping."

"Yes. So you might as well just accept it. We have decided to be the backers for this adventure. We're invested now in finding the treasure. Just consider it a little payback for-oh, I don't know-that time you saved our lives in Mexico," Alex said.

"Well, if you put it that way," Jeff said chuckling. "I graciously accept. But I'd say we're kind of even, given my recent experience. And I'm afraid your clothes will never be the same, Liz. I'm sure all that blood will never come out.

"No worries," Liz replied. "Alex just considers it a good excuse to do a lot more shopping before we go home. I guess your getting shot was the best thing that could happen."

"I didn't say that exactly," Alex said, "but I think it falls into the lemon/lemonade category."

"Yeah, okay," Jeff said, nodding his head. "Good recovery."

"So how are you feeling?" Liz asked, with genuine concern.

"Oh, I'm fine. I'm definitely ready to continue our search. Laying around isn't really my style."

"Glad to hear that," Alex said. "I was beginning to think you'd gotten lazy over here in France. Picked up the thirty hour work week mentality."

"No, Ms. King. I am still the hardworking young man you both know and love," Jeff said. "In fact, you'll be happy to know that I was just offered a teaching position at USF for the fall semester. My commitment to Simône ends August 1st, so it looks like I'll be heading home soon."

Liz raised her eyebrows at Alex, who ignored her sister. "Well, I guess then we better get cracking on solving the Templar treasure mystery so that you don't leave any loose ends here in France, right?" Alex asked.

"Right," agreed Jeff, giving Alex a quizzical look.

Sensing the awkwardness that seemed to be developing, Liz jumped in. "Why don't we find someplace to eat dinner? I'm starving!"

"Sounds like a plan," said Jeff, obviously glad for the change of subject. "Actually, I heard that the restaurant connected to the hotel is really good; it's a pet project of a Michelin-rated chef."

"That sounds great," Liz said.

"Yes, we haven't had a really good dinner since you took us to that restaurant in Montmartre, and that seems like ages ago," Alex said.

"I'll go ask the concierge if she can get us in," volunteered Liz.

After she had disappeared around the corner into the lobby, Jeff said in a low voice, "So what's up? I'm getting a weird vibe off you right now."

"It just seems like you have gotten very comfortable in your life here. It made me wonder if you had any plans to come back to San Francisco."

"Hey, you heard what I said. And I thought you knew I always intended to come back to San Francisco." He hesitated a moment before adding, "for a number of reasons."

"Well, that's good to know. I just..." Alex stopped talking when she saw Liz returning. In a low voice, she said, "I think we should talk about this later... so Sis, what's the verdict?" Alex asked brightly, when Liz reached the table.

"We're set. Tasting menu for three at 7 PM. My treat."

"Why is tha...?" Alex asked, before stopping when Liz gave her a 'don't ask' look. Once they finished their wine, they agreed to meet Jeff in the restaurant a few minutes before their reservation.

When they reached their room, Alex asked, "So what was that about? Why are you paying for dinner?"

"Because," Liz said, as she took off her clothes and got ready to step into the shower, "the dinner is 200 euros per person. I'm pretty sure Jeff didn't realize how much it would cost when he suggested it, and I didn't want to make him feel badly by saying it was too expensive. I mean, obviously, it isn't for us. And yes, I still have a difficult time accepting that I am spending 600 euros on one dinner. That's what I used to spend on three months of meals before..."

"Before you found your real life. Like it or not, our parents were rich, their parents were rich, and now you are rich. Wealthy. Whatever. And it just proves what I am always saying: you have a lot of catching up to do. So hey, start spending. Or one of these days, I'll be broke and living off your charity."

"Sorry, I didn't realize you were having to pay for everything," Liz said, a hurt expression on her face.

"I'm kidding, Liz. Go shower," Alex said, as she launched a pillow in her direction.

"He is dead."

"How?"

"Gunshot-I don't know."

"Where?"

"The morgue in Bruges. A believer there alerted me. Nothing to be done. Authorities watching."

"The diary?"

"Not in his possessions with the body."

"The woman, dead?"

"I don't know. Probably not unless he'd already dumped the body before he died."

"Find out, NOW!"

The man looked at the last text message, frowning. *Merde, what a screw up. I'm glad I'm not the one who had to tell Al-Bazheeri,* he thought, as a shiver ran up his spine. After quickly surveilling the area, he began walking up the street.

An hour later, Alex and Liz found Jeff already sitting in the small, sleekly appointed restaurant, about to peruse the wine list. Alex deftly extracted it from his hand as they sat down.

"Don't worry about that, buddy. You heard the lady; she's paying."

"Yes, I am. And I think that all of the wine already comes with the tasting menu," Liz said. "But don't worry-I didn't pick it out," she added. "The chef did. I may know what I like, but I'm not a wine connoisseur-yet."

"You know, I've been thinking, one of these days we should all take a Napa wine tour. I mean, it's right outside of the city," Alex said. "We should take advantage of it."

"Great idea," Jeff said. "And we could stay in the guest house at my parents' vineyard. My mom's been asking when I am going to bring the beautiful King girls around again."

"It's a deal," said Alex, as the waiter arrived with three glasses of champagne and an amuse-bouche to start the meal. "Bon appétit!" she added, as they raised their glasses in a toast.

Three hours later, they finally left the restaurant. "I've never been so full in my entire life," said Liz, grimacing. "I had no idea that there would be twenty different courses. I mean, they were small, but I really didn't think I was going to be able to eat the last course."

"Oh, you mean the foie gras sorbet. Yes, that was rather unusual," said Alex, with a nod.

"Hey, good, nonetheless. But it was something of a Monte Python moment-'one thin mint.' I was thinking I might explode," said Jeff.

"So maybe we should go take a walk around the Tuileries Garden, to burn off some calories," suggested Liz.

Alex and Jeff looked at each other quickly before Jeff said, "I don't know, Liz. I still think we should be cautious. Hopefully all of the boogeymen are gone but we can't be sure."

"Okay, you're probably right," Liz said, sounding disappointed.

After agreeing to meet at 7:45 the next morning, they headed up to their rooms, to bed, and unsettling dreams prompted by their feast, and recent experiences.

CHAPTER TWENTY-SIX

"The two girls haven't left the hotel since they got back around 5 PM. And I haven't seen the guy since they arrived the other day; probably still recovering from the gunshot."

The voice on the other end of the call said, "Okay, then call it a night. They aren't going anywhere. The clerk who is working for me says they have their rooms booked for another five days. Seems like maybe they have given up their amateur detective activities."

"Let's pray for their sake that you are right. I will check in with you tomorrow morning, Brother; bon soir," said the caller before ending the call and pocketing his phone. Within a minute, only the rear light on his scooter was visible as it weaved in and out of traffic on the street skirting the border of the Jardin de Tuilleries.

"Good morning, everyone," Liz said cheerily as she joined Simône, Alex and Jeff, who were sitting in the lobby enjoying pastries and coffee.

"Well, good morning, little Miss Sunshine," said Jeff. "I understand you got up early and went and got us a car."

"Yes," said Liz, "because I really want to stop at Giverny, if that's okay, so that we can see Monet's house and gardens, so I thought I would save us some time."

"Excellent plan," said Simône. "It truly is beautiful and worth the visit. Have you eaten?" she asked, pointing toward a plate of chocolate croissants.

"Oh, yes, thank you. I grabbed something at the corner café when they opened. I have to admit, they look tempting." She hesitated before adding, "But given the 10,000 calories I'm pretty sure I consumed last night, I think I'll exercise a little self-control, or I will have to buy an entire new wardrobe before we go home."

"Ah, oui," Simône said, nodding sympathetically.

"Anyway, the car is outside. I asked the valet just to keep it at the curb. But if it will be a while before we leave, I can have him park it," offered Liz.

"No, I think we are ready to go," Simône said, before taking a last sip of her coffee.

Having already paid, they gathered their belongings and each pulled a small overnight bag out to the curb.

"Ooh, nice ride," said Jeff, as Liz pointed out the black BMW X5 SUV she had rented. "Glad to see we'll be traveling in style."

"I don't really know cars-not like Alex-but this one comes with all of the bells and whistle, GPS, satellite radio, and looked pretty comfy, so I decided to go for it," Liz said.

"Très bien, very nice of you," said Simône. "It is about 80 kilometers to Giverny. It should take us about an hour and a half if the traffic isn't too bad. Would you like me to drive?"

"That would be great, but because of the way I rented the car, I think only Alex and I are insured to drive it. Sorry," said Liz.

"Pas de problème. I like having a chauffeur."

"Why don't you sit in the front passenger seat, Simône, and I'll drive; you, of course, can be the navigator," said Alex. "But be prepared to hold on. I do like to drive kind of fast. I'll probably beat your estimated time."

"Thanks for the warning; but we French are pretty fast drivers as well," Simône said, amused.

"So how do we get there?"

"We will take the A3 for about 55 kilometers and then we will turn onto a toll road. When we get to the town of Vernon, we'll cross over the Seine and arrive in a few kilometers."

Once they cleared the city traffic, they made excellent time. Liz, who was seated in the backseat by the already sleeping, inert form of Jeff, looked up periodically. True to her word, Alex was driving in her normal speed demon manner. A few times, Liz saw Simône flinch as Alex accelerated up to the bumper of a car, before passing quickly.

After they left the highway, Liz set aside her guidebook in order to take in the beautiful, bucolic French countryside lining the two lane road: rolling fields of multicolored crops, timeless, quaint stone farmhouses, and sheep and cows grazing contentedly. The passing scenery was such an anachronistic postcard of another era that she experienced a jarring snap forward to the present when they passed a town square occupied by a group of cell phone tethered, skate boarding teenagers.

A few minutes later, Alex turned their car onto the Rue de Claude Monet, and into the parking lot for Monet's house.

"One hour twenty minutes, from when we left the hotel," Alex said, looking at her watch with satisfaction.

"Perhaps you should consider driving in the Monaco Grand Prix next year. I thought I drove fast, but you are on another level. Truly! I had to shut my eyes a few times when you were passing."

"Sorry-I didn't mean to scare anyone," Alex said, with a slightly evil grin on her face.

Simône gave them a brief history of Monet and his famous paintings, as they locked up their car and walked up the pathway into the artist's former homestead. The house, a typically French, two-story gray stoned dwelling with dark green shutters, and ivy climbing the walls, sat just off the main street running through the village.

"As I am sure you know, Monet was one of the founders of the Impressionist Movement," Simône said. "In fact, the name comes from one of his paintings entitled, 'Impression, Sunrise,' first exhibited in 1874 in Paris. He moved to Giverny in 1883, purchased this house in 1890, and began creating the amazing landscape you can still see here today. By the late-1890's, he was painting the water lily pieces for which he is most famous."

When they had finished touring the house, with it's large dining room and huge kitchen that had been maintained in the same condition as when Monet regularly cooked and entertained there, they exited and passed through a green wood trellis onto the pathway leading through the gardens.

"Oh my God! It's beautiful! Even more beautiful than his paintings," gasped Liz, as they followed the meandering path encroached by every color and species of flower imaginable, to the water gardens.

"I know. I've never seen so many different varieties of flowers," agreed Alex. "But the water lily gardens really do look just like his paintings. Down to the Japanese-styled bridge. Seeing it, you appreciate the reason for his obsession with these gardens as the focus of his paintings."

"Yeah, a little obsessed, I'd say," said Jeff. "But it is beautiful; I agree."

They spent about an hour wandering through the gardens, and documenting their visit with their cell phone cameras. Once they had completed circling the property, Jeff said, "I'm starving; let's get something to eat."

"Look who is getting his appetite back. You must be on the mend," said Alex, smiling.

"We passed a little café on the way into town," Liz said. "What do you think, Simône?"

"Actually, I have eaten there before. It is simple food, but quite good."

"Perfect," said Alex. "All of this strolling through nature has made me hungry, too."

They walked a short way down the main road to the café and grabbed seats at an umbrella-covered table on the patio. The bottle of Provence rosé wine selected by Simône arrived just as they had begun to strategize about their visit to Mont St. Michel.

"I love this wine," Liz said after a sip. "I think it may be my new favorite.

"Yes, rosé wine in the summertime is my favorite as well," agreed Simône. "Very refreshing."

"Let's face it, Liz. You have become a true wino, and I mean that in the nicest possible way. I mean, my parents do own a vineyard, as you know. The more people who drink wine, the rosier my future. Get it?"

"Yes, Jeff, we get it. Rosy, rosé," said Alex, rolling her eyes. "Hey, but to get back to the subject at hand, what did you find out from your professor friend about Mont St. Michel, Simône?"

"Well, unfortunately, he agreed with what Sister Angelique told us. Given both its use as a prison, and the major restoration in the past century, it seems unlikely that anything concealed in the abbaye at the Mont could have remained hidden."

"Oh," Liz said, disappointment drawing her face into a frown.

"But, a true scientist does not proceed on guesses and assumptions. We shall make our own search before, as you Americans say, 'we cry uncle!'"

"Sounds good to me," said Jeff, as he raised his glass in a toast. "Here's to our success!"

The four clinked glasses, before Alex asked, "So Simône, did he have any ideas where we should begin our search?"

"Bien, you heard Sister Angelique. The church or chapel of Notre Dame sous Terre, which translated means, 'Our Mother Underground,' was buried with later construction and only rediscovered and restored in the last century." As Simône spoke, she pulled up a digital map on her phone showing the various levels of the Mont's abbaye.

"My colleague, Professeur Ormonde believes that someone wanting to hide something may have chosen this area of the abbaye," Simône said as she pointed to the lower level where the chapel was located. There could still be undiscovered alcoves, passages, which could have been employed by the mystery man…"

"Or woman," interjected Alex.

"Or woman who left the message at the Abbaye D'Orval," said Simône.

"But how do we search with all of the tourists around? There must be thousands of visitors this time of year," said Liz.

"You are right, of course," admitted Simône. "But I have an idea. I have gotten us a private tour for tomorrow morning. We will have plenty of time to get the lay of the land. If necessary, we can take turns distracting our guide while we explore. I will email you each a copy of this map. And then, tomorrow night…"

"Wait, how do we get in at night?" Alex interrupted.

"Turns out that they do limited night tours in July and August. It is actually quite lovely. A theater production company illuminates parts of the abbaye with stage lights and various musicians-cellists, violinists, electric keyboardists-play in various rooms of the abbaye that are open for the tour. Luckily, they are doing a practice tomorrow. We will have the opportunity to wander through the abbaye and hopefully sneak away for some private viewing," said Simône, a mischievous grin on her face.

"So I take it we are doing this *sine licentia*?" asked Jeff.

"Yes, without permission, as you say," Simône agreed, as she put a finger to her lips as if to silence him. "But I think it is the best way to do the search without attracting attention."

176

"So what happens if we get caught?" asked Alex, eyes narrowed.

"Je ne sais pas, precisement (I don't know precisely). I think it is most likely that we would just get kicked off of the Mont. Worst case scenario, I will call my ex-husband and have him bail us out of jail," she replied, with a shrug. "You might end up persona non grata in France, but probably not. I have some connections."

"Great," Alex said sarcastically, while Liz looked worried.

After a few moments of silence, Simône looked at each of them before asking, "So what do you think?"

"I'm in. I'm leaving France soon, anyway," Jeff said.

"Me too," Alex said, after a dramatic sigh.

"Me three," said Liz after a slight hesitation. "All for one and one for all, right?" she asked, a pensive look on her face.

"Absolutely!" Alex said. "Let's just hope they put us all in the same jail cell. I'm kind of picky about my cell mates."

Everyone laughed nervously, before taking a sip of wine to seal the deal.

CHAPTER
TWENTY-SEVEN

"Saint Michael, when he came to me, told me that Saint Catherine and Saint Margaret would come to me and that I should act by their advice, that they were bidden to lead me in what I had to do and that I should believe in what they would say to me and that it was by God's order."

Saint Joan of Arc, speaking at her trial

On the walk back to the car, Liz said, "So, it's only 12:45. Since we don't have a tour until tomorrow morning, do you think there is any chance that we could take a detour to the American cemetery in Normandy? It's one of the places Alex and I had talked about visiting while we are here in France. And if we are about to be thrown out of the country..."

"That's a wonderful idea," Simône said. "We might as well use our free afternoon. It will take us less than three hours to drive there, especially with Alex driving. We could spend an hour or so, and then drive to the Mont, which is about an hour and a half south of the memorial."

"Thanks, we appreciate you being a good sport about our tourist activities," said Alex.

"Pas de problème. It is I who am appreciative. For both your company, and our fine transportation."

After driving for about 45 minutes, they arrived in Rouen, where they stopped briefly to visit the square where Joan of Arc, at the young age of 19, had been burned at the stake in 1431.

"I think it is apropos that you see this. Obviously, there are no signs here now of poor Joan, other than the cross that marks the site of the execution."

In fact, the town square seemed completely ordinary to the Americans. There was no image of Joan other than a weathered photo opportunity wood cutout of the saint to suggest that it had been the location of such an infamous event.

"But," Simône continued, "it is significant because Joan was put to death by officials of the English church, at least in part because she claimed that she had been called by the Archangel Michael himself to lead the French armies against English domination during the Hundred Years' War."

"So Joan believed in St. Michael. Then maybe we should say a prayer that she helps us in our search at the abbaye," said Alex.

"It couldn't hurt," agreed Jeff, as the group walked back to their car to continue their journey to the Normandy coast. In less than two hours, they pulled into a parking lot congested with behemoth tour buses.

"Wow, this place is packed," exclaimed Liz.

"Oui, it is very popular for tourists, not just Americans and French. People come from all over the world to see this plot of land donated to the United States for their help rendered to France during World War II, and in memorial to the many American lives lost on the beaches and farmlands of Normandy during the days and weeks after the invasion on D-Day."

Once they reached the memorial grounds, they spent a few minutes admiring the massive bronze statue of a man reaching skyward, centered on a plaza partially encircled by a two-story colonnade. When the plaza began to fill with a newly arrived busload of Japanese tourists, they surrendered their spots, bought tickets and stood in line for entry to the museum. Inside the cool marbled hall, they found interactive videos and timelines of the D-Day invasion, a lone helmet balanced atop a rusted infantry rifle buried in sand, and photos, letters and other memorabilia of the soldiers involved, from the lowliest private, to Dwight D. Eisenhower, the general tasked with guiding those soldiers to victory.

An hour later, they exited to walk through the green-carpeted cemetery, past row after perfectly aligned row of white marble crosses and markers topped with Stars of David, standing in silent attention and memorial to the souls whose remains were interred there. At the edge of the property, which dropped steeply down to the infamous Omaha Beach, their small group stood silently staring out into the vast Atlantic, imagining the bloody arrival of the many brave soldiers who had crossed the shore below, never to leave.

Finally Jeff broke the silence. "It's incredible-the amount of emotion people still feel for something that happened over seventy years ago."

"I know what you mean. I saw a young woman weeping at one of the graves," Alex said quietly. "I wonder what her connection to that soldier was? Maybe her sadness was just for soldiers generally, people who continue to die for freedom, at the hands of modern day tyrants," she pondered aloud. "So sad."

"But it is hauntingly beautiful," Liz said.

"I know what you mean," Alex said. "I almost expect to see a ghost or two drifting through the rows of crosses. Eerie, really."

"Not exactly Disneyland Paris," Jeff said, breaking the mood.

Simône, who had remained silent, finally said, "When you are ready, let's head down to the Mont. I have taken the liberty of making a dinner reservation for us at the famous restaurant, La Mère Poulard, known for its lofty omelets. And then I have reserved us rooms at a hotel there on the island. The rooms are small but nice and most have views of the tidal basin."

"Sounds wonderful, Professeur. I'm starving again, even though we just ate a few hours ago. Must be something about the fresh air," Jeff said.

"You're always starving, Stahl. I thought I ate a lot until I met you. You're mother told me one time that she and your father were able to cut their grocery bill in half when you moved away to college," Alex said, teasing him.

"No, she didn't!"

"Oh, yes she did!" Alex said, laughing. "Should we call her and you can ask her yourself?"

"Uh, no thanks, 'cuz she would ask how I'm doing and I would have to lie. I don't plan to tell her about the gunshot thing until I get home. You know how mothers are."

Alex and Liz looked at each other, before Alex said, "Uh, no, not really. But that's okay; we get what you mean."

Jeff reddened when he realized his gaffe. "I'm a big jerk. I will now extract my foot from my mouth."

"It's okay, Jeff," said Liz, graciously. "No big deal- we're used to it."

Again, Simône remained silent, but looked amused as the three continued their banter as they weaved their way past rows of vehicles to their parking spot.

A few minutes later, after Alex had pulled their car back out onto the main road leading south, they encountered a heavy rainstorm, which forced her to decelerate to 40 km an hour. Twenty minutes later, the storm, which at one point caused them to slow to a crawl as hail pelted their windshield, passed through, and Alex sped up to a normal highway pace.

"This car handles great in the rain, but I didn't want to scare anyone, so..."

"We are grateful for that sister. I'd rather get there later and in one piece," said Liz.

"The storms can be quite fierce here coming off the ocean. If you remember what we read at the museum, the

D-Day invasion was delayed several times because of bad summer storms," Simône said.

"Also, the Americans didn't have the German engineering of this Bimmer," Alex said.

"Not very politically correct of you to point out," Jeff said, grinning. "Thankfully, the Americans had the will-power to win, despite the great German engineering. And as you know-Nazis, neo-Nazis-none of those guys are my favorite people, even though my family tree is about 99% German."

"Well, we will not hold that against you. We are not responsible for our family heritages. And some of my best friends are German. Hopefully, the world wars, I and II, were anomalies that the world will never experience again," Simône said. "Unfortunately, Fascism is an evil that infects segments of mankind in every age. Then it was the version propagated by Hitler and Mussolini and their evil followers. Now it is the terror wrought by Ji-hadists and radical Islamism. Anything good, whether it is national pride, or a religion, can be perverted by those motivated by evil."

"Throughout history, authoritarian movements and dictators have flourished whenever a vacuum created by a lack of human opportunity has existed. Want or need leads to envy, jealousy and misunderstanding, which can manifest itself in hatred of others. Presently, a lack of ed-ucation or cultural assimilation and/or scarce economic opportunity in both the Middle-East and Europe seem to lead some young Muslims, especially the poor of these communities, to be easy targets for radicalization."

"That's true, Professeur, but not all Jihadists come from poor families. Look at Bin Laden; he came from a wealthy Saudi family. So people like him must be motivat-ed by religious intolerance, not poverty," said Jeff. "The guys that kidnapped you were dressed pretty well, I no-ticed. Just saying."

"So what's the solution?" Liz asked, sitting forward and looking expectantly at Simône.

"I wish I knew," Simône said. "It is a conflict that has remained unresolved for fifteen centuries. But certainly, our efforts can only help, I would think. Anything to create some common ground between the Judeo-Christian West and Islamic Middle East could only serve to benefit the situation."

Liz nodded in agreement, before sitting back in her seat, silently considering the significance of their quest.

CHAPTER TWENTY-EIGHT

Seeing who was calling, Jamaal hesitated, dreading the conversation to come. On the third ring, he stood up and forced himself to hit "Accept."

"Sabahu al-khair, assalamu alaikum, *(good morning, may peace be with you)* Sheikh."

"Wa alaikum assalam *(and with you also)*, Jamaal."

"I've called to thank you and congratulate you on the martyrdom of your son," said the sheikh, his voice warm.

"He has given his life for our faith, and for that I am grateful. But..." the caller said, letting the word float heavily in the air, before continuing. And now even over the phone, Jamaal could feel that the tenor of the call had changed dramatically.

"Yes, Sheikh?" asked Jamaal.

"But... It should have been you, you coward!" yelled the sheikh, his anger radiating through the phone. "You left a boy to do a man's job."

Jamaal, his voice quivering, said, "But the meeting that night..."

"Was meant for the faithful," continued the angry voice, "not those that had failed in their tasks. You told me you were taking care of it!"

"I will take care of it," Jamaal said quietly.

"Yes, you will. Find the woman and her little gang of Americans. I have been told they left Paris. Find them! And get me the document, or proof that it has been destroyed. Do not bother to return to Paris until your task is complete, and if you fail..." The speaker did not bother to finish the sentence, his meaning clear.

"Inshallah," the sheikh said, ending the call, before Jamaal had a chance to respond.

His hand shaking, Jamaal laid down his phone and picked up a pack of cigarettes. It took a few seconds for him to steady himself before he was able to light one. Finally, as the tip flared with life, he took a long drag, before collapsing down onto his chair.

CHAPTER
TWENTY-NINE

OCTOBER 1793, L'ABBAYE DU MONT ST-MICHEL

The two ruggedly clad soldiers, until recently still peasants toiling in the fields that flowed down to the coastline, dragged their charge through the rough stone-lined corridor to the one open door, before dumping him unceremoniously onto the straw covered floor of the clammy, dark room, lit only by a thin needle of moonlight, which sliced the darkness through the thick iron bars in an opening high up on the exterior stone wall. Just because he could, the younger of the two spat upon the ragged heap and delivered a swift kick before slamming the cell door shut with a resounding clang. Moans and cries echoed down the corridor as the two men walked away laughing, presumably as oblivious to the agonized cries as the imprisoned had once been to their own pleas for mercy and succor.

Inside the cell, the heap slowly sat upright, revealing himself to be a man in his late fifties or early sixties, his face, torso and feet a mass of bruises and cuts after years of abuse at the hands of the revolutionary guard. The man, a Cistercian monk, knelt and crossed himself before beginning to pray silently, attempting to block out the cries echoing throughout his hell on earth. But soon a pitiful wailing erupted in the cell next to his. After a few minutes, too distracted to continue his prayers, he stopped and strained to hear the sound of water lapping on stone, somewhere far below.

Even though he had been brought here blindfolded during his weeklong journey after being captured by the revolutionary soldiers who had come to the Abbaye D'Orval, his abbaye, he knew the location of his prison:

Mont St-Michel. As a young monk he had traveled here on a pilgrimage to celebrate the feast of the Archangel, St. Michael. He still remembered his first images of the majestic Mont rising out of the sea, as if placed there by the Archangel Michael himself. The entire abbaye seemed to glow with a special light coming down from the heavens, and as he and his fellow travelers reached the rough stone street, which led up to the abbaye's entrance, they had heard a beautiful choir of angelic voices, echoing down from above.

The memory faded as the man surveyed his mean surroundings. Wet moss covered the stone walls, and rats darted freely about, stealing the crumbs from the one piece of daily bread on which he now barely survived. *How far we have fallen*, he thought, not only of himself but also of this abbaye, and his abbaye, and his many brothers and sisters in Christ, murdered or exiled in the name of the revolution.

Liberté, égalité, fraternité-what lies, he mused, bitterly. He had tried to tell the parishioners, the peasants that he and his brothers had served, but they been caught up in the fervor of the revolution, in the promise of equality for all. Instead, as far as he could discern, the revolution had only brought death and destruction.

He had heard from fellow prisoners that some of his brothers had knelt bravely inside the gate as a ragged band of soldiers, a few with long guns, most brandishing pitch forks, knives and torches, had arrived, seeking what they claimed was the crown's, and now, the people's treasure.

One of the brothers, Andrew, who had escaped but had later been captured and imprisoned here, said that Brother Luc had willingly opened the main gate, thinking that cooperation might save the abbaye. But certainly, as the commander had said, the fact that the monks were known to have helped Austrian troops had not helped the abbaye's cause.

And truly, the revolutionary soldiers, really more of an uncontrolled mob than disciplined troops, had been intent on destruction, the cumulative anger of their shabby existences fueling their every action. Not content with ransacking the abbaye for anything of value, Andrew had told him that they had razed the entire religious compound to the ground after failing to find the treasure for which they had come.

The old man laughed, without mirth. He supposed Leonard's treasure of silver might still be concealed on the grounds of the abbaye, unless it too had been destroyed. *But,* he thought ruefully, *the Queen's treasure-the true treasure-was surely consigned to the flame.*

CHAPTER THIRTY

Once they reached the highway that turned west toward the coast, their glimpses of the Mont, through the stands of trees lining the sheep-dotted farmland that sloped down to the ocean, were replaced with their first full views of the medieval monastery atop the island, which seemed to be floating out on the bay. The closer they drove to the parking area located directly across from the bridge leading to the island, the more majestic the abbaye appeared. Sitting just .6 kilometers off the coast, the granite and limestone of the abbaye walls appeared to glow in the late afternoon sun.

"It really does just rise out of the sea, as if by magic," Liz said.

"You can see why it was used as a prison," Alex said.

"Yes. But not really a very secure one, I wouldn't think, since you could just walk across the sands from the island at low tide," Simône said. "In fact, before the new bridge was completed just a few years ago, there was an old land bridge, or causeway that connected the island to the mainland and there was parking just at the foot of the Mont. So much silt had been deposited around the island that it was no longer truly an island, even at high tide. So they dredged out some of the silt and built a new bridge on pilings, which allows for the unimpeded flow of water under the bridge and completely around the island. The plan is that over time, more silt will be washed away."

"So, without the new bridge, the island would ultimately have become part of the mainland?" Liz asked.

"Yes, that was the fear," agreed Simône. "It is such an important tourist attraction and part of its magic is that it is an island. The French government was determined not to let that happen."

"But it looks like you can still walk on the sand at low tide, right?" asked Alex.

"Yes, but you must take care. There is more water flowing through than in the past, and the tide can reverse quite suddenly. Over the centuries, many people who have been caught out on the sands when the tide changed have drowned," Simône explained.

"So where should I park?" asked Alex as they reached the entrance to multiple parking lots.

"Pull into that one on the left. It's closest to the stop for the shuttle bus that will drop us off at the base of the Mont. Luckily, it is late enough that most of the day tourists will have started to leave the island. As you can see, people are already loading up the tour buses that will head back to Paris tonight. Only those fortunate enough to spend the night on the Mont will remain in a few hours. But it won't be as desolate as it was when the old causeway was in place. Then you had to leave by late afternoon because the tide would fully cover the causeway and all of the cars had to be removed from the parking lot or they risked being submerged. Back then, once the tide came in, you were stuck on the island for the night, with or without a place to sleep."

From the next shuttle bus, which pulled up as Simône and her group were heading toward the stop, spilled dozens of tired tourists who walked, laden with backpacks, cameras, and souvenirs, toward their waiting air-conditioned chariots that would transport them back to the City of Lights. Once it was emptied, they climbed aboard to the rows of abandoned seats. When the driver pulled the bus around for its return journey back across the causeway, it seemed to be swimming upstream against scores of tourists who had chosen to walk in multicolored clumps back to the mainland, having absorbed all the sights and sounds available to day trippers to the magnificent Mont.

After alighting from their bus within feet of the arched stone entrance to the walled interior of the Mont, they immediately encountered a fairly steep cobblestoned street, the Grande Rue, which passed between rows of stone flanked store fronts, their windows displaying souvenirs of every type and quality, from tacky plastic replicas of the island to expensive one of a kind paintings by accomplished artists. Interspersed amongst the shops were restaurants, including single windows hawking street food. The window of one shop proudly displayed an advertised 'first edition' of *Les Misérables* by Victor Hugo.

"I wonder if that is authentic?" Liz asked, pointing at it as they passed.

"Possibly. The owners of that shop are an old, well-known family who have lived here for centuries," Simône said.

Further up the winding thoroughfare, they passed a bar that boasted views of the bay below.

"Should we stop? I'm getting thirsty," Jeff said, looking longingly at the bottles of wine lined up in rows behind the bar. "I'm off my meds-I could use a glass, strictly for medicinal purposes."

Simône looked at her watch. "It's 6:45. Dinner isn't until 7:30. I have a couple of calls to make. Why don't you three grab that table that looks out over the water, and I'll meet you in 45 minutes at La Mère Poulard. It's just a little further up the street."

The three Americans looked at each other before Alex said, "Sure, but you should join us."

"No, it's okay. Work issues. I'll see you soon."

When the hostess approached to seat them, Simône waved goodbye before heading back out on the street. Once she was out of sight, she stepped into an empty doorway and dialed a number on her cell phone.

"Yes, it's me. I said I would call."

She listened for a moment before saying angrily, "I remember exactly what you said."

"Merde! Je comprends. If we find it, you will be the first to know." Several seconds passed as she listened to the raised voice emanating from her phone. Finally she said, "Now leave me alone. I'll call you, don't call me. You bastard," she added, whispering the last two words under her breath. Before the voice could answer, she ended the call, and then looked around surreptitiously to ensure that no one had been listening.

Satisfied that she had not been overheard, she walked quickly up the street and entered their hotel. After quickly surveying the empty lobby, she passed through to the bar where she grabbed a seat and ordered a whiskey from the elderly bartender. With a slightly shaking hand, she raised the glass slowly to her lips as she looked at the reflection of a pale frightened woman in the long horizontal mirror behind the bar.

Simône had given up smoking almost a decade earlier, but as she sat there, the desire for a cigarette was almost overwhelming. She shivered unconsciously, which partially dispelled the gnawing urge, before taking a large gulp from her glass and signaling the bartender for a refill. Fifteen minutes later, the drinks had achieved the desired effect. She paid her bill and wheeled her small suitcase down the street into the restaurant.

"Bon soir. I have a reservation for Madame Bertrand pour quatre personnes," she said, holding up four fingers.

"Ah yes, welcome. Etienne said I should expect you. You are a few minutes early, Madame," the hostess said, looking up at a nearby wall clock, "but fortunately, the table has just cleared. We have a lovely table for you looking out at the bay. Are your companions here also?"

"They should be here any moment," Simône said, also glancing up at the clock.

"Bien, wait here just a moment, s'il vous plait."

Jeff, Alex and Liz had just entered the restaurant when Simône turned to look toward the main door opening on to the street.

"Here you are. Everything good? Got your calls made?" Jeff asked, as they reached her.

"Oh yes. Pas de problème," Simône said, with a shrug. "Actually it took less time than I thought so I had a drink in the lobby bar in our hotel while I waited."

"Excellent use of your time, then," Jeff said, with a grin.

"Well, we had a lovely glass of wine and enjoyed the view of the water," Alex said.

"Yes, and we saw a couple riding horses across the sand. The tide is just starting to come in so they were splashing quite a bit. The horses seemed to be enjoying it, although it is a long ways down there," said Liz.

"Yeah, so we couldn't ask them," Jeff said, jokingly.

"Ha ha. I really wish I'd had my camera with the telescopic lens. It would have made an amazing picture," said Liz.

"I'll bet you can find the same picture in one of these shops. They probably do the same ride every afternoon just to entertain the tourists," Alex said.

"Maybe." Liz said, frowning at her sister. "But mine would have been better."

"Oh, no doubt," Alex said, with a sly smile toward Jeff.

"Our table is almost ready. I thought we could eat first and then check into our hotel," Simône said.

"I'm good with eating first, as long as they are holding our rooms," Jeff said.

"We have a reservation so I am sure it is fine. We can just pick up our keys after dinner."

While they waited to be seated, they watched through a window into the open kitchen where beefy men with bulging muscles whisked egg whites in large copper bowls, before adding the yolks. Soon the eggs, which had started as a syrupy liquid, began to bubble, doubling in size as the men rhythmically beat the golden froth.

"No wonder their muscles are so huge," Alex exclaimed. "Talk about an upper body workout!"

"I know, they look like an ad in a body builder's magazine," Liz agreed, nodding.

At their table, they ordered various versions of the famous omelet, some with meat and cheese and some with jam. A few minutes later, they were presented with fluffy golden half-moon shaped piles of cooked egg, completely covering their plates.

"Wow, maybe we should have shared one," Liz said, looking at the huge omelet on her plate.

"Maybe," said Alex, eying her own plate of food.

"Don't worry, mes chers. It is mostly air-all of the whipping makes it more like a soufflé."

"Hmm, interesting," Jeff said, after a few bites. "It is quite airy, as you said. Not quite like the ham and cheese Denver omelets you can get at the Over the Moon café in San Francisco."

Simône smiled slightly. "Yes. It is probably not like those at all. But when in France…"

After doing some damage to their food, and a half hour of conversation, mostly between Alex, Liz and Jeff, they paid their bill and headed up the street to their hotel.

"So I got a room for Alex and Liz, one for you, Jeff, and one for me," Simône said after retrieving their keys from the front desk. "Your room is the largest but still quite small with twin beds," she added apologetically. "Space is at a premium here on the Mont. So no large suites here, I'm afraid."

"I'm sure it's fine," Liz said, taking one of the proffered keys.

"Guess we should decide what time we're meeting tomorrow," said Jeff.

"Let's say 7:00 AM. In the dining room. That will give us time for coffee and a croissant before we meet our guide up in the abbaye at 8. It will take about 20 minutes to walk up there."

"Sounds good, Professeur. Well, good night, ladies," he added, before grabbing his bag and quickly climbing the flight of stairs toward his room.

"Bon noir. See you in the morning," said Simône before turning to follow Jeff. Alex and Liz, who were located in another wing, wheeled their small bags down the hall before picking them up to climb the stairs leading to their room. Inside they found what could only be described as a very compact room with only a foot separating the beds and a two-foot passage into the equally small bathroom.

The young women looked at each other before laughing. "Hey, Simône warned us," Alex said. "Good thing we are both skinny."

"And our bags are small," Liz responded, laughing. "Otherwise... But hey, look, we have a window that looks out to the bay. And the room décor is pretty," she added, surveying the gold and green bedspreads and the flowered wallpaper.

"Oui, very French. I feel like one of Marie Antoinette's maids-living in the attic in Versailles."

"Yes, well, we are sort of working for the queen, aren't we?" asked Liz, as she pulled on an oversized t-shirt and grabbed her toothbrush from her bag.

"How so?" asked Alex, who also had changed into a t-shirt to sleep.

Liz, who held up a finger, stepped into the small bathroom to spit out toothpaste before answering. "Well, she was the one who bothered to have the 'Accord,' assuming it exists, hidden. Otherwise, it might have been destroyed-lost forever during the revolution."

"Sure, but I don't think her motives were particularly altruistic. It's not as though she was saving the document because of its historical value, or anything. You heard Simône and Jeff. They think she was planning to use it to save her own skin, presumably by using it to blackmail, or should I say, 'persuade' the Pope into helping rescue her and Louis from the revolutionaries."

"And their poor children, of course," Liz said sympathetically.

"Sure, true. But again, Marie-Antoinette, I doubt cared about uniting the three religions. She was a Catholic-maybe not a good one, but Catholic nonetheless. I'm pretty sure there weren't many Jews or Muslims in her close social circle."

"Oh, I'm sure you are right about that," said Liz, with a laugh. "But whatever her motives, we wouldn't be on this adventure if it weren't for poor Marie-Antoinette. But on another subject, what do you think is up with Simône? She was really quiet at dinner. Hardly said anything, except when we were talking about the omelets."

"Yeah, I noticed that, too," agreed Alex. "Maybe she is just tired. It has been an exhausting few days, after all. I'm beat," Alex said, stifling a yawn as she crawled under the down comforter topping her small bed.

Liz turned off the overhead light and crawled onto her bed. "Me too. Good night," said Liz, as she reached over to turn off the bedside lamp.

"Bon noir," said Alex, in a sleepy voice.

Within minutes, the muted sound of water lapping at the base of the Mont, hundreds of feet below, had lulled them to sleep.

CHAPTER
THIRTY-ONE

JUNE 21, 1796, DOVER, ENGLAND

He had awoken just as the first light of dawn filtered through the one filthy window in his tiny attic room. Upon opening the window to lean out, his senses immediately were assaulted with the strong smell of fish coming from the docks below, and the screeching cries of seagulls circling overhead. He had been happy to see that the sky had cleared after the previous night's pounding wind and rain, a good harbinger for his voyage to come.

He thought back to his crossing almost three years before from Calais to Dover. He had never before been aboard any type of ship and he had suffered seasickness as the boat was tossed about by strong winds from a summer storm. When they reached land and he disembarked, his first instinct had been to kneel down and kiss the land, stable beneath his feet. He had not been on a boat since, and had prayed that this crossing would involve calmer seas.

Bernard, no longer Brother Bernard-he had left his vows behind the day he walked away from the Abbaye D'Orval-pulled his head back inside and began packing his modest collection of belongings into his knapsack. The ship would depart in three hours, and the quartermaster had told him to be there two hours early in order to secure a spot onboard. He spent a few moments looking around the room, his home while he had lived in exile in England. *Truly God had provided*, he thought, with a job in the fish market and a second as a cleaning man in the pub below, which had given him places to eat and sleep in lieu of wages.

When he first left the Abbaye D'Orval, Bernard had trekked west for several weeks, narrowly avoiding revolutionary patrols and finding shelter haphazardly with still true believers, kind souls who risked everything to help a poor displaced monk. After too many barely avoided encounters with the revolutionary guard, he had soon come to realize that he could never be safe as long as the revolution raged in France. So with the help of a widowed farmwoman, and attired in clothes that had until recently been worn by her deceased husband, he had headed toward the coast.

Once he had reached the port, he had discovered that he was not the only refugee seeking to escape from the horror of the revolution. The first night, as he sat eating in a pub overlooking the harbor, he heard innumerable harrowing tales of travelers, some like him, who were fleeing for their very lives. Although all local clergy in the town were gone, either to prison, death or exile, one of his dinner companions had sent him to speak to a godly man, formerly the mayor of the town, who took pity upon him and gave him some francs for the voyage. The man had even agreed to take Lucky, his little companion who had kept his spirits bolstered in his darkest of days. *Monsieur Molyneux,* Bernard mused. He hoped that the man had survived the ravages of the reign of terror and had not been carted off to suffer the cold metal of the guillotine. Bernard had hoped to see him again one day and thank him for his kindness.

JUNE 22, 1796, CALAIS, FRANCE

Now, these many months later, having arrived safely back in Calais, and after spending a day futilely searching for his benefactor, Bernard headed south along the coastline, intent on fulfilling the promise he had made to God that last day in the abbaye. He would take the 'treasure' to the abbaye at Mont St-Michel and hopefully deliver it to the Abbott-his Abbott-himself. And failing that, he intended to turn the prize over to some other man of God that he deemed worthy of the burden.

Bernard, who no longer considered himself that man, thought with a heavy heart of the man he had killed that last night in Calais before boarding the ship to freedom in England. The ragged beggar, with a scar running from his left eye to the corner of his mouth, reeking of cheap rum, who had accosted him as he left the home of Monsieur Molyneux, had attacked him with a knife, demanding the money that the miscreant somehow knew the merchant had given him.

But Bernard, who had been younger and more agile, had managed to wrest the man's weapon from him and stab the thief instead. Once he saw with horror what he had done, albeit in self-defense, Bernard had fled the bloody scene, never looking back. But the look on the man's face, shock, terror, and finally, resignation, as Bernard thrust the knife into his heart could never be erased from the monk's mind. It regularly haunted his sleep and, he knew, always would.

As he walked, Bernard shook his head to dispel the ever-present image. He consciously redirected his dark thoughts to the small metal box he carried, the box that had never left his presence for even a moment in the past three years. Afraid to leave it in his room during the day while he worked, he had fashioned an interior pocket inside the back of his shirt to hold the box. This addition to his clothing had earned him the nickname 'hunchback" from one of his fellow workmen. He had spent almost three years fending off the entreaties of the man to reveal the secret of his hump. But nonetheless, Bernard and James had become friends, and he would miss the light-hearted banter and companionship of the man who was now a sea away.

Despite being intent on his mission, Bernard knew that it was unlikely that his Abbott was still at the Mont since most of the imprisoned clergy had been released with the restoration of some religious freedoms in February of the previous year. But he hoped the journey would provide him with at least some information as to the fate of the old man. A newly arrived French traveler he had met in Dover a month before had assured him that many clergy had survived and had recently been released. Others, too battered by the years of torture and abuse to leave, still resided at the prison, cared for by some of the clergy who remained. When Bernard questioned him on the source of the information, the man admitted that he had until recently been a jailer there, but that he had been sacked after the formal declaration of separation of church and state by the newly formed government.

It was that man's information that had finally caused Bernard to decide to return to his native land. Until that moment, he had assumed that anyone he had left behind was long dead. But now, he had a renewed hope that at least a few of his brothers, truly the only family he had ever known, still lived. And so his decision to pursue this quest, not only to fulfill his vow to the Abbott, but also to find any remnants of his past-and perhaps his future-had been made. Bernard knew that the trek might take several weeks but he was determined and hopeful that the Lord would continue to provide as he had over the past three years. And then perhaps his efforts might earn him absolution, or at least clemency for his unforgivable sin.

CHAPTER
THIRTY-TWO

"Wake up, sleepyhead," Alex said in a low voice as she gently pushed on the shoulder of her still sleeping twin.

The floor at the foot of their beds was bathed in a sliver of muted light slipping between a break in the curtains covering their small window.

"What-what time is it?" asked Liz, as she rolled over, and began to get her bearings.

"It's about 5:45. The sun will be up in about 30 minutes. Put on some running clothes. Let's run up to the top of the Mont and we can catch the sunrise."

"Okay," said Liz, as she got up and began to rummage through her bag. "But since when did you become the Farmer's Almanac?"

"Oh, I Googled it last night. It looks like it will be a beautiful day. It is light enough already that we shouldn't have any trouble seeing."

"So I don't need a flashlight or night vision goggles?"

"No. I think we'll be okay. Why, do you have night vision goggles?"

"No, unfortunately, but they might have come in handy in our search tonight."

Five minutes later, the two passed through the deserted lobby and stepped out onto the cobble-stoned street. They stretched for a few minutes before jogging up the street leading to the abbaye; several times they diverted to explore stairways and alleyways leading to hidden courtyards and gardens, landings which provided views out to sea or land, and upper ramparts encircling the outermost edges of the walled Mont.

They had just finished a sprint up a steep winding stairway when they reached a main rampart, giving them a view not only of the bay, but also of the vast open water to the northwest. Within a minute, they were momentarily blinded as the sun rose above the eastern horizon, and the water below them sparkled as though it had been lit on fire.

"Wow, I'm glad we didn't miss this!" exclaimed Alex, as they watched the sun ascend into the sky, growing ever bluer as the rosy fingertips of dawn gave way to daylight.

"I'm glad I got my lazy butt out of bed," Liz said, giving her twin a half hug with her arm around the shoulder.

"Pas de problème, as Simône would say," said Alex, with a grin.

The two watched until the sun fully illuminated the abbaye walls before turning to run back down the stairs.

"I'll race you," said Alex, as she picked up her speed.

A few minutes later, they stopped, hands on knees, to catch their breath at the hotel entrance.

"That was fun, but I thought I was going to lose it coming down those stairs, we were going so fast."

"Yeah, definitely wouldn't meet the San Francisco building codes. But actually running here sort of reminds me of running on the city hills in San Fran," said Alex, before looking at her running watch. "Hey, it's about 6:30. We should probably go get ready for breakfast."

Up in their room, they took turns showering in the broom closet sized bathroom. Liz, who had grown up in such modest surroundings, showered and was ready to go in less than ten minutes. While Alex got ready, Liz perused the guidebook she had bought the evening before that contained descriptions of the various abbaye buildings.

"Are you ready to go down?" asked Alex, as she spritzed herself with a small bottle of perfume.

202

"Sure," said Liz, tucking the book in her purse.

Downstairs, they found Jeff and Simône studying an iPad intently.

"Whatcha looking at?" asked Alex, as she slid into a space on the couch next to Jeff.

"This is the digital map of the abbaye. We are trying to figure out where we should try to search today." Jeff pointed to a GPS spot at the bottom of the map. "See, we're here."

"So, where do we start?" asked Alex, squinting at the iPad's screen.

Jeff started to answer but was interrupted by Simône. "We will take the tour, which ends at the large western terrace at the top of the abbaye. Then perhaps you, Jeff and Liz can break off and make your way down to the Notre Dame sous Terrace. I will engage the guide in conversation and then explain that you went to get something to eat. Most French think Americans have poor manners so he will not be surprised that you left without thanking him."

The three Americans looked at each other silently, eyebrows raised, as Simône continued.

"This area, here," she said, pointing at the map, "was most recently excavated. It is possible there are alcoves, closets, not yet uncovered. We will need to look for any changes in stone or brick that would not be obvious to the casual tourist, or even workmen. If such a thing exists, it will be very subtle."

"But I think it is very important that we do not exhibit too much interest in the area while we are on the tour. I don't want to draw any attention to our quest."

"Okay, Professeur, whatever you say; sounds like a plan," Jeff said.

"Alex, Liz, do you want to grab something to eat before we head up to the abbaye?"

"Yes!" They answered together. "I'm starving. Alex woke me up early and we did a run up around the top of the Mont."

After they had ordered chocolate croissants and coffee from the passing waitress, Alex said, "It was beautiful! We got to see the sunrise from one of the top ramparts. Pretty spectacular."

"Well, aren't you two industrious? I'm impressed. I'll just have to live vicariously through your exercise. Don't think I'll be running for awhile-at least until I get this sling off," Jeff said, gesturing to his left shoulder.

"Oh, poor baby," Alex said. "Guess you'll have to cut down on your eating then. We don't want you getting pudgy. You don't want a spare tire hanging over your water polo swimsuit. From what I've seen, a six-pack is a pre-requisite for guys on your team."

"Oh really?" Simône asked, smiling.

"Yes, I have seen his team play lots of times. The guys are all hot! C'est magnifique, as you would say, Simône."

"Then perhaps one day I will come to visit the three of you in San Francisco, and meet some of these magnificent men."

"I don't know," said Liz. "They may be great physical specimens, but some of them are real idiots! Jeff set me up on two different blind dates-try having a conversation with one of those guys. Ugh!"

"Yes, Jeff is something of an exception to the rule, I admit," said Alex, laughing.

"Well, thank you for that," Jeff said, turning red. "But I think you are being a little bit harsh, Liz. Ryan graduated from Stanford with a degree in engineering."

"Okay, fine," admitted Liz, "not an idiot. But when he told me that Dumb and Dumber was his favorite movie, I realized that we didn't have much in common."

"I don't know, Liz. That movie is considered something of a classic," Jeff said, grinning.

"What is this Dumb and Dumber?" Simône asked, with a look of puzzlement.

"An American movie with lame humor-teenaged boys love it," Alex replied.

"Oh," said Simône, still clearly confused by the reference.

A few minutes later, having finished their breakfast, they paid and headed out onto the street, which was already teeming with large groups of tourists speaking every language imaginable.

"Wow, where did all of these people come from?" asked Alex, as they slowly made their way up the packed thoroughfare.

"Many early morning tour buses from Paris," Simône said, sidestepping a group of Japanese documenting the minutiae of their visit with iPads, cameras and cell phones. "That is why our tour starts an hour before the abbaye opens for general admission. My plan is to stay well ahead of the massing hoards."

"Good plan," said Liz, who just had almost been knocked over by a zaftig German man intent on shepherding his wife and daughter through the throng.

"It took them another fifteen minutes of zigzagging and sidestepping before they emerged from the crowd into the relative calm of the landing below the broad steep stairs, the Grande Dagrè, leading up to the abbaye.

"Over there," Simône said, pointing to a small door fronting an alley to the left of the staircase. "Brother Francis will meet us there, I think."

With his good arm, Jeff pulled open the heavy wooden door to allow the three women to pass through. Inside, they found a small stone-walled room with high set windows filtering dusty light, and a wooden table bearing the scars of innumerable centuries of carved graffiti, strewn with some brochures about the abbaye, surrounded by a mismatched set of wooden chairs.

"Fancy," said Alex with a chuckle. Liz picked up one of the brochures and began to read, while Jeff and Simône took another look at the digital map. Only a minute or two had passed before the door in the far wall was opened by a tall, goateed, dark-skinned man, wearing a scarlet red, floor length robe and rope sandals.

"Bonjour," he said, as he stepped forward to shake their hands. "Welcome to Le Abbaye du Mont St. Michel. Thank you for coming to visit our beautiful home. My name is Brother Francis."

They each introduced themselves as the monk launched into a brief introduction to their tour.

"Why don't we go back through this door and we will begin our tour before the crowds ascend in about 45 minutes, I imagine," he said, briefly glancing at an inexpensive plastic watch on his wrist.

They stepped through the door into the main entrance hall. Huge blocks of light colored stone comprised the two-story high walls. But the effect was marred by the metal detector and security guards blocking ingress to the upper hall.

Ignoring the 21st century anachronism, Liz exclaimed, "Beautiful!" The echoes of her voice bounced from wall to wall, meeting again where the group stood.

"As you just heard, great acoustics. Perhaps that is why most cloistered orders rarely raise their voices-in anger or joy," Brother Francis said.

After they had passed through the security station, the monk began recounting the history of the abbaye, starting with the visitation of the Archangel to St. Aubert, the Bishop of Avranches, and the angel's multiple exhortations to build an abbaye on the island. "He ignored the angel until Michael used his finger to burn a hole in the Bishop's skull. Soon after, a small church was constructed, and consecrated in October 709 A.D."

"After the Normans annexed the area in 933 A.D., the Mont gained importance as the new frontier with Brittany. In fact, if you have seen the over 900-year-old Bayeux tapestry, which commemorates William's conquest of England, you saw it depicted."

"I've seen pictures of it in one of my art history classes," Liz volunteered. "Truly amazing!"

The monk smiled at her enthusiasm before saying, "Yes, it is. We are blessed that it has survived the many

206

wars in which our country has been involved over the past millennium."

"But back to the history of the abbaye; for those same millennia, pilgrims have traveled here as one of many sacred sites. However, especially during medieval times, this, along with Rome and St. Jacque de Compostelle, in Spain, were particularly revered as centers of spiritual and intellectual enlightenment. Unfortunately, such pilgrimages ceased before the French Revolution when the abbaye was converted into a prison to hold clerics and other enemies of the state."

"When we go below, you will have an opportunity to view a few of the cells where the clergy and later political prisoners were held. Because of lobbying by well-placed members of French society, such as Victor Hugo, the government finally closed the prison in 1863, and the Mont was declared a national monument in 1874."

"In 1966, the celebrated year of the 1000th anniversary of the monastery, a religious community moved back to the Mont. In 2001, my order of monks and nuns, Les Fraternités Monastiques de Jérusalem made the Abbaye our home."

"So there are monks and nuns living here together now on the Mont?" asked Jeff.

"Oui. But of course, we have separate quarters," answered Brother Francis, with a grin.

"Of course," said Simône quickly.

Jeff and Alex smirked at each other, but said nothing.

"Now that you know some of the history of our precious Mont, please follow me and I will lead you through the various levels of the abbaye, and continue with the history lesson as we go. We will take parts of the tour backwards, in order to avoid some of the other guided tours that will head straight for the Western Terrace."

After passing through the Knights' Hall (the work and study room for the original monks), and a covered walkway, they descended what Brother Francis called the

North-South stairs. Near the bottom of the landing, he used a key to open a wood door barely visible in the low light, before ushering them inside.

"This small chapel beneath the church is known as Notre Dame-Sous-Terre (Our Lady Below Ground). You are fortunate to get to see this; the chapel is not open to the general public. You can only visit on specially arranged guided tours."

Simône smiled and nodded in thanks as Brother Francis began to recount the history of the space.

"The chapel was constructed by the Benedictine monks who settled here in 966 A.D. Most historians believe it was built in the exact location of the grotto, which St. Aubert allegedly carved out of the western side of the main rock of the Mont in 708 A.D. As such, it is the oldest existing monument on the Mont. It has a double sanctuary, with two naves with individual apses, those recessed areas with the arched roofs, which is separated by this wall with the arches running the length of the chapel. One of the naves, probably the right one, is believed to have been a meeting place for devotees to St. Michael. As you can see, the backside of the right apse is comprised of the solid rock of the Mont."

"Archeologists believe that between 1776 and 1780, the monks had to erect a supporting wall to carry the weight of the church above, which blocked access to the two apses. It wasn't until 1960 that the supporting wall was torn down and replaced with pre-stressed concrete beams, thereby reopening access to the two apses."

"The altars that you see today were installed in the apses at that time. The left one is dedicated to the Virgin Mary, with the inscription 'Virgo Maria mater Dei (The Virgin Mary, mother of God)' and the inscription on the right altar on the right apse is dedicated to the Holy Trinity: 'Gloria tibi Trinitas aequalis, una Deitas, et ante Omnia saecula, et nunc, et in perpetuum (Glory to you, Trinity; Equal to one God; And before all worlds; Now, and for all time.)'"

"The chapel originally had windows that must have provided brilliant light before they were walled up when the chapel was surrounded by the foundations of the main church above, which was constructed in the 11th century. Until the late 19th century when renovations were undertaken, it is unlikely that the chapel was actively used."

As he had been speaking, Simône had stood listening intently while the other three casually inspected the two naves and surrounding areas for any potential hiding places.

Liz, who had wandered back to hear the conclusion of his presentation, asked with a look of disappointment on her face, "So, it would not have been accessible during the time that the abbaye was used as a prison?"

"I would think not; it was essentially buried until the excavations began in the late 1800's."

Jeff and Alex, who were still casually wandering through the chamber, missed this comment. However, their search was cut short when a group of Chinese tourists and their guide poured into the small space. Jeff looked toward Simône, who shrugged her shoulders and motioned slightly with her head, indicating that they should leave.

Fifteen minutes later, having passed through a number of high-ceilinged stone rooms, and encountering several stairways, they entered the beautiful garden cloister sitting atop many other levels of the abbaye, and from which they were able to enjoy the magnificent view of sand and sea below. Brother Francis allowed the group a few minutes to take photos before leading them from the cloister to the church.

"As you can see, the church is fairly austere, but still is used for worship to this day."

"So is this the church that the Archangel Michael ordered Aubert to build?" asked Alex, as they entered the many storied stone structure, comprised of a huge cross shaped sanctuary with rows of simple wooden benches facing a main altar area. A few small groups of visitors sat in silence, contemplating the majesty of their surroundings; near the altar, a tour guide spoke through audio headphones to a group of about thirty French tourists.

"No, that structure would have been down below in the area of the chapel. It was destroyed by fire before the chapel was constructed in the late 10th century. But as I briefly mentioned earlier, in the 11th century, construction here was begun when Richard II, Duke of Normandy, hired an Italian architect to design this Romanesque church. Interestingly, the architect chose to place the transept crossing at the very top of the mount, which explains the massive crypts and many chapels below necessary to support the weight of the church. At the same time, some of the original portions of the monastery were built."

"But the entire abbaye structure was not built at that time, correct?" asked Simône.

"No, that is correct. It was built in many phases over the centuries. A supporter of Henry II of England, Robert de Thorigny, paid to reinforce the structure and façade of the church in the 12th century. Sadly, in 1204, Guy de Thouars, acting on behalf of the Duchess of Brittany, laid siege to the Mont. In addition to burning the village below and killing most of the inhabitants, he lit much of the existing abbaye on fire."

"Oh no! That's horrible," said Liz, looking around sadly.

"Yes, but very typical of warfare, in the past, and regrettably, the present. Fortunately, Philip Augustus of France provided funds for the repair of the abbaye and the addition of the refectory and cloister, which we just visited. And then two centuries later, Charles VI, who reigned as the king of France from 1380 to 1422, fortified the Mont with additional courtyards, towers and strengthened ramparts. Of course, often, additions to the Mont were made for military, not religious reasons. Remember, the Mont sat right in the middle of the lands disputed in the Hundred

Years' War, which raged between the English and French from 1337 to 1453 for control of the throne of France."

"In the 15th century, Louis XI, who had founded the Order of Saint Michael in 1469, tried to have the church recognized as the chapel for the order, but ultimately the distance from Paris made it impractical. But allegedly, the Order did meet here from time to time. Historians have also recorded that almost every French ruler for the last 1000 years has come here on pilgrimage to worship," their guide   said.

"And regardless of the ruler in power, throughout the past millennium, this place and its inhabitants have been not only observers but also participants in the rich and often bloody history of France," added Simône, solemnly.

They completed their tour on the large stone plaza adjoining the church, the immense Western Terrace. After following Simône and Brother Francis outside and stopping to take a few pictures, Jeff, Alex and Liz joined a group of tourists who were filing back into the church, while Simône, as promised, engaged the monk in further conversation.

"I feel badly about not thanking him," said Liz, as they made their way out of the church and back downstairs to the chapel.

"Oh, don't worry," said Alex, you know us 'rude Americans.' He probably won't even notice, at least according to Simône."

"So how are we going to get back in?" Liz asked. "You heard him-you can only go into the chapel on specially guided tours."

"What?" asked Alex and Jeff at the same time.

"Oh, maybe you both missed it. Yeah, he said it isn't open to the general public."

"Great!" said Alex, sarcastically. "So now what do we do?" she asked Jeff.

"Let's not give up yet. Maybe we can sneak in somehow."

They took turns trying the door, which was definitely locked.

"Can you pick it?" Liz asked hopefully.

"Uh, that would be a no-I left my trusty lock picking set back in the room, and this lock looks pretty hefty, anyway."

They were about to admit defeat when they heard the deadbolt grinding open. As the door swung open, they stepped aside as a small group of French-speaking tourists, and their equally French guide streamed out. The guide eyed them suspiciously before saying, "Private tours only!"

Jeff hesitated a moment before responding in French, "Yes, we know. We were here earlier with our guide. My friend thinks she left her cellphone inside near one of the altars. We just need to go in and check."

The woman looked around, as if to ask, "Where is he?"

"Oh, he had to get back up to meet his next group. Told us it was okay to come back on our own."

The guide considered his less than credible story, before glancing at her watch and her retreating charges. "Fine, but be quick. And close the door tight when you leave," she said, scowling at them for emphasis, before turning to catch up with her group.

"Oui, certainement! Merci beaucoup, Madame," Jeff yelled after her.

"Come on, before she changes her mind," Alex said, grabbing his arm.

The three stepped quickly into the chapel and Jeff turned the lock to secure the deadbolt in the heavy wooden door.

"Let's split up; we probably don't have much time until the next tour group arrives," suggested Jeff. "Why don't you two each check out the separate naves; I'll search around the rest of the chapel.

212

As though on cue, Alex and Liz both pulled flash-lights from their purses to begin searching the mortar and stone walls, which enveloped the ancient space, while Jeff began to walk around the perimeter.

"I'm not seeing anything that may have been a hiding place," said Alex, after about ten minutes of searching.

"She's right. All of the walls look uniform, and I am guessing that they were repaired anyway whenever the chapel was uncovered. Remember Sister Angelique told us that the chapel had been hidden for centuries."

"I know, it is strange, don't you think," said Liz, who had stopped her search and joined Alex and Jeff.

"What do you mean?" asked Jeff, who had abandoned his search to stand beside them in the center of the chamber.

"Oh, maybe you didn't hear Brother Francis, because you and Alex were over in that corner when he was finishing his talk, but he said these naves, and particularly the apses were probably totally closed off from the late 1700's to the late 19th century so it wasn't accessible when the abbaye was being used as a prison. So it seems strange that Simône would have us searching here."

"Yes, Liz, that seems very strange," said Alex, who had turned to look at Jeff questioningly. "Is there something going on with Simône that we ought to know about? It sounds like she sent us on a wild goose chase," she added, a note of irritation in her voice.

Jeff was about to respond when they heard voices in the outer corridor. "Let's get out of here and go find Simône, and we can ask her. It sounds like someone is coming."

Jeff unbolted the lock and the three slipped out just as another French tour guide and a group of elderly Americans, some wearing hats and vests identifying them as WWII veterans, came spilling into the chamber.

CHAPTER THIRTY-THREE

"Where did your Americans wander off to?" Brother Francis asked, after Liz, Jeff and Alex had disappeared into the crowd.

Simône shrugged her shoulders as if to say, "They're Americans, who knows?"

The monk nodded in silent agreement, as Simône added, "I want to thank you for the tour, Brother Francis. Very informative. I would like to make a contribution to your Fraternités, as a thank you for your time."

"That isn't necessary, I assure you, Professeur."

"Oh, but I want to."

"But you may not feel that way once I tell you my real purpose in being your guide today."

"What do you mean?" asked Simône, her brow furrowed.

"I'm here to ensure your attendance."

"Attendance at what?" Simône asked, suspiciously.

"With the 'Monseigneur, of course. You knew he would be contacting you at the end of the tour, oui?" he said, looking at his watch.

"And why would I want to meet this Monseigneur?" Simône asked angrily.

"It isn't for me to say."

"Are you the person who called me last night?" asked Simône.

The monk laughed. "No, Professeur, I am a mere foot soldier in the Order."

"The Order of Jerusalem?" Simône asked, even more confused.

"No, you misunderstand. It is true that there is a Brother Francis in the Fraternités Monastique de Jérusalem. But unfortunately he fell ill today, so that I could conveniently take his place."

"Then who are you?" asked Simône, tension in her voice.

"My name is unimportant. All you need to know is that my true devotion is to the Order," he said, smiling broadly.

"What Order?" Simône asked, exasperated.

"The Order of St. Michael, of course," he said, pulling from underneath his robes a chain upon which hung a pendant of a dragon being stabbed with a sword in the shape of a cross.

Simône looked at it for a moment as comprehension dawned.

"And now," he said, again looking at his watch, "it is time for us to go." He grabbed her arm to steer her back toward the open church door.

"And why should I just willingly go with you?"

"Because," the monk said, now looking amused, "the sinner must pay for her sins."

Simône's eyes narrowed as she looked at him with a mixture of fear and resentment, before pulling her arm from his grasp. "I don't need your assistance," she said, not hiding her anger.

"As you wish," he said, before leading her through the church and down through several levels of the abbaye, clearly following a route he had traveled before. Simône followed reluctantly behind him, considering her options.

After climbing down a very narrow circular stairway, concealed behind a small locked wooden door, they reached a corridor in what Simône guessed must be the very bowels of the abbaye. As their footfalls echoed through the dark, dimly lit stone corridor, Simône briefly considered turning back. As if with some sixth sense, the monk reacted, stopping and turning to look at her.

"Too late, Professeur," he said, again grabbing her arm and steering her to the right into a cell fronted by rusted iron bars and an ancient rusted door, which anachronistically bore a shiny new brass lock in the handle. Simône again started to resist until she realized that inside the cell stood a gray-haired, goat-teed man in his late 50's or early 60's, attired in fashionable, expensive clothing, a well-tailored shirt and pants, and Italian leather loafers. Immediately she noted the only aberrant part of his appearance, which suggested that he might be of the clergy, the ecclesiastical looking ring on his right hand.

"Ah," said the man as he stepped out of the shadows, "finally I get to meet the famous and equally lovely Professeur Simône Bertrand. Thank you, Brother Francis, you may go."

Simône's escort nodded and smiled obsequiously as he backed out of the cell, before retreating down the corridor.

Simône, who had recoiled when she realized that this man's voice was the one she had heard in last night's phone call, decided to ignore the baiting compliment. "And who are you?"

"Oh, pardonnez-moi!" the man said, sticking out his hand, with a slightly smarmy smile. "I am Monseigneur DiLorenzo; among other things, I am presently head of the Order of St. Michael."

Ignoring the proffered hand, Simône asked, "Am I supposed to be impressed? I have never even heard of such an Order, and the title 'Monseigneur' is usually just an honorific lacking in any authority."

"Vraiment (really)?" asked the man, regarding her as one might a cute animal caged in the zoo. "And yet, here you are. But to be fair, perhaps I should tell you a little bit about our Order and then, perhaps you will understand the necessity of the request I made of you last night."

"Request? I recall that it was more of a blackmail demand," Simône said, her voice shaking slightly in anger.

216

"Well, perhaps. But nonetheless, it only seems fair that you understand the basis of my-shall we say-adamant request."

"Would you like to sit?" he asked, gesturing to a stone bench that lined one wall of the cell.

"No, this isn't a tea party; I'll stand," Simône said brusquely. "Let's get on with it."

"As you wish," he said. "Well, as I mentioned earlier, I am the head of the Order of St. Michael, originally founded by Louis XI on August 1, 1469. Unfortunately, officious, heathen French authorities abolished the Order in 1830. We are Christian knights, warriors if you will, dedicated to St. Michael and the continued existence of the Christian religion."

"You just said that your order was abolished in 1830. Seems like you and your friends are almost 200 years too late."

"And that is where you would be wrong. Even though it was abolished in 1830, it served as the basis for the creation of the Order of Arts and Lettres."

"But that's just a civil award that the government gives artists, people of letters," retorted Simône.

"Yes, that is true. In my opinion they are just poseurs and degenerates of every sort who dishonor the memory of the original Order. But, what few people know, and now you are one of the few, is that the true Order still exists. We are hundreds strong, and we serve both the Archangel and the one true church, not the modern version being polluted by liberal ideas of the present pretender to the Papacy, who dishonors the shoes of the original fisherman, Saint Peter."

"Oh, got it, you don't like Pope Francis and his policies, and this is your little protest."

"Non!" the man said forcefully. "Our goals are much greater. He is a mere man, one who quickly will come and go, unimportant in the historical scheme of things."

"So what are you after, or should I ask, trying to achieve?" asked Simône, who had been pulled into the conversation, despite the bizarre circumstances under which it was taking place.

"Straight to the point; I like that. You must be a good teacher. Bottom line, we have NO interest in the Church, the true Church, aligning itself with the heathens mentioned in the document we know you are seeking."

"And by heathens, you are referring to?"

"The jihadists, the savages running rampant through many parts of the world."

"But not all of Islam supports jihad or the actions of..."

"We are in an existential struggle," he interrupted, his voice getting ever louder as it echoed into the corridor beyond.

"You can't be blind to what is happening even here in Europe, in Germany, in Belgium, in our beloved France."

"So you see yourself as modern day crusaders, intent on preventing any kind of rapprochement with the savages, as you refer to them," Simône said scornfully.

"Your analysis, not mine. But yes, such an 'Accord,' if it ever existed, which it surely does not now, would give support to the dangerous ideas of the 'Coexist' crowd," he said, making air quotes with his fingers. "And that is something we don't intend to let happen."

He looked at her briefly before continuing. "So you must turn over the diary, and the rubbing, which I would contend you obtained illegally anyway."

"I don't know what you are talking about," said Simône.

"Oh, Professeur, surely you don't intend to play that game."

When Simône just continued to look at him blankly, he continued. "Of course you know what I am talking about: the diary of Leonard's nephew and the rubbing you made at the Abbaye D'Orval during your little adventure in Belgium."

"How do you know about either of those?" asked Simône, wide-eyed.

"As I've have been trying to explain, my Order is both strong in numbers, and well-placed. Nothing goes on in or concerning the Church of which we are unaware. Surely you didn't think that your discoveries had remained secret. You and your American friends have been much too indiscrete, much like the proverbial bulls in the china shop."

"Which brings us to your present predicament. It was, in fact, your rather indiscrete actions with your previous graduate assistant, Thomas Dubois, if I recall the name correctly, which made you susceptible to my entreaties."

As her cheeks began to burn, Simône was suddenly glad that the cell was dimly lit.

"Unfortunately, it was your carnal behavior that also led to your divorce, I understand."

Simône silently fumed as the man actually "tsk,tsk"ed at her from across the cell.

"Sadly, some people and, of course, educational institutions can be so unforgiving of infidelity, particularly with a student, even in this day and age."

Simône glared at him, before asking, "How do I know that if I turn over the diary and rubbing, I will be assured that my 'indiscretion,' as you referred to it, won't still be revealed to the administration at the Sorbonne?"

"Why would we want to do that? By protecting your secret, and thus your tenure, we insure your silence and loyalty."

"Even if I give them to you, how do I keep my friends quiet?"

"Perhaps you can tell them that they were stolen from your room, after you bring them to me tonight."

"But they will still know about them, and what they say."

"Yes, but without the physical proof…" he shrugged his shoulders as if to say, 'who will believe them.'

"As to how you get them to give up the search, that is your problem, n'est pas?" he asked, smiling cruelly. "That is, if you want your secret to stay a secret."

His visage hardened as he said, "Meet me in the Church of St. Pierre at 10 tonight with the diary and rubbing. Don't be late."

Without waiting for a response, he brushed past her and walked quickly down the corridor.

Within a minute, Simône heard him running up the stairs.

When she was sure he would not return, she slumped down heavily on the stone bench and began to sob.

CHAPTER THIRTY-FOUR

JULY 3, 1796, NORMANDY, FRANCE

Bernard stopped beside the small tree-lined stream that he had been following since late morning. He dipped his hand in the cool flowing water and brought it to his mouth before splashing some water over his sweating brow. Squinting toward the sun, which was still quite high in the sky, he guessed that it must be almost 5 PM. He realized that were he still at this abbaye, it would be time for evening prayers before dinner. Shaking his head to dispel the memories that still only brought him sorrow, he looked around for a place to rest. The hunger, which he had purposely ignored for the past few hours, was now producing actual pains in his empty stomach. The cold water he had just consumed seemed to have made the feeling more excruciating.

Sighing, he settled under a large tree with roots extending like jagged fingers into the flowing water. After a habitual quick look around to check for potential dangers, he opened his knapsack and extracted a half-eaten loaf of sour dough bread wrapped in a small piece of cloth. Before taking a bite, he bowed his head and uttered a prayer of thanks for the sustenance that God had provided, not just today but during all of the days since he had begun his trek from Calais. Thinking back over the past 10 days, he offered a further prayer, grateful as he was for the food and lodging that miraculously had appeared regularly, as if by providence, on his journey. After taking a few more bites, he rewrapped the bread, before stowing it in his knapsack, which he then shouldered to continue on his way.

He smiled slightly as he thought about the weathered old man, roughly clad in ragged clothes and boots, he had met just as he had reached the outskirts of Calais, who had befriended him and told him about a number of houses and churches, which in the past had offered shelter and sometimes even food to pilgrims headed to Mont St. Michel. Though the man had acknowledged that pilgrims were no longer headed to what was now a prison, he assured Bernard that friendly believers along the way might still offer him aid.

Strangely, now that Bernard thought about it, he realized the old man had gone as suddenly as he had come. They had journeyed south together for several hours on the main road leading out of Calais. When they reached a small ville that afternoon, Bernard had stopped at the village well to refill his animal skin bag with water. Having finished his task, he turned around to offer some water to the man, but he was gone. Seemingly vanished.

Bernard had wandered around the town for a few minutes before giving up the search, and continuing on the road out of town, putting the man from his mind. He had walked steadily for several more hours. As evening approached, he had begun to think not only of something to eat, but also of where he should shelter for the night. Bernard knew of no wild animals that might be found in the surrounding countryside; rather, he feared the possibility of encountering ones of the two-legged type who might sorely treat a lone traveler.

As he had topped the next hill, he had felt relief and said a silent prayer; down below him, a village with 10 or so houses, thatched roofs glowing red in the early evening sunset, had come into view. Even better, in the middle of the town square stood the village church, looking to be in sad disrepair, yet still intact. For Bernard, a church, even if it was no longer in use, meant refuge, a place to rest his weary body until the morn, without likelihood of molestation, if only because of the still remaining beliefs of most of the populous, and the superstitions of the unwashed who might be passing by.

Now that the revolution had entered a slightly less bloody phase, and the Reign of Terror had mercifully passed, some of the lawlessness that had pervaded his homeland for the last several years had started to recede. And with that recession came a return of the values that had been inculcated in the average poor, rural parishioner since birth: fear and respect of God, and all things godly, including places of worship.

His eyes had welled up as he walked slowly down the hill toward the village in the fading light. Bernard knew it would be years before every parish in the country again had a priest, an operating place of worship. But for him, a church, operating or not, offered at least a semblance of safety, of respite.

When he reached the stone steps of the church, he saw that one of the two double doors hung slightly battered and open on its hinges. Bernard looked over both shoulders before gently pushing the heavy oak door partially open. Stepping through the small space he had created with his efforts, he waited as his eyes adjusted before continuing into the dimly lit space. He flinched slightly as the musty smell of neglect, and a high-pitched scraping of wood against stone accosted his senses.

Looking for the source, he noted that the shutters on a window near the right side of the altar swung slowly back and forth, moved by a breeze that flowed rather musically through the oratory, summoning various creaks and sighs from the ancient structure. Now that his eyes had fully adjusted, he also saw, thankfully, that the place was uninhabited, except by a small black cat that had slunk past him resentfully as he had entered. Based on the overall evidence of disuse, overturned pews, leaves on the floor, and piles of dirt in the corners, Bernard felt certain that he would find no priest kneeling in prayer in the shadows of the altar.

"So no food here," he had said aloud to the rafters where a lone pigeon sat eyeing him. *And no way to get that winged rat down*, thought Bernard, who would have happily made a meal of the wary bird.

Bernard had closed his eyes for a moment as he mentally counted the coins he had tucked into a small pouch at the bottom of his knapsack. He had managed to save most of the meager wages he had earned over the past three years, since his two jobs had provided him with room and board, but he was hesitant to spend any of the money, since he had no plans beyond delivering the 'treasure' to Mont St. Michel, and only the Lord Almighty knew what his future would hold. But after reluctantly acknowledging that the grumbling in his stomach would not be ignored, he had retraced his steps out into the now purple tinged dusk and considered his options.

From a few of the several, thatched roof dwellings emanated light and sounds of occupation; others seemed long deserted. After a few more moments of surveillance, Bernard took a deep heavy breath to summon courage before heading toward the one that seemed most welcoming, a two-story dwelling with an opened door spilling light out onto a small side street running off the square where he stood. Drawing closer, he could hear several voices raised in what he hoped was friendly conversation.

As his foot fell on the first stone step leading into the house, Bernard, who had spoken rarely in the past several days, cleared his throat and then shouted, "Bon soir. Comment-allez vous? Je suis un voyageur inoffensive. Puis j'entrer, s'il vous plait? (Good evening. How are you? I am a harmless traveler. May I enter, please?)

After a few seconds of silence, Bernard had heard some whispered conversation being exchanged, before a man of immense girth had stepped into the light, virtually blocking the doorway.

"Harmless, well let me see," said the man, as he eyed Bernard intently. It seemed to Bernard as though minutes passed before he added, "Show me your hands."

Bernard complied immediately, and voluntarily turned all of the way around to demonstrate that he carried no weapons. He even lifted his tunic to reveal the top of his trousers, and the absence of anything threatening. Finally, seemingly satisfied, the man asked jovially, "So harmless traveler, what can I do for you?"

"Kind sir, I am on a pilgrimage to Mont St. Michel. I merely seek some food for which I would gladly pay. I hope to rest tonight in the church before continuing my trek at daybreak."

"Well, traveler," the man answered, after looking over his shoulder to someone inside, "if that is all, my better half says you are welcome to our humble house, and the rabbit stew we have leftovers from our evening meal. But no, you cannot pay; that is not how we treat guests in this ville."

"Entre vous," said the man, smiling broadly, as he swept his hand through the air in a gesture of welcome.

Inside near the glowing hearth, Bernard spied the 'misses,' a petite woman in broad cloth dress and apron, and three others, a boy of twelve or thirteen sitting at a table, and two younger girls on the floor in the corner, engaged in a game of spilikin (pick up sticks), who Bernard assumed to be the children of his hosts. The two girls eyed him momentarily before apparently deciding he was of no interest; soon they rejoined their game.

The boy, however, who had been inspecting Bernard with acute interest, asked, "Mont St. Michel? But isn't that a prison now?"

Bernard, who had been invited by the mistress of the house to sit at the table, and was already greedily slurping down the bowl of steaming aromatic stew he had been served, smiled before answering.

"You are correct, young sir."

"Then why are you going? You aren't a jailer are you?"

Bernard, taken aback by the question, laughed and then said, "No, far from it. But I hope to find some answers there."

Intrigued, the boy leaned forward, chin in hands, before asking, "What kind of answers?"

"Well, that is quite a long story," Bernard answered, his eyes downcast as his thoughts flooded with the memories of the past few years.

At this, his host guffawed and said, "Wonderful, we love a good long story. And as you can see," he added, sweeping his beefy hand around the room, "we have no other pressing matters."

Bernard used a piece of bread to sop up the last few bites of his stew, with a nod to his hostess, before taking up the invitation. Soon he was deep into the tale of all he had experienced in the past three years, albeit without revealing anything about the real reason for his present journey.

When he finished his recitation an hour later, the boy was wide-eyed, and the husband and wife sat shaking their heads. Finally the man broke the silence that engulfed the group.

"So sad and yet not surprising. Yours is unfortunately a very common tale. You may have noticed the empty houses when you came into town."

Bernard nodded as his host continued.

"My poor neighbors, killed or carted off by the revolutionary guard. Those godless monsters," he said, before crossing himself, spitting on the floor with disdain, and then looking at his wife who reacted with a slight sound, and a nod to the two girls, who still played in the corner.

"And poor Father Laurent, we have no idea. They came for him in the night, poor man. Dead, imprisoned, shipped to one of the devils' penal colonies. Only God knows," he concluded, crossing himself again, before raising his hands and eyes to heaven.

The wife, who had not yet spoken, finally was roused by this last recitation to ask, "Monsieur, perhaps, when you reach Mont St. Michel, you could ask about him as well as your Abbott? Perhaps they took him there?"

"Of course, Madame, I will inquire. But I fear the prospects of finding my Abbott or your priest are quite poor. The stories that have travelled over the sea to England these past few years have been terrifying, equally terrifying to what happened at my abbaye."

The four fell back into silence, each nodding sorrowfully. The crackling fire provided a cheery glow, and the girls chattered happily at play, at odds with the horrors they had just been discussing.

But finally his host said, "But life goes on, oui?"

Bernard nodded in answer.

"You have been through enough, more than enough. At least let us give you shelter for the night," offered the man.

"Celeste," he said, turning to his wife, who seemed startled to be called by name, "get Brother Bernard some blankets. He can sleep by the last of the fire, and we will send him off with a full belly in the morning."

"As I said before, you are very kind, all of you. A good Christian family. May God bless you," Bernard said.

"He hasn't been around much recently," the man said with a snort, as he pushed his chair away from the table. "Mais tant qu'il y a de la vie, il y a de l'espoir (but if there is life, there is hope)."

"Ah oui," agree Bernard.

Without further discussion, the family filed upstairs, leaving Bernard alone. He had looked around with a grin before snuggling into the pile of down quilts that Celeste had placed on the floor near the dying fire. *Much better than sharing the floor of the church with the mouse catcher*, he thought, before drifting off to sleep.

Bernard had awoken with a start as a cock greeted the dawn. He sat up in the muted light filtering through the one window of the cottage, and stretched to relieve the knots knitted by a night spent on the stone floor. After exiting the house to perform his morning ablutions, he returned a few minutes later to find a still taciturn Celeste already tending a pot over a newly lit fire.

As promised, before letting him continue on his journey, his hosts had fed him a simple but tasty porridge, and filled his knapsack almost to overflowing with a portion of goat cheese, a small baguette and a leather flask of wine.

"This is too much, truly a feast," Bernard had protested, as he shook hands with Alard-he had finally learned the man's name-then Celeste, and Clement, their son. He also bid adieu to the two girls, who still slumbered upstairs.

As he turned from the house to begin his trek, the woman, in a hesitant voice, called after him, "remember us in your prayers, s'il vous plait, Brother Bernard."

Bernard, who had paused for a moment upon hearing the address, shrugged-to correct her would ruin what had been a wonderful encounter, then turned to give them a wave and a nod before continuing down the road.

The next ten days had passed in much the same manner, with God-fearing people providing him with food and shelter. Always he told his story in payment; frequently he heard about the equally horrific experiences of the people he met. Yet despite their sorrows, these simple country folks remained stoic, for the most part their faith still strong, unextinguished.

On a few days he had been forced to dip into his bank to purchase bread, cheese and wine, and twice he had rested his head on dirt beneath hedgerows. But Bernard knew he had been blessed and protected, if not by God himself, then at least by his archangel, Saint Michael, to whom the young monk had dedicated his quest as he stood in the ashes of the abbaye. And he hoped, based on information from a fellow traveler he had encountered two days ago, that tonight he would reach his journey's end at the foot of Mont St. Michel.

CHAPTER
THIRTY-FIVE

After indulging in a few more minutes of self-pity, it occurred to Simône that voluntarily sitting in a damp, dark prison cell in the depths of Mont St. Michel was not going to solve any of her problems. Fumbling in her purse, she retrieved her cell phone and using the light, retraced the route she had followed a half hour before. When she finally stepped out of the dark corridor she had followed through a small wooden door onto the main stone steps of the Grand Dagré leading downward from the entrance to the abbaye, she stopped for a moment to get her bearings.

In a few minutes time, she had traveled from the 10th to the 21st century. The contrast was mentally jarring. Here, tourists clad in t-shirts, shorts and Nikes, stood taking pictures with cell phones and sophisticated cameras with zoom lenses, objects that could never have been envisioned when the magnificent structure behind her had been constructed. Despite what had just occurred, her training as an archeologist and anthropologist briefly overcame her very raw emotions as she momentarily marveled at the amazing scientific accomplishments of mankind on display at this 1000-year-old edifice.

The blare of someone's cell phone ringing brought her out of her reverie. Glancing at her watch, she saw that it had been almost 45 minutes since she had parted company with Jeff, Alex and Liz.

"Merde," she muttered under her breath, as she quickly descended the multiple flights of steps leading to the main thoroughfare. Given the large numbers of tourists who had swarmed onto the island since she had hiked up to the abbaye that morning for their tour, it took her a good 15 minutes to thread her way through the morass of sightseers laden with backpacks, vacationers struggling to pull their wheeled suitcases up the steep cobblestoned passageways, a group of robe clad monks, heads bowed in prayer, and even past a hand cart being used by one of the local restaurateurs to resupply his establishment with paper goods.

When she finally reached the lobby of their hotel, she was relieved to learn that the three had not yet returned. Attempting to shrug off the feelings of anger, guilt and embarrassment she been experiencing since being shanghaied by the 'fake' monk, she passed through the hotel to its back entrance, which opened onto the rampart skirting the outer edge of the Mont's stone fortifications. She lit a cigarette from the pack she guiltily had stopped to buy at the store next door, and drew deeply from it, holding in her breath for a few seconds before expelling the smoke. Feeling slightly calmer, she leaned forward on the rampart wall to look at multicolored dots, guided groups of tourists making their way by foot across the sandy, now waterless bay below.

As she stared down at the tranquil scene, she mentally struggled with her predicament. After about 15 minutes, and another cigarette, Simône took one last drag, violently stubbed out the cigarette on the rough stone wall, and then vehemently shouted, "Screw them," garnering stares from a passing couple, before heading back into the hotel bar to wait for her three companions.

Having made their way back up to the main entrance to the abbaye, Jeff, Alex and Liz, stopped to take a few pictures before descending the staircase down to street level.

"Simône must be back at the hotel by now," said Jeff, after looking at the time on his cellphone.

"Yeah, and we can ask her why she has been wasting our time," added Alex, still sounding annoyed.

"Maybe she didn't know about the history of the chapel and didn't have a chance to tell us not to bother, because the monk was there," said Liz, trying to give Simône the benefit of the doubt.

"Maybe," said Alex, sounding unconvinced.

When they reached the hotel lobby, they found Simône at the bar, nursing a glass of wine, apparently lost in thought. Once she heard the three, she swiveled her chair toward them and said enthusiastically, "Come. Sit. So tell me, did you find anything?"

In response, Alex gave a sidelong glance at Jeff who almost imperceptibly shook his head.

"Unfortunately no, Professeur," said Jeff. "We managed to sneak back into the chapel when another tour group was leaving but we didn't find any evidence of a hiding place."

"Yes, and we spent a good thirty minutes there," added Liz. "I suppose with the renovations they did in the 1960's, anything hidden there over 150 years before would have been discovered or destroyed."

"Yes, I suppose you are correct," said Simône. "Well, at least we looked."

"Was there any other room you saw on the tour that you thought might have been used as a hiding place?" she asked, changing the subject.

Alex, who had remained silent to that point, said, "Not really, Professeur. But what about you? Don't you have some other ideas? After all, you know the history of this place, so much better than the three of us."

There was an awkward silence before Jeff said, "I'm sure if you had any other ideas of where to search, you would tell us, right, Professeur?" he asked, looking intently at Simône.

"But of course. Unfortunately, I am at as much of a loss as the rest of you. I guess I must apologize; perhaps this trip has been a waste of everyone's time."

"Oh no, not at all," interjected Liz, diplomatically. "This place is spectacular. Even if it may have been a dead end regarding the Templar treasure, we wouldn't have missed it for anything. Right, Alex?"

"Uh, right," said Alex begrudgingly.

Another few seconds of uncomfortable silence followed, before Jeff broke the tension by saying, "As usual, I'm starving; it's been hours since breakfast. Let's find somewhere to eat."

"What an excellent idea," said Simône, sounding relieved. "My treat. I saw a restaurant two or three doors down that serves crepes and salads. It is out on the terrace adjoining the rampart; it should have a beautiful view. We can get to it through the rear door," she added, pointing to the back of the lobby.

"Sounds great," said Jeff, enthusiastically.

Within a few minutes, they had secured a table, ordered, and were well into their first glass of wine.

"Once again, the wine of France does not disappoint," said Liz, who was holding her glass aloft to capture refracted rays of sunlight glinting through the delicate pink color of the liquid. "From now on, whenever I drink a glass of rosé, it will remind me of French summers, and the beauty of this place."

"Well said; I'll drink to that," said Jeff, who raised his glass in a toast, prompting the others to follow suit.

The waitress appeared at that moment with plates of golden crepes filled to overflowing with shrimp and a cream sauce generously laced with sherry.

"This looks delicious," said Liz, before taking a forkful.

"What do you think, another glass of rosé?" asked Jeff, looking at their now empty glasses.

232

"Sure, why not? If it's okay with Simône; she's paying," said Alex, with a glance at Simône, who was busy looking at a text on her phone.

When she did not respond, Jeff said," Simône?"

"Yes, of course," said Simône distractedly, a furrow creasing her brow, without looking up from her phone.

Jeff caught the waitress's attention, pointed at the empty glasses, and held up four fingers, before asking, "everything alright, Professeur?"

Simône, who had just slipped her phone into her purse, looked up and replied, "Yes, just an administrative problem at school. Nothing to worry about," she said, shaking her head and smiling.

"By the way, before you got back, I made us a dinner reservation at 7 PM at the restaurant next door. Unfortunately, there isn't much fine dining on the Mont, but I imagine their seafood is pretty good," she said apologetically.

"And then, of course, we are booked for the evening musicale and light show up in the abbaye. I believe it starts at 9 PM."

Once they finished their leisurely lunch, and Simône had paid, she said, "You know, I've got a bit of a headache. I think I will go to my room and rest for a while. So I will see you at dinner, oui? Au revoir," she said abruptly, as she stood up and quickly headed toward an archway marked "EXIT," before any of them could reply. Within seconds, she had disappeared down a set of winding stairs leading to the street.

CHAPTER
THIRTY-SIX

JULY 4, 1796, THE SOUTHWESTERN COAST OF FRANCE

Determined to complete his journey as quickly as possible, and blessed with agreeable weather, Bernard pressed on through the deepening dusk until he reached the shoreline abutting the bay in which the 'wonder of the medieval world' awaited him, just as the first evening stars began to glisten in the night sky. Squinting, he could just make out the abbaye's outline against the ink stained horizon. But a short while later, he sat watching in awe as the moon rose in the night sky, sending rays of light dancing across the water, and illuminating the pale colored stone of the abbaye to a beautiful silvery glow.

Finally, when exhaustion overcame him, he made a bed of sorts in a hollow where the grass of the pasture running down to the bay's edge met the sandy shore. His sleep was restless, punctuated by disturbing dreams of the last time he had seen his Abbott, and interrupted by the sound of the tide rushing into the bay, dogs barking at some nearby farmhouse, and finally the chattering of seagulls as the first light of day lit the outline of the distant horizon.

Shaking off the dregs of sleep, Bernard sat up and rubbed his eyes before looking seaward to insure that the Mont truly was before him, and not just an image from a fevered dream. He stood up to stretch and then collected his belongings: a coat he had laid down to afford some protection against the damp sand, the walking stick he had found near the stream he had traveled beside for a day, his animal skin water bag, which he had refilled before he left the stream and turned toward the coast, and his knapsack containing the reason for his journey.

Bernard realized he felt both excitement and not a small measure of trepidation about what he might encounter that day on the Mont. *Was Abbott Godard still alive, and if so, was he still at the Mont? And if not the Abbott, could he, Bernard, find some other man of God to relieve him of his three-year burden. And if he did, then what?*

Until now, Bernard had purposely refused to think about what his future might hold. He knew that whatever future lay before him was in God's hands, not his, and that as just a tiny speck of creation, the story of what would become of him was unimportant to anyone other than himself. Wasn't it St. James who had written in his gospel that we are but "a mist that appears for a little while, and then vanishes."

Yet Bernard could not help feeling anxious now that he was almost at his journey's end; *what would become of him?* Once he was finished delivering the treasure, he would have no holy mission or vow to sustain him, no brotherhood or monastic way of life to which he could turn. He was truly a fallen man, one who, he prayed daily, God would take mercy on at the end of days.

As he always did when faced with an insurmountable problem, Bernard fell to his knees and began to pray, asking for God's guidance to lead him to the future for which he was intended. After about 30 minutes, he arose, feeling somewhat renewed and ready to face the task before him.

Bernard looked toward the Mont, and considered the best way to approach it. He had heard many cautionary tales of pilgrims caught in the bay's quicksand, or by fast changing tides in which they drowned. Gratefully, Bernard saw that the tide that had risen during the night had begun to recede, exposing the sandy bottom of the bay. He was confident that the water would not return before he reached the island, but he would have to rely on the grace of God and the guidance of the Archangel St.

235

Michael to whom he had just prayed to keep him clear of the deadly quicksand. Stowing his boots in his knapsack, he stood barefooted for a few minutes watching where the seagulls landed, and looking for areas where the sand seemed dryer and firmer. To his right he could see a darker area that bubbled and rippled, sure signs of treacherous sand.

Summoning his courage, he was about to begin walking on the path he had mentally mapped out, when he heard the neighing of a horse. Turning to look behind him, he saw off in the distance a horse-drawn cart headed down the nearby road leading to the bay's edge. Thinking that a tradesman in a cart probably did not present a danger, he said a quick prayer of protection, and hoped that this was an answer to his earlier prayers.

When the cart was about 100 yards away, he shouted to the driver, "Bon jour, Monsieur. Are you by chance going to the Mont?"

He received no answer until the driver of the slow-moving cart pulled beside him a few minutes later.

"Bon jour," said the driver, who had removed his cap and used his sleeve to wipe his brow, before squinting down at Bernard.

"Oui, I am going to the Mont. What business is it of yours, Monsieur?"

"Pardonne, Monsieur. I am but a pilgrim traveling to the Mont. I am seeking news of my Abbott who was imprisoned there a few years ago."

"Your Abbott, so you are a monk?"

"A former monk, Monsieur."

"A former monk? Ah, I have never heard of one of those. I thought your vows were for life. Strange. But of course, everything is strange these days. And it is no business of mine. So if you need a ride out to the island, climb in the back. Duchess won't mind, will you girl?" the driver affectionately asked his steed.

"You like the name?" he asked, looking back over his shoulder at Bernard who was awkwardly climbing into the bed of the cart. "My little joke-not a lot of Duchesses these days, at least ones who still have their heads."

Bernard recoiled at the mention of the guillotine, knowing that some from his own abbaye may have shared the same fate. But he did not respond to the jibe. Instead as he climbed into the cart, he said, "You are so kind, Monsieur; I am grateful for your assistance. I was a little worried about falling victim to the quicksand."

"So, a smart 'former' monk," the driver said, laughing. "Yes, we lose a few people to the sand and tides every year. But who can question God's ways, eh, Monsieur Former Monk," he added, as he urged Duchess to "get up."

The horse responded by slowly pulling the cart out onto the sand.

"Do not worry; Duchess knows the way. We deliver supplies to the prison three days a week. And Duchess always keeps her head," he added, laughing again.

Bernard crossed himself before sitting down amongst several bags of grain. After several seconds of holding his breath, waiting for the cart to drop out from under him, he relaxed and began to enjoy the gently swaying motion as the cartwheels bumped across ridges in the sand.

Twenty minutes later, he found himself drafted into unloading the driver's cargo onto a hand cart parked at the base of the Mont outside an open drawn gate set into a massive stone archway.

"Would you like me to help you pull the cart up to the abb-the prison?" asked Bernard. "It is the least I can do in return for my safe journey across the sands."

"Oh, no, they will be down shortly to collect the cart-you know, cheap labor, the prisoners," the driver said, gesturing up toward the abbaye towering above them. "I don't ever go there. I stay as far away from that hellhole as possible."

"But if I wanted to go inside the prison?"

"Inside?" asked the man, surprised. "Why would you want to do that? Your kind was just recently released from there, at least the few who were still alive. I wouldn't think you would want to go back."

"Yes, I understand but I must try to learn of the fate of my many imprisoned brothers and my blessed Abbott."

"Well, for God's sake," the man said, crossing himself, "don't go up to the prison. No good can come of it. There are still many revolutionaries, jailers there who hate the clergy."

"But I have traveled so far. Isn't there anyone who I can talk to about the released prisoners?"

The driver thought for a moment before responding. "Well, I don't know if he can help you but I have heard there is still a priest on the island. One who was held in the prison himself. Maybe he may know something. You might be able to find him at the village church. L'eglise Saint-Pierre. Halfway up the Grande Rue. It is Sunday after all."

"Sunday? I had lost track..." said Bernard, his voice trailing off. "Well, thank you again," he said to the driver.

"De rien (it was nothing)," the man said, dismissively, turning to tend to his horse.

Bernard shouldered his pack, before heading through the stone archway onto the steep cobblestoned road that stretched before him up through the heart of the Mont. From the position of the sun in the sky, Bernard knew that it was not yet 7 AM. As he walked slowly up the still quiet Grande Rue, he passed numerous shuttered shops, and even one building front signed as an inn. A few women, busily sweeping their stoops, used to seeing strangers passing through on a daily basis, considered him briefly before going about their business.

Repeatedly, as the street curved first left, then right, providing a view, Bernard found himself stopping to look upward to the imposing structure that he had traveled so far to reach, yet could not visit. He also thought sadly of

238

the countless pilgrims to whom the abbaye no longer offered refuge. As he continued to follow the snaking street, he reached an area where the storefronts were less frequent and the buildings seemed to take on a character similar to the structures of a monastery. Looking to his left, Bernard spied a raised terrace dotted with the tops of stone crosses of varying ages and sizes. Realizing that this must be the graveyard for the parish, he gazed further left at stairs that ended in a small stone courtyard; looking up, he saw a plain metal cross mounted above the entrance to what he knew must be the village church, L'eglise Saint-Pierre, the saint of fishermen.

Taking the stairs two at a time, he reached the front door of the church and pulled on the large protruding ring, only to find that the door was locked.

So, not a place of sanctuary, he thought, ruefully. *Well, it is Sunday. Surely someone will arrive soon for morning mass. I guess I will just have to wait.*

Settling himself on the stone stoop, he pulled a piece of dried meat from his backpack to make his morning meal. After finishing the last morsel, he leaned back against one of the double doors and closed his eyes, listening contentedly to the morning sounds issuing from the street below, of the island coming to life. Perhaps due to his overall fatigue from the many days of travel and the little rest he had gotten the night before, he soon was asleep.

Unsure of how long he had slept, Bernard awoke to the sound of church bells ringing, summoning parishioners to Sabbath mass. Without warning, one of the double doors beside him was swung open, and he found himself looking up into the bemused face of a young priest.

"Oh hello, Father," Bernard said, embarrassed, as he jumped to his feet. "I was just waiting to talk to you, and for mass, of course."

"Of course," said the priest, still amused by his discovery. "Well, come in, you no doubt get the prize for most eager attendee at any of my masses. Normally I have to scour the streets to gather a group of even 10."

Bernard grabbed his backpack and followed the priest into the intimate candle and sunlit interior of the church. Bernard decided he should wait until after the service to attempt a discussion with the priest, who had put on his sacramental robes and already was busy lighting candles upon the altar. Bernard stopped to admire the beautiful stained glass windows set high up in the stone walls of the church, before depositing his knapsack on a wooden bench, and kneeling in prayer.

Within a few minutes, a few other faithful souls, a family of four, three elderly women, and surprisingly, a group of four young men, clothed in what Bernard recognized as monks' habits, joined him in the wooden pews. The priest, who had been sitting to the side of the altar, slowly strode forward to stand behind the altar, and began to chant in Latin.

Bernard glanced at the family, who had reverently bowed their heads, despite clearly not understanding a word of what was being said. Bernard, who, on the other hand, had been schooled in Latin since childhood, listened intently, soaking in the beautiful words, which he had not heard for many years. Dover, like the rest of England, was Protestant. During his three years in exile there, Bernard had on a few occasions attended private prayer meetings with other French refugees from the "Jacobins" violence, but there had been no church to attend and certainly no priest holding mass.

As he listened, Bernard realized that this was truly the first time since he had left his abbaye three years before that he had felt at home. The terror and turmoil of the past had finally been lifted from his shoulders, and he felt for the first time in a long time that he could breathe. He bowed his head to utter a silent prayer as tears flowed freely down his cheeks.

Once the service ended, all of the attendees except Bernard filed silently out of the sanctuary. The priest

240

quickly snuffed out the altar candles, and put out away the remaining communion host, before stepping into a side room to remove his sacramental robes.

Clothed now in his simple black habit, the priest came and sat beside Bernard, who had not moved since the end of the service. He sat quietly beside Bernard for several minutes, before saying, "Bonjour. I am Father Pierre, no relation to St. Pierre, of course," he said, smiling slightly at his own joke.

"I am Bernard," he said quietly.

"I noticed that you did not take the sacrament, yet I saw you silently mouthing most of the liturgy along with me. Are you a man of God?" the priest asked, looking intently at Bernard.

"I am... I was a monk at the Abbaye D'Orval, before it was burned to the ground three years ago."

The priest, who could hear the pain in Bernard's voice, did not respond, sensing that to do so would silence the young man. Bernard, who could feel the empathy flowing from the priest, began to recount his entire story from the imprisonment of Abbott Godard, to his arrival on the Mont that morning. But unlike those times when he had told his tale for room and board, he included the real reason for his journey, 'the treasure' still residing in the knapsack lying between them.

"Oh my! That is quite a story. And here I was thinking that I had endured a lot because I had been imprisoned here for six months. And yet, in truth, by the time I was brought here, some of the most brutal jailers were gone. And the jailer for my corridor was still secretly a practicing Catholic. In fact, I regularly heard his confession," Father Pierre admitted, shaking his head at the irony.

"My imprisonment, though uncomfortable, and certainly not desired, was, I hesitate to say easy, but not as brutal by any measure to what your Abbott and brothers suffered. And you as well."

"But Brother Bernard, you still have not explained why you did not take the sacrament today."

"I am no longer in a state of grace," Bernard said, with anguish in his voice. "There is one part of my story I left out."

"Because?"

"Because I am so ashamed and full of guilt."

"What could you possibly done?" the priest asked with concern.

"I killed a man. In self-defense," he added quickly, as the priest looked at him with surprise. After regaining his composure, Father Pierre asked, "Would you like me to hear your confession?"

"Yes, Father," said Bernard, who fell on his knees beside the priest who remained seated in the pew.

Once Bernard had finished, Father Pierre asked, "Were you intending to kill your attacker or just defend yourself?"

"To defend myself. I never meant to kill him," Bernard said quietly, with despair.

"Then, my son, you are without sin. Every man has the right to defend himself, and if you are unsure of what was in your heart at the time you acted, then I absolve you of your sin, as it is clear that you have suffered and truly repent for any ill will or malice you may have had in your heart against that man who attacked you."

Bernard kissed the hands of the priest, who gently urged him to sit down beside him on the bench.

"But what of my act of contrition?"

The priest let out a low chuckle, before saying to Bernard, whose face was a mask of confusion, "I don't mean to make light of this, but wouldn't you agree that your journey of the past three years, and certainly since you landed back in France, constitutes enough contrition for one lifetime?"

Bernard, who smiled for the first time since entering the church, said, "Yes, Father. Thank you."

"Well," said Father Pierre, rubbing his hands together to indicate that the matter was settled, "I am starving. I have a small cottage behind the church. Would you care to join me for a midmorning meal? I usually don't eat until after mass."

"Yes, if you're sure I am not imposing," Bernard said.

"Not at all," said the priest, after patting him on the shoulder. "And besides, I want to hear more about this 'treasure.' And I have something to share with you as well. I met your Abbott when I was imprisoned up in the abbaye. Unfortunately, he died from the abuse and torture he had suffered."

"When?" asked Bernard, the smiled vanishing from his face.

"Only a month before we were all released last year. I am so sorry. He was a good man, no doubt a great man. I actually was called upon to take his deathbed confession."

Bernard sat weeping silently, his body rocking back and forth on the bench, for the loss of his Abbott, the only father he had ever known. The priest sat silently beside him, as the other man's sorrow poured out in waves. Finally, after the monk's grief seemed to have subsided, Father Pierre said, "I am so sorry for your loss. But take comfort in the fact that he has truly gone to a better place."

A few minutes later, Bernard asked in a quiet voice, "I don't suppose he ever mentioned anything about the abbaye, about what had happened there before he was taken?"

"Unfortunately, I did not have much time with him. But while we were talking just now, I remembered something he said which has remained a mystery to me to this day."

"Something he said?"

"While he gave his confession, the guard, upon my insistence, allowed me to be alone with your Abbott for a few minutes. Just before he died, he whispered to me, 'If

243

he comes, tell him to take it to the place where the heathens plundered, the penitents prayed in poverty, and the falcons still soar at the end of the world. One day mankind must know the truth.'"

"Having now heard your story, he must have been talking about you and your treasure."

Bernard looked at him, mouth agape. Finally, when the shock of what he had just heard began to recede, he asked, excitedly, "But what does it mean? Where is this place he described?"

The priest shrugged his shoulders, palms facing upward. "I have no idea. Until today, I didn't even know what 'it' was. I thought perhaps just the ramblings of a dying man. But now I am not so sure. When he whispered the words, it was almost as though he had memorized them so that he would not forget them, even in extremis."

Bernard fell silent as they entered the small cottage. Father Pierre busied himself with setting the table for the meal, while Bernard, overwhelmed by the priest's revelations, sat trapped in thoughts of the abbaye and Abbott Godard.

"Come, let us feast," said the priest, who had placed bread, wine and a hearty seafood stew before Bernard. "The parishioners here don't have much, but what they have, they share, and as you can see, they keep me quite well fed."

"When we have finished, perhaps we can try to tease out the meaning of your Abbott's words. But for now, let us give thanks for what God has provided."

They both bowed their heads, and Father Pierre said a brief prayer before both men fell silent as they ate.

CHAPTER
THIRTY-SEVEN

"Am I the only one, or did the two of you think that was extremely weird? What's her deal?" Alex asked, nonplussed.

"Uh yes, I have to admit that was pretty strange," agreed Liz.

"Don't look at me," Jeff said. "I have no idea what is going on with her. It is like she has turned into an incredible flake, and believe me, that is not the way I would ever have described her until now. Maybe being kidnapped affected her way more than we realized. Maybe PTSD, or something."

"You got shot and you haven't lost it. I mean, she was so gung-ho about finding the treasure, the 'Accord,' whatever it is, and now she has a 'slight headache' and she can't be bothered? I mean, come on! Really?" Alex asked, clearly perturbed.

"I agree, Al, but there is no point getting upset about it," Liz said, trying to calm her sister. "I think we all feel let down."

"I know I do," Jeff said. "I've been working on this for months. But I'm not ready to give up yet. Because I've been thinking; if the person who left the message in the abbaye was a monk, a priest, a man of the cloth, it seems pretty unlikely that he would take any sort of treasure into the actual abbaye once it had become a prison. Sort of like Daniel voluntarily walking into the lion's den, right?"

"Oh, look at you, making Biblical references," Alex said, teasing him.

Jeff gave her a dirty look, but Alex just grinned at him.

Liz, who was practiced at ignoring their banter, said, "You're probably right. Even if he wanted to bring it here to the island because of the connection to St. Michael, he would have needed to be a little more ingenious."

"Maybe we've been thinking about this wrong," said Alex, getting excited. "This whole island is dedicated to St. Michel. It literally could be anywhere on this huge hunk of rock."

"Yeah... "Liz said slowly. "But what makes more sense? That –let's call him Brother B (I like the alliteration), anyway-Brother B carries this treasure all of the way from the abbaye in Belgium and then sticks it in some random place because he can't get in this abbaye, or, that having travelled all of this way, he finds some place special, significant, to stash it, assuming he stashed it here at all."

"Uh, well, I would guess the latter," said Jeff, grinning at Liz.

"He could have somehow snuck into the abbaye/prison, but I imagine access was either limited or impossible," Alex said.

"So," Jeff said, "what else was on this island in the 1790's?"

"I don't know but I think we should find out," Alex said, with a wink at him.

"Let's all go get our laptops and reconvene at that pub further down the rampart. Looks like a good place for research and some thought provoking wine."

"Agreed," said Alex and Liz, in unison.

While they went to their rooms to gather their laptops, a summer squall with heavy rain moved over the Mont, causing every tourist out on the ramparts to scurry for cover. By the time they arrived at the bar, they were fortunate to grab the last remaining unoccupied table sheltered by the metal canopy. As the rain drummed steadily above them, they researched potential hiding places, looking up every so often from their digital libraries to enjoy

246

sips of wine and the view of seemingly solid sheets of rain pelting the bay.

After about 15 minutes, Liz said enthusiastically, "I think I might have a winner!"

"Do tell, Sister," said Alex, looking up from her computer screen.

"L'eglise Saint-Pierre. It's the parish church here on the Mont. We must have passed it on our way up the Grande Rue this morning. It's almost as old as the abbaye. It was mentioned as far back as 1022 A.D.: 'the monastery of Saint Peter, prince of the Apostles, situated on the side of the hill.' According to this article, it has been enlarged and renovated-redone really-numerous times over the centuries, but it has always been an operating church."

"Looks like a real possibility," said Jeff, who also had Googled information about the church as Liz was speaking.

"And to top it off," Liz said, with satisfaction, "there is a little side chapel in the church with a silver statue of St. Michel."

"Wow, really?" Alex asked.

"Yes, but..." Liz paused for a moment, "but the statue only dates back to 1873 A.D."

"That's okay," Jeff said. "It establishes a connection, between the church and St. Michel. Who knows, maybe there was some earlier tribute to St. Michel, which the statue replaced."

"At least it gives us another place to look," Alex said, agreeing.

"And unlike in the abbaye, Brother B," she paused to grin at her sister, "would have had access to it."

"Let's go take a look at this church," Jeff said, as he placed a 20 Euro note beneath the empty wine bottle. "I'm guessing the best route would be to go back through the restaurant to the Grande Rue."

The church, it turned out, was only a two-minute walk up the street. They found the red, front double door of the sanctuary on a small raised terrace facing up toward the abbaye. Next to the door stood a statue of Joan of Arc, clad in armor.

"I didn't even notice this building this morning. It is sort of hidden if you aren't looking for it. But I can't believe we missed Joan here," Alex said, posing for a selfie beside the elevated statue.

"If you recall, we were fighting our way through massive crowds this morning. I almost got squished by some German guy."

"True," said Alex.

Jeff, who had climbed the church stairs, was about to grab the handle of the red door when the sound of voices raised in song came floating toward them.

"Damn," he said, as he noticed a schedule posted on the stone surround to the right of the door. "It looks like mass just started. I guess we'll have to come back later."

"Now what do we do?" asked Alex, frustration sounding in her voice.

"I have an idea," Liz said, as they climbed down from the churchyard terrace onto the Grande Rue. "It's something I've been wanting to do anyway. The rain has stopped. Let's go down and walk across the sand in the bay."

"And why would we want to do that?" asked Alex, amused.

"Because it is part of the pilgrimage experience of Mont St. Michel, and it is our only chance to do it since we will probably be leaving here tomorrow."

Jeff, who had been silently observing this exchange, decided to jump in. "I think Liz is right. You should do the whole tourist thing while you are still here. I, on the other hand, am going back to my room to do some online grading of term papers. I'm way behind and I know, Templar treasure or not, there is no way Simône is going to let me out of the country until I finish them and get the grades posted."

"But don't you need a guide to, you know, avoid that whole nasty sinking into quicksand thing?" asked Alex.

"This is sort of weird," Liz retorted. "Usually you're the risk taker. I'm sure we'll be fine. I was looking down there earlier. There is a pretty well-established path from all of the guided tours that have crossed the bay today already."

"So will you go with me?" asked Liz imploringly. "Please?"

"Well, I guess so," Alex said, "but I'm still not convinced it is safe."

Jeff shook his head at the two of them and said, "Okay, then I guess I will see you two later. Call me when you finish playing in the sand and we can go back and check out the church before dinner."

"Sure, see ya," Alex said, giving him a quick kiss before pushing him playfully down the street.

"So should we change into shorts and flip flops," asked Alex, looking down at their capris and sandals.

"Sure, just in case we get sucked into that mean quick sand. You wouldn't want to ruin the new Chanel sandals you just bought."

"No, I wouldn't," Alex said, laughing, as she gave her sister a playful punch on the arm.

"You've certainly gotten flirty again with Jeff," said Liz, as they reached their room to change clothes. "What changed?"

"Well, you heard him."

"Heard what exactly?"

"Until today, since we got here, he has seemed just a little too cozy with Simône, finishing each others' sentences, etc. I mean, they have spent a lot of time together."

Liz looked amused as her sister continued, "But given the conversation we just had, I can see that he was just being the devoted TA, trying to get a good recommendation, I suppose. Now that he agrees she's being weird…" Alex said, her unfinished thought obvious to Liz.

"Okay, I get it-you're happy that Simône is being weird, flaky."

"No," said Alex, an embarrassed look on her face. "I'm just happy that he thinks so too; shows that there is nothing going on between them."

"Well, praise the Lord!" said Liz, raising her hands above her head. "He hasn't fallen under the spell of the evil temptress, Simône. We wouldn't want her turning him into a pig, like Circe did in the Odyssey."

"Oh, ha ha, very funny," Alex said, launching a pillow from the bed at her sister.

"Come on, let's go before the tide comes in and I have to rescue you from the quicksand," Alex said, already out the door before Liz could reciprocate.

Jeff posted the grade from the final term paper and closed his laptop, satisfied. He pushed back the rigid wooden chair he had been occupying for the last several hours, stood up and stretched. Looking at his watch, he saw that it was after 5 PM.

I wonder why I haven't heard from Liz and Alex, he thought, as he headed out of his room and down the stairs to grab a drink at the lobby bar before dinner. He was surprised when he reached the bottom of the stairs to see Simône just entering the lobby.

"Oh, hello," Jeff said, as she approached. "Are you feeling better?"

Looking confused, Simône asked, "What?"

"You know, your headache, is it better?" Jeff asked, looking at her quizzically.

"Oh, yes, thank you. I started feeling better, so I went for a walk. I'm going to head upstairs and get ready for dinner."

As she passed him, he asked, "You haven't seen Liz and Alex, have you?"

"No, why?"

"Well, they were going to do the pilgrims' walk across the sand."

"Don't worry. There are lots of people down there; I'm sure they're fine."

"I'm not worried. It's just that we were…Oh, never mind. We can talk about it later," he said, when he saw that Simône was eager to end the conversation. "See you in about an hour down at dinner."

"Bien," said Simône, already headed up the stairs without a backward glance.

Jeff shook his head, again surprised by her abrupt, almost off putting behavior. "Oh well, I'll be leaving soon-not my problem," he said aloud, as he headed to the bar and ordered a locally brewed hard cider. The friendly bartender, Alan, also suggested a small plate of bread, brie and sausage, and Jeff happily indulged. *Must be the sea air*, he thought. *I'm definitely going to have to get back to my fighting weight before I go home. But I've still got a few weeks.*

He ordered a second glass and pulled out his phone to check his emails. A few minutes later, he was relieved to hear the voices of Liz and Alex coming from the rear of the room.

Turning in his chair, he said, "There you two are. I was about to send out a search party. You've been gone for hours. What happened to our plan to return to the church?"

Alex and Liz looked at each other guiltily before Alex responded, "sorry," as she checked the time on her phone. "I guess we sort of lost track of time, but you won't believe who we ran into. After we made our way over to shore-without falling into any quicksand, I might add-we decided to go over to the shops near the shuttle bus stop."

251

"Nothing special, by the way," Alex said, continuing the tale. "In fact, the locals call it Las Vegas. Apparently it and many of the shops on the island are owned by one businessman, so maybe just some professional jealousy."

"But we found a café with really good coffee and pastries, so we decided to take a break," Liz said. "We were almost finished when in walked..."

"Jamie Crenshaw!" interrupted Alex.

"Who?" asked Jeff, a blank look on his face.

"You remember Jamie Crenshaw. That guy in my class who disappeared a few days after graduation. Everybody thought he was dead or something. He was one of our top runners. Some people even thought he might end up training for the Olympics."

"Anyway, he just disappeared without saying good-bye to anyone. His parents, who live somewhere on the east coast, even filed a missing persons' report. You must have heard about it."

Jeff shrugged as Alex continued, "The police interviewed a bunch of people on campus. I think they initially thought his fraternity was involved somehow, but turned out no one knew anything about what had happened to him. The police finally just gave up. And because he had already graduated, the university didn't get involved. I did hear that his parents came to town about a month later and cleared out his apartment because his lease was up."

"And he just now walked into a coffee shop at Mont St. Michel?" Jeff asked, his interest piqued.

"Yeah, he was in line waiting to order. I first noticed him when he came in, but he looked so different, longer hair, beard, I wasn't sure it was him. When he saw me, he sort of turned away. I think he had recognized me but he was hoping I wouldn't notice him."

"But when he did that, I knew it had to be him. Otherwise, why would he try to hide?"

"So let's guess what Alex did," Liz said, with a smirk.

"Oh, I have a pretty good idea," Jeff said, with a chuckle.

"Yep, she walked right up to him and said, 'Jamie, what a surprise seeing you here.'"

"And did he deny that it was him," Jeff asked.

"For a few seconds, I thought he might, but then his face turned red. He knew he was busted, and he said, 'Hi, Alex. Yes, this is a surprise.' Although it didn't sound like a very happy surprise."

"Then Alex invited him to sit with us. I saw him hesitate for a moment, but you know Alex. She can be pretty persuasive," Liz said.

"Yes, I know," Jeff said, laughing.

"And I think maybe it was a relief to be able to tell someone from home his story. It's like something out of a novel. The guy was a straight A computer and math geek. He graduated Summa Cum Laude. And now he is working on a fishing boat," said Alex.

"Why? Is he in witness protection or something?" Jeff asked.

"He wishes. Apparently he is on the lam from some very 'bad dudes.' His words, not mine. I personally don't know any bad dudes."

"Except for that neo-Nazi scumbag Anthony, may he rot in prison forever!" Liz interjected.

"Definitely," Jeff agreed. "But that's a story for another day; what's Jamie the geek fisherman's story?"

"Well," said Alex, who along with Liz had taken a stool beside Jeff at the bar, and ordered ciders, "it turns out poor Jamie had a rather severe online gambling habit. And he got into really big debt-like to the tune of $500,000-to those 'bad dudes,'" emphasizing the term with air quotes.

"They threatened to kill him if he didn't pay within a week of graduation. They probably were afraid he was going to skip town."

"Good thinking," said Liz.

"Now, Jamie," Alex continued, "who didn't have $500,000, figured the only way he was going to stay in vitae, you know, alive, was to do just that-skip town. And the east coast wasn't an option because the 'bad dudes,' apparently, have associates there too. So he bought the cheapest ticket he could find and flew to Paris. He was there for a couple of years working odd jobs until he fell in love with a local girl. They got married, and he ended up here in her family's business, fishing.

"Kind of a change of circumstances. Private school in San Francisco to fishing boat," said Jeff, shaking his head.

"No kidding," agreed Alex. "But it turns out his story sort of has a happy ending. With his prodigious math skills, he turned around his in-laws' business, which was almost bankrupt. They've gone from one small boat in disrepair, to a thriving enterprise, with several new state of the art boats.

"So all's well that ends well," said Jeff, taking the last gulp of his cider.

"I guess you could say that, but I sensed when he was telling his story that he really misses his parents, the U.S.," Liz said.

"He hasn't told them where he is? That he's alive?" Jeff asked.

"Says he's still afraid it might put them in danger. Now they can honestly say they don't know his location, if anyone comes looking for him," Alex explained.

"But it's been four years!" Jeff said, shaking his head.

"Yeah, that's what I told him, but he made us swear not to tell anyone."

"I think it's really sad," Liz interjected. "But he seems pretty happy. He lives with his wife in a really quaint farmhouse about 5 miles away."

"And you know this because?"

"Oh, he took us by. We met his wife, Anne-Marie. She's awesome. Beautiful, nice and smart. And about six months preggers."

"Yes, really sweet," added Liz.

"No wonder you were gone for over 4 hours. Quite the adventure," said Jeff.

"Yep," Alex said. "Liz, it's almost 6. We better run upstairs and shower before dinner."

"I probably should shower too," Jeff said.

"Yah, probably," Alex agreed, pretending to smell him.

"I'll meet you two down here in about 20 minutes."

"Okie, dokie," said Alex, who threw 40 euros down on the bar.

Before Jeff could object or return the bills, Liz and Alex went running up the stairs leading to their room.

CHAPTER
THIRTY-EIGHT

When they reached the restaurant at about 7 PM, they found Simône already seated at a prime table with views out toward the bay.

"Bon soir," said Simône, seemingly happy to see them. "I hope you all had a good day after we parted."

"Actually, we had an adventure, but we can talk about that later. How are you?" Liz asked, grabbing Simône's hand sympathetically. "I hope you are feeling better."

"Yes, much. I think I just needed some rest and then, some fresh air. I don't know if Jeff told you, but we ran into each other earlier. I had just come back from a walk. But that's enough about me. Jeff mentioned there was something we should talk about," she said, looking at him.

"The thing is, Professeur, we aren't ready to give up on finding the 'Accord.' We did some research this afternoon and concluded that the person who left the message, if he came here, probably wouldn't have been able to get into the abbaye," said Alex,

"Yes, that's right," said Liz, enthusiastically. "It occurred to us that maybe we might consider other potential hiding places that might have some significance to a priest, a monk."

"And did your research turn up any results?"

"Yes," said Alex. "Liz gets the credit. The village church, L'eglise St. Pierre. It's just a short ways up the Grande Rue."

"But unfortunately, there was a mass going on when we got there. So we didn't have a chance to go in," Jeff added.

"Do you know anything about it?" Liz asked Simône.

"Coincidentally, I was there this afternoon. When I woke up from my nap, I had the same thought. So I went into the church. Luckily there was no one else there so I was able to spend about 30 minutes, undisturbed, looking around the sanctuary. There is a beautiful silver statue of St. Michel in a small chapel inset in the wall opposite the main doors. But from what I read, it wasn't placed there until the second half of the 19th century, so it wouldn't have been there at the end of the 18th century when our mysterious message writer might have traveled here."

"Yes, we read the same information. Although I thought perhaps it might've replaced some earlier tribute to the Archangel," Jeff said.

When Simône did not respond, Jeff asked, "So, you didn't see any other place in the church where something might've been hidden?"

"Unfortunately no," said Simône. "Although great minds do apparently think alike, it appears to be another dead end. If the 'Accord' was brought here, it was most likely discovered long ago and destroyed, or it is still hidden here and will remain so for time immemorial." Simône added, seemingly ending the discussion, "I guess we should take a look at the menu. I understand the mussels in garlic wine sauce are divine."

The waitress shortly arrived to take their order. After deciding to share a family order of the mussels served with freshly baked bread, they each chose various seafood entrées for their dinners.

"Simône, why don't you choose some wine for us? You are the expert after all," Jeff said, with a smile.

Simône perused the menu before ordering two bottles, a French Rhone, to be followed by a Bordeaux. Once the waitress left, Simône said, "Voilà, that is done. Now tell me about your adventure."

"Well, I may have oversold it," said Liz sheepishly, "but we did walk across the bay over to the mainland; we wanted to get the full Pilgrim experience while we're here."

"Excellent," Simône said, clapping her hands together. "I am happy you had the opportunity to experience that. No problems I take it-no quicksand mishaps?"

"No," said Alex, joining the conversation. "By the time we went, there was a well-established route. Even the heavy rain storm didn't obliterate it."

"It rained?" Simône asked, surprised. "I had no idea. I must've slept really soundly."

"You've been through a lot in the past few days. You deserve some rest," said Liz.

"I suppose we all do," Simône said, sounding weary.

Jeff looked at her appraisingly, but said nothing.

A moment of awkward silence ensued before Liz said, "But we didn't tell you about the rest of the adventure."

Alex gave Liz a look as if to ask, "What are you doing?" But Liz continued talking.

"While we were over on the mainland, we went into a coffee shop and ran into one of Alex's friends from college."

"Liz?" Alex said, glaring at her sister, but Liz ignored her.

"Really, how extraordinary," Simône said.

"Yes, a weird coincidence that he would be vacationing here at the exact same time that we are here," Liz agree.

"I haven't seen him in years, since graduation, in fact," Alex said.

"So not a close friend?" Simône asked.

"Not really, although we were on the cross country and track teams together. Nice guy. It was good to catch up."

"It truly is a small world we live in," Simône said, before taking a sip of the white wine that the waitress had just poured for her to taste.

"That will be excellent," she said to the waitress, who then poured wine into all of their glasses.

Soon after, the wonderful smells of wine and garlic enveloped them as the waitress placed the large steaming bowl of mussels in the middle of the table.

Simône raised her glass before saying, "So let us toast to the four musketeers. We might not have succeeded in our quest but you must admit it has been quite an adventure."

Liz, Jeff and Alex exchanged glances, but made no comment as Simône continued, "and I hope you will enjoy the tour tonight. It is quite magical."

The four toasted and took a few sips of wine, before donning bibs to begin the messy process of de-shelling and devouring the aromatic sea creatures.

"Once again, I think we've ordered too much food. I'm stuffed," said Alex, wiping her hands and mouth with one of the fresh napkins that had just been replaced by the very efficient waitress.

"Speak for yourself," Jeff said. "I'm ready for my lobster, with lots of butter."

"I may need a to-go box for my Sole Meunière," Liz said.

When their entrées appeared, the three women took only a few bites, but Jeff, true to his word, dug into his lobster with glee. When he finished, he pushed his chair back slightly from the table and said, "Now, I'm finished."

Everyone laughed, which helped to dispel the awkward feeling that had permeated the meal to that point.

"Dessert anyone? Cafés?" asked the waitress, who had arrived to clear the dishes.

"No, no way, that would be a no," said the three Americans, while Simône ordered an espresso, thinking of her night ahead.

A few minutes later, having paid, they headed up to the abbaye, arriving just as the main gate at the top of the Grand Dagré was being raised.

"Perfect timing," said Simône. "It's always good to get ahead of the crowd, even if only limited tickets are sold to this nighttime event."

At the top of the stairs they passed through security before following the lighted route up to the Western Terrace. Beautiful theatrical lighting in a rainbow of reds, oranges and blues lit up the face of the church. Inside a cellist, a violinist and a pianist played Bach, which echoed to the church rafters that also were expertly lit.

"Oh, it's fantastic!" exclaimed Liz.

"Yes, it truly is. And as you wander through the various chapels and rooms, there will be more lighting, as well as individual musicians playing at various points. It really is the best way to appreciate the beauty of the abbaye, particularly because as I said, they only sell a few tickets to this event so it doesn't get nearly as crowded as during the day."

"We'll, thank you for arranging this for us," said Alex. "You were right. It is spectacular at night."

After listening to the music for a few more minutes, they left by a side door and went out to the cloister, which also had been lit, and where a single musician played a haunting Medieval tune on an instrument that looked like a cross between a harp and a guitar.

"Oh look, she's playing a psaltery," said Liz.

"A what?" asked Jeff, amused.

"A psaltery, like a zither. I learned about them in a medieval history class I took. Although the ones from the Middle Ages didn't include bows. I think they just plucked them like a harp," explained Liz.

"You really are a fount of esoteric knowledge," Jeff said, teasing her.

"I do my best," said Liz, with a smirk.

"So where do we go from here?" asked Alex.

"I believe from here you go to the refectory, which is where the monks ate their communal meals. If you remember, it's the one with the lovely tile floor and the rows of arched windows on each side. It will be obvious because certain rooms are roped off and not open for the nighttime tour," said Simône, before glancing nervously at her watch.

"Aren't you going with us, Professeur?" asked Jeff, who had noticed her checking the time.

"You know, my headache has returned. I have been on the nighttime tour a number of times. If you don't mind, I think I'll just leave you to finish without me."

"Do you want someone to go back with you, Simône?" asked Liz, concerned.

"No, I'll be fine. And I don't want to spoil your evening. So I think I will just say good night and plan to see you in the morning for breakfast. D'accord?" said Simône.

"Well, if you're sure, Professeur. Hopefully a good night's sleep will make you feel better," said Jeff.

"No doubt. Thank you and good night," Simône said, before turning to head back through the church toward the exit from the abbaye.

CHAPTER THIRTY-NINE

Once she was out of sight, Alex turned to Liz and Jeff and said, "I'm not buying it. Did you see her looking at her watch? She's going somewhere to meet up with some-one."

"I think you may be right. I've never known her to have a headache the whole time I been working for her, and now two in one day," said Jeff.

"So let's go," Alex said, with a sense of urgency.

"Go where?" asked Liz.

"I think we should follow her and find out what she's up to," said Alex.

Jeff grimaced for a moment before saying, "Okay, but there goes my reference. We better hurry before we lose her but let's not get too close. I don't want to spook her," said Jeff.

"I agree," said Alex.

When they reached the top of the Grand Dagré, they saw Simône at the bottom of the stairs. She stopped to recheck her watch, before walking quickly down the Grande Rue.

In the fading light, deep shadows covered most of the stairway. Alex had already started to run down the stairs when Liz called out, "Slow down, you're going to fall and kill yourself."

Alex stopped for a moment to let them catch up. When they reached her, Liz and Jeff both turned on the flashlights on their phones.

"Good idea. I don't have mine. It was out of juice, so I left it charging in the room," said Alex.

262

"I was wondering why you were stumbling around in the dark," said Jeff.

As they reached the bottom of the stairs and turned right down the Grand Rue, they spotted Simône, who had stopped at the stairs leading up to the churchyard of St. Pierre. She appeared to be hesitating, as if she was unsure about continuing.

The three stepped into a doorway to avoid detection as Simône turned to look back up the street.

"Do you think she saw us?" asked Liz.

"I don't think so. She looks like she's nervous; it seems like she's looking around to make sure no one is following her," said Alex.

"Look, she's going into the church," said Jeff, nudging Alex.

After the door had closed behind her, the three went running down the street, no longer feeling any need to be sly in their movements.

Upon reaching the stairs leading up to the churchyard, Alex asked, "So who do we think she is meeting in there?"

"I suppose it could be as someone as innocent as the village priest. Maybe he was busy when she was there and she made arrangements to meet him this evening to talk to him about the church," said Jeff, unconvincingly.

"No, she said there was no one there when she was looking around," said Liz.

"And if she is just doing some research, why would she lie and tell us she wasn't feeling well, and going back to her room?" asked Alex, skeptically.

"You're right. How she is acting makes no sense," agreed Jeff.

Without further discussion, the three clambered up the stairs and scurried over to a shadowed area at the corner of the church.

"So now what do we do? We can't just walk right into the sanctuary," said Alex.

"You're right," said Liz. "And I'm not really in favor of going in there without knowing what's happening inside."

"When we were doing our research earlier today, I found a map of all the buildings on the island. There is a back door to the church that opens onto an alley of sorts. It's one level up from this courtyard. If we go back down to the street, I saw some stairs that we passed; I think they might lead us up to the upper-level," Jeff said.

Once they reached the alleyway, they walked quietly back toward the church. "I think this is the right door," Jeff whispered.

Jeff put his hand on the handle, and instinctively held his breath as he slowly turned it to the right. As he did so he could feel the lock disengaging. Pushing ever so lightly, he moved the door open about an inch, breathing a sigh of relief when no creak sang from the hinges, then leaned forward to look through the small crack he had created.

Alex and Liz, who were standing behind him stood up on tiptoes to try to see over his shoulders.

"What do you see?" Alex whispered in his ear.

"All I can see is the back of the church. But I hear people talking. Be quiet so I can listen," Jeff said, his voice barely audible.

"Okay, sorry," whispered Alex.

"Shh," said Jeff. "I can hear Simône, but they are speaking French and I need to concentrate."

Alex was about to say something else but Liz silenced her with a poke in the ribs.

"Nice, add insult to injury by keeping your blackmail victim waiting for you," said Simône, angrily.

A male speaking French, in an undefined accent said, "My apologies, Professeur. Do you have someplace more important to be?"

When she did not respond, the man said, "I thought not. I, on the other hand, was in a very important meeting with my colleague, actually someone you know quite well."

264

"Who?" Simône asked, incredulously.

"That's not important at the moment. What is important is that your little discovery-or perhaps not so little-" he said upon seeing the look on her face, "has led me, us, my compatriots and I to an even greater discovery."

"What are you talking about? Had a little too much communion wine this evening?" she asked, sarcastically.

He glared at her with narrowed eyes. "Let me tell you a very interesting tale about the person who left the message that you and your 'helpers' found at the abbaye in Belgium," his voice betraying the disdain he held for the three Americans.

"Were it not for the diary, and then the rubbing..." he mused, "the secret may have stayed hidden forever. It should have," he added, as if to himself. "Oh, that reminds me, before we continue, let me see that you brought the diary and the rubbing."

"Merde!" Jeff, Alex and Liz heard Simône say, before the conversation was muffled by Simône rummaging around in her purse.

"Mon Dieu, woman, what all do you have in there? Stop stalling, give them to me if you want your secret to remain a secret."

Simône hesitated for a few seconds more, her face contorted with emotion, before she pulled her gun from her purse and aimed it at the Monseigneur.

"Well, you are full of surprises, Professeur," said the man, sounding more amused than afraid.

"Do you even know how to use that thing?" he asked, laughing.

"Oh, she knows, don't you, Simi?" asked a second male voice, as a man who had been standing in the small storeroom to the left of the front doors stepped into the light beside the Monseigneur.

"What are you doing here, Philippe?" Simône asked, her voice shaking with anger.

"You must forgive me again," said the Monseigneur. "How impolite. Let me introduce my colleague. But, of course, you already know him as Mr. Maçon, n'est pas?"

"Did she just pull out her gun?" Alex whispered to Jeff.

"I think so," Jeff whispered back.

"If she has her gun, then we should go in," Liz said. "You know, for back up."

Simône, who was staring with hatred at the second man, said, venom in her voice, "So that's how they found out about my affair, my research, you bastard! But you're not even religious," she added, eyes narrowed, a question in her voice.

"Turns out you don't know me very well at all," said Philippe, sounding almost sad. "I wore this pendant the entire time we were together," he said, pulling out a chain, with a pendant of a dragon being stabbed by a cross-shaped sword, from inside the collar of his shirt.

"That? I just thought it was a family heirloom or something," Simône said dismissively.

"And you never even bothered to ask!" Philippe yelled, deep anger in his voice.

"So, what, this is payback because I didn't ask about your necklace?"

"Well that, and your whoring around with that student. Should I continue?" he asked, as Simône shook her head no. "But I warned you to stop your search; told you that I couldn't protect you."

"And so here we are," said the Monseigneur with a smarmy smile.

The two men stood sneering at her, as Simône, her hands shaking, pointed the gun toward her ex-husband.

"Oh, come on, Simi; we both know you aren't going to shoot me, as much as you might like to," he said, mockingly.

"Alex, Jeff, we have to get in there, before she does something stupid!" Liz said frantically.

"I..." Jeff began to say, but Alex had already pushed past him, and stepped into the room. Jeff and Liz,

266

seeing no other option, followed her inside. Simône, momentarily distracted, turned to look for the source of the noise behind her. Seizing the opportunity, Philippe lunged forward toward Simône as Alex yelled, "Simône, watch out!" Simône jerked her head back around just as Philippe grabbed for the weapon, but in the ensuing struggle, the gun went off.

"Mon Dieu," screamed the Monseigneur, the sadistic tone completely gone from his voice, as Philippe gasped, "Simi," before clutching at the circle of crimson spreading across his shirt, while his legs crumpled underneath him.

"I didn't mean…" cried out Simône, dropping to her knees beside him. She looked desperately around at Alex, Liz and Jeff who stood in shock viewing the bloody scene, like something out of a movie. The Monseigneur, bravado faded, who had scurried backwards as Philippe lunged forward, now stood silently, looking like a slowly deflating balloon.

After a few seconds, the reality of what had happened sank in, and Jeff finally reacted. "Simône, put pressure on his chest. Liz, call 112, the emergency line. Alex, go out onto the street and see if you can find someone to help. Try our hotel."

"Yes, of course," said Alex and Liz, who both looked as though Jeff's words had been cold water thrown in their faces. But as Alex headed toward the front door and Liz pulled her phone from her purse, they heard repeated loud shouts of "Allahu Akbar" and "Go!" as four gun-wielding men, dressed all in black, burst through the front and back doors of the sanctuary.

One of the four then yelled in English buried in a strong accent, "Put up your hands, now!" The Monseigneur seemed to shrivel even further in size as he tried to dissolve into a corner at the back of the altar. Simône, kneeling in a pool of blood, started to comply but then stubbornly returned to compressing the wound in the chest of the now unconscious Philippe. Liz quickly dropped her phone into her purse before raising her hands. Alex, who was directly in front of the two gunmen who had come through the front door, backed up, hands raised, until she bumped into the corner of one of the wooden pews.

While the two gunmen who had entered from the back of the church remained silently on guard, the same man who had shouted before, said loudly, "Sit down on the benches. Keep your hands up. No talking."

Before anyone had an opportunity to comply, he leaned down and picked up the gun still lying beside Simône, before grabbing her by her hair, hauling her away from Philippe, and throwing her roughly onto the front pew.

Simône screamed, "No, if I stop, he'll die!"

"He's already dead," said the man, as he returned to the inert figure of Philippe. Without hesitation, he pointed her gun at Philippe's head and pulled the trigger. "See?"

Simône screamed in horror, before slumping over on the floor, her body wracked with sobs.

Liz made a move to go to her, but stopped when the teenaged gunman at the front of the church pointed his gun at her, and said, "No, you stay, there," pointing at the far end of the bench.

Alex, who now was seated next to Jeff, whispered, "It's the same guy-the one from Bouillon," she added, almost imperceptibly using her chin to gesture to the gunman giving most of the orders.

The second gunman, seeing the motion out of the corner of his eye, stepped toward her and hit Alex in the head with the butt of his gun. "Next time I'll use the other end."

"Hijo de puta!" Liz screamed at him. The gunman, who clearly did not understand Spanish, just laughed.

Jeff started to stand up to retaliate but Alex, slightly dazed but conscious, said, "No!" forcefully, as she pulled him back down. "You've already been shot once this week."

"Listen to your girlfriend, foolish little American boy, if you don't want to end up like that guy," said the lead gunman, pointing at the lifeless body of Philippe. Simône moaned in anguish at the brutal comment, but said nothing.

The Monseigneur also made a slight sound, prompting the leader to swing around to face him. "Oh, did you think we had forgotten about you? Monseigneur, is it? You don't seem so important now, hiding in the corner like a scared rat."

"Come out, Monseigneur Rat," he said, motioning with his gun at the frightened man. "Now that we have your audience seated, it is time for your performance. I believe I heard you say that you had a very interesting tale to tell us about this blasphemous document that you all have been seeking."

The Monseigneur, wearing a look of sheer terror, shook his head in denial.

"Oh come now, don't be shy. You were so proud before-tell us your story. And, if you lie, I assure you I will know it. I have a knack for detecting liars," he said coldly.

"Go stand right there beside the altar. It seems appropriate, non? You are a priest, correct? Or so you say," he added with a cruel laugh.

The Monseigneur stepped uncertainly from his corner before stopping at the altar, on which he leaned for support.

"After we learned about Professeur Bertrand's finds-the diary and the message at the abbaye..." he said, his voice shaking with fear.

"Now, Monseigneur, I know you can do better than that. Speak up, but make it quick. We do not have all night."

"And..." said the Monseigneur, starting again. "And when we learned that she believed the 'Knights' Call' as she refers to it, might have been brought here, I did some research," he said, his voice growing stronger, as if mesmerized by his own tale.

"Yes," said the gunman encouragingly, even shooting a smile at the Monseigneur.

"I, well, I did some research in the church archives. During the revolution, there were no priests here at the church for several years, but after most of the clergy had been released from the prison," he said, nodding up in the direction of the abbaye, "a young priest named Father Pierre took over the duties here at St. Pierre's. He served here for many years. Was beloved by the parishioners here on the Mont."

"So what?" asked their captor, growing impatient.

"Well, it turns out that Father Pierre was a prolific diarist. In fact, I found 40 years of diaries he had written from 1795 to 1838, most likely the year he died. I guess he was quite a young man, in his 20's, when he first came to Mont St. Michel as a prisoner in 1794."

"Again, perhaps this may be interesting to the historians in our audience, but what does it have to do with an 'Accord?'" asked the lead gunman, pointedly.

"It is believed that a document may have been found by the Templars in their excavation of the Temple Mount in Jerusalem in the 12th century. The document was an 'Accord,' which, like it or not, had been entered into in approximately 850 A.D. by the Grand Imam of Jerusalem, the head Rabbi of the Jewish community and the Eastern Orthodox Patriarch, representing the Holy See."

"We think there were at least three copies signed, one for the head of each of the three religions. No one knows what happened to two of the copies or whether they were ever made public, but we believe the third copy, the Muslims' copy, was kept in a secret vault below the Temple Mount, and when the Templars took control in the 1100's and began excavating, they discovered it. Some have even hypothesized that it was this discovery, and not the Templars' immense wealth, that gave them such power over not only the Papacy, but also many European

270

monarchs. Such an explanation makes sense because once the Crusades began, no Pope nor any of Europe's kings would have benefited from the revelation of a document which purported to proclaim a truce between the three religions."

"There have been rumors for centuries about such an 'Accord,' even whispers that a second copy-the Christian copy-was hidden somewhere in the Vatican library, but I've searched for it for years, and I never found any evidence to support that rumor," he said shaking his head.

Their captor, said, "We care nothing about your failures. Again, what does this have to do with your village priest?"

"That's just it-everything! In his diary for the year 1796, he wrote about a young monk, a Brother Bernard."

At the mention of the monk, Liz and Alex looked at each other wide-eyed.

"Apparently, the monk had lived in exile in England for three years after his Abbott had been taken and imprisoned at Mont St. Michel in 1791, and his abbaye, the Abbaye D'Orval, in what is now southern Belgium, had been put to the torch by the French Revolutionary guard in 1793."

Jeff, Liz, Alex and even Simône, who had stopped crying, were now listening raptly to the Monseigneur's tale.

"He arrived here at Mont St. Michel in July 1796, and with him, he carried what he referred to as 'a treasure' that he had been instructed by his Abbott to guard with his life."

"Turns out that someone representing no less than the ill-fated queen, Marie Antoinette, had been instructed to hide this 'treasure' at the Abbaye D'Orval, in anticipation of the royal family's flight from the Jacobins. This servant of the queen, according to young Brother Bernard, came and went just hours before the Revolutionary guard arrived to drag away the poor Abbott."

"That might have been the end of Brother Bernard's story, at least as told to Father Pierre, but coincidentally, the priest while imprisoned, had met the Abbott in question. Father Pierre revealed to Brother Bernard that he had taken the old man's last confession before the Abbott's death."

"So what did the Abbott tell the priest? Get on with the story," demanded the gunman impatiently.

"I will tell you, but you must guarantee my safety. And hers," he said, pointing at Simône. "Only she, I think, can solve the riddle."

"What riddle?" screamed the man, cursing in Arabic as he looked around at his three companions.

"It was what the Abbott told the priest as he was dying. And I quote, 'if he comes, tell him to take it to the place where the heathens plundered, the penitent prayed in poverty, and the falcons still soar at the end of the world."

"So where is this place?"

"That is the mystery, and why you need her. Us," he added quickly.

"Neither the priest nor the monk knew what or where the Abbott was talking about. But I'm sure she knows, or can figure it out, with the help of her brain trust," the Monseigneur said sarcastically, pointing at Jeff, Liz, and Alex, who all wore looks of surprise.

The lead gunman muttered something again in Arabic before walking over and putting his gun barrel against Simône 's temple.

"You remember me, don't you, Professeur? I saw it in your eyes when we first came in. You were supposed to be dead several days ago, but perhaps Allah, in his infinite wisdom, had a reason for keeping you alive. You are going to help me find this 'Accord,' so that I can destroy it, or you can die on the floor beside your dead dog of a husband."

"But I don't know what it means," Simône said, choking back a sob as her eyes strayed to the corpse of Philippe.

272

"Well, that is unfortunate for all of you," he said, cocking the trigger of his gun.

"No, wait," begged Liz. "We can figure this out together," she said, looking first at Simône, and then at Alex and Jeff. "Right?"

"Sir, what is your name?" Liz asked, timidly.

"You don't need to know my name," the man said, menacingly.

"But I just want to know how to address you properly," Liz said.

"Then just call me 'Jesus,' like your savior," said the man with a chuckle, "because making me happy is the only way you're going to survive."

The other gunmen laughed obsequiously at his joke, before Liz asked seriously, "Okay, Mr. 'Jesus,' then may I ask the Monseigneur a question?"

"Fine, one question."

"Monseigneur, did Father Pierre write about what happened later to Brother Bernard?"

"Yes, actually, he did. In his diary for the year 1837, he included a letter he had received from the monk. I guess over the years they had engaged in correspondence from time to time."

"I made a copy of it; it read as follows," said the Monseigneur, looking at a piece of paper he had pulled from his pocket. "Dear Father Pierre, like you, I am no longer a young man, but I have not given up on my quest. I have always held close to my heart what you said that day that I met you, that the contrition for my act of unspeakable evil was to fulfill the task that Abbott Godard gave to me. Because our order continues to be suppressed, I'm setting out on a final journey to take 'the treasure' to where the falcons soar at the end of the world," guided once again by the archangel. Keep me in your prayers. And it was signed Brother Bernard."

"In earlier diaries, Father Pierre had recorded some of the Brother's story. It turns out that while Brother Bernard was here at Mont St. Michel, he met up with another group of monks who had also been rendered homeless by the revolution. He ended up traveling with them back to England where they joined a monastery in Dorset, England, Lulworth, I think. What's interesting is that then a group of French monks from that abbey, who had been expelled from France, during the revolution of 1830, decided to relocate to Mount Mellaray Abbey, a Cistercian Trappist monastery founded in 1832, and Brother Bernard went with them."

"Cistercian, just like the monks at Abbaye D'Orval," Simône said.

"Where is Mellaray?" Simône asked excited, momentarily forgetting her grief.

"In his letter to Father Pierre, Brother Bernard said that the monastery was located on Knockmealdown Mountain, in Cappoquin, in the diocese of Waterford."

"Waterford, why that's not that far from..." Alex said, before stopping, realizing she'd spoken aloud.

"Not far from where?" asked 'Jesus,' turning to point his gun at her.

"Oh, it's nothing, I was just thinking about a trip I took once to Dublin, that's all."

"Remember, I told you," he said, waving his gun at Alex, "I am a human lie detector, and you, Blondie, are lying."

"Adad," he said, looking at one of the two men guarding the back door, "look it up on your phone."

As instructed, the young man pulled out his cell phone to Google the abbey in question. After about a minute of total silence, he said, "It is in southern Ireland, but nowhere near Dublin, lying bitch!"

'Jesus,' his face turning red with fury, strode over and slapped Alex, before yelling, "Tell me the truth, or you all die now!"

The fourth gunman, who had remained silent during the exchange, said, "Brother, think for a moment. If you kill the Americans, it means more trouble. Shoot the Professeur-we've already got one dead Frenchman, what's another?"

"You're right," said 'Jesus,' regaining his composure.

He placed the barrel of his gun directly between Simône's eyes as the second younger gunman stood guard over Jeff, Alex and Liz. "Now tell me where you think we should be looking in Ireland, you stupid American girl, Alex, right-or I will splatter Professeur Bertrand's brains all over this church."

He had counted to two, when Alex screamed, "Skellig Michael."

"What?"

"Skellig Michael; it's an island off southwestern Ireland, not that far from Waterford."

"Why there?" 'Jesus' asked, his gun barrel still crammed against Simône's forehead, as he turned toward Alex to appraise the truthfulness of what she was saying.

"Because the description fits, and more importantly, because of St. Michael," Alex answered, speaking to him as though he was a small child.

The man looked at her blankly, before she said with exasperation, almost yelling, "Saint Michael? Follow the arrow of Michael? Mont St. Michel? Skellig Michael? See any common denominator there, 'Jesus?'" she asked sarcastically, her anger fueling her courage.

Ignoring the sarcasm, he said, "Thank you. That wasn't so hard, was it?" he asked, dropping his gun hand down to his side.

"Okay, so now we have a plan," the man said with glee.

"What?" Jeff asked.

"We are going to take a little trip to this Skellig Michael, and you," he said, pointing at Jeff, "and you," waving his gun at Simône, "are going to be our guides."

"There's no way I'm leaving Alex and Liz," Jeff said angrily.

"Oh, don't worry, they'll be fine; you heard my brother: we don't want any more trouble," he said.

Then he turned toward the Monseigneur and said, "Thanks for your help, too," before shooting the man in the head. The Frenchman slumped over the altar, as blood spilled to the stone floor.

"You're a monster!" Alex screamed, which just caused 'Jesus' to smile more broadly. He then shouted directions in Arabic to his companions.

"And now we really have to go; that shot, unlike the one from your pea shooter, Professeur, may have woken up the entire village. Get up, let's go," waving his gun at the four remaining hostages.

"Here," he said, handing Simône's gun to the second gunman. "Wipe off her prints and put it in the Monseigneur's hand. And this one," he said, wiping his prints from his own gun, "we will give to Philippe here. That ought to confuse the gendarmes for a while," he added, as he placed the gun in the dead man's cold hand.

"We can't just leave Philippe here, like this," Simône said, again crying. Liz went over to comfort her as Alex and Jeff stepped toward the body, intending to at least lay him on one of the benches.

"No!" shouted 'Jesus.' "You are messing up my perfect crime scene. "Let's go," he said, gesturing with his gun toward the door leading out into the courtyard.

Three minutes later, walking quickly and unimpeded down the Grand Rue, the group of eight, Alex, Liz, Jeff and Simône, and their four captors, passed through the unguarded gate to the Mont.

'Jesus' said something else in Arabic to the two men guarding Alex and Liz, before he directed Jeff and Simône to climb into the black windowless panel van parked in the shadows at the island end of the causeway.

"I'm not going without them," Jeff said, refusing to get in.

'Jesus,' his voice icy, said, "You will, or I will shoot all four of you right here and drive away before anyone finds you. Your choice."

Alex said, pleading, "Jeff, we'll be okay. They just want to keep us for... insurance until they get the 'Accord.' You heard them, they don't want trouble with us."

"If you hurt them," Jeff said threateningly, before 'Jesus' interrupted him, "Okay, Superman, get in the back of the van," waving his gun again. Finally, Simône and Jeff complied. After the doors were shut, 'Jesus' roughly placed duct tape over Liz and Alex's mouths.

"Give them some knockout shots, like you used on those girls last night in Paris. That will keep them quiet for a while."

Alex and Liz began to struggle, as 'Jesus' climbed into the front of the van beside the other gunman and the van sped away. As the taillights of the van receded across the causeway, they both felt pricks in their necks, before everything around them faded to black.

"What do we do with them now? Just leave them here?" asked the younger of the two remaining gunmen.

"No, throw them into the back of your truck. Luckily they are both skinny bitches-just like those girls last night."

"Should we have some fun with them first?" asked Adad.

"No, better not," said the older of the two, who seemed to be in charge. "We can't do anything obvious to hurt them. It needs to look like an accident."

"So what then?"

"We'll throw them over into the bay about halfway across the bridge. They'll either drown-the tide's coming in-or get sucked into some of the quicksand. That's if they don't break their necks from the fall. Even if they do make it to shore, hours from now, we'll be long gone. It's 11 now, there's nobody on the roads, so we'll be back in Paris by 3:30."

The men, satisfied with their plan, pulled the tape from the girls' mouths, and loaded the unconscious Alex and Liz into the back of the truck before lighting cigarettes and climbing into the cab.

After stopping to throw the limp bodies of Alex and Liz feet first over the railing, the men waited to hear two splashes, then tossed in their purses as well, before climbing back into the truck, and driving away.

CHAPTER
FORTY

Alex's first sensation, as she came to, was of soaking in a tub of ice water, like she used to do after track meets. And then the throbbing in her head began, like the rhythmic beat of someone incessantly pounding a nail, or on a drum. Opening her eyes, her only view in the dim light was of some type of structure above her. As her senses began to awaken, she realized that she was shaking violently, and then she remembered, the men, the church, Simône, Philippe. "Oh my God!" she screamed.

Moving her arms and legs around, she realized she was floating in only a few feet of water, which had been gently rocking her in the ebb and flow of the tide. Putting her feet down to stand, she experienced an immediate sensation of sinking. It took her still fogged mind a moment to put a name to the sensation. "Quicksand," she finally said aloud, as she began flailing in the water while struggling to pull her feet free. After a momentary panic, she took a deep breath as she remembered that struggling was the wrong reaction.

I've got to swim out of it, Alex thought, as she lay back in the water and began to move her arms. For several seconds, she stayed in place, her feet held fast. But finally, after a few minutes of effort, the sand's grip on her lower limbs loosened and she began to move backwards out into open water, no longer under the metal canopy that she now realized was the underside of the causeway leading to Mont St. Michel.

Fully clear of the bridge, Alex stopped swimming and relaxed into a float, willing her breathing to slow and her heart rate to drop to a normal range. Looking at her watch, which thankfully was not only waterproof, but also had a luminescent dial, she saw that it was about 2 o'clock in the morning.

"Jesus," she said out loud, before realizing, in horror, the name she had just uttered. But saying the name seemed to act like smelling salts, fully alerting her to her situation. Straining to turn her still-pounding head to the right, and then to the left, she saw that she was much closer to shore than to the Mont. Using her hands as paddles, she pointed her body headfirst toward shore before beginning a rhythmic backstroke. As she swam, she repeatedly yelled out, "Liz, Elizabeth, D, where are you? Answer me!"

The words became a mantra, a meditation, which helped her to avoid thinking of the one thing she feared the most, that perhaps her sister, her twin, her other half, was not answering because she was so severely injured that she could not speak, or worse, that she was dead, drowned, sucked into the treacherous quicksand that they had joked about just 12 hours before.

When she finally reached the shore, she steered herself to the area of sand where she and Liz had exited the bay the previous afternoon, confident that it provided solid footing. Pulling herself up to a sitting position at the edge of the water, Alex took deep gulping breaths, both to clear her head, and to restore the oxygen her body craved because of her exertion, and unceasing screaming.

Looking back toward the Mont, she was surprised to see that there were a few lights twinkling amongst the dark outlines of the abbaye and surrounding buildings. *Burning the midnight oil*, she mused, irrelevantly, before looking again at her watch. Realizing that it taken her only 10 minutes to swim to shore, Alex felt heartened, thinking that Liz, despite not being as strong a swimmer as Alex, could have done the same thing, and was already ashore looking for help.

As she stood up, pain shot throughout her body, but she was relieved to discover that everything seemed to be in working order and unbroken. She walked back and forth along the shoreline for about 10 minutes, constantly calling for her sister, before deciding that alone, without a light, her chances of finding her were minimal. *I've got to get help*, she finally resolved. Grateful that Liz, ever practical, had convinced her to wear tennis shoes for their visit to the abbaye the night before, she began running down the road that would pass the parking lot where their now useless car was parked.

With each pounding step, the extent of the abuse she had suffered from being thrown off the bridge became mercilessly clear; every muscle, every nerve ached and burned, but she pushed on relentlessly. 30 minutes later, exhausted, desperate, she began beating on the farmhouse door of her long-lost teammate. What Alex had failed to notice as she sprinted the last 50 feet toward the house was that not only the porch light, but also several interior lights were already illuminated, at 3 o'clock in the morning.

"Okay, I'm coming," a male voice said, as the door swung open to reveal a grinning Jamie. "Boy, you King girls just won't leave a guy alone, will you?" he asked, opening the screen door to allow her to enter.

Realizing what he had said, Alex asked, "What?" before her eyes focused on the blanketed figure of a person seated in the middle of the room, her back to the door.

"Liz?" Alex cried, tears streaming down her face as she rushed to wrap herself around the huddled figure of her sister.

"I thought I lost you," Alex said, still crying as she stepped back a few feet to look at her still seated sister.

"I'm not that easy to get rid of," Liz said, as the sisters inspected each other. Alex saw what she had missed in her initial rush to embrace her sister. Blood oozed from a significant gash in Liz's forehead, and her left arm was raised to shoulder height in a seemingly locked position, the victim of either a break or shoulder dislocation.

"Is it broken?" Alex asked, concern in her voice.

"Well, we were just about to determine that when you arrived," said Anne-Marie, standing near the kitchen door in a nightgown, hair disheveled. Alex looked doubtfully at the pregnant woman, who, seeing her concern, said, "Don't worry. I was a paramedic in Paris, before I met this scoundrel, and he had his way with me," she said reassuringly, with a loving glance at her husband.

After gently unwrapping the blanket to inspect Liz's shoulder, Anne-Marie said, "The good news is that I don't think your clavicle or your arm is broken, Liz. I think it is dislocation; you must've landed on it when you fell."

"Try thrown!" Alex interjected, angrily.

"Yes, those bastards did a number on you two," Jamie said, with disgust. "I imagine though, that it was being drugged that saved you both. Like the drunk that is so loosey-goosey that he walks away from his totaled car."

"You're probably right," agreed Alex. "So what is the bad news you referred to Anne-Marie?" she asked, with another look at her twin.

"The bad news," said Ann-Marie," is that if I don't reduce the dislocation to put it back into place, Liz will continue to be in horrible pain, and any further movement of her arm could do more damage to the surrounding ligaments and muscles. So what do you think?" she asked, kneeling down with some difficulty to look at Liz face-to-face.

"Just do it," Liz said, grimacing with pain.

"Okay," Anne-Marie said as she slowly stood up. "Jamie, please get that silicone cooking spoon we have."

Jamie reached into a drawer behind him, and like a well trained OR nurse, deposited the spoon in his wife's outstretched hand.

"Now, Liz, you can bite on this, or you can just scream. It doesn't matter to me, but sometimes biting on something helps you focus your attention away from the pain."

"Okay," Liz said, before placing the handle of the spoon between her teeth.

Anne-Marie, who had positioned herself behind and to the left of Liz's chair, said, "Liz, look over at Alex," who was standing holding her sister's right hand.

"Now I'm going to…" Before completing the sentence, Anne-Marie grabbed Liz's forearm and upper arm, and with her two hands, forcefully yanked them backwards, causing the head of the humerus to slip back into place. As Anne-Marie completed the sentence, "pull on your arm," Liz let out a muffled scream between her clenched teeth.

With tears flowing freely, Liz pulled the spoon from her mouth, and began to laugh. Realizing that her sister was okay, Alex joined in.

"You are one sneaky pregnant lady," Liz said, putting her right hand gently on her left shoulder.

"How does it feel?" asked Anne-Marie, who had circled around to stand before her patient.

"It still hurts, but nothing like before," Liz said. "Thank you so much!"

"Glad to help," Anne-Marie said modestly.

"Yeah, she likes to cause pain, whenever she can," Jamie said, beaming broadly at his wife. In response, Anne-Marie picked up a kitchen towel and snapped him on the butt.

"Ouch, see I told you," he said with a grin.

"Bien, take these," Anne-Marie said, picking up two Tylenol, two Advil, and a glass of water from the table and handing them to Liz. "I don't want to give you anything stronger since we don't know what those animals used to drug you."

Without any further prompting, Liz immediately swallowed the pills.

"So now let's take a look at that gash," said Anne-Marie, with the caring but efficient bedside manner of someone used to treating much more serious injuries. After examining the wound under a flashlight, she said,

283

"Thankfully, it's not actually very deep. Head wounds just bleed a lot because of all of the small capillaries. I don't think you need stitches, and if we clean it up well and close it with some butterfly steri-strips, it should heal in a few days with no scars, only a bad memory."

"Jamie, can you go get…" She said, turning to look for her husband, who-the former running champ he was-had already left the room and returned in lightning speed, carrying a very impressive first aid kit.

"That looks more like a deep-sea fishing tackle box," Alex said, impressed.

"That's my wife, always prepared," Jamie said, with pride. "She was a Girl Guide, like Girl Scouts, but better according to her."

"Yeah, whatever," Anne-Marie said, perfecting a Valley girl drawl, as she worked on Liz's head wound.

"Voilà! That should do it," she said, admiring her handiwork. "If you have a scar after that, you can sue me," Anne-Marie said, laughing.

"Oh no, I would never…" Liz exclaimed, before getting the joke and joining in the laughter.

"Sorry, I'm not usually so slow, but you know, head wound, dislocated shoulder, drugging," she said, pointing to her various body parts.

"You have been the perfect patient, ma cherie," Anne-Marie said, giving Liz a gentle kiss on the cheek.

"So, what can we fix on you?" Jamie asked, turning to Alex.

"Nothing, thankfully, but I will take some of those," she said, shaking two Advil into her hand and swallowing them down with a gulp of Liz's water.

"Pardonnez-moi," Anne-Marie said mortified, hitting her forehead with the palm of her hand. "You must be thirsting to death," she said to Alex. "We were so concerned with your sister when she arrived. Here sit down," she insisted, steering Alex to another chair.

"Now," said Jamie, plopping down on a third chair at the kitchen table, "tell me what happened."

284

"Yes, Liz had just begun to tell us when you arrived," said Anne-Marie.

"I bet you made good time getting here, though, King, didn't you?" Jamie asked. "Broke some kind of land record," he said teasing, giving her a wink.

Within five minutes, Liz and Alex, excitedly talking over each other, and completing each other's sentences, had described the horrible scene that had unfolded at the church before Jeff and Simône had been spirited away, and they had been drugged.

"And I guess the tide coming in washed me up onto the shore," Liz said, "because that was where I woke up. Good thing because I never could have swum to shore with my dislocated shoulder. I called and called to Alex but she didn't answer, so I came here," she said, concluding her part of the tale.

"Thank God you did. And now," Alex said, speaking rapidly, "I have to get in touch with Natalia-you know, remember, the UCLA runner, Israeli." Jamie, recognizing the name, nodded as Alex continued. "Turns out she's a Mossad agent."

"What?" Jamie exclaimed, before shrugging. "I guess everybody has a story," he said.

"You have to hear ours one day," Alex said with a wry look toward her twin. "But right now, I've got to call Natalia, and arrange for a plane from Saint-Malo to... I don't know, someplace in Ireland, near Skellig Michael, and maybe a helicopter, or a boat."

Jamie and Anne-Marie stared at Alex, who seeing their looks of confusion, realized she should explain. "Again, a long story for another day, but it turns out we," pointing to herself and Liz, "are filthy, and I mean with a capital F, rich. So, do you mind if I borrow your phone?"

"Why don't you call the police?" Anne-Marie asked.

"What would they do about Simône and Jeff? They are probably already out of the country. The police would just end up taking us in for questioning about the murders, and we need to go rescue Jeff and Simône," Alex said. "No police."

"Oh," said Liz, "and we can't use our rental car because the keys were in my purse, which I assume is somewhere out in the bay."

"Got it," Jamie said, "you need a ride." Turning to Anne-Marie, he said, "Honey, go back to bed; you're pregnant," he said, before kissing her on the forehead.

"Right, I hadn't noticed," said Anne-Marie, with a smirk.

"I am going to drive these King girls, like a speed demon, to Saint-Malo. I'll be back in a few hours. Keep the bed warm. See you," he said over his shoulder as he followed after Alex and Liz, who had already bounded out the door, leaving Anne-Marie speechless.

CHAPTER
FORTY-ONE

An hour later, using Jamie's cell phone, Alex had recounted the events of the last two days to Natalia, who had agreed to hire a helicopter to meet them at 6 AM at Saint-Malo airport, and had arranged through their attorney and manager of their estate, William Murray, for air transport from Saint-Malo to Kerry airport, the closest one to Skellig Michael. Jamie pulled his Jeep into the empty parking lot of the general aviation terminal at Saint-Malo airport. After the three of them exited the vehicle, Alex and Liz repeatedly thanked him, insisting that they would pay him for the kind aid and medical treatment he and Anne-Marie had provided to them.

"Now you're just insulting me," Jamie said gregariously, refusing their offer. "In fact, here, take these euros," he said, handing them money through the window. "But someday, now that I know you are swimming in dough…" he said, leaving the sentence unfinished.

"Take care of that amazing wife of yours; she's a keeper," said Liz, before giving him a hug with her uninjured arm.

Alex kissed him on both cheeks, in the classic French style, before saying, "You're going to be an awesome dad; call your parents; I'm sure they miss you."

After he got back in his car, he rolled down his window and yelled, "Hey, Kings, next time you run into those bad dudes, I expect you to kick their asses," before peeling out and speeding back down the road leading to the main highway.

"He always was a speed demon," Alex said, shaking her head.

Liz, who was starting to look worse for wear, said, "Al, I need to find something to eat. All of those pain meds are making me nauseous."

"Sure, let's go inside. Although given the way we look, covered in blood and sand, and smelling like fish, I wouldn't blame them if they refused us service."

"Yes, I hope Natalia remembers to bring us some clothes to change into," Liz said, looking at the sad state of their attire.

"Why is it that we always seem to end up looking like bizarre hobos on our vacations?" Alex asked, shaking her head as they headed toward the terminal.

Inside, they discovered that the one small cafeteria did not open until 6 AM, so they were reduced to eating a breakfast of soda, candy bars and chips from vending machines. After finishing their less-than-healthy snack, they went into the bathroom and did their best to wash away the fishy, salty smell permeating their hair, skin and clothes.

"I will never again complain about having a bad hair day," Alex said, laughing, as she inspected her mirrored reflection: hair dripping wet, plastered to her head, and the remnants of her mascara ringing her eyes, like a raccoon.

"Are you kidding? Look at me," said Liz, who had been forced to try to rinse the salt, seaweed and blood out of her hair without wetting the large bandage taped across her forehead.

"Thank God we turned down that Vogue photo shoot," Alex said, before the two began to laugh, venting an uncontrollable mixture of emotion fueled by exhaustion and the sheer relief at being alive. After a few minutes, when the overwhelming wave of emotions had ebbed, they gave each other a long silent embrace.

Finally, Liz said, "Okay, enough of this sloppy emotional stuff. Let's go find our ride to Ireland."

288

Out in the passenger lounge, they found a gray-haired man in his late 40's, dressed in khakis and a blue buttoned down shirt, flipping through a general aviation magazine. Looking up, he said nonchalantly, clearly making an effort not to notice their appearances, "I take it you are two of my passengers. Mr. Murray, your attorney, told me the basics of your situation, so no explanation is necessary," he added. "I understand we are waiting for three more passengers to join us."

"Yes," said Alex, as she turned around, alerted by the noise of the helicopter that had just landed. "That must be them," she said, pointing out the window, as the craft's pilot powered down the spinning rotors. Natalia, Davide, and a second man, popped out of the copter and ducked, before running toward the entrance to the lounge.

Once inside, Natalia introduced herself, Davide and Aaron, the second man, to their pilot.

"A pleasure to meet you," he replied, shaking hands all around. "My name is Jerry; our plane today is a Gulfstream G650 with a cruising speed of almost 600 mph. Kerry airport is less than 500 miles west of here. Wheels up in five minutes. I'll have you on the ground in Ireland by 7 AM."

He paused for a moment before asking, "Does everyone have their passports?" and looking specifically at Liz and Alex, who both turned to Natalia.

"My friend at the US Embassy loves being woken up at 4:30 in the morning," she said. "But hey, no worries. I helped him pass his final exam in chemistry our senior year; he still owes me," she added, handing each of them faxed copies of their passport photo pages. "He made me promise to remind you that you need to go back to Mont St. Michel and retrieve the real ones before you try to fly home from France."

Alex and Liz nodded at Natalia, who said intensely, eyes narrowed, "But first things first; let's go get Jeff and Simône!"

CHAPTER
FORTY-TWO

Once they were locked inside the back of the van, Jeff switched on his cell phone light. "At least they didn't take this," said Jeff. "Other than the head guy, the others seem to be amateurs."

"I think you're right," agreed Simône. "But I wish I had managed to get my purse. I wasn't able to grab it when we left the church. I had a Swiss Army knife in there that could have come in handy."

After trying to open the back door, which refused to budge, Jeff used his light to examine the interior of their prison. Holding up his phone in the four corners of the van, he unsuccessfully attempted to obtain a cell signal.

"No luck," he said, sitting down beside Simône on the filthy floor, littered with candy wrappers and soda cans.

"Not exactly neat freaks," Jeff said, randomly.

"But they definitely are freaks," Simône said. "Especially 'Jesus,' I can't believe what he did to Philippe," she said, choking back a sob. "And even the Monseigneur. He was evil, but he didn't deserve to die like that."

"You're right, of course," Jeff said, "but it is kind of hard to feel sorry for him. He was blackmailing you, after all."

Simône felt her face burn, before asking, "So you heard that?"

"Uh, yeah," said Jeff, sharing in her embarrassment. "But my lips are sealed. No one will ever hear about it from me. As far as I'm concerned, it's your personal business, not mine, not the Sorbonne's, and certainly not some renegade religious cult's."

"Thank you, Jeff," said Simône, "but I can't help but wonder, if Philippe would still be alive…"

"You need to stop thinking about it, Professeur. Let's try to get some sleep. I assume we are headed for an airport somewhere. When we get there will need to have our wits about us. It's 11:30. I'm going to close my eyes for a little while," he said, as he turned off his phone to save the battery, before slipping it into his back pocket.

"Probably a good idea," said Simône, wearily, who slid next to Jeff, who was already sitting in one of the back corners, eyes closed. Within a few minutes, they were both asleep.

They both awoke with a start, when the back door to the van was thrown open by the second gunman, who shown a flashlight directly into their faces, momentarily blinding them.

Jeff turned his head and blinked a few times, before surreptitiously glancing at his wristwatch. 3:15 AM.

"We've been traveling almost four hours," Jeff whispered.

"They must've brought us back to Paris," Jeff guessed, as Simône nodded.

"No talking," said their captor, waving a gun at them. "Time to get out," he added, motioning for them to climb down from the van.

"Where are we, Paris? Seems like you're going in the wrong direction," said Jeff, unable to keep from taunting the man.

"I said shut up!" screamed the teenaged gunman, enraged, before knocking Jeff to the ground and kicking him in his wounded shoulder.

"Ahh, you son of a bitch," Jeff grunted in pain, glaring back at the teen, who said, "Get up. Next time, I'll shoot you."

Jeff continued to stare at him, but decided that further conversation with the brute would serve no useful purpose. Simône helped him to his feet, as 'Jesus' walked around to the back of the truck.

"I just got off the phone with Al-Bazheeri; he's got the plane waiting. The pilot is doing his preflight now. What's going on here, Khalil?" he asked, surveying the scene. "I told you, we need them in good shape until we get to the island, so try to control yourself."

"Yeah, but he was talking," Khalil said, defensively.

"And you were yelling. Let's try not to wake up security. This airfield is closed at night but I'm sure it's patrolled. We don't need any nosy security guards showing up to ask why we are holding these two at gunpoint."

"Okay," said Khalil, clearly embarrassed by the dressing down in front of his captives. "Let's go," he said gruffly, putting the barrel of his gun into Jeff's side, in an attempt to regain his feeling of control.

As they walked around the corner of the hangar where the van had been parked, Jeff and Simône could see the outline of a good-sized private jet, already lit. They exchanged glances, as Khalil, eyes shining, reacted like an excited little kid. "Wow, cool! I bet it has an awesome sound system."

'Jesus' gave him an annoyed look, before turning to Simône and Jeff and saying, weirdly, "After you, Professeur Bertrand, Mr. Stahl," treating them as if they were honored guests. Jeff followed Simône, as they climbed the plane stairs. At the top, Jeff had to duck his head to enter the cabin, before stifling a laugh as he saw that the plane was gaudily decorated with a bizarre combination of Middle Eastern, and, what he assumed were meant to be, contemporary fixtures. Antique woven rugs covered the floor, in contrast to bright yellow leather seats and gold lighting fixtures.

"Must have bought it from a drug dealer," Jeff whispered to Simône, who responded by rolling her eyes.

After handcuffing them, Khalil pushed them into seats near the back of the plane. Soon, they could feel the engines powering up, but the pilot had not raised the stairs or closed the cabin door. Several minutes passed without any movement of the aircraft, during which 'Jesus' and Khalil huddled together, speaking in hushed tones. Finally, another man climbed into the cabin, closed the door and took a seat by the pilot, after greeting the other two men in Arabic.

Jeff whispered, "Who do you think that is?"

"Another thug, no doubt," Simône said, not bothering to lower her voice.

Khalil turned around to give them a menacing look, but then quickly swiveled back around in his seat when the newest addition to their group leaned out of the cockpit and asked him something in Arabic. Given his immediate and seemingly deferential response, Jeff guessed that the new man was clearly someone in charge.

"I wish I spoke Arabic," Jeff whispered, to which Simône nodded in agreement.

After take-off, they soon learned that Khalil had located the sound system, which he used to blast a hideous selection of music during the course of their flight.

"I don't think I can stand it-truly is a form of torture," Simône said, groaning.

'Jesus,' it seemed, was oblivious, deeply engrossed in something he was reading on his tablet. The pilot and the other man were protected by aeronautical headphones, presumably unable to hear the musical carnage.

"Yeah, definitely a form of torture," Jeff agreed out loud, sure that Khalil would not hear them over the racket. Finally, after about an hour, they begin to feel the plane descending. Jeff looked at his watch, which read 5:25 AM.

"Do you have a sense for where in Ireland we landed? We've been flying for about an hour and a half."

"I don't know," Simône said, lowering her voice as Khalil turned down the music at the direction of ''Jesus'.'

293

"Could be Shannon, or Kerry, which is closer to Portmagee."

After the aircraft rolled to a stop, 'Jesus' and the new man had an extended conversation, before Khalil came back to remove their handcuffs. "We don't want to draw any attention to you, but don't forget," he said looking at Jeff, who had risen from his seat, "I still have my gun."

"Yeah, got it," Jeff said, conveying by his tone of voice that he was less than impressed.

The pilot, 'Jesus' and the third man all disembarked, before Khalil shepherded Simône and Jeff off the plane and onto the tarmac to stand beside the other men. 'Jesus,' they saw, had obtained a new gun, which he pointed in their general direction.

Looking around, even in the dim predawn light, Simône and Jeff could see that they were at a good-sized airport. In the distance, they could make out the outline of full-sized commercial jets parked alongside jet ways. Simône leaned over to Jeff and whispered, "I'm pretty sure it's Shannon, which means we are about a 3-hour drive from Portmagee."

Her suspicion was soon confirmed as 'Jesus' said to the new guy, "You know, Rashid, Kerry would've been much closer."

"Yes, Jamaal," Rashid answered, scathingly, "and would have drawn a lot more attention since it is a much smaller airport. According to the sheikh, I am now in charge of this operation. You and that mongrel nephew of yours, Khalil, left quite a mess back at Mont St. Michel from what I understand, not easily brushed under the rug. We will have to roll up several of our cells, given the intense scrutiny we will now be under throughout France. You killed a cop and a priest!"

"Yes, but..." Jamaal ('Jesus') started to say before he was silenced by a look from Rashid.

"I'm here to make sure that no further messes are left behind," Rashid said ominously, glancing at the two captives.

"At least now we know their names," Jeff whispered to Simône.

"May not be a good thing," Simône said, anxiety in her voice, "since we can identify them, and they don't seem to care."

Jeff nodded glumly, acknowledging the dire nature of their situation.

Khalil, who had mysteriously disappeared immediately after they exited the plane, soon returned, driving a dark colored food delivery van, with the words "Paddy's Pride Pastries" emblazoned on the side in large white letters.

"What is this?" Jamaal asked angrily as Khalil pulled the van to a stop near them and stepped out. "I said to get something nondescript, discreet."

"It was the only one I could find that didn't have a security system that would alarm when I broke in," Khalil said, almost whining.

Rashid shook his head in disgust, while Jamaal continued to berate Khalil in Arabic. Finally, he stopped as though weighing the risk, before looking at his watch and saying, "We've got to go. It's going to take us almost 3 hours to get there," glancing resentfully at Rashid, who, busy looking at his phone, missed the insubordination.

"We'll have to use it. There's some grass over there at the edge of the tarmac. Smear some dirt around to dirty up the paint. Maybe we will go unnoticed. You better hope so for your sake," Jamaal said, shooting a look like daggers at Kahlil, who was already running toward the edge of the tarmac to pull up some turf.

Jeff and Simône, despite their situation, observed all this in amused silence. Finally, unable to contain himself, Jeff muttered under his breath, "Keystone cops."

Simône, who didn't understand the reference, just shrugged silently. After a few minutes, when Jamaal seemed satisfied with Khalil's efforts, Jeff and Simône were forced to climb into the back of the van and heard the outside lock being engaged, before the engine roared to life and the van began to move.

Turning on his cell phone, Jeff burst out laughing as he realized that they were completely surrounded by multiple carts piled high with trays of freshly baked pastries, and pallets stacked with a variety of bottled fruit juices.

"Wow, it was nice of Khalil to provide us with breakfast!" Jeff said.

"Ah, oui, très sympathique," agreed Simône.

"Shall we?" Jeff asked. "I doubt that Paddy would mind. We can't let them all go to waste."

"I agree," said Simône, who had already opened an orange juice and was gulping it down.

Jeff gobbled down a scone and a cherry tart before finishing with two bottles of apple cider.

"Not quite as good as the hard cider we had on Mont St. Michel, but it will do," he said, with a grin.

Simône, eating at a much daintier pace, finished a croissant, before wiping her fingers on her clothing.

"They can't get any dirtier," she said, looking at her once black pants, which were encrusted in areas with Philippe's dried blood.

"I feel like I will never be clean again," Simône said forlornly, wiping tears from her eyes. "Even if we live long enough to..." she added, her voice trailing off, as tears spilled onto her once white blouse.

"Oh, my scarf," she said, noticing as she looked down that it was gone, unaware that the beautiful silk scarf she had worn to dinner the night before and then used to stanch Phillipe's bleeding, would soon be bagged as evidence by agents of the Department of Sûreté, Securité Territoriale, who had responded to a call from Mont security officers. Security had arrived at L'eglise Saint-Pierre at 11 PM after being awoken by a frantic call from a Mont St. Michel shopkeeper who claimed to have heard shots fired in the vicinity of the church.

"We can't think like that," Jeff said, trying to console her.

"Who knows? Alex and Liz are very resourceful; those other two guys were instructed not to hurt them. I have to believe they'll be okay," he said, his voice breaking slightly, before clearing his throat to continue. "If I know Alex and Liz, they probably already got away. Or maybe, despite what she said to us in Paris, Natalia was having us watched."

"Peut-être," Simône said, not sounding convinced, her voice betraying a combination of exhaustion and resignation.

Hearing that, Jeff said, "Maybe we should try to get some more sleep. If you're right, we have at least another two and half hours before we get to Portmagee. These scumbags have been up all night too. If we get some rest, maybe we will be able to outthink them when the time comes."

"That shouldn't be too difficult," Simône said, smiling for the first time in many hours.

"Yeah, not exactly rocket scientists," said Jeff, "although that new guy worries me. He seems a lot smarter."

"Yes. I was thinking the same thing," Simône said, as she attempted to cover a yawn.

"You are right, though; I need sleep," she admitted, pulling a packing blanket away from one of the juice pallets to curl up in a corner.

"Wake me up if anything exciting happens," she added, sardonically.

"Will do," Jeff said, before propping himself uncomfortably against one of the stainless-steel carts, and willing himself to sleep.

He was surprised when he awoke an hour later as the van came to a stop. When someone swung the back door open, he heard Jamaal say sarcastically, "You had to steal one without petrol."

Rashid stuck his head into the enclosure and asked, "Professeur, Mr. Stahl, do either of you need a bathroom break? I see you already had breakfast," he commented, amusement in his voice, as he surveyed the pile of wrappers and empty juice bottles placed neatly in one corner.

"Oui, yes, thanks," said Simon and Jeff, surprised by the unexpected kindness.

After climbing out of the van, to the sights and sounds of Khalil cursing as he pumped diesel into the van, they also saw Jamaal, who was smoking a cigarette while engaged on his cell phone in what seemed like an angry conversation. Nevertheless, he watched closely as Rashid escorted the two prisoners to the public toilet, accessible by a door, which opened to the outside of the minimarket where they had stopped.

Rashid, who looked into the windowless interior of the bathroom, before gallantly holding open the door as Simône passed through, said to both of them, "Don't try anything. You've probably already learned that my companions have rather itchy trigger fingers."

Simône and Jeff both nodded in silent acknowledgment.

When Simône finished, Jeff took her place, securing the door behind him. He tried for several minutes to get a signal on his phone, but realized that he was not connecting to whatever company provided local cell service.

When Rashid finally knocked on the door, and said, "Are you setting up camp in there? Time to go," Jeff muttered, "Dammit" in frustration, before quickly using the facilities and exiting.

"Thought you'd fallen in," said Rashid, which struck Jeff as strange, since he would have thought that was something of an American joke.

As Rashid escorted them back to the van, Jeff surreptitiously observed the man. Although he seemed Middle Eastern and spoke Arabic, there was something about

298

him, the way he carried himself, that seemed different, distinct from their other captors.

Once they were locked back inside, Jeff asked, "Does something seem off about Rashid?"

Simône almost snorted as she sputtered, "Off? I'd say there is something 'off' about all of these soulless thugs!" she retorted with anger.

"No, I know, but he seems..." Jeff stopped, searching for the correct word.

"Not quite as brutal," Simône said, finishing his thought.

"Maybe you're right, but murderers and kidnappers, all of them fall into one category, in my mind," Simône added.

"I guess so," Jeff said, settling back against the cart as he felt the van start to move.

About 90 minutes later, they heard the tires slipping on gravel, and the van came to a stop. Jeff and Simône stood up, fully alert, adrenaline pumping, to mentally prepare for fight or flight. When no one came to open the door immediately, Jeff again turned on his phone to illuminate their lightless box.

"What do you think they are doing out there?" Jeff asked.

Simône shrugged before answering, "If we are at Portmagee, maybe they're looking for a way to get over to Skellig Michael."

They didn't have to wait long before they heard Rashid, Khalil and Jamaal conversing loudly.

"I talked to the only boat captain I saw down there," they heard Khalil say. "He says that the boats aren't going out to the island today, too rough."

Someone, *probably Rashid*, thought Jeff, spoke in a quieter tone before Jamaal exclaimed loudly, "I don't care. We are going out there today! Al-Bazheeri told me not to come back to Paris without it, or proof that it doesn't exist. We've come this far."

Again, Rashid responded at an indistinguishable volume before Jamaal again erupted. "It's not your head on the line; we are all going out. You saw that guy, Jeff, at the Abbaye D'Orval, he can climb. That's why we brought him, and whether he finds it or not, it will be his last climbing expedition."

Someone said something in response before Jamaal continued. "The fact that it is dangerous makes it even better. Once he comes down, we can make it look like a climbing accident. Problem solved," Jamaal concluded, sounding proud of his plan.

"Khalil, go back to the boat, tie up the captain, but make sure you aren't noticed," he continued. "We will follow in a few minutes. We don't want to linger on the dock and cause a scene."

"Okay, Uncle," said Khalil, sounding happy to have another opportunity to brutalize someone.

When Kahlil reached the dock, he encountered the captain he had spoken to earlier.

The fisherman standing on the water side of the locked gate to the jetty, clad in a rain slicker, his face weathered into patinaed leather by long years spent on the ocean, frowned as he saw Kahlil approaching.

"Oi, laddie," he said with a lilting Irish brogue, "like I said before, afraid the boats aren't going out today. Better luck to ya tomorrow."

"Too bad; my wife and I were really looking forward to it. But you're right, maybe tomorrow," Kahlil said, shrugging with disappointment.

"Here, let me get that for you," Kahlil offered helpfully as the fisherman struggled to hold open the heavy gate, while pulling all of his fishing tackle through.

"Much obliged, boyo," said the old man with a crinkled smile, as Kahlil stepped past him into the secure area of the dock, to hold the gate open.

"Listen, if you are looking for someplace to stay tonight, the folks at The Moorings are nice. Good food, too, in the pub. Maybe a little touristy since all of the Star Wars movie hoopla, but good just the same. Tell them Fergal sent you."

"Oh sure, thank you," Kahlil said, forcing himself to smile at the man, who had become much too chatty. Kahlil stepped back through the gate and pretended to latch it, as the fisherman hoisted his tackle onto his shoulders and headed toward the parking lot.

Kahlil continued to watch as the Irishman stowed his gear into the back of a small, beat-up sedan, before driving away. Pulling out his phone, he texted,

> "Come to the dock, all clear. The one guy who was here just left."

Simône and Jeff, who had exited the van and were forced to sit on the ground, so that they could not be seen by passersby, watched as Jamaal read the text, and then exploded into what was clearly a string of Arabic expletives, including the phrase, "ya ibn el sharmouta (son of a bitch)," one that Jeff recognized.

"What's wrong now?" asked Rashid, sounding annoyed.

"That idiot. I told him to tie up the boatman-instead Kahlil let him go."

Rashid shook his head but said nothing.

"Now there is a witness that we were here," said Jamaal, before muttering further profanities under his breath as he texted back.

> "Stay there. We're coming."

From the cabin of the van, Jamaal then grabbed a backpack that Jeff had noticed on the plane. Reaching inside, Jamaal retrieved a silencer and attached it to his handgun, before gesturing with it toward Simône and Jeff.

"Get up, let's go!" he said angrily. "As you can see, if I shoot you, no one will hear. So don't even think about trying to yell for help or run away.'

301

"Besides, where would you go in this dump of a town?" he asked, looking around dismissively.

Simône and Jeff realized he was probably right as they walked down the main street toward the dock. A few quaint, multicolored buildings lined the narrow road. Centered prominently in the main block of buildings was a pink-faced restaurant/pub/hotel, The Moorings.

But the street was deserted, Jeff noted. Sneaking a glance at his watch, he saw that it was not yet 8 AM.

When they reached the gated entrance to the dock, Kahlil, who had been hiding in a small dinghy tethered to one of the moored tourist boats, clambered up onto the dock and swung the door open.

"Come on, quick," Jamaal said, looking around furtively to make sure they had not been observed, as his two captives and then Rashid filed into the supposedly secure enclosure.

Kahlil clanged the gate closed, before leading the group to a boat at the end of the dock.

"So," Jamaal asked sarcastically, "are you now the boat captain, since you let ours go?" before cuffing Kahlil violently on the side of the head, almost knocking him into the water.

Kahlil, who had fallen and turned bright red at the abuse, stood up slowly before saying," But Uncle, I thought you would be pleased. I drew no attention, as you directed."

"Pleased? How are we going to get out to the island, you imbecile? Do you know the way?" Jamaal asked, spitting with anger, his gun now pointed at Kahlil.

Rashid remained silent, busily typing something on his phone, before finally stepping in to diffuse the situation.

"What are you going to do? Shoot him for his stupidity? What would his mother, your sister, say?"

"So what's your brilliant idea?" Jamaal demanded, turning toward Rashid.

"While the two of you have been bickering, I have looked up the coordinates to Skellig Michael. I've been there before. I will pilot us out."

"Fine!" said Jamaal." Al-hamdu lillāh (Praise be to Allah)!"

"Certainly no thanks to you," he said scornfully to Kahlil, who had positioned himself behind Rashid for protection.

CHAPTER
FORTY-THREE

"I hardly feel real again... I tell you, the thing does not belong to any world that you and I have lived and worked in: it is part of a dream world."

*George Bernard Shaw, Irish author,
writing in 1910 about a visit to Skellig Michael
(SCEILG MHICHÍL)*

Simône and Jeff, who had climbed aboard and were seated, handcuffed, on a bench in the cabin, watched as Rashid, seemingly at ease on the vessel, hotwired the engine, which started with a purr, before turning on the navigation system. Within minutes, he had programmed in the digital coordinates to Skellig Michael, and the group of reluctant treasure hunters was underway.

Looking out at Khalil and Jamaal, who were both seated on the open benches out on the boat deck, Rashid said, "That guy you spoke to was right, Khalil; the water is really rough today. And it will be worse when we try to dock at the island. Look in those benches you're sitting on; there should be lifejackets."

Jamaal gestured to Khalil, who opened the top of one of the benches and pulled out three lifejackets from the cache. After pulling one on and giving one to Jamaal, he leaned into the cabin to hand one to Rashid, who frowning, asked, "Can't you count?"

Khalil glanced at Jeff and Simône, before responding. "Oh, for the infidels? What does it matter? Let them fall into the sea!"

Rashid, eyes menacing, took a deep breath, as if swallowing his anger before saying, "If you were in charge, we'd all be in the sea long before we reached the island. Give them lifejackets, now!" His voice boomed, even over the sounds of the engine and the non-ending series of large swells through which the boat was struggling.

Khalil, obviously unused to Rashid raising his voice, scurried to comply. Once he had retrieved the jackets, he fumbled and dropped his keys, before finally managing to unlock Jeff and Simône's shackles.

After they put on the jackets, Khalil made a motion to recuff them, before Rashid, who was manning the wheel, yelled, "No, leave it!"

Khalil started to respond, but upon seeing Rashid's face, silently slunk back to his position out on the wave-washed deck.

"Thank you," Simône said, as Rashid nodded silently, his gaze never leaving the horizon.

An hour later, after they had passed the bird-covered sister island of Little Skellig, Simône and Jeff climbed out onto the deck to watch as the boat slowed toward the landing at Skellig Michael. The island, a massive, jagged, molar tooth shaped rock covered in splashes of green between steep cliffs, and rising improbably out of angry waves which buffeted its base, seemed at first glance to be impenetrable. But as they got nearer, they could see a concrete dock with steep steps descending directly into the water.

"This is why the boats didn't come out today," Rashid shouted, over the wind and crashing water. "Prepare to get very wet," he said as he slowed the engine in an attempt to steer the boat along the wave-splashed steps, which lacked any type of railing or handhold.

Now that they had slowed, the pitching of the boat had become much more violent, like being on a mechanical bull that had been turned up to the highest speed.

Rashid, who was doing his best to hold the boat steady, yelled to Khalil, "You will have to time it; get ready to jump over to the steps as the boat rides the top of the wave. If you're off, you'll be crushed between the dock and the boat. Once you're on the dock, we'll throw you the anchor lines."

Khalil, a look of sheer terror on his face, hesitated, before looking at Jamaal, whose facial expression conveyed the fact that Khalil had no choice. Balanced up on the edge of the side of the boat, holding fast to a metal rail running around the top of the roof the cabin, Khalil waited, getting the feel of the syncopated rise and fall of the boat before finally throwing himself over to the steps.

Even Jeff and Simône watched breathlessly as he landed face first on the wet steps, before his body began to slide, accelerated by the slipperiness of his yellow rain slicker that he had gleefully donned when they first started their voyage. Three steps from the bottom, he finally stopped sliding when his fingers found a hold in a crack, four steps up. He narrowly avoided losing his right leg, which hung over the side of the stairs, when he yanked it in, a split second before the boat violently banged against the side of the stairs.

Khalil lay on the steps, trying to catch his breath, before slowly standing up and giving an idiot's grin and thumbs up toward the boat. Once he had managed to climb up to solid ground, Jamaal tossed over a line tied to each end of the boat, which Khalil then secured to concrete cylinders sunk into the dock.

Jeff and then Simône both managed to jump to the stairs while incurring only a few bumps and bruises, after following Jamaal, who had landed in a heap near the top of the stairs, arms flailing before climbing onto the dock, gun cocked.

Rashid, after cutting the engine, put on his backpack, effortlessly jumped up onto the deck railing, and with what could only be described as acrobatic grace, perfectly timed his leap over to the stairs, landing solidly on both feet. Jeff and Simône, impressed by the man's catlike balance, looked at each other with eyebrows raised, before pivoting around to the sound of yelling behind them.

"Hey," yelled a fit, twenty-something, red-haired man, rapidly descending the steps that led from the dock up to the stone path (the lighthouse road) surrounding the base of the island.

As he continued to walk toward them, he asked, sounding exasperated, "What are you doing out here? We said no boats today..." His voice trailed off as he saw the guns that Jamaal and Khalil were holding.

"Shut up!" Jamaal said menacingly. "We were hoping to go unnoticed, but now that you're here, you can guide us up to the top," he added, momentarily looking up at what loomed above, before re-fixing his gaze on the man.

"But what... What are you...?" The man sputtered, totally confused.

"You don't need to know, infidel dog!" Khalil yelled, spilling out the worst insult he could imagine. "Put up your hands, keep your mouth shut, and do as you're told."

Jeff and Simône looked back at Rashid to see if he might intervene, but he remained mute, as though the pedestrian details of their little adventure were not his concern. The guide immediately complied, as Khalil circled around, gun pointed at his back.

"Hey, I'm just a guide here. I don't want any trouble, but I should tell you, it's pretty windy up top today; going up could be dangerous."

"If we want your advice, we will ask for it," said Jamaal. "Let's go," he said, motioning to Jeff and Simône who then followed behind Khalil and the guide as they began to climb the stairs up to the lighthouse road.

Rashid, after checking the knots that Khalil had tied for anchorage, followed the group.

Despite their situation, both Jeff and Simône found themselves admiring the beauty of their surroundings, as they followed the limestone path circling the base of the island. After passing under a canopied area, no doubt erected to protect tourists from potential rock fall from above, and by a helicopter pad balanced precariously on a cliff above the water, they reached the bottom of the 661 steep stone stairs, which Jeff knew had been erected starting some 1500 years before by Augustinian monks who had chosen to live in the harshest of conditions on this remote island. The steps, in most areas about 4 feet wide but only a foot or less deep, stretched up above them before turning to the right and vanishing out of sight.

As they climbed, the steps grew steeper and steeper until it felt as though they were actually climbing a ladder. Numerous times, Khalil, the youngest of their group and leader of their procession, stopped to catch his breath, giving the rest of them, including Jeff and Simône, a chance to look around. The sharp rock outcroppings, both above and below them, were punctuated by the island's verdant green vegetation, and the crashing surf hundreds of feet below. The few clouds, which had covered the top of the skellig when they first arrived, were being pushed away by strong gusts of wind, causing a swirling design in the sky above the island's highest peak.

"This is incredible," said Jeff, unable to resist commenting during one of their rest stops.

"I know," said Simône, revealing labored breathing. "I wish I were seeing it under different circumstances."

"Me too," Jeff said, before continuing to climb.

Some 30 minutes passed before they reached the last pitch of stairs, so steep that a metal chain to provide a handhold had been bolted into the rock wall to their right. The stairs ended on a rough stone path bordered by a sheer drop to the sea some 600 feet below. Jeff and

Simône both avoided looking down to the right, instead focusing on carefully placing their feet until the path turned away from the cliff, dropping down through a series of rock lined terraces, before passing through a stacked stone passage topped by a massive flat lintel.

On the other side of that passage, they saw that they had reached the monastery comprised of six bee-hive-shaped, ancient stacked stone structures, presumably built for habitation, intermixed with two other larger beehive dwellings that probably had served some communal purpose, an area which appeared to be a raised graveyard topped by a number of roughly carved crosses, and a separate, partially standing ruin that Simône and Jeff immediately recognized to be St. Michael's church. It was distinct, both because of the larger rectangular design, and also, because its stones were held in place by a whitish looking mortar, in contrast to the beehives, which structures and shapes solely relied on the weight of each successive level of stone bearing down on the levels below.

Looking through the doorway of the church as they were marched past, they saw headstones, which Jeff from his earlier research, knew marked the graves of deceased children of 18th-century lighthouse keepers. Separated from medical care and living in the most rugged of conditions, these children had lived their short lives, and died on the island.

When they reached an open area in the middle of the compound, Jamaal turned to Simône and said, "So Professeur, you're on. What are we looking for?"

Simône, looked at Jeff before answering. "I hate to tell you this, but I doubt that you are going to find anything here. The diary described a small metal box, probably brass, but now discolored. Inside there was a carved wooden tube with a metal top. Look around you. Even if this is where Brother Bernard brought that box in the 1830's, there have been countless visitors since then. Someone surely would have found it by now."

"Let's hope for your sake that you're wrong," Jamaal said, with a quick glance back at Rashid. Opening his backpack, he pulled out small LED flashlights, leaving them in a heap on the ground.

"We don't have all day," he growled. "Everybody grab a flashlight and start looking. At some point, someone is going to sound the alarm that..." He stopped, looking at their guide. "What's your name?"

"Dan," croaked the man, nervously.

"That Dan here is missing," Jamaal added.

"Khalil, go stand at the entrance to the terraces. Make sure no one followed us."

"Okay," said Khalil, glumly.

While they had been climbing, the wind had shifted direction, bringing with it large dark cumulus clouds that blocked the sun and dropped a fine mist, quickly dampening their clothes and shoes.

Jeff and Simône began to thoroughly inspect each beehive structure, looking for any crevice in the walls or stone floors, which might have served as a cache or vault. After examining the six beehives, the two larger beehive shaped dwellings and the raised burial grounds, they entered the ruins of the church of St. Michael, which despite missing a roof, was clearly recognizable as a once large rectangular structure.

Finally, Jamaal who had been following them around, wandered away to a different area of the ruins to keep a close eye not only on Dan, but also on Rashid, who seemed to be rather aimlessly wandering around the structures.

When they finally were alone, Jeff said, "There's no way it's here in the monastery. Millions of people have come to these ruins since the 1800's."

"But what about the Hermitage?" Simône asked. "It's up on the South Peak. From what I've read, it is where the most religious of the monks went to pray, and possibly even live to be closer to God, at the top of the world. I

310

think it best meets the description from Abbott Godard and Brother Bernard, 'where the penitents prayed and the falcons still soar at the end of the world."

"You may be right," Jeff agreed. "Pilgrims were going up there in the 1800's, but in the 20th century, it became accessible only for serious rock climbers and archaeologists. Although even with the smaller numbers, you would have expected something hidden up there to have been found by now. Maybe we should ask Dan. I bet he's been up there," suggested Jeff.

Stepping out of the church, they spotted Jamaal, disrespectfully leaning against one of the beehives, smoking a cigarette as he conversed with Rashid. Khalil, they saw, still manned his post leading down to the stairs.

"Look, he's over there," said Jeff, pointing to the guide who had taken a seat in a remote corner against one of the exterior rock walls. "If we go around the backside of this larger beehive, maybe they won't see us. Keep an eye on those two. I'll go around and try to get his attention."

"Okay," said Simône. "But be careful. Rashid is right; Kahlil, and probably Jamaal, are just looking for an excuse to shoot us."

Jeff walked silently around the structure, and then crouched down, so that he was no longer visible to his captors, before waving his hand, trying to get the attention of Dan, who was bleakly looking at the screen of his service-less cell phone. Finally, Jeff resorted to pitching a small stone toward the man, who flinched when it landed at his feet. Jeff put his finger against his lips, willing the other man not to cry out.

Dan subtly nodded his head, before slowly standing up to stretch. For about a minute, he appeared to wonder aimlessly in the area, stopping to look at stones on the ground, before ending his rambles at the back of the beehive, also hidden from the view of their captors.

"I have to make this quick, to the point. You must've figured out that we are here as prisoners, too. They are looking for a thousand-year-old document that a monk might've hidden here in the 1830's when pilgrims were still coming to the island. It can't be hidden here in the monastery; every inch has been combed over. Do you think it could be up at the Hermitage on the South Peak?" Jeff finished, breathlessly.

Dan took some time to consider the question he had been asked before whispering, "I guess it is possible. There have been a lot of climbers and archaeological teams up there since the 1970's, but it still hasn't been completely excavated or explored."

"Can you think of anything up there that could mark a hiding place, like a cave or grave anything?" Jeff asked, sounding desperate. "I'm hoping that someone down below has noticed you are missing and called the police, National Guard, whatever, but in the meantime, we need to stall, give them something, or we will quickly become expendable."

"Okay, I understand," said Dan. "I can't think of anything like what you've described, but..."

"But what?"

"But a number of years ago, before the surveys were done up there in the 1980's, in fact, someone did find a hand carved cross. At the time of the find, they thought it might actually have come from monks who'd been using the area for praying, centuries ago."

"Where?" Jeff asked, his voice rising in excitement.

"Where what?" came the voice of Jamaal, who with his gun crammed in Simône's back, had just snuck up to interrupt their conversation.

"We were just talking about places where Brother Bernard might have hidden the 'Accord.' Dan thinks he might know a place to look."

"Where's that?" asked Rashid, who had joined the conversation.

"Yes, well, I was telling Jeff that a number of years ago, a hand carved cross was found up near the end of the Outer Terrace. Nobody knows its origin but I guess it would make sense for your monk to put something up there," Dan said, a question his voice. "I don't know," he continued. "It is the most remote of the three terraces, almost at the peak and pretty difficult to get to without special climbing gear. Who knows what it was like in the early 1800's, and over the years, part of the terrace appears to have collapsed. I've been up there, but..."

"Hear that, Rashid," Jamaal said, "the Outer Terrace. Luckily, we have Jeff here, with his climbing skills, and Dan who knows the way. It should be no problem."

"Wait a minute!" Jeff said, alarmed. "I've done some climbing at the wall in my gym, not on a sheer rock face 600 feet above the ocean."

"Lucky for you, then, that I brought some rope." Walking over to his backpack, Jamaal reached inside and pulled out a length of climbing rope, which he threw at Jeff, who reflexively caught it. "Also lucky for both of you that you're wearing your trainers."

"So how do we, or I should say, you, get to this South Peak?" he asked, looking at Dan.

"Well, it's right over there," Dan said condescendingly, pointing to the higher peak to the south.

Jamaal's eyes flashed as he leveled his gun at Dan's chest. "Answer my question, if you want to keep breathing."

"Okay, fine, chill out. We have to go about halfway back down the stairs we just came from, and then go up the intersecting path to Christ's Saddle, that depression between the two peaks that you could see to our left as we were climbing up."

"And then?" prompted Jamaal.

"From there, we follow a ledge around to the west to the Needle's Eye; it's like a chimney with an opening at the top to reach the other ledges and terraces on the

South Peak. Then it is about a 40 foot climb up a steep gully to the Garden Terrace."

"So that is where…?" Jamaal began to ask.

"No man," Dan interrupted, not realizing the danger. "I told you, there are three terraces. From there you have to climb up a 20-foot high rock face to a path that leads to the southeast to the Oratory Terrace. Or you can go up to the summit which is another 45 feet up, using hand and foot holds to the upper traverse, and from there over to the Outer Terrace. But like I said, parts of that terrace at the end have partially collapsed. There's no way to know whether it looks like it did in the 19th century."

"And yet," Jamaal said, "you two college boys are going to go up there and take a look."

"Khalil," Jamaal yelled down to the teenager, who stood leaning against a stone wall, playing a game on his phone.

Khalil, happy to be relieved of his watch, sprinted up to join the group. "Yeah, what's up?"

"These two are going up there on the South Peak. And you're going with them."

"But Uncle, I can't climb," said Khalil, fear evident in his voice."

"Don't be such a coward," Jamaal screamed, slapping the young man in the face. "Allah wills it."

Khalil, his face now bright red with shame, muttered, "Yes, I'm sorry. Praise be to Allah."

Rashid, silent as usual, nodded approvingly.

Jamaal, seeing that Khalil's face had now gone from red to white, blanched with fear, relented, saying, "You do not have to go all the way up. Wait for them at the base of this Needles' Eye the guide spoke about. It's the only way for them to come down."

"Yes, uncle," Khalil said gratefully, clearly relieved.

"We will stay up here," Jamaal added, "to avoid being seen from below. When they come down, bring them back up here." Again Jamaal looked at Rashid, who nodded his approval.

CHAPTER
FORTY-FOUR

As the three young men prepared to leave, Rashid said, "Wait, you must take water." Reaching into his backpack, he handed them each a bottle of water.

Both Jeff and Dan look surprised, but said, "Thank you." Khalil gave a sideways glance at Rashid, trying to understand his motives, before accepting the water and quickly looking away.

"Let's go," Khalil said, engaging in a renewed display of bravado as he brandished his gun, indicating they should begin their descent.

Once Jeff, Dan and Kahlil had disappeared down through the stone entrance to the first terrace, Jamaal turned to Simône and said, "You better hope they find your 'Accord.' Otherwise..." He left the word hanging menacingly.

Refusing to be intimidated, Simône just stared at him, willing him to look away. Jamaal finally broke eye contact but continued to glance at her frequently, as though he thought she might attempt to escape. Rashid, on the other hand, seemed to have lost interest in their captive; he walked to the far end of the terrace, lit a cigarette and stared out to sea.

Finally, after several minutes had passed, punctuated only by the screeching of sea birds overhead, Simône seated herself on the steps leading up to the terrace in front of the various beehive structures. Jamaal watched her movements suspiciously, before pulling out his phone and positioning himself a few yards from Simône's perch. A fine mist soon enveloped them, leaving her shivering, her knees tucked to her chest in an effort to keep warm.

After almost an hour of silence, Simône turned to Jamaal and said, "I don't know what you have been told, but the document we are looking for isn't dangerous, or something that should be feared. If it still exists, it is, in fact, a miraculous gift."

Jamaal looked up from his phone momentarily, eyes narrowed, appraising her words, but not wanting to overtly show his interest.

Rashid, who in the past hour had not strayed from his silent contemplation of the horizon, wandered closer once Simône began talking.

Seeing that they were listening, Simône said, "Think about it. Wise men-Christian, Muslim and Jewish leaders-1000 years ago realized that continued conflict between their three religions would just lead to further bloodshed and tragedy."

When neither man rebuked her, she continued. "We don't have to believe the same things about God, but the fact that all three religions believe there is a God, the God of Abraham, ought to be the basis for some type of agreement. We are all on this planet for such a short time. Think about how wonderful it would be if everyone could just agree to live and let live, and let that same God sort it out in the end. That's what's going to happen anyway, isn't it?"

"Why not let the world decide the value of the document, instead of destroying it?" Simône asked, beseechingly.

Jamaal, who momentarily had seemed seduced by what Simône had been saying, belatedly rushed forward and shoved his gun in Simône's chest.

"Shut up, you heathen bitch! There is only one true religion and all infidels must convert or die! There is NO reason for the blasphemous compromise you speak about! The document WILL be destroyed, just like you and

316

all other infidels! Allah wills it!" Jamaal yelled, spitting his words in her face.

Rashid, hearing the uncontrolled anger in Jamaal's voice, walked slowly toward them.

"Calm yourself, Brother," Rashid said, speaking in a low, steady voice. "She is a mere woman. Do not concern yourself with her blasphemous words. Just ignore her. Soon this will be finished, and we will be on our way back to Mecca."

"Sit there and keep your mouth shut," Jamaal said finally, pushing his gun deeper into Simône's chest for emphasis, before turning his back on her.

Realizing that any further effort to persuade them was futile, and probably life threatening, Simône shrugged, and turned her attention to the angry ocean below. Periodically, as the minutes slowly passed, she made surreptitious checks of her watch, and whispered increasingly fervent prayers for some sort of miracle.

Dan, who was used to daily climbs on the island, quickly descended the stairs, in some places, two at a time, until he reached the trail leading up to Christ's Saddle. Jeff followed at a moderate pace, seemingly at ease despite the steep staircase below him. Khalil, in contrast, seemed to hesitate after leaving the relative safety of the chain handhold, before carefully sidestepping down, one at a time, to each narrow piece of stone.

By the time he had reached the trail leading up to the right to Christ's Saddle, Dan and Jeff were halfway up the slope.

"Stop at the top and wait for me," Khalil demanded. Dan, who had already finished the climb, said to Jeff as he reached the top, "You know, we could just push this Khalil guy off the ledge higher up."

"You're probably right, and believe me, I would love to," Jeff said, "but they've got Simône. I can't risk it. In case you haven't figured it out yet, these guys are killers. They killed two men last night in the village church at Mont St. Michel."

"What the hell?" Dan asked, looking down at Khalil who, eyes downcast, was nervously focused on his climb. When he finally reached them, Dan said, "Let's go," affording Khalil no time to rest.

"Wait a minute," Khalil demanded, gasping for breath as he leaned forward, hands on his knees, but with the gun still pointing at them.

"Okay, can we get on with it?" Dan asked after about a minute.

"Fine, go," Khalil said wildly waving his gun up the trail.

"I hope you have the safety on," Jeff suggested. Khalil ignored the jibe as he struggled to keep pace with the other two men who were already several yards ahead. As they walked along the lower traverse, a narrow path edged by a sheer steep cliff, they could see that Khalil was experiencing vertigo; his steps were unstable, and he seemed to be trying to glue himself to the rock face, even as he inched along.

By the time Khalil reached the base of the Needle's Eye, Dan and Jeff had already climbed halfway up, using the centuries' old foot and handholds carved into the rock. They quickly reached the top of the columnar structure, where a series of steps led up to the gully ascending to the Garden Terrace.

Dan stopped to take a swig of water, and Jeff followed suit.

"That guy's a killer?" Dan asked skeptically.

"Maybe not him. I think he just likes to talk a big game, and wave his gun around. But his uncle, Jamaal, is a stone-cold killer."

"What about the third guy, Rashid?" Dan asked, as they started their ascent up through the gully leading to the Garden Terrace.

"I don't know," Jeff said, pausing to look for his next foot and handholds. "I can't quite figure him out. He seems to be in charge, but since he showed up, he's been-I hesitate to use the words-almost kind, to Simône and me, like he's watching out for us or something. He seems to have his own agenda."

Dan grunted, as he pulled himself onto the Garden Terrace. "At least he doesn't seem to be a thug like Jamaal, and that little creep, Khalil."

"Yeah, I think you're right," said Jeff, who had just climbed up beside the guide.

Jeff stopped for a second to admire the view, before following Dan to the other end of the vegetated terrace, where the trail continued.

"If you went that way," Dan said, pointing over to the southeast, you'd get to the Oratory Terrace, but that we'll have to leave that for another day. Were going up," he said, gesturing with his thumb, "to the summit."

As Jeff looked up, his brow creased. Dan said, "Don't worry. I made it sound worse than it is. I've been watching your technique; you'll be fine. Just watch me and use the same hand and foot holds I do."

Jeff concentrated as he watched Dan, who paused every so often to look for his next position, scale the rock face with ease. Jeff took almost twice as long but ultimately cleared the top of the face. Following the upper traverse past the Spit (the rock outcropping where pilgrims once crawled to kiss an upright stone pillar hanging out over thin air, to express their religious fervor), they finally reached the partially collapsed Outer Terrace.

"Be careful," Don warned. "There is a lot of loose rock here. Maybe it wouldn't be a bad idea if we tied together, just in case. Nice of Jamaal to bring us rope, but some harnesses and carabiners would've been better."

"Yes," Jeff agreed, "I'm pretty sure he knows nothing about technical climbing."

"Well, this will have to do," said Dan, as they each used figure eight knots to tie opposite ends of the rope around their waists.

"So where was the cross found?" Jeff asked, as he surveyed the terrace.

"Over there, past the end of the retaining wall, on that lowest ledge. You can see what I mean." Dan said. "It looks pretty unstable. You're going to have to climb down, on your stomach, I think, just in case."

Once they had descended to the upper portion of the lowest level of the terrace, with yet another cliff face dropping down hundreds of feet, Dan said, "Let me sit down and dig in some foot holds, near the end of the retaining wall, and then you can crawl out. The cross was found a few meters out, midway between the rock face on your right and the cliff face on your left, near the end."

"That's a sheer cliff," Jeff said, swallowing hard. "Is there anything marking the spot now?" Jeff asked, looking with doubt in the area the Dan head indicated.

"No, I just saw it marked on the map, actually, on a survey sketch, done back in the 80's."

Jeff took a deep breath before saying, "Okay, well, I guess I'm either going to die here, or back down there, so here goes."

Dan, who had created deep divots in the dirt, dug his heels in and leaned back to prepare, should the line go taut with Jeff's weight.

"What is this vegetation with the little flowers? It's really dense," Jeff yelled back to Dan, but his words floated away on the wind.

"What?" Dan yelled back.

"The vegetation," Jeff said, trying again.

"It's called Sea Campion; it grows all over the island. Dig down through it and there should be some soil, or at least decomposed rock underneath."

320

Jeff began to inch forward on his belly. When he reached what he thought was the location in question, he found a good-sized rock with a sharp edge and began to to dig through the thick, matted vegetation. Once he had cleared an area of approximately 2 meters square, he used the edge of his stone tool to scrape through dirt and broken rock. He labored for almost 30 minutes, before stopping to gulp from the water bottle stuffed in his jacket pocket.

"How's it going over there?" asked Dan, who had been browsing through pictures on his phone, as Jeff dug in the soil of the 1200-year-old ruins. "Well, there seems to be a lot of rock on this rock," Jeff said, wryly, "but not much else. Oh, the hell with it," he said, as he sat up and poured some of his precious water over his dirt covered face.

"Are you sure this is where they found the cross?"

"Pretty sure," Dan said. "I've got the island survey maps on a PDF in my phone."

Jeff looked back at Dan, who had opened the file before confirming, "Yeah, I'd guess within half a meter of where you've been looking."

As they spoke, the sun, which had been hiding behind dark clouds, peeked out, sending spiked rays of sunlight to pierce the corners of the terrace. Out of the corner of his eye, Jeff saw the merest glimmer of a reflection, before the clouds again blocked the sun, casting the area where he sat in shadow.

Jeff stared intently down at the area, not sure whether he had imagined the reflection.

"What do you see?" Dan asked, leaning forward to try to get a better view.

"I'm not sure, but just now when the sun came out, I thought I saw something, just for a second, shining in the dirt. I think it was in this area where I poured my water."

"Pour the rest then!" Dan said excitedly. "I'll share mine with you, if that's what you're worried about."

"All right," Jeff said, sacrificing the remainder of the bottle, before digging, using his now bloodied fingers to probe the soil. Making little progress, he returned to using his Stone Age tool. When he had reached a depth of about 3 inches, he stopped for a moment to wipe away the sweat that had begun to drip into his eyes.

"I hope this corner of the ledge isn't about to collapse from my excavation."

"I think we're okay; it's held the weight of the rock wall for over a thousand years. What are you, about 12 stones, 170-I'm guessing-you're okay. Keep digging," Dan said.

"Easy for you to say," Jeff said, before resuming his efforts, forcefully plunging his rock deep into the soil. He stopped short when he felt an unfamiliar scraping sensation.

"Did you hear that?" Jeff asked.

"What?" Dan asked, getting up on his knees to try to see over into the shallow hole that Jeff had created.

"Be quiet," Jeff said, before again plunging his stone shovel into the dirt and pulling it toward his body in a scraping motion, creating the distinct sound of stone scraping on a solid object.

"That," Jeff said, before repeatedly plunging the stone into the hole, bringing out what appeared to be uniformly small pieces of stone. Again resorting to using his hands, he scraped away a 4-inch square area of dirt to reveal a pile of similar stones, arranged in a rectangular shape.

"I think there's something under here," Jeff said, as his heart began to beat rapidly.

"Should I come help you dig?" asked Dan, who had stood up, and was standing on his tiptoes to try to see.

"No, I don't want to risk it. The side of this mountain could slide out from under us. Stay there as my anchor. I'm going to try to use my feet to push this layer of stones away. My hands won't take much more abuse, and my shoulder where I was shot is killing me."

"What?!" Dan exclaimed, as Jeff said, "Same creeps, different country, a few days ago," before concentrating his efforts on his excavation.

After pushing away all the loose stones with his feet, he returned to his knees and used his hands to clean away another inch of dirt, stopping when one of his fingers caught on something sharp.

"Dammit!" screamed Jeff, as he looked at a sizable gash in his middle right finger. He held up his hand to display the wounded digit, to which Dan said jokingly, "Thanks a lot."

Looking back down, Jeff whooped out loud as he saw the source of his injury: the corner of a dark metal object protruding from the soil.

"Oh my God! I think this might be it!" Jeff said, now pawing frantically through the dirt to fully uncover his find. Once more he used his stone to dig around the edges of what appeared to be a small metal box 5" x 3" in size.

Although seemingly cemented into place, the box finally came loose after Jeff kicked at it with the heel of his running shoe. The box flew through the air, landing mere inches from the sheer cliff face.

"Steady bro," Dan said. "Someone is going to have to crawl out there to get that; you want me to go?" Dan volunteered.

"No," Jeff said, silently cursing his actions. "I'm the one who stupidly drop kicked it, and I'm already out here. But sit back down; I really do need an anchor now."

As requested, Dan sat back down and firmly planted his feet, bracing himself, should the worst occur.

Back on his belly, Jeff, barely breathing, inched far enough out that he could almost touch the corner of the box with his outstretched hand. With blood pouring freely from his injured finger, he made several unsuccessful at-

323

tempts before his slipping fingers grabbed a raised edge on the hinged side of the box. He carefully pulled it toward his body. Once he had secured his grip on his prize, he awkwardly inched back until he reached relative safety in the area where Dan was seated.

"Good job," said Dan, who had been taking video of Jeff throughout the ordeal.

"What the hell?" asked Jeff, annoyed, when he realized that his actions have been recorded.

"Hey, I work here. I had to record this for posterity, so we know exactly where you found it. Besides, your crawling out there and back, that was epic! If we survive this, you'll be showing it to your grandkids one day."

"Yeah, okay, whatever," Jeff said, now more embarrassed than annoyed. Standing up, he saw that his shirt, pants and jacket had been shredded from crawling across the rocks. He also realized that he had multiple small cuts and scratches on his legs, torso, arms and face.

"Death by a thousand cuts, eh?" Dan asked, laughing.

"Better than a gunshot," Jeff said, looking at his shoulder wound, which had begun to ooze blood again.

Finally realizing the seriousness of Jeff's condition, Dan said, "Wow. You're pretty banged up, and we still have to climb down. It's about 11:30 now," he said, looking at his phone. "We've been gone for two hours; do you think your friend Simône is okay?"

"God, I hope so," Jeff said. "And I hope Alex and Liz..." he said, not completing his sentence, realizing that he had no idea if they were dead or alive.

"Who?" asked Dan.

"Friends of mine; some of those terrorist creeps kept them on Mont St. Michel."

"Last night," he added, in response to a blank look from Dan.

"Right, got it, more bad guys," Dan said.

"So aren't you going to open it?" Dan asked, eyeing Jeff's discovery.

"Oh, yeah, right," Jeff said. After carefully examining all sides of the box, he unsuccessfully tried to pry it open with his hands, and then with a rock sliver jammed between the metal edges where the top and bottom joined.

Finally, admitting defeat, he said, 'It's not budging. Not surprisingly, the hinges are rusted shut."

"Want me to try?" Dan asked, his hand extended.

Jeff hesitated, looking at his watch, before replying. "No, I think we better go. We've been up here too long; I'm worried about Simône."

"Okay, it's your treasure hunt," Dan said, with a shrug.

As they began their dissent, Dan asked, "So what's going to happen when we get down? You mentioned something about being expendable."

"I was hoping you were about to tell me that by now, your buddies down at the bottom would have brought in the cavalry."

"Unfortunately, no," Dan said, frowning. "All of the guides do seven day shifts on the island. Everyone left yesterday evening. I agreed to stay in case of an emergency-but not this type of an emergency. The new shift was supposed to show up this morning, but they couldn't come out because of the rough water. The contingency was that they would be flown over tonight by helicopter."

"Oh, that sucks! So, no rescue."

"Probably not, and the only contact with the mainland is a SAT phone down at base. When I came down to the dock this morning, I didn't bring it. I thought I was just going to find some local kids screwing around, not a gang of terrorists."

"I know what you mean," Jeff said. "My whole week has gone like that," he said, sardonically, as they reached the Garden Terrace.

"So what should we do? Try to jump Khalil, get his gun?" Dan asked, as they reached the top of the gully that would lead them to the Needle's Eye, where Khalil was waiting.

When Jeff didn't answer, Dan said, "Look, I'll go down the Needle's Eye first. I can do it quickly, maybe catch him off guard. If not, I'll tell him you were injured but that you have the box and you're bringing it down. Maybe he'll get distracted waiting for you and I can get away, get down to the SAT phone and call for help."

"Okay, we've got to try something," said Jeff, reluctantly agreeing to the plan. "And then if you do get down, take the boat, so they can't leave the island. Head back to shore, send help. At least you'll be safe that way. And you can warn your fellow guides to make sure they don't come over."

"Okay, thanks man, good luck," said Dan, giving Jeff a fist bump before climbing down the gully and into the Needle's Eye.

Only a few minutes later, Jeff heard a shout from Khalil, and then a gunshot, followed by a pause, and then another shot, which reverberated up through the Needle's Eye and into the gully.

Jeff stopped for a moment, but continued his descent when no further sounds echoed up to him. *Either Khalil is dead, or Dan is dead,* he thought grimly. *Guess I'm about to find out.*

At the top of the Needle's Eye, he stopped to retie his jacket, which held the box, around his waist. After climbing down the steep steps at the top, he began his descent, expecting any moment to be shot, which would cause him to fall to his death. Instead, when he reached the bottom, he encountered someone sitting on the trail, in a pool of blood. Looking closer, he saw that the blood flowed from a wound in Khalil's left arm. Khalil had made a tourniquet with his belt, but Jeff could see that he had not entirely stopped the bleeding.

When Khalil saw Jeff, he jumped up unsteadily and began to waive his gun wildly, while shouting in Arabic. After yelling uncontrollably for several seconds, he finally switched to English. "I should shoot you right here!" he said, agitated, waving his gun. "Your friend did this," pointing at his wound.

"Who are you talking about?"

"Your friend, Dan, that son of a dog."

"My friend?" Jeff said. "I just met the guy today. So where did he go?"

"I don't know... Down there somewhere," Khalil said, motioning vaguely toward the sea. "But it doesn't matter. I know you found the box. And now Jamaal and I will be rewarded. And you..." he said, leaving Jeff's fate hanging in the wind that had begun to gust around them.

"Give me the box or I'll kill you!"

"Relax," said Jeff, trying to calm the seemingly delirious boy. "No problem," he said, untying his jacket to extract the blood covered object, which he offered to Khalil.

"This-this is the piece of crap that we've all been suffering for? That my cousin died for?" Khalil ranted, as he grabbed the box.

For a moment, Jeff thought he might actually throw the box out into space, but then Khalil seemed to realize where he was, and what he was holding in his hand.

"Let's go. I have to take this back to Jamaal. You go first," he said, to Jeff, stating the obvious.

"Okay," Jeff said, before running around the ledge toward Christ's Saddle, hoping that perhaps he might be able to lose Khalil, or that in his weakened state, Khalil might lose his balance and fall off the ledge.

But surprisingly, perhaps because of his altered mental state, Kahlil seemed to have forgotten about his fear of heights. He managed to match Jeff's pace, staying only a few feet behind, with the box tucked under his right arm, and his gun tucked into his waistband.

Jeff, looking back, couldn't help but wonder if this time, Khalil had remembered to engage the safety. When they reached the stairs leading back up to the monastery, Khalil pulled his gun and brandished it threateningly.

"I've already shot someone," Khalil said. "I'm not afraid to use it," he added, sounding less like a hardened thug, and more like a frightened child trying to convince himself of his own ruthlessness.

"Yeah, okay," said Jeff, adding under his breath, "you shot yourself, you little psychopath!"

But realizing that he and his friends were still in great danger, he added a silent prayer, "Lord, if you're going to help out, now would be the perfect time."

CHAPTER FORTY-FIVE

By the time they landed in Kerry, exactly an hour later as Jerry had promised, they had both changed into clean clothes provided by Natalia and used her satellite phone to hire a helicopter to fly them to Portmagee, the main port for boats headed out to Skellig Michael.

After they had all climbed down from the plane, Alex said, "The helicopter pilot agreed to wait around Portmagee in case he has to fly us out to the island. Apparently, the water is often too rough for the boats to go out."

"I checked," said Natalia. "They usually leave around 9 AM so we should get there in time. We may even get to Portmagee before the Syrians take Jeff and Simône out to the island. And if we don't, then we will fly over."

"Yes, but if we fly over on the helicopter, they'll see us coming. I'd rather avoid that," said Davide.

"But if they've already headed to Skellig Michael, we can't waste any time. These guys are brutal; they won't keep hostages around once they've gotten what they want. And I should add, they're not afraid to die and take everyone around with them," Aaron interjected.

Alex and Liz looked at each other, fear etched on their faces.

"Jeff," Alex moaned, prompting Liz to squeeze her hand for reassurance.

"Now you see why we brought Aaron along. He's been tracking Al-Bazheeri's group for several years," Natalia said.

"They are a splinter group that formed at the beginning of the Syrian civil war. They're not that well organized but they are murderers, very violent, and very determined. They no doubt see this 'Accord,' if it exists, as an affront to their entire faith."

"Yes, we saw that last night," Alex said, grimly. Liz nodded, rubbing her left shoulder unconsciously.

Inside the terminal, they quickly found their pilot, James Brannigan, who had already completed his flight plan.

"Follow me, the helicopter is out this door," he said, holding it open as they walked out directly onto the tarmac.

As they climbed aboard the helicopter, their pilot said, "This is a Eurocopter EC 145; it can hold nine passengers plus crew. It can fly about 150 mph. Portmagee is about 50 miles to the southwest; we'll be there by 8 AM. There is a field at the edge of the village where I have secured permission from the owner to land. It is a couple of minutes' walk to the dock from there."

Turning from his seat to look at them, he asked, "Alex, right?"

"Yes."

"You've got my cell number. Give me a heads up if it looks like you're going to want to fly over to Skellig Michael. I will try to call the guides on the island to let them know that we are going to be using the helipad."

"Okay," Alex said. "I will call you as soon as we get into the village and determine what the situation is."

"Alright everyone, please fasten your shoulder harnesses for takeoff."

Once airborne, it seemed as though only a few minutes passed before they looked down to see the small colorful portside village of Portmagee, with a dozen buildings lined along the waterway and about the same number of boats on the two-sided dock which ran directly perpendicular to the town's only real street. They landed, and Natalia and Alex jumped out of the helicopter while the rotors were still turning.

At the dock, it was readily apparent that the Syrians and their hostages had come and gone. Beside a lone police car, parked in the lot adjacent to the dock, stood a small crowd of what appeared to be local residents. Natalia visually scanned the crowd before approaching the one uniformed policeman.

"What happened here?" she asked.

"Who are you?" asked the disgruntled man, who clearly had dressed in a hurry.

"Hello, I am an Israeli Mossad agent but I am currently under assignment to Interpol," she said, quickly flashing her badge before he could inspect it.

"We are currently searching for several Syrian men with two hostages, a man, blonde, mid-20's and a woman, brunette, 30's, who may have come through here. Has anyone seen them?" Natalia asked, looking toward the crowd, who were trying to listen in on the conversation.

"You could say that. Seems they stole Ryan Callahan's boat this morning and headed out into the ocean, destination unknown. It's a mystery," he said, shaking his head.

"Actually, it's not," Natalia replied. "They went to Skellig Michael. It is a very long involved story, but take my word for it; they are out there," she said pointing out to sea.

"And I and my fellow agents are going to fly out and rescue the hostages. We've got a helicopter at the edge of town. You're welcome to join us if you'd like to," added Natalia as the patrolman just stared at her, mouth open.

"But you have to decide quickly because we're going now," she said, looking at her watch which read 11:15 AM.

"What time was the boat stolen, approximately?"

"Around 7:30 AM, they think," he said, his ability to speak restored, as he gestured to the crowd.

"So, they've already been gone almost four hours! We've got to go," she said, looking around to Alex.

"Yes, the chopper is powered up. Let's go!" said Alex, who had already alerted their pilot.

As they took off at a run back toward the helicopter, where Liz, Davide and Aaron were waiting, the policeman yelled, "But what should I do?"

"Call for some backup," Natalia yelled back to him, but her words were swallowed up by the swoosh of the helicopter's rotors whipping through the wind.

Standing outside of the helicopter, Natalia said, "Alex, I think you and Liz have done enough. We are trained professionals, you're not."

"But they are my friends."

"Yes, but…" Natalia said, trying to reason with her, "you don't even have weapons or body armor, and you and Liz have suffered enough. If you don't care about yourself, at least think about Liz."

"I have. Neither of us could forgive ourselves if we didn't go, and something happened to Jeff… and Simône," she added, after a moment's hesitation. "And," Alex said, clearly ending further argument, "besides, I paid for the helicopter."

Aware that she was not going to change Alex's mind, Natalia said, "Fine, it's your neck. End of discussion."

CHAPTER FORTY-SIX

Dan stopped to catch his breath, having come down the mountain at a full run. Several times he had almost lost his balance, recovering equilibrium at the last possible moment. When he reached the communications shack, he entered the five-digit lock code before throwing the door open. Rushing to the desk, he grabbed the SAT phone, before running back outside as he dialed. Based on experience, he knew he had to head to the bottom of the Monks' stairs to get a clear line of sight. He had already begun to run back up the lighthouse road toward the stairs before realizing that the phone was dead.

In a panic, he ran back down into the shack, only to discover that someone, *probably Bridgette*, he thought bitterly, had failed to place the backup battery into the charger.

"Son of a bitch!" he screamed in frustration, as he threw the phone savagely onto the desk.

He took a deep breath, trying to calm himself, before heading down the trail at a sprint. *Plan B*, he thought, wondering if he would be able to get the engine started in the boat. *I'm guessing our loser kidnappers didn't have the key either*, he thought, as he reached the dock.

"At least the swells have calmed down," he said aloud, grateful for small favors. He had no trouble boarding the vessel, but soon discovered that he had no idea how to hotwire anything. *What a crappy education*, he fumed, briefly considering his 17 years of private school education. *I know how to dissect a frog, conjugate a compound sentence, tell you the value of Pi out to six digits, but I can't get a damn boat started without the key.*

He kicked the captain's chair in frustration, and then yelped in pain.

Okay, Dan, time to get your shit together, he thought.

Stepping back out onto the deck, he considered his options. *I could go back up to the monastery and try to play hero.* "Nope," he said out loud, "not going to do that."

Or I can find a place to hide until the next guide crew shows up. Only sane choice, Dan thought, reconciling himself to the fact that he wasn't James Bond.

He headed back up the lighthouse road, toward his hut, stopping frequently to listen for sounds of anyone coming down off the mountain. He was about to pass the locked gate leading into the enclosure for the helicopter pad, when the wind shifted, and he heard the unmistakable whop whop whop sound of helicopter blades slicing through the sea air.

Looking toward the mainland, he saw that the chopper was coming in low and slow, presumably to avoid being seen by anyone up at the monastery ruins.

"Finally!" Dan said, as relief flowed through his system. He opened the coded gate lock, to wait for the helicopter to land. Because of the wind gusts, it took several minutes before the pilot was able to safely set the aircraft down on the pad balanced precariously over the crashing waves below.

Thinking it was the guide crew coming in early, Dan was very surprised when out climbed Natalia, Davide and Aaron, guns drawn, followed closely by Liz and Alex.

Dan, who, by now, really hated the fact that he had not left the island the night before with his fellow crewmembers, raised his hands, making it clear that he was offering no resistance.

Natalia, who was leading the charge, saw him and said, "Relax, soldier, we're the cavalry."

"Oh, thank God!" Dan reacted by lowering his hands and breaking into a huge smile.

"You won't believe what's been going on..." Dan began, before being interrupted by Natalia. "Sorry, not to be rude, but I need the Cliff Notes' version."

"Oh, right," Dan said, before recounting everything that had happened since he had encountered the boat thieves and their hostages that morning on the dock.

"Thank you," Natalia said. "Well, at least we know Jeff and Simône were alive the last time he saw them. Stay down here," she added. "Hopefully the local constabulary has organized some reinforcements by now. If they show up, let them know what's going on, but tell them they cannot go up to the monastery. We don't need the wrong people getting shot. Do you understand?"

Dan looked at Davide and Aaron, who were wearing bulletproof vests and guns strapped to their thighs, before saying, "Got it, 10-4."

"Oh, one other thing," Dan said, looking at Alex and Liz, who had started to ascend the stairs up from the dock.

"Jeff mentioned two girls, women," he said, correcting himself quickly, "that the bad guys had taken hostage on Mont St. Michel. Is that you?" he asked.

"That's us," Alex said, flashing him a smile.

"I can see why he was concerned," he yelled, as they disappeared on the path above him.

Moving at a quick sprint, the five of them reached the bottom of the Monks' stairs, before pausing for a moment to look up at the imposing climb.

"Wow, those monks were tough SOB's," Natalia said, with admiration. "No disrespect intended," she added, looking at Alex and Liz, who burst out laughing.

Having released the pent-up adrenaline and tension they had all been experiencing, Natalia said, "Okay, here's the plan. Based on what Dan said, I'm guessing they are all back up at the monastery, even Jeff and Khalil."

"Alex and Liz, stick close to us. You don't have any body armor. When we get to the top, wait until we let you know it is safe to come onto the grounds of the ruins."

"Here," Natalia said, showing them a sketch of the monastery grounds that she had pulled up earlier on her phone.

"No worries. It's only Jamaal and his punk nephew," Davide said, sounding confident.

Aaron nodded in agreement, as though this was a training exercise.

"But," Liz said, "Dan mentioned a third guy, Rashid."

"Yes, Rashid," Natalia said, smiling.

"Wait, I don't understand," Alex said, a look of bewilderment on her face.

"You will, you will," Natalia reassured her.

The group of five began rapidly climbing the stairs up to the monastery ruins. 15 minutes later, having finished the ascent at a record pace, they stopped at the bottom of the last pitch with the chain-link handhold, to catch their breath.

"What's all this, 'it's easy to run at sea level stuff?'" Davide asked, causing them all to choke with laughter.

Natalia, suddenly serious, said, "Davide, you've got Jamaal; Aaron, Khalil. I'll take Rashid and secure the perimeter," she said, a mysterious smile on her face.

Alex and Liz followed them to the outer perimeter of the monastery grounds, before waiting as the three Mossad agents slowly moved forward.

Three minutes later Natalia stuck her head out of the passage that marked the entrance to the monastery, and "Okay, you can come up."

Alex looked at her watch, and mouthed, "Three minutes. Bad asses!" to her twin, who nodded in response.

Inside the monastery grounds, Alex and Liz stopped for a brief moment to admire the otherworldly beauty of the place.

"Amazing!" Liz said.

Alex wanted to pull out her phone to take a picture, but then she recalled that she had left it charging in their room at Mont St. Michel. Climbing up past several terraces, they entered the main area of the compound, where they saw, with great satisfaction, that Jamaal had been subdued, bound and gagged.

"Where's that other guy, Rashid?" Liz asked, looking at Davide. He smiled, before pointing toward Natalia, who, bizarrely, was talking to the man in what looked to be an intimate conversation.

"What that f...?" Alex began to say, before stopping herself, her voice much louder than she'd intended, as she realized she had no right to defile the sacred space.

Davide, seeing her distress, strode over and whispered in her ear. Alex's face beamed, as she turned to share the information with her sister. But before she could, Natalia said, "Attention everyone, based on what Dan told us, Jeff and Khalil should be up here any minute. Dan said they found what they think is the 'Accord.'"

"What? You're kidding, right?" Liz asked in disbelief.

"Anyway," Natalia continued, "Khalil expects to find Jamaal and Rashid in charge here. Aaron and Davide are going to stand at each side of the stone passage opening. Assuming that Jeff enters first, Aaron will pull him to safety, giving us a clear shot at Khalil."

"But..." Liz said, starting to protest.

"Only as a last resort. Liz and Alex, I want you to stay inside the church. We'll let you know when it's all clear. Until then, stay there!" she added, with emphasis.

"Sure, okay," they agreed, reluctantly.

Once inside the crumbling walls of St. Michael's church, the women began to explore their surroundings.

"How sad, look at that," said Liz, pointing at the flat gravestones, marking the births and deaths of little children.

"Life was hard back then," Alex said, as she stood by her sister and wrapped her arms around her.

"What about now?" Liz asked, as they burst into laughter, before covering their mouths when they realized that the sound had echoed around the stone walls.

"Did you hear what Dan said?" Alex asked, joining Liz, who had sat down in a corner of the ruin. "He thinks Jeff found the 'Accord.'"

"I'm not getting my hopes up, but it would be pretty incredible, wonderful really," Liz mused, before lapsing into silence.

Seduced by the silence, and overcome with exhaustion, they sat down, leaned against one another and closed their eyes. Only a few minutes passed before they were roused by a scream, "No!"

They both jumped up, hearts pounding, trying to identify the source of the sound.

"Come on, we need to see what's happening," Alex said, pulling her sister to the opening to the church to look out. They saw that the central area of the monastery, where the beehives, St. Michael's church and the graveyard converged, was empty.

"It must've come from down by the terraces," Liz whispered.

Walking as quietly as possible on the loose stones, Liz and Alex stopped to peer around the corner of the church wall toward the lower terraces. They were elated to see that Jeff, bruised and battered but alive, stood with his back to them.

"Oh my God!" Alex whispered, as Liz hugged her, before looking back at the unfolding scene.

Jamaal was still tied up, sitting propped up against one of the stone retaining walls, but his gag had been removed.

338

Natalia, Aaron, and Davide had formed a semicircle around a very frightened Khalil, who gun in one hand, and a small metal box in the other, had backed up as far as he could against the retaining wall, which prevented the terrace from falling hundreds of feet to the sea below.

Rashid, handcuffed but unattached to either group, stood alone, seemingly neutral.

Alex and Liz watched with fascination, as the three Mossad agents formed an even tighter circle around the wounded Khalil.

"Stop!" he said. "Come any closer and I will throw this into the sea."

Jamaal, who somehow had managed to struggle to his feet, shouted, "Do it, Khalil. The document is blasphemous. It threatens our entire religion. Allah commands it!"

Khalil hesitated, thinking, rightfully, that control of the box was the only thing that kept the Israelis from shooting him. "Why should we keep it? Why should any of us want it?"

Liz, who heard the terror in his question, stepped forward to answer.

"What are you doing?" Alex whispered, trying to stop her.

"He deserves an answer," Liz said, calmly.

"She's right," said Simône, who, leaving her hiding place behind one of the beehive structures, stepped forward.

Khalil, who was now bleeding profusely from his gunshot wound, chose in his confusion to climb up on the wall, the one thing protecting him from certain death.

"Khalil, no, listen," Liz said, stepping forward to join the semicircle. Alex hesitated for a moment before stepping forward as well.

"You don't realize what you have," Liz said, speaking in soothing tones. "It's not evil; it's not blasphemous; it's an instrument of healing, of peace," Liz said, moving even closer toward him.

Simône, joining in her plea, asked, "Khalil, you come from Syria, correct?"

When Khalil did not respond, she said, "I know you must have lost friends, family to the Civil War."

Khalil, standing precariously on the wall, began to sway, but appeared to be listening.

"But your leaders have lied to you-your war is not a war between different religions. The bad guys aren't the Christians, Jews; they are the fellow believers who have been led astray and want to kill their fellow Muslims," said Simône.

"It's true," said Alex. "There's no reason the three religions can't coexist. Leaders over 1200 years ago recognized that fact. Shouldn't we honor their foresight, their wisdom?"

"Don't listen to them, nephew," Jamaal pleaded. "Your duty is to Islam, not to infidels. That document is blasphemous!" Jamaal said, before Aaron raced over to silence him by slapping a piece of tape over his mouth.

"Wouldn't you like to be the person to bring peace to the Middle East, to Syria?" asked Simône, thinking to appeal to his childish pride. "Yes, we have disagreements, but as trite as it sounds, can't we agree to disagree?"

"Think about your countrymen, what you could do for Syria, all of the people who are suffering there," said Alex.

"I...maybe," Khalil, who seemed to be wavering, said, looking as though he might surrender the box.

Everyone stood silent, not moving as Khalil swayed on his precarious perch. As they watched him, the sun, which had emerged a few minutes earlier to illuminate the entire terrace, ducked behind a cloud. Just as they were cast in shadow, the cry of a huge bird soaring above them caught their attention. For a split second, the entire group focused on the splendor of the solitary bird, before it swooped down below their line of sight.

"What do you think, Khalil?" asked Jeff, who had remained silent until that point in time.

"I don't know..." he said, looking first at his uncle, then toward Rashid, his face an inscrutable mask.

"Look," Natalia offered, "Just come down. We won't hurt you; unlike Jamaal, you haven't done any permanent damage to anyone."

"And with what you're holding, you could do so much good," Simône said, offering her hand.

"Just let us look at it," Liz said, pleading, as she stepped even closer to Khalil's position, also offering her hand.

Overcome by his blood loss and their arguments, Khalil appeared to be surrendering as he began to bend his knees, looking as though he would sit down on the wall.

"If I give you this, you have to let me go," Khalil said, still coherent enough to bargain, as he slowly squatted down, looking now as though he intended to jump down from the wall.

"We will..." Natalia began to say, but she stopped midsentence, when a monstrous gust of wind came whistling through the monastery compound. Momentarily, everyone reflexively looked behind them toward the force of the wind, before turning back around in a split second to the sight of Khalil flailing, balance lost. Both Liz and Jeff lunged forward in an attempt to grab him, his face cast in exquisite fear, before he fell backwards into unending space, holding tightly onto his gun and the box, as if they somehow still could save him.

His cry, as he fell, seemed to continue, carried on the wind-a memory, an echo-long after he had reached the rocks and sea below.

Jamaal, who had managed to remove the tape that Aaron had slapped across his mouth, cried out in anguish, "Rashid, why didn't you save him?"

"But you got what you wanted brother, right? The "Accord,' if in fact that is what it was, is gone, lost to the world and humanity, a chance to bring peace between the religions," Rashid said bitterly, before turning, with disdain, to look out to the sea.

After several moments of silence, in which each individual attempted to reconcile him or herself to the reality of what had just happened, Natalia said, looking around at each of them, "Okay, enough. Now's not the time. Get those lowlifes out of here," she said, nodding toward Jamaal and Rashid.

Davide and Aaron grabbed both men roughly and steered them toward the stairs leading down to the sea, while Simône, Jeff, Alex, and Liz, who had instinctively huddled together, stepped apart as Natalia approached.

"You're in shock, it's understandable," Natalia said, gently, "but we need to get out of here. The Irish Defense Forces, their federal police, will be arriving soon. Too late, of course, but nevertheless they will come. Unless you want to spend several weeks being interrogated for answers that you don't have, it's time to go," she said forcefully.

"D'accord," Simône said quietly, "nous comprenons, we understand."

Silently, following Natalia, they hiked down, not once stopping to appreciate the singular beauty of their surroundings. When they reached the helicopter, their pilot said, "I was beginning to worry; I almost sent Dan up to find you."

"I'm coming with you? Right?" asked Dan, as he saw with satisfaction that both Jamaal and Rashid had been taken into custody.

"Where's that jackass, Khalil?" Dan asked, looking up the path behind them.

Jeff shook his head, before finally saying, "Unfortunately, he didn't make it."

"Unfortunately? What?" Dan asked, confused.

"I'll tell you later," Jeff said, attempting to end the conversation.

Looking around, Dan noticed with surprise the looks of loss and sorrow on the faces of the three women.

"It's like the John Donne poem, 'each man's death diminishes me, for I am involved in mankind. And therefore, never send to ask for whom the bell tolls, it tolls for thee,'" Liz said, trying to explain.

"Yeah, Kahlil was a very troubled kid, but..." added Alex.

"Oh, right," said Dan, not wanting to admit that he didn't understand the reference.

Once they were all aboard the helicopter, the pilot expertly steered his craft back toward land; it took only 10 minutes to reach Portmagee, where the afternoon sun glinted off the boats bobbing peacefully at the dock.

The pilot landed back in the field, but left the engines running as Natalia, Alex, Jeff, Liz and Dan climbed out.

"We need to take these guys back to London, turn them over to Interpol," she said, nodding up at Jamaal and Rashid, who were still inside the aircraft, under the guard of Davide and Aaron.

"So, Rashid," Liz asked in a whisper, as though sharing a secret, "is he even Muslim?"

Natalia nodded "yes," before Liz asked, " And he really is MI6?"

"Yes, but he's undercover, and we're trying to keep it that way, so you need to keep that bit of information to yourself. By the way, I wasn't lying; I really am an adjunct agent for Interpol. You know, when the need arises," Natalia said, with a grin.

Alex laughed, before saying, "Who knew that when I used to run against you in college and beat you, repeatedly, you would save my life, not once, but several times. I'm so sorry; if I'd known, I would've let you win," Alex said, with a wink toward Natalia.

"Are you kidding, King?" Natalia asked, indignantly. "I only saved you because of all those times you kicked my butt. You were worth saving," she said, with a slight catch in her voice.

"Oh, Simône, I spoke to the Paris bureau chief for Interpol and the head of the Sûreté. That's who I was talking to on my headset while we were flying back from the island. I explained to them what happened at the church on Mont St. Michel. They understand that it was Jamaal who killed Philippe, and that the gunshot that you were involved in was just an accident."

"It also helps that the gun that Philippe was shot with was his own gun. As a consequence, they are not interested in pursuing any illegal gun charges against you."

"Pourquoi? I don't understand. That was my gun," said Simône.

"Well, technically, no. It turns out that the gun was actually registered to Philippe. Even though he'd given it to you to use, he kept it in his name. So as far as they are concerned, he was shot with his own gun while trying to subdue a group of terrorists that Interpol and the French government have been after for quite a while. So that is the end of it."

"But you are still going to have to give a statement at some point in time; they are willing to wait until after Philippe's funeral."

"I don't know how to thank you for that, Natalia. And to thank you for saving our lives. I think I'm going to give up being an adventurer-go back to just being a boring university professeur."

Natalia smiled at her before turning to Jeff, Alex, and Liz.

"They also want to take a statement from the three of you. But you can do that back in San Francisco with your lawyers at the French Consulate. I will text you the information of the individual that you should get in touch with, so you can set up an appointment. I also was asked on behalf of the French government to thank you for your role in capturing Jamaal and bringing down their cell."

"You're kidding, right?" asked Alex.

"No, I'm serious. After I told them everything that you went through, they decided for purposes of international relations, it would be better to consider you heroes than troublemakers. But don't expect to get any medals," Natalia said, laughing.

"So no Purple Heart for Jeff's gunshot wound?" asked Liz.

"No. You're just going to have to be satisfied with the fact that the bad guys are either dead or going to jail for a really long time," said Natalia.

"But what about Al-Bazheeri?" asked Alex.

"Unfortunately, when he heard what happened at Mont St. Michel, he left the country. But I'm sure he'll turn up again."

"Too bad. That guy needs to be in jail," said Jeff.

"I am confident that Aaron will find his trail and we will ultimately get him. Sooner or later these guys all are captured or killed."

Alex and Liz both gave her prolonged hugs, before Natalie stepped back and said, "But do me a favor. Stay out of Europe for a while. I have a vacation coming up, okay?"

"Okay," said Alex and Liz together, laughing.

"Oh, by the way, I hear that the hotel and pub at The Moorings, that pink building, is great," said Natalia. "If it is okay by you, I'm going to use the helicopter to fly these guys to London. Rashid and MI6 can deal with Jamaal from there. I will make arrangements for a car-a very nice car-to pick you up tomorrow morning and drive you to Kerry airport. From there you can catch a flight back to France. Don't forget you have some passports to retrieve."

"Oh, we won't," said Liz, holding up three fingers. "Girl Guides' honor."

"What?" Natalia asked.

"Oh nothing, private joke," said Alex, grinning at her sister.

At the edge of town, the four musketeers, plus one, watched as the helicopter lifted off.

"There go our worst nightmares," said Alex, "and our best friends," added Liz. "Right?"

Alex and Jeff both nodded before the five of them headed back into the village toward The Moorings pub, where an early dinner of fish and chips, and Irish whiskey awaited. Within 10 minutes, they had claimed seats at the bar; soon several of his Dan's fellow guides joined them to toast their luck, the luck of the Irish.

Simône, who was not in the mood for a celebration, ate only a few bites of her dinner before excusing herself to return to her room.

"I'm sorry. I will see you all in the morning. Bon soir."

By the time Jeff paid their bill, they had become fast friends with their black-haired, blue-eyed bartender, Gavin, and everyone in the bar, tourists and locals alike, had heard their harrowing story.

"We've been up for 36 hours, not counting a few cat naps," Liz said, once they had reached their room and dropped exhausted onto their beds.

After a few minutes lying silently in their darkened room, Liz asked, "Do you think it really was the 'Accord'?"

Liz waited for an answer, but all she heard was the gentle breathing of her sister, asleep, and for a while, at least, at peace.

CHAPTER
FORTY-SEVEN

When Alex awoke the next morning, it took her several seconds to realize where she was and why. Rolling over, she saw that the bed in which her sister had gone to sleep was empty.

"Oh, it's already 8:45," she exclaimed, looking at the clock on the bedside table. *Natalia said the car was coming to get us at 9:30. I guess I better get my butt up.*

Alex hurriedly showered and redressed in the borrowed jeans, T-shirt and tennis shoes that Natalia had provided, before heading downstairs to the dining room next door to the bar where they had dined the night before.

Inside she found Jeff and Liz, heads together in an intense conversation.

"Well hello, Alex. I was just about to come up and roust you before you missed breakfast. Jeff and I just had homemade bread slathered with local butter and honey. Really yummy!" said Liz. "And, we have eggs and bacon on the way."

"And the coffee is great too," said Jeff, as he handed Alex an empty mug from the table.

"Maggie, over there, is our waitress. She should be by any minute with a fresh pot."

"So where is Simône? Still asleep?" Alex asked, looking around.

"That's what we were talking about when you came in," Jeff said. "She left me a note. Apparently, she caught a ride early this morning with some local guy who was headed up to Shannon. She arranged to have a copy of her passport and some euros overnighted to her at the airport."   "She decided she needed to fly back to Paris as soon as possible. I guess Philippe is being flown from Saint-Malo to Paris today and she wanted to be there to meet the body. His only relatives are his elderly parents, and she didn't want them to have to deal with it."

"Poor Simône. I hope she realizes it's not her fault that Philippe is dead. We all know the first shot was an accident. And I imagine that Philippe would've survived if we could have gotten him help right away," Alex said.

"And if that monster, Jamaal, hadn't shot him in the head," Liz said angrily.

At that moment, their waitress Maggie, a friendly middle-aged woman with dark curly hair and green eyes, stopped by their table to pour Alex a cup of coffee.

"And what else can I get you, my lady?" she asked, looking at Alex.

"Oh, I would love some of that bread with honey and butter that they had. And I'll take some eggs and bacon as well. Thank you."

"I'll get it ordered right away; let me know if there's anything else you need, my lady," said Maggie with a smile, before turning to greet another couple who had just entered the restaurant.

"She's nice," said Alex.

"Everybody's nice around here," said Liz. "I wouldn't mind coming back someday under different circumstances and touring this area. They call it the Kerry Ring. It really is beautiful and rugged. And so green."

"I agree. But that will have to be another trip. When I talked to Mr. Murray last night, he said he would have a chartered flight waiting for us at the Kerry airport at 11 to fly us back over to Saint-Malo. And then he also arranged for a car so that we can drive to Mont St. Michel, pick up our luggage and our passports, and then drive back into Paris."

"Doesn't it seem like we just did this?" Jeff said.

"No kidding; it's like we're stuck in Groundhog's Day," said Liz, nodding her head.

348

"So, when you get back to Paris, what are you going to do? Are you going to finish your trip through Italy and Germany?" asked Jeff.

Liz and Alex looked at each other, seemingly engaged in some type of silent communication. Finally, Liz said, "No. I think we'll save Italy and Germany for another trip. We just want to go home to San Francisco."

"What about you?" Alex asked, looking at Jeff.

"I talked to Simône last night briefly. She said since I've completed all of my paperwork, I don't need to stay around until August 1st. I'm going to go clean out my office tomorrow and pack up my apartment. My plans are to fly back to San Francisco within the week."

"Oh, that's good news! Right?" Liz asked her sister.

"Absolutely. I think you've spent enough time with the French," Alex said, with a slight smirk.

After breakfast, Jeff, the only one who still had a wallet, paid and checked them out of the hotel. At exactly 9:30 AM, their car and driver arrived to take them to the Kerry airport. Dan, who had stopped by as they finished breakfast, shook hands with Jeff, and gave Liz and Alex each a big hug, before promising to come visit them in San Francisco when he finished his summer guide job on Skellig Michael.

"We'll show you all around the city, and we promise you won't be kidnapped or held at gunpoint," Alex said, as she climbed into the back seat beside Liz.

"Sounds kinda boring," Dan said, laughing. "I will definitely take you up on it," he yelled after them, waving, as their car pulled away and headed out of Portmagee.

Seven hours later, having flown to Saint-Malo, driven to Mont St. Michel, and collected theirs and Simône's luggage and belongings at their hotel on the Mont, they reached the outskirts of Paris.

Alex, who was driving, turned to Jeff and asked, "Why don't we drop you off first at your apartment? That way, Liz and I can keep the car and use it to drive to the airport tomorrow. We fly out of Charles de Gaulle airport at 10 AM. It's a direct flight to San Francisco, so we'll be home by tomorrow night."

When they reached Jeff's apartment, both Liz and Alex stepped out of the car to say goodbye. Liz gave Jeff a hug with her good arm, before saying, "I still owe you that bottle of wine; you'll just have to come visit us in San Francisco to collect, I guess," she added, before getting back into the passenger seat of the car.

Finally alone, Jeff and Alex stood looking at each other for several seconds.

"So, Ms. King," Jeff said.

"So, Mr. Stahl," Alex said as she put her arms around his neck and stepped in to give him a kiss.

When they finally parted, Jeff said, "Wow! Maybe I should try to pack up all my stuff tonight so I could fly home with you tomorrow."

"No. Take your time getting back to San Francisco. When you get there, you know where to find me," Alex said, before getting in the car, and driving away, leaving Jeff standing on the curb, grinning and shaking his head.

CHAPTER FORTY-EIGHT

"There's an envelope for you on the table," said the pretty, petite woman, eyes shining, as she rocked the infant in her arms.

The man, who had just entered the house, shrugged off his jacket and boots.

"Who is it from?" he asked, as he grabbed a bottle of beer from the refrigerator.

"I don't know; see for yourself. Some law firm in San Francisco," she said, amusement in her voice.

"Hmmm," said the man as he grabbed the envelope and examined it briefly, before using a kitchen knife to slit it open.

After taking a sip of his beer, he pulled out a single piece of paper from the envelope. Unlike the envelope, which appeared to be official stationery from the law firm, this was a yellow piece of paper torn from a legal pad, with a woman's handwriting, scrawled on the first few lines.

When he finished reading the message, he walked across the kitchen to kiss his wife and newborn son.

"What does it say?" she asked.

He silently handed her the note, as a smile spread across his face.

"Your debts have been paid, with interest.

They say, 'no hard feelings.'

Take your wife and son to visit your parents.

Life can come and go, in an instant.

Take care,

A & L"

The End

Acknowledgements

* * * *

To my editors, Paige and Alex,
Your ideas, corrections, suggestions and
criticisms helped me separate the wheat
from the chaff, cross the T's and dot the
I's. Thank you.
To Rich, thank you for the hours you
spent helping me format the manuscript
for publishing.
And to Peaches, my reader and friend,
thank you for your invaluable insights.
Sometimes an image is worth
a thousand words.

* * * *

St. Michael's Line

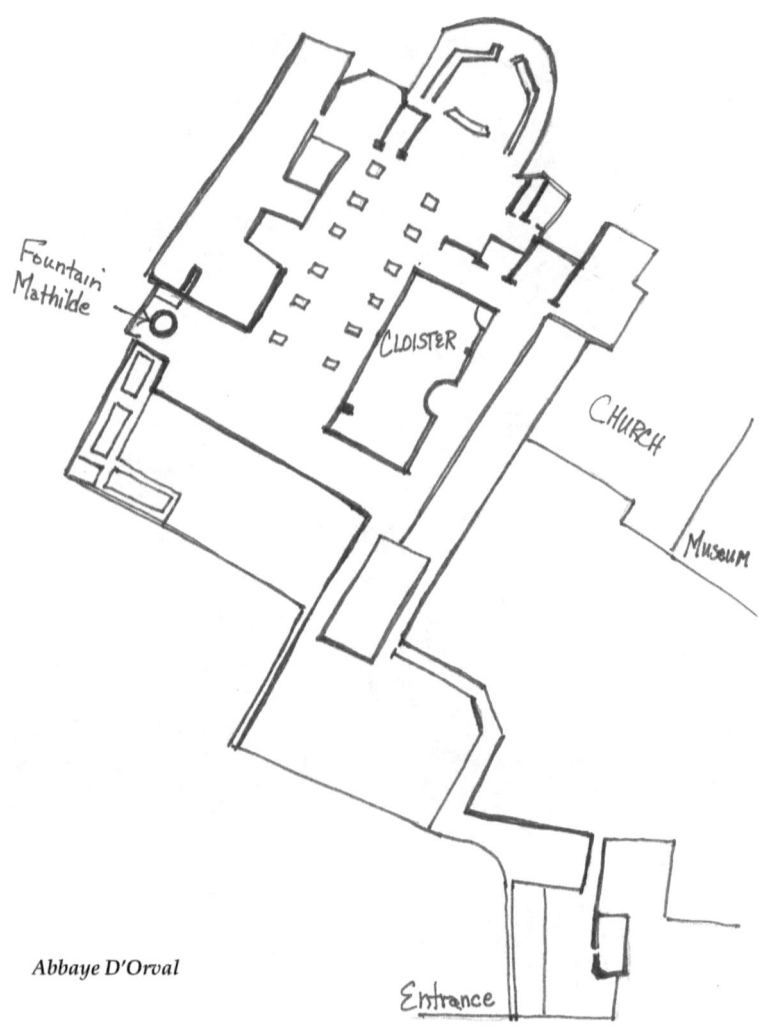

Fountain
Mathilde

CLOISTER

CHURCH

Museum

Abbaye D'Orval

Entrance

356

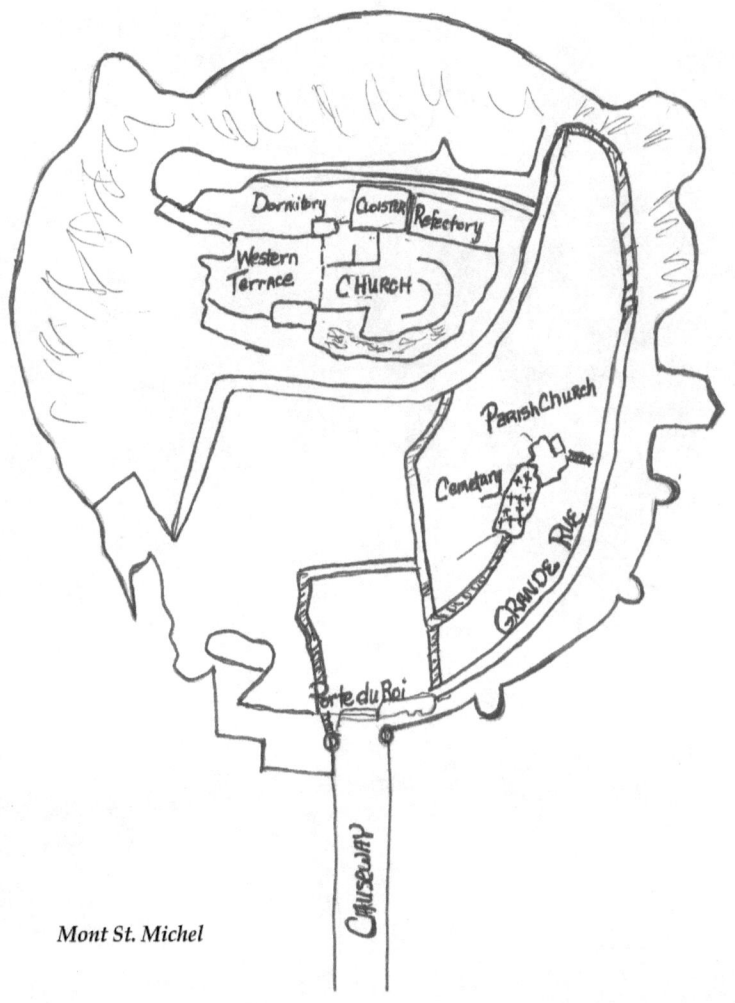

Mont St. Michel

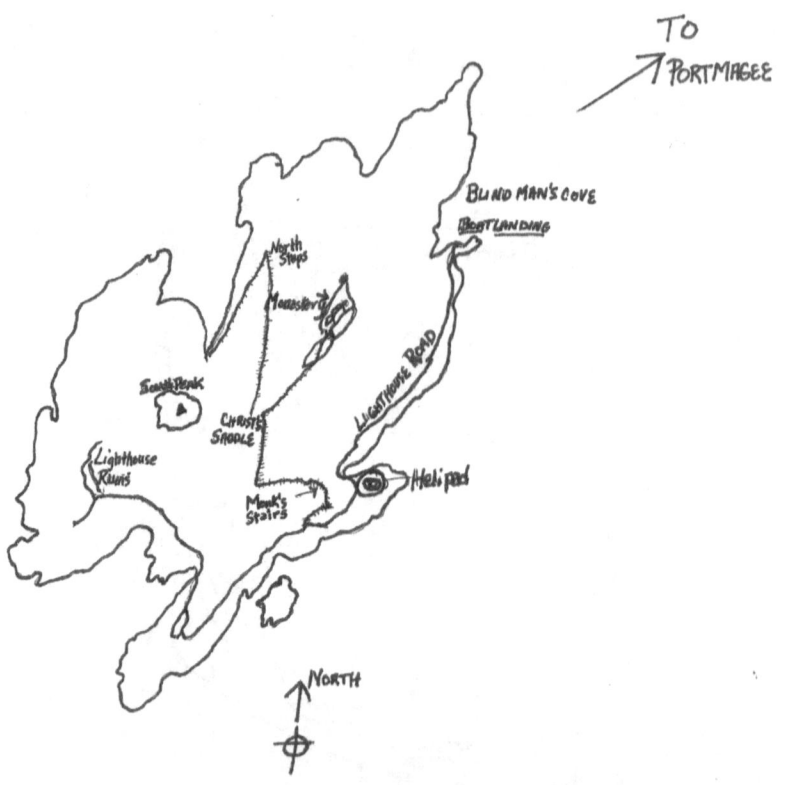

TO PORTMAGEE

BLIND MAN'S COVE

BOAT LANDING

North Steps

Monastery

LIGHTHOUSE ROAD

Seagull Peak

CHRISTS SADDLE

Lighthouse Ruins

Monk's Stairs

Helipad

NORTH

Skellig Michael

358

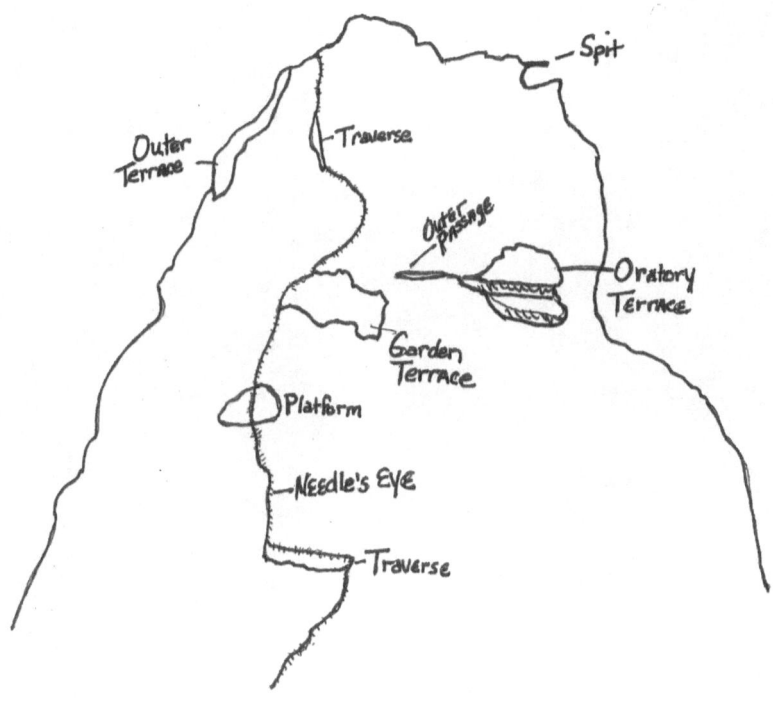

South Peak of Skellig Michael